PRAISE FOR
Silas House and *The Coal Tattoo*

"House is a master at rendering his characters' emotional terrain as real and accessible. In fact, he inhabits his characters so thoroughly, so concretely, they almost feel like little places themselves, little living places. . . . In *The Coal Tattoo*, Silas House, a writer of startling abilities, has no time for hopelessness, writing as he does toward the passionate center of his characters' lives."

—*The Atlanta Journal-Constitution*

"One of the truest and most exciting new voices in American fiction."

—ROBERT MORGAN, author of *Gap Creek*

"The talented House continues his long love letter to Kentucky in this starkly beautiful third novel. . . . Whether describing the sight of dozens of redbirds or the taste of moonshine, House does so in prose that is both lovely and cadenced."

—*Booklist*

"*The Coal Tattoo* is Silas House's most brilliant novel to date. . . . The characters of the two sisters and their mates are engagingly complex, and the psychological insights into maturation, family, and talent have an impressive depth and originality."

—SENA JETER NASLUND,
author of *Four Spirits* and *Ahab's Wife*

"It's a real pleasure to pick up a book by Silas House. A native and current resident of Appalachian Kentucky, House writes glittering prose about his home region and the people who inhabit it. . . . But what makes House appealing isn't just his work's unique setting. His literary craftsmanship and well-wrought characters foreshadow the emergence of a master novelist."

—*Nashville Scene*

"Evocative prose and unforgettable characters mark this haunting novel. . . . The titular image of the coal tattoo— a bluish tinge that seeps under a miner's skin and leaves a permanent stain—is a perfect metaphor for the novel's depiction of the indelible imprint the land leaves on the human soul."

—*Publishers Weekly* (starred review)

"House's beautiful third novel is both a story of survival and sacrifice and a stirring testament to the love of the land."

—*BookPage*

"[House's] characters are unpretentious, his prose un- cluttered and his message unmistakable. House writes from his heart . . . it's no wonder, then, that the characters in *The Coal Tattoo* slip under your skin and cause you to ponder the meaning of sacrifice and survival."

—*Mobile Register*

"The characters in *The Coal Tattoo* are so real to me and their love of their land comes through strong and powerful."

—LARRY BROWN,
author of *The Rabbit Factory* and *Father and Son*

"Powerful."

—*Lexington Herald-Leader*

"A gentle tale with appealingly flawed people and an exquisite sense of the quotidian."

—*Kirkus Reviews*

"Count on *The Coal Tattoo* to make a mark of its own."
—*Cincinnati City Beat*

PRAISE FOR
A Parchment of Leaves

"A SEAMLESS WORK OF FICTION, entrancing in the manner of a vivid dream . . . The novel is steeped in details of place—the sounds, smells, and quality of light in House's native Kentucky."

—*Newsday*

The Coal Tattoo

Also by Silas House

Clay's Quilt

A Parchment of Leaves

The
Coal Tattoo

a novel

Silas House

BALLANTINE BOOKS
NEW YORK

2005 Ballantine Books Trade Paperback Edition

Copyright © 2004 by Silas House
Reading group guide copyright © 2005 by Random House, Inc.

Published in the United States by Ballantine Books,
an imprint of The Random House Publishing Group,
a division of Random House, Inc., New York.

BALLANTINE and colophon are registered trademarks
of Random House, Inc.
READER'S CIRCLE and colophon are trademarks of Random
House, Inc.

The author is grateful to the University Press of Kentucky for its generous permission to use lines of poetry from James Still's *From the River, From the Valley* (© by James Still) and to Iris Books for its generous permission to use lines of poetry from Ron Rash's *Among the Believers* (© by Ron Rash).

Excerpts from this novel appeared in slightly different form
in *Nantahala Review*.

Originally published in hardcover by Algonquin Books of
Chapel Hill, a division of Workman Publishing, Chapel Hill,
North Carolina, in 2004.

This edition published by arrangement with Algonquin Books of
Chapel Hill, a division of Workman Publishing.

ISBN 978-0-345-48005-7

Printed in the United States of America

www.ballantinebooks.com

6   8   9   7   5

Book Design by Anne Winslow

For Lee

and all the family I have made at
the Hindman Settlement School

It is this land that makes us kin

The Coal Tattoo

PART ONE

....

Many Rivers Converging

Sharp, sweet spring eddies
through generations, streams
merge in churning unity—
one believer in blood and bone.

—Jane Hicks, "Ancestral Home"

One
....

Little Sister

ANNETH WAS DANCING in her tight red dress and everyone was watching her, the way she closed her eyes and felt the music running up and down the backs of her legs, the way the curls trembled down in her eyes as she threw her hair about, stomping her feet with one leg proudly thrust through the high slit that ran up one side of her dress, and it was like seeing joy made into a human form that could travel across the dance floor—it was like seeing the music itself. Every part of her was moving. Her hips met the beat of drums; her bare feet matched the riffs on the guitar. She had kicked off her shoes as soon as the first strains of "Maybellene" came on the jukebox. She didn't wait for anyone to ask her to go out on the dance floor with them, and she didn't stop to grab a man. She liked dancing to this song alone, although no one ever danced by themselves at the Hilltop. There was a scattering of couples along the edges of the floor, but she was in the middle and all eyes were upon her.

Anneth's sister, Easter, stood within the shadows near the door. She wore a long wool coat, and the cold drifted off it in thin little wisps as she was enveloped by the body heat inside the club. Her mouth was gathered in a tight knot and she looked much older than her twenty-two years. She had watched as Anneth jumped up, leaving her shoes and purse behind. She had watched as Anneth ran out onto the dance floor, snapping her fingers, shaking her body.

Now people were clapping along with the song, and men were holding their fingers to their mouths to fashion wolf whistles. Those leaning against the back wall tapped their feet and twisted at the waist. The other dancers turned to look at her and clapped in rhythm. "Look at her go," a man yelled, unwrapping a long finger from the neck of his beer bottle to point at her.

Easter watched her sister and all of the other people, too. She saw the way men were looking at Anneth, their eyes on her hips, on her long legs. She saw the women trying to get their men's attention. One of them reached up and grabbed her husband's chin, pulling his face around to her. He laughed and pushed her hand away, went back to watching Anneth. He leaned back and hollered, unaware that his wife was now walking away with the car keys in her clenched hand.

When the wild breakdown of guitar and drums started, Easter lurched across the honky-tonk and plucked Anneth's purse up off the table. She snatched Anneth's jacket from the back of a chair and then hooked two fingers into the red heels her sister had left behind. She didn't know any of the people sitting at Anneth's table and they didn't even notice her; they were all drunk and laughing and caught up in the music. Easter marched out onto the dance floor and took hold of Anneth's arm as it arched over her head. She jerked Anneth around hard and grabbed her by the crook of her elbow.

"Let's go," Easter said, but her words were lost to the loudness of the place. She pulled Anneth across the floor and hustled her out through the milling crowd. Easter hit the door with a flat palm and it swung open, just missing two men standing on the other side. Outside, it was cold, and all was covered in a starless night sky. The air smelled of an oncoming snow.

"Take your damn hands off me!" Anneth screamed. She pulled away from Easter and took three steps back. She didn't seem to notice the cold gravel under her bare feet. She touched her elbow lightly with her fingertips, as if Easter had harmed her there. "What the hell do you think you're doing?"

Easter took a long time to collect herself. She was so mad that she was out of breath. She was too angry to speak right now, anyway; if she said anything too quickly, words would spew out that she wouldn't be able to take back. She stood there looking Anneth in the eye, breathing hard, for a long moment before she spat out her words. "You are seventeen years old, Anneth."

"So what?"

"Seventeen-year-old girls don't go in no bar. You've been sneaking off since you were fifteen and I'm tired of it," Easter said. "You want to be the talk of the county?"

Anneth crossed her arms against the cold and ran her hands up the undersides of her bare arms. "Maybe I do," she said.

Easter let out a sigh and tossed Anneth's jacket toward her. Anneth caught it with one hand and shoved her arms into it furiously. Easter fumbled around with one of the two purse straps she had on her arm. "I got your purse, too," she said, trying to pick the tangled straps apart. "Here," she said. "And your shoes." She let the heels fall onto the ground between them. They landed perfectly, side by side and upright.

Anneth slipped her feet into the shoes and jerked the purse from Easter's hand and unlatched it. She bent over it like someone staring into a deep kettle and fished around inside, looking for a cigarette, then fired her Zippo and breathed a line of smoke. She put her purse strap on her arm, turned, and walked away.

"If you think you'll get a man acting thisaway, you're bad wrong," Easter said.

Anneth twirled on one heel. "You think I care about getting a man?" she said, smirking. "I don't want no *man*."

"What else would you come to a bar for? We've all been worried to death, and I've been out all night looking for you."

Anneth rolled her eyes and exhaled smoke like a movie star and crunched through the graveled parking lot, her heels grinding.

"Answer me," Easter said, almost in a holler. "Why'd you come here?"

"To dance," Anneth said. "That's why."

Anneth got into Easter's car. She slammed the door hard and the glass rattled in the doorframe. The windshield had frosted over and Easter had to sit there a minute and let the glass warm up. The wipers scraped across in long, monotonous moans. The radio played low with the strains of a country song, a fiddle and a mournful cry. She sat there for a long moment without saying anything, concentrating on the groaning wipers. There were Christmas lights hanging from the eaves of the honky-tonk and they glowed big and smudged through the frost on the windshield.

Anneth sucked hard on her cigarette, and the tobacco cracked and popped. She pressed it into the ashtray and fished out her pack of Lucky Strikes and lit another one. The lighter lid snapped like a pistol being cocked.

The window was only half defrosted, but Easter put the car in reverse and backed out, anyway. She drove slowly down the mountain, hunched over so she could see out of the spreading clear spot on the window. When they got down to the main road, she sighed heavily once more. "I'll tell you what, Anneth. You are going to get destroyed. Running off to bars and worrying us every one to death. Who took you up here, anyway? I looked for Gabe in there but never could find him."

"Gabe's off gambling somewhere."

"How'd you get here, then?"

Anneth looked out her window, although it was still fogged up. "I was walking up the road when I seen Lonzo Morgan drive up. He brought me up here."

Easter slapped the steering wheel. She wore a small silver ring that snapped against it loudly. "I'll have me a talk with Lonzo tomorrow."

Anneth turned quickly, her curls sticking to her eyelashes. "You won't do it," she said, the scent of whiskey traveling from her lips.

"And you've been drinking," Easter said. "I ought to call the law on them for selling liquor to you."

Anneth leaned her head back against the seat and laughed. "Some feller bought me a shot."

"You're just a little girl," Easter said. She ran her palm over the windshield, blurring the road. "The mind of a little girl in a woman's body."

Anneth leaned forward and turned the radio up loud. Ray Price was singing and she pushed the buttons until she found another station. She was in the mood for some rock 'n' roll. Since they were surrounded by the mountains, there was nothing but static. She found a station that was playing something fast and grinding, but before the song could make itself known, Easter snapped off the radio.

"Ain't you ashamed of yourself?"

"I don't intend to be like you," Anneth said. "I'm not going to set in that house with you on a Saturday night. Not going to lay down early so I can get up and go to church. I want to live, Easter. Why don't you?"

They came down the mountain and then they were in town. Easter stopped at a red light and looked around. There were no cars out on the streets, and all the stores were closed. Dim lights burned in the plate glass windows. Easter leaned her arms on the steering wheel and looked at Anneth while she waited for the light to change. She couldn't stay mad at her, even when she tried. She wanted to conjure more hateful words, but she didn't know if she could muster them.

"That ain't no kind of life," Easter said at last. "Drinking and carrying on. Smoking. What makes you want to act such a way?"

Anneth looked at her lap, unable to meet Easter's eyes. "I don't know," she whispered, and Easter believed her. "Sometimes I feel so full up of something that I think I'll bust wide open. Don't you know how that feels, to want more? I just want to have a big time."

The light turned green and Easter tapped the gas. "You'll have a big time for the next few months because you won't be going anywhere."

"I don't have no boss," Anneth said, shaking her head. "You think you'll tell me what to do? I'll leave and never will come back."

Easter laughed out loud without meaning to. She couldn't help it. "I don't know where you intend to go."

Anneth didn't say anything. Now they were out of town, and the mountains pressed big and black on either side, misshapen without their leaves. It was late but some people still had their Christmas lights burning; they lined the porches of houses that seemed to hang from the mountainside. Trees blinked in the windows.

Anneth slipped her shoes off and put her feet on the seat. She pulled her knees up to her chin, and her dress rode up, exposing her white panties. They glowed in the dim green light from the dashboard.

"Don't you want to have fun?" Anneth said. "Didn't you ever want to get out and dance and go on? You're twenty-two years old and never done a thing I can remember except go to church. We're *young*."

Easter held tightly to the steering wheel. She hated these conversations with Anneth. They never led to anything. There was no name she could put to the difference that stood between them. She regretted that she and Anneth weren't more alike. One night, about a year before their grandmother Serena died, Anneth had left her pew in the middle of church. Serena found Anneth at the creek, running her hand through a man's wavy hair and kissing him on the mouth as they sprawled out on a big rock. Serena had taken her back to the house, Anneth's face too beard burned to go back into the church.

Easter didn't want a gulf to open up between them, for she loved Anneth more than she loved anyone else in this world. But it seemed that was going to happen. There was a wild blood in her sister. Sometimes Easter fancied that she could see it pulsing right in Anneth's veins.

"Say?" Anneth said. "Did you hear me?"

"We're different, and that's all there is to it. Not all sisters are just alike."

And all at once Anneth was crying. She scooted over on the seat until she was sitting right beside Easter. She laid her head on Easter's shoulder. Easter didn't flinch and kept her eyes firmly upon the road. It was curvy here, with the creek on one side and sharp cliffs on the other. She could feel her jaw clenching.

"I never meant to worry you," Anneth said. "I just wanted to dance."

Easter wanted to bring her hand up to Anneth's face and hold it there, but she didn't. Anneth always did this — she always did wrong and was forgiven. She knew just how to get Easter in the gut. And the worst part was that Anneth really meant what she had said. But Easter didn't say a word. She relished the feel of Anneth's face on her shoulder and drove on, watching the yellow slants of the headlights as they guided her toward Free Creek.

Two

·············

Living with Ghosts

EASTER LAY IN her bed, listening to Anneth cry. She started to get up several times but knew it would be best if she didn't.

Anneth had wanted to talk it all out, but Easter had simply taken down her hair, put on her gown, and said, "Good night," in a practiced, empty voice, Anneth standing in the hall with her hands on her hips as Easter shut the door in her face. It was the first time in years that she hadn't kissed Anneth on the forehead before lying down. Easter was more worried than angry. Still, she knew how Anneth's mind worked. The only real way to get to that girl was through her heart. Anneth had a good heart that was easily startled, and Easter could have shamed her by crying and exaggerating how worried she had been. But Easter wasn't about to act like the feeble one, crushed because her wild sister had sneaked off. That would be too easy. She wanted Anneth to think she was angry with her, when in fact Easter could not find it in her heart ever to be very mad at her sister.

Easter was twenty-two years old and she was raising her seventeen-year-old sister and that was all there was to it. Sometimes it amazed her when she thought about her situation, but here she was. Their uncle and aunt, Paul and Sophie, lived just up the road and had of-fered to have Anneth and Easter move in with them two years be-fore, when Serena died. Easter had refused.

"I don't want to leave the house where we've lived all our lives," Easter had told them. "I don't believe Anneth could stand it."

Nobody disputed her. The family saw no reason why the girls couldn't keep right on living there. After all, Easter had always been responsible and was plenty old enough. Nobody said aloud that most girls her age were married with children. They knew she would take care of Anneth. Even as a child, Easter had worked alongside her grandmothers in the garden or canning the beans. She had insisted on Paul's teaching her how to quilt, had gone to church with Sophie every Sunday. She had once planned on going away to the college in Berea, but when Serena fell sick with cancer, that was all forgotten, like a long-ago dream that she couldn't remember correctly. Nobody in their family had ever been to college, but Easter's grades had been good enough to get the attention of the scholarship committee made up of old coal barons' widows who made themselves feel better by sending poor girls off to school. But it wasn't meant to be. It was like a tune in her head that she could stop humming: *It wasn't meant to be, wasn't.*

After the cancer had grown too large for Serena to bear its weight anymore, Easter took a job in the high school cafeteria. It wasn't so bad except for the heat in the kitchen and the awful plastic aprons that they had to wear. She had wanted to go to college and become a teacher, but her job in the cafeteria allowed her to be one, anyway. She studied the faces of pale, hollow-eyed girls and knew which one needed someone to talk to, which one needed some money shoved into her hand. She could see trouble brewing behind the eyes of disheveled boys. The kids all knew her by name and came to her whenever they felt their lives were falling apart. She always knew what to say.

Everyone agreed that she had done right by Anneth. Their brother, Gabe, sure hadn't done anything. He was wild, always running the roads, drinking or gambling, a different woman on his arm every time she saw him. Mostly Easter felt as if she didn't even have a brother. He had always been so separate from her and Anneth. Different, too, in all ways. Gabe's eyes held nothing but secrets. Maybe it was because he had stayed with Paul as much as possible rather than be raised by all those women. He had been working in the mines since he was seventeen, and she hardly ever saw him since he had moved over to Pushback Gap. He tried to give her money every time they got together, but Easter always refused it. She would take care of her little sister without anyone's help, and she didn't care if that seemed prideful or not. She made sure that Anneth went to school every morning and that she didn't go too awfully wild, except for the occasional lapse, like tonight.

Easter rolled over, put her fist into her pillow, and pulled the quilt up to her neck. She still couldn't get comfortable. She sat up and put her feet over the side of the bed, listening. Apparently Anneth had cried herself to sleep. Easter couldn't hear anything except the house. The old wood murmured as it settled into the night. Sometimes she thought the lumber of the house held ghosts. She imagined those creaks and moans were the whispers and sighs of the dead, even though she knew better. She was as still as she could be, even going so far as to hold her breath. She could hear the whip-poor-will out there in the backyard, perched up in the locust tree it loved so much. She listened to its lonesome song and tried to ignore the other sounds she heard. She didn't listen to the ghosts if she could help it.

The cold floorboards felt good as she put her feet down, and a shiver ran up her back, but it was a comforting feeling, this coldness. It reminded her that she was alive. She padded down the hallway and slid her feet into Anneth's lined boots, standing by the door as if at attention. She hustled on her coat and latched all the buttons, then pulled a wool cap down over her ears. She needed the night air, even if it was freezing outside. Her thoughts were running too wild for her to sleep.

She stepped out into the blackest night she had ever seen. She looked at the sky and saw no trace of silver. There was not one star or even so much as a slice of moon. She had never seen a sky so void and still, like bottomless water. As soon as she stepped out, the whip-poor-will stopped singing. Maybe it was a ghost, too; everyone knew that whip-poor-wills didn't come out to sing in December. She wondered if anyone heard its song except for her and Anneth. Sometimes they went to sleep listening to it.

"It's not normal," Easter often said. "A whip-poor-will hollering through cold weather. They're supposed to leave for the winter."

"He's magic, though," Anneth would say. She looked for magic anywhere she could find it.

There would be snow soon; Easter could smell it on the air. She walked close to the creek and listened to its music. If she concentrated, she could be completely lost in that sound. Across the creek stood the mountain, noticeable only because it was blacker than the black sky, huge and looming like a gigantic animal.

There was no doubt about it: ghosts lived here. Nobody saw them but Easter—not even Anneth, who was on constant lookout for such things—and she tried to ignore them. Sometimes she was aware of them on all sides of her, crowding around and breathing down her neck. There were her grandfathers, loud and rambunctious, always in motion. Her grandmothers. Her father's mother, Serena, reared back in laughter, her big hands clapping together. And her maternal grandmother, Vine, standing in the shadows of redbud trees, her eyes cast down, as if that strange mixture of sadness and joy she had carried with her in life had followed her into death as well. There were people Easter didn't know, too. Tall men with black eyes stood amongst the blue-leafed corn in the garden. A man who played the banjo and whispered a song. A whole gang of squat women with bunned-up hair who scurried along the creek bank, peeking back at her nervously. She had no idea who they could be. Sometimes she caught a glimpse of a child running. The children were a comfort, although she was always unsettled to see their unnaturally pale features. There was one child in particular, a boy who made her stomach ache. He bothered her the most because she had the strange sense that he did not exist yet. She had to close her eyes and pray for him to go away. Sometimes it was unbearable. But it was inevitable that ghosts would live here, considering everything that had happened.

THEIR FAMILY HAD been marked by death, as if they were cursed. Their family history was a convoluted affair. Had it been a solid, visible thing, it would have looked like many rivers converging, seen from high above. It was a water crowded by secrets and lies. Only Easter knew all of it. Serena had told her some. Sophie had told more. But most of this history Easter simply knew, the way she knew when a flood was going to come or when someone was going to die in a car wreck.

Serena and Vine had been two forces of nature. Serena was a large, loud woman whose presence filled up the entire room and overtook it; everyone in the county knew her and liked her, despite or perhaps because of her habit of telling everyone exactly what she thought of them. Serena worked all the time, even when it wasn't needed, and had a boisterous laugh that people recognized. Vine was a full-blooded Cherokee with hidden stories tucked in her eyes. Easter's most vivid memory of Vine was walking behind her as she moved like a ghost through the woods, examining the leaves of every tree. Serena and Vine had been best friends for years when their children—Serena's Luke and Vine's Birdie—joined their two families, making them all kin.

Birdie had been a bashful, withdrawn girl, scarred by growing up alongside her first cousin, Matracia, who was so beautiful she moved old men to lust in such a manner that they ended up cutting themselves in shame. And then Matracia had run off to East Tennessee to find her mother, which caused Birdie to withdraw even further. She had loved Matracia like her own sister—they had been closer than even two sisters can be—but Luke brought her back from this grief. Once Luke set his eye on Birdie and began to court her, everyone was shocked to see that they were unnaturally alike. They really did seem like they were two halves of one person.

Luke urged Birdie's true spirit forth and she opened like a window being eased up. A whole new girl emerged. She had a fiery temper that matched his. Her beauty was made plain once joy showed on her face. She was a twig of a girl, in sharp contrast to her big-boned parents. She loved to dance and laugh and sing at the top of her lungs, although she had done none of these things before Luke started getting her out of the house. He was like that, though—the kind of boy who couldn't be refused. He was always laughing and cutting up and having a big time. He was the joy not just of Serena's life, but of everyone who knew him.

Still, when they announced their engagement, their mothers begged them not to marry. Luke was eighteen and Birdie only sixteen and both the women knew that she wasn't old enough. Neither of them had married so young. But there was not much choice in the matter once Birdie came into the kitchen and told Vine that she had not bled in three months. Luke took a job in the Altamont mines and moved Birdie to Free Creek, where they built a house above Serena's on the mountainside.

Anneth and Easter's father was beautiful. Easter was six years old when he died, but strangely she could not recall ever having seen him. She knew his face only through the pictures that Serena kept on her walls. He had wavy red hair and a square jaw, and thick lips that were full of color. She knew all of this even though the picture was in black and white. When Anneth was small, Serena had always told her that she had her father's eyes—green as redbud leaves, so bright they nearly glowed in the darkness. He was a tall man with corded forearms and a cleft in his chin. Anneth studied this picture all the time, as if trying to recall his face, but there was no way she could remember him. She was only one year old when he died. When Easter saw her carrying around the picture, she knew what Anneth was thinking: *I wish I had known him. His eyes have fire in them, like mine. Maybe he could tell me something about myself.*

When Luke died, it nearly killed every one of them. The Altamont mine caved in, and it took the crews three days to dig the men out. That whole time, families stayed at the mine entrance, praying and crying, drinking coffee and smoking, standing near the fire that was built in a rusted rain barrel. The state brought in a long yellow school bus for them to rest in, but nobody slept. For three days they waited, mostly women standing in the February wind. Often there was complete silence. Easter was there, but she was not sure if she could really remember it. Sometimes she believed she could simply remember her grandmother's retelling of that day, and when she thought of it all, she saw it not only through her own eyes but also through Serena's.

It was just becoming dawn and the sky was the color of copper when the crew finally got to the chamber of dead miners. By the time they packed the bodies out, peach light was splitting the sky, and thin tufts of snow were falling. When they brought out Luke's body, Serena did not cry or holler out in pain. She simply fell to her knees and stared off into the distance, at the snow-covered mountains, at the horizon, at nothing. But Birdie started screaming and didn't stop. She tore at her hair and moaned. A pack of women tried to hold her still, but she pushed them away. Serena couldn't move to do anything.

Birdie stumbled around the hardened mud, the bobby pins falling from her hair, curls making their way into the corners of her mouth and eyes. And then she hushed long enough to lean over and begin to search for pieces of coal. She walked along, hunched over, the way Easter imagined someone on the beach, looking for seashells washed up in the tide. She found five squares of coal, then threw her head back and let them each slip into her mouth like pills. Easter knew that her mother had lost her mind. The madness had been instant, like a candle being lit.

After they buried Luke, Birdie left the little house he had built for her on the mountainside and moved in with Serena. Birdie couldn't stand the thought of being in that house without him, and for this Serena and Vine were glad. Serena didn't like the idea of the girls' being left alone with Birdie up there, because she didn't know what to expect of Birdie. In those first days after the funeral, Vine moved in with Serena, too, since they were both widows now. They had used each other's houses over the years, anyway. By that time Vine was already sick herself and not able to help much, but each night she was present to comb out the girls' hair, to stand in the doorway while Serena sung them to sleep, to sit by Birdie's side when she wouldn't allow anyone else to console her.

Birdie had stayed in her room most of the time, talking to herself, shuffling and reshuffling the stack of postcards that had been Matracia's prized possessions, singing, dusting her dresser, and remaking her bed dozens of times before she would come out and eat. She cried all the time. "I didn't know it was possible for a person to have so many tears," Serena said. Birdie got so bad that one day

Easter found her standing in the middle of Free Creek completely naked. Easter was seven and didn't know what else to do but run and get her grandmother. Easter crossed her arms over her chest—each hand holding on to the opposite shoulder—and sat on the creek bank while Serena went to Birdie.

"Here, now," Serena said, and took off her own shawl to wrap around Birdie's nakedness. The shawl was too short and didn't cover anything except Birdie's breasts. She walked up out of the creek with her head leaning on Serena's shoulder, and Easter watched as they made their way up the road and into the house. Birdie's rump and legs were marked by a dozen small blue marks, as if she had pinched herself over and over.

Easter hated to remember what had happened shortly thereafter. Her beautiful mother, dead and cold in the ground. She realized now that she'd never get over it. There were so many times when she wanted just to go to her mother and tell her all of her troubles, to crawl up on her lap and lay her head on her mother's shoulder, to smell the lavender oil Birdie dotted behind her ears, to hold her mother's hand in her own.

As a child, Easter sometimes walked out into the garden so silently that Serena wasn't even aware of her until Easter stood just behind her grandmother. She had always possessed an abnormal talent for moving without making a sound. Serena would start but never let out so much as a yelp, and then Easter would realize that the old woman was crying. Easter would squat down in the garden beside her and take her hand. "There's just too much death in our family. It's too much," Serena would say.

Vine and Serena had told the girls much of this old history. They were always telling about Birdie and Luke's wedding day, always going into one of the old tales when they were cutting corn off the cob or peeling potatoes in the kitchen or were holed up in the house during a bad snowstorm. But her grandmothers left so many things out that Easter had to fill in with her unexplainable knowledge. Serena had a whole other life that she never talked about, too. Easter knew, though. She knew about Serena's scandalous divorce and the way she used to drink with the men and curse like a sailor. But Easter also knew what a good friend Serena had been to Vine and how they had helped each other to survive all their troubles. And she knew about Serena's midwifing half the people in the county, too.

Serena rarely talked about her midwifing days, and Easter couldn't understand why. Every time they went to town, someone came up to Serena and said that she had delivered them from the womb, and she grew more and more distraught that she couldn't remember all of them. This bothered her greatly, especially in the weeks before she became so sick that she was bedfast.

After Vine died, Serena never was the same. It was as if a little part of her had been sucked away with Vine. That was when the real trouble had started with Anneth. Anneth was only eleven, but she'd taken to Vine in the same way that Easter took to Serena. When Vine died, Easter had seen the flicker of epiphany on Anneth's face. Anneth had been too little to really understand either of their parents' dying, but she had watched Vine be eaten up by the cancer. Vine's last words were a gurgle in the back of her throat: "I am paying for my sins." Easter had seen Anneth's mind working, trying to figure out Vine's past, wondering what she had done to deserve such a horrible death. Serena had laid her head on Vine's chest and cried great heaving sobs. But Easter had watched Anneth: the color draining from her face, the understanding of death clear in her eyes. It was almost as if Easter could read Anneth's thoughts: *I have to live all that I can. Look at this, how fast life goes. Everybody dies one day.* Anneth already had wild blood, and here was a seed that had been planted that day.

But it was worse when they lost Serena. Easter remembered that night when she had sat up with Serena, listening to her die in that cold hospital. Anneth had been just a child, but couldn't she have been there with Easter and Sophie and the other women cousins? Couldn't she have been there instead of back home, helping Paul with a quilt? She didn't even like to quilt.

If Easter thought too much about it, she became furious. Because Anneth had not been there to see the realization in Easter's face, to see how Easter suddenly knew that she had to spend every day of the rest of her life trying to do the good that Serena always hoped to do. The day Vine died, Anneth had decided to be as wild as possible; when Serena died, Easter had decided to walk through life like a whisper.

That night, Serena had held her hand so tightly that she thought her fingers would break. And then, when the life began to seep out of Serena, Easter could feel it being sucked away through her fingers, too. She had held on to Serena's hand so long that Sophie had to pry their intertwined fingers apart.

Easter had had enough of death. Standing on the porch in the cold, she realized that her face and hands were completely numb. The night was so silent that even the creek was nothing more than a low rumbling that sounded very far away, like the sound of blood in one's ears. *This must be what death sounds like,* Easter thought. Above the mountain stood a gray line of light, like smoke. Daylight was approaching from the other side of the world.

Three

···············

Everyday Magic

ANNETH COULD NOT believe she was seeing a redbird at night. She had been given this gift only once before, as a child, and had thought that sort of magic was reserved for the innocent. Redbirds did not stir after dark, yet there it was, sitting right in a square of moonlight in the middle of the path, as if someone had posed it there.

Anneth took careful steps toward it, not moving anything but her feet. She thought it was most likely hurt. Perhaps it had been asleep and had fallen from its nest in the middle of the night. That was the only thing Anneth could figure. She squatted down as she got nearer the bird, bending her knees and pulling in her body so that her chin rested on her chest. She could see the moonlight in its feathers. Its tiny head moved around nervously, like the head of a blind person trying to figure out who is nearby.

When she was five years old, Anneth had been awakened in the middle of the night by Vine. Vine had whispered, "Get up. I want you to see something," and had positioned Anneth on her hip and carried her outside. Unlike tonight, that night had been very warm — so warm that the earth seemed to hiss and steam against the darkness, the air filled with the faint scent of baking soil. She put her face in the heat of Vine's hair, which smelled like clothes that had been hung out to dry. She wanted nothing more than to go back to sleep, but then Vine patted her back and said, "Look here."

There was a long moment before she understood that they were standing in the middle of the yard in front of Vine's house, where Anneth was spending the night. And then she saw: the ground was covered by redbirds, dozens of them. They were perched in the smaller trees in the yard—young redbuds and dogwoods—but mostly they sat on the ground, looking up at the mountain as if something stirred there. They were so silent, so still, yet a low hum arose amongst them, the way it does at a church meeting when everyone's head is bowed in prayer.

"This must be magic," Vine said.

After a while Vine sat Anneth down on the ground and moved near the birds, holding out her hand as if she held a fistful of seed. Vine ran her finger down the back of one of the birds, but it did not move. Then she stood quickly, withdrawing her hand as if this touch was almost too much to bear. She came back and squatted down with her arm around Anneth's waist.

And then, one by one, the redbirds rose from the steaming ground and sailed away on quiet wings. When they were gone, the valley seemed impossibly silent, a silence only rocks knew.

"Remember this," Vine said, looking up at the sky. "You'll never see anything else like it in your life."

But now Anneth was bearing witness once again. Tonight it was only the lone bird, but somehow this seemed even better. She pushed her hair back under her beret, arched her body close to the ground, and brought her hands out very slowly, cupping them together so she could scoop up the little redbird or at least touch its feathers, the way Vine had. It didn't move as she drew near. She was so close to it that she thought her hands could feel its tiny heat. And then she stepped into the moonlight, casting a shadow over the redbird. At that, it flew away on wings that sounded like soft crinolines.

Anneth stood in the middle of the path and looked at the treetops stupidly. No matter the amount of moonlight, she was never going to be able to see that little redbird again. She eyed the moon and thanked it for the chance to see this sight. She knew that she had been given this moment. It *was* magic—she was sure of that—and magic was the thing that Anneth looked for every day. She did not wonder what this meant or why it had happened, but accepted it as something she was blessed to see.

Anneth had sneaked out of the house. Only a week before, Easter had forbidden her to be running wild, but it was Christmas break and there was a party at the pine patch tonight. She wasn't about to miss it. As she went farther up the path, the sound of the creek behind her became quieter and she could hear people's voices as they drank and talked by the bonfire. Somebody had brought along a transistor radio, and Anneth could hear its music. But then she heard the strum of a guitar and she began to walk a little faster at the thought of a song actually being created right there on the ridge.

Anneth drew a cigarette out of her coat pocket and fired her Zippo. She was almost up the ridge and wanted to make sure she had a Lucky hanging from her lips when she came into the clearing. She tried to blow out her smoke the way Natalie Wood had in *Rebel Without a Cause.* She wanted to be Natalie Wood, the most beautiful girl she had ever seen, all hugged up with James Dean. Really she wanted to be James Dean. She still got choked up when she thought about that movie; it had nearly killed her to see the longing in his eyes, the yearning he carried around so plain for everyone to witness.

She shoved her hands into the pockets of her long coat and walked a little faster, glancing back once to where the spot of moonlight had lain on the path. There was nothing but darkness down there now.

Everybody was up there at the pine patch—Lonzo Morgan and Lolie and Israel and several cousins and all her friends. People she had known all her life. The flames of the bonfire caught in the glass of the jars and bottles that were being passed around. Everyone sat on felled trees, laughing and carrying on so loudly that it took her a moment to hear the music again. There was a boy sitting on a stump, strumming on his guitar; he was playing a song she had never heard before. It was such a soft, light sound, like slow-moving waves washing up onto rocks. He was tall and long fingered and had thick black hair. He wasn't much to look at, really. But there was something about him, something about the way he held his eyes shut as he ran his thumb over the guitar strings. She liked the way he leaned into the guitar, cradling it against his chest. The way he seemed to be swept away by the song, as if he could feel every mournful note running through his body. She wanted to be like that. She wanted to get up on a stage and let everyone see her passion playing out on her face.

She stood there frozen for a moment, tuning out all the voices and laughter so she could focus on his music. It was as if he had been playing music that everyone loved, then had lapsed into his own composition and lost the interest of the others. But he had Anneth's attention. When the song was over and he opened his eyes, she saw that they filled out his whole face. They made what was once a plain, regular face into something altogether different, and she could see that they were outlined in black, like all of the coal miners'. Anneth loved the way the coal got into a miner's eyelashes like mascara and stayed there permanently. His eyes were so blue they nearly glowed, the way Serena's iridescent candy dish shone when sunlight fell on it through the window.

Lolie was suddenly beside her, holding a bottle in front of Anneth's face. She had known Lolie so long that she thought of her as family.

Lolie wore too much eye makeup and too much perfume—so much that it settled on Anneth's clothes when she stood near—but she was the wildest girl that Anneth knew, and Anneth appreciated that about her.

"Easter will kill you for sneaking out," Lolie said, and forced the bottle into Anneth's hand. "You might as well be drunk when you face her."

Anneth took a long pull on the bourbon and wiped her mouth on the sleeve of her coat. She didn't take her eyes from the guitar player. He was looking at her as if he was memorizing her face.

"Who's that?" she said, pointing the mouth of the bottle his way before handing it back to Lolie. She wanted him to know they were talking about him.

"Matthew Morgan," Lolie said. "I don't know who invited him up here. He's sort of quiet, but he sure can sing."

"He's pretty," Anneth said.

Lolie arched her eyebrow and studied him for a moment. "If you say so," she said, then tapped Anneth's arm with her knuckles. "You going to party with me or not?"

Anneth looked up at the sky. There were so many stars that she thought she could feel their heat. She scanned the tops of the trees, looking for the redbird. Perhaps it had followed her here.

"Might as well," she said, and took another drink. The warmth of the liquor spread out through her arms and into the tips of her fingers.

They tuned in a good AM station on the transistor radio and they all sang along when "Sixteen Tons" came on, their arms wrapped around one another's shoulders. Anneth was so drunk that she felt as if she could simply put her arms out like wings and float away from the whole crowd. She wished she were the redbird. She wanted to drift up, up where she could look down and see them standing there together, all of them a little in love with one another.

But then the song was over and everyone started to scatter. She noticed the fire was getting lower and lower. She picked up a small log and poked at the flames for a time. She took a deep breath of the woodsmoke and stood close to the fire so the scent would soak into her coat. The smell of the pines pushed at her from all sides, too, as soothing as menthol. She could feel the cold seeping through the back of her coat and thought about moving away from the fire so she could keep that sensation, but instead she took out a cigarette and held it against the embers. She sucked in the hickory flavor when she drew on the Lucky Strike.

She tried to shake away thoughts of Easter, lying asleep back at home. She hated that she was betraying her sister. She looked up at the sky for some comfort. The moon was nearing in on being full, and millions of stars spilled out on the blue blackness. The sky was always changing, but most people didn't notice this. Every night there was something different about it, whether it was the size of the moon or the number of stars or the texture of the blackness. Looking at the sky, Anneth thought, was like seeing God. When it was at its most beautiful, she sometimes had to turn away because it seemed too intimate.

All at once the guitar player was standing very near. She saw him only out of the corner of her eye, but she had memorized his shape by now. She could even make out his stance—hands shoved into the pockets of his coat, feet set apart as if he were firming himself against a strong wind. "Hey," he said.

She turned her head and met his gaze. "Hey, yourself."

"I been watching you this night," he said. He stood very close to her and she thought she could feel the heat of his body moving off him in waves. She looked again at his eyes. They made her feel as if she were peering over a high cliff that she couldn't resist jumping off.

"I hope you enjoyed yourself," she said, and took a hard draw on her cigarette. She let the smoke curl from her lips.

He smiled. "I believe you're the best-looking girl I've ever seen."

She tried not to grin and looked back up at the sky. It seemed lit from behind now, a sign of snow. She could feel the bourbon rise in her throat and catch there, hot and acrid, before going back down.

"Have you quit talking to me?" he asked.

"Do you believe in magic?" she said. "Do you think there really is magic in this world?"

"Yeah," he said without a pause. He stepped closer and put his big hand on her arm. "I do."

"Me, too."

She had a sudden image of Easter waking up and looking about her dark bedroom. She could almost hear her hollering out, "Anneth?" to the emptiness of the house and only the creaks of the wood answering her.

"I have to get going," Anneth said. "It was nice to meet you, Matthew Morgan. I like the way your name sounds. Like it's a made-up name, the two *M*s."

"How'd you know my name?"

"I asked," she said, and slipped into the woods, finding the path easily. Even though the moon wasn't completely full, it gave off light that touched the limbs with silver. She ran through the woods, aware of everything on either side of her. She could hear the creek, its sound intensifying as the water gained momentum on its way down the mountain. The trees seemed abnormally large; she expected their limbs to reach out and grab her. She smelled the coal smoke of the houses down below and the metal scent of cold. By the time she had made her way back down to the creek, she could hear Lolie up there calling for her. She liked the idea of their not knowing where she had run off to.

The houses were all dark. She hurried up the road and ran around to the back of their house and eased the back door open, but it creaked anyway. She stepped into Easter's room and saw her lying there, so still. She leaned down and kissed her on the forehead.

"I love you, Sister," she whispered. Easter's skin was warm. She had feared it might not be. She worried all the time about discovering Easter dead. Any day, she might find herself completely alone in the world.

EASTER AWOKE TO the smell of woodsmoke. It overtook her bedroom—a rich, hearty smell, the scent of warmth and light. She lay there without moving, staring out her window at the ghostly image of a gibbous moon that hung just above the mountain. Behind the old glass its shape was distorted and seemed to shimmer on the December sky, lit with the strange blue black of approaching daylight.

The scent of woodsmoke was one of knowledge. Anneth, she knew, had sneaked out the night before, and when she'd returned, she had come into Easter's bedroom to see if she was awake. Easter could picture her sister stepping carefully to avoid the planks in the floor that screeched the loudest, easing the door closed. But still Anneth had chanced getting caught just to come in and check on her. She wondered how long Anneth had stood there watching her sleep.

Four

....

Midnight and Lonesome

ANNETH TOOK THE SHOTGUN out of Easter's bedroom closet, balanced it on her shoulder, and set out for the mountain. She whistled a tune she couldn't name and thought of what Serena had always said: *A whistling woman is pure of spirit.* Anneth eyed the gray, moving sky that gathered low and threatened snow, her feet finding their own way on the familiar path up the mountain. She wrapped her bare hand around the metal of the gun and savored the coldness that lived there.

She spied a clump of mistletoe and planted her feet firmly. She brought the gun up to her shoulder, set her sights, and pulled the trigger. The mistletoe broke away and dropped down, clattering against limbs. She left it lying on the ground as she shot out another clump in the high branches of a gum tree.

Anneth shoved the mistletoe into the pockets of her coat and went on up to the top of the mountain. She stood on the outcropping of rock with her fists on her hips and looked out over the valley. The sky moved low and gray over the curls of smoke that rose up. Far across on the opposite ridge she saw a new mine. The company had cleared off a whole shelf of land to make a parking lot for the miners and it was a raw place on the earth. She looked away, remembering how that land had belonged to some of Lolie's people before it had been taken away from them. Coal companies could do that. It made Anneth too mad to think about. She closed her eyes and drew in the winter air, then turned without looking anymore.

She drew the butcher knife out of her pocket and hacked off the limb of a young cedar, then went back down the ridge, gathering boughs of holly and pine and laurel. She had so much Christmas greenery she could barely carry it all. Easter would die over Anneth's getting the shotgun out—it had been their father's and Anneth knew it was not to be touched—but she didn't care. That was the best way to get mistletoe out of the trees, and it was time to decorate the house. Easter was always getting upset over something these days, anyway.

They had fought the last two weeks without end, but now it was almost Christmas, and Anneth had no intention of squabbling through the holiday. Easter still refused to let her go out, even though school was not in session and everyone else was at the pine patch every night. A few days ago, Anneth had lain down in her clothes, waited until past midnight, and then carefully crept from her room, planning on joining the others for another party. But when she got to the kitchen, there sat Easter, drinking a cup of cocoa and waiting for her. She had found out about Anneth's last trip to the pine patch. "You carried the smoke home with you from the bonfire," she said.

Anneth whistled while she hung the greenery from the doorframes. She placed the cuttings all over the house, got out the red candles that they only burned at Christmastime, and popped corn to put on the tree they would go get later in the evening. She didn't want to fetch it without Easter. That would have been far too lonesome, to go cut a tree by oneself. Anneth was standing on a chair, nailing the mistletoe over the door between the kitchen and the living room, when Easter returned from town with Sophie.

The gun was still lying there on the kitchen table, but Easter didn't say a word about it. "Well, the house sure does look Christmassy," she said.

At least they could put the arguments aside to celebrate Christmas properly. Later, when they went to cut down their tree, Anneth had to bite her tongue to keep from mentioning the New Year's Eve party again. Easter had said that Anneth could not go, that she had to be punished for sneaking out to the honky-tonk. Anneth didn't mention it as she watched her sister walking in front of her, made big and round by her double layer of coats, carrying the big end of the tree.

On Christmas Eve they walked to Sophie and Paul's with their arms interlocked. Sophie met them at the door with her Christmas apron on. She was small and kind faced, her hair pulled up into a neat bun on the back of her head. What remained of their family was there. There was Paul, of course, sitting in his usual chair and entertaining everyone with his stories. Lolie brought her fiancé, Israel, but never hushed long enough for him to talk. She was still going on about how her cousin had lost his whole mountain to the coal company. They had a broad form deed and Lolie explained what this was, over and over, as if all of them didn't already know. Gabe came over from Pushback Gap with his new wife, Jimmie, who wore a tight skirt and drank liquor from a red aluminum cup that Gabe kept going outside to refill, as if every one of them didn't know any difference. No one said a word about it, even though Sophie set her mouth firmly and kept giving knowing looks to Easter. Jimmie watched them all with wet eyes. Her people had moved to Detroit to find work, and she kept saying, "I miss them terrible bad." Then she'd hand Gabe the red cup again and say, "Fix me another one, baby."

When the men went out to set off fireworks, Anneth went with them, although the rest of the women stayed inside. She begged Gabe for a drink of bourbon and he finally let her have a sip from the fifth he had hidden beneath the driver's seat in his car.

"That's enough," he said, snatching the bottle out of her hands. "Wild-ass."

AT MIDNIGHT, ANNETH and Easter walked back up the road to their own little house. The heat of the coal stove hit them when they got inside.

"Let's open our presents tonight," Easter said.

"Can we?" Anneth said, and clapped her hands.

Anneth had done enough babysitting to buy Easter a bottle of Heaven Sent perfume. Sophie had helped her make a bookmark for Easter's Bible out of quilt scraps. Actually, Anneth hadn't done anything except choose the colors—which Sophie had thought were too loud and bright for a Bible marker—but it was beautiful and Easter claimed to love it.

Anneth sat on the floor like a little child and opened her presents, carelessly ripping away the wrapping paper. When Anneth spread everything out before her, she knew that Easter had spent too much on her. There was a lipstick, a sweater set, a pair of galoshes, and a stack of movie magazines tied up with a length of twine. Easter sat on the floor beside her, watching her face.

"Why are you so good to me, Easter," Anneth said, "after all I put you through?"

"I've got something else for you, too."

"What is it?" Anneth said, and looked around the tree for another box.

"I'm going to go to that New Year's Eve party with you," Easter said. "You know I don't like to go to things like that, but I know how bad you want this."

Anneth wrapped her arms around Easter and held her close. She thought she could feel the blood running through both of their veins. She promised herself to never, ever betray Easter's trust again.

She would try, at least.

ANNETH INSISTED THAT they walk. It wasn't far to the old schoolhouse, anyway. The wind came up the valley in great gusts, blowing their skirts flat against their knees and smoothing back their hair. Easter had let Anneth fix her hair tonight. Anneth had fashioned Easter's hair into a fancy bun, although she usually just wore it pulled up in a knot on the back of her head. Her hair was too long—all the way down to the small of her back—and she sometimes thought of cutting it, but the Bible said a woman's hair was her glory, so she let it keep growing. Anneth had put little sprigs of holly all over the bun, and Easter actually thought it was pretty when she held the hand mirror up to look at herself in the chifforobe mirror. She had wrapped a gauze scarf around her head, but Anneth let her own hair fly. She never spent much time getting fixed up or fooling with her hair, and Easter loved this lack of vanity in her sister.

They walked on the side of the road next to the creek and watched the white water tumble over the rocks. It had rained all morning and now the mountain was sending down its flood. The rushing water sounded like a great fury unleashed.

"Hold on a minute," Anneth said, and squatted down behind a rock. When she arose, Easter saw that she had bent down there to get out of the wind long enough to light a cigarette.

"It looks so ugly for a woman to smoke," Easter said, walking along and looking straight ahead.

"I don't think it does," Anneth said. "Susan Hayward smokes, don't she?"

"How would I know?" Easter said. She never went to the movies.

"Every time you see her in a movie, she's smoking. And she's as pretty a woman as you're likely to see."

"Well, every man I ever knowed said it was ugly for a woman to smoke."

"I'm not out to impress nobody," Anneth said, and picked up her pace so she could pass Easter.

"You know the only reason I'm going to this is on your account, don't you?" Easter said.

Anneth put her arm around Easter's shoulder and walked along like that. "Yes, I know it, and I'm grateful to you always." She squeezed Easter's shoulder. "You never know, though. You might have some fun if you'd let yourself."

"I doubt it," Easter said.

Anneth laughed and the sound curled out in front of them, echoing up over the ridge.

"I never did like to be away from home on New Year's Eve," Easter said. "I always get sad on New Year's. It's a lonesome time, somehow."

"How could you be lonesome when you're with me?" Anneth said.

A gray winter dusk with a mist of rain on the wind came down and settled over the land. The air smelled of the sandy creek bank. Up ahead they could see the lights burning in the schoolhouse windows. Already cars lined the road, and even over the wind they could hear the music.

Outside, men stood around a barrel that was meant to hold fire, but tonight it was too windy. The men always gathered around a fire, though, and seemed not to know where else they should get together. The light falling from the window caught in a bottleneck's glass and sent out a little glint across the yard. The men nodded to Anneth and Easter, and a couple of them elbowed each other in the ribs. Easter knew they were taking note of Anneth's looks. Everybody always did.

Inside, the music overtook everything. The band was assembled in front of the wall of blackboards. Someone had taken chalk in hand to scrawl "Happy New Year's" across the boards in a tight, hunchbacked cursive. There were two guitar players and a banjo picker, a fiddler, and even a pianist. A woman sat in a folding chair amongst all the men, taking long slugs from a bottle of orange Nehi and holding a tambourine capped over her knee. They knew a lot of mountain music but were most famous for covering Hank Williams's songs. One of the guitarists had RIP HANK WMS embroidered on his guitar strap.

People were milling about in a great frenzy, as if they hadn't been out of the house in ages. There were feisty girls running after boys, and older women who walked through the crowd looking for someone to call down.

Easter was hustled into a corner by Lolie. Lolie was short and thick bodied, both traits made more noticeable by the beehive hairdo she wore tonight. Her face exuded kindness. Easter loved her wide green eyes and the way Lolie put her hands on people's arms when she talked, but Easter also found her to be exhausting. Lolie talked so fast that Easter didn't know how she had time to catch her breath. Lolie was telling her about Israel and how they were planning to run off to Jellico, Tennessee, where they would elope.

"They say everybody there is a justice of the peace, that the town makes half its living off marrying folks," Lolie said. "And Israel drove all the way to Hazard to buy a dress. You ought to see the one he picked out. Looked like something Mamie Eisenhower would wear. But I ended up getting the one I wanted."

Israel was leaned against the far wall, telling jokes to some of the other boys. Lolie had on too much perfume, and it got into Easter's mouth and made her feel sick. Lolie hadn't given Easter the chance to respond, even when she asked her a question. Anneth stood close by and watched the dance floor. She moved her hips to the music, snapping her fingers.

As soon as the first licks on the guitar announced "Hey, Good Lookin'," a boy asked Anneth if she would dance. He was about the same age as Anneth but a head shorter, his face sprinkled with freckles.

"This song was wrote special for you," he said, smiling with crooked teeth. Anneth put her hand over her mouth and looked back at Easter, making her amusement plain to see. Easter rolled her eyes.

"Are you a good hand to two-step?" Anneth said.

"Best in the county," he said, and put his arm out.

"We'll see about that, hoss," Anneth said, and hooked her arm into his. She walked beside him out onto the dance floor. Easter tapped her foot to the song, watching them as they moved about the floor. She didn't really follow country music, but she had liked Hank Williams. She'd cried when they told on the radio about his being found dead in the backseat of his car.

Israel strutted across the room, nodded to Easter, and took Lolie's hand. He wore his hat cocked down on his forehead and was wearing a necktie, although no one else was. "Let's dance, baby," he said, and finally Lolie was gone. Easter held her elbows in her hands and watched the dancers. There was a big stove at the front of the building and she could smell the sweet scent of hickory burning. The room was so hot and close that she felt beads of sweat popping out on her forehead. She didn't know why they kept loading the stove with wood; there were enough people in here alone to make the place warm by way of body heat.

Easter located Anneth on the dance floor and watched how perfectly she two-stepped. The boy was pulling Anneth to him as they danced, and she kept pushing him back, all the while wearing a big smile on her face. The boy whispered in Anneth's ear and she leaned her head back and laughed as if he were the funniest person she had ever met.

When the song was over, Anneth made her way back to Easter, scanning the crowd and hooking her hair behind her ears. The boy followed along but Anneth waved him away without even turning around. "I don't want to dance to no old slow song," she said.

Anneth grabbed Easter's hand and led her back to the concession table. Here sweating women sold peanut butter fudge and bottled drinks and popcorn that smelled so good Easter became suddenly hungry. Anneth asked for two bottles of Dr Pepper.

"I seen the best-looking man while I was up there dancing," Anneth said as she plucked a half-dollar out of her little change purse and paid the woman. She looked over her shoulder at the crowd. "Now I can't find him nowhere," she said, holding her bottle against her chest as she clicked the purse shut with a thumb and forefinger. "Lord, he looks just like Elvis Presley."

The drink was so cold there were little flecks of ice floating around in it. Easter held it against her forehead for a moment to cool herself down. Anneth scanned the crowd, looking for the man.

"Oh, there he is," Anneth said. She leaned closer to Easter, pointing. "See him standing against the wall there, smoking?"

There were at least a dozen men lined up against the wall, all of them with cigarettes hanging from their lips. But then one of the men looked up and Easter realized that he was looking right at them. Easter grabbed Anneth's finger and forced her hand down. "Quit pointing," she said. "He's seen us looking at him."

"Good," Anneth said. "Ain't he pretty?"

He had black hair that was too long on the top, combed up with Vitalis that shined beneath the bare bulbs hanging from the ceiling. His eyes were very dark and his lips were so full and curved that they looked like a woman's. He did favor Elvis Presley a bit, but only Anneth would have noticed the resemblance. There was something about him that seemed very confident yet out of place here. Easter felt the way he looked: like she wanted to be somewhere else. The man held their gaze a moment—neither smiling nor frowning— then looked away.

The woman in the band was so short that she had to stand on a wooden box and wave her arms around to get everyone's attention.

"We're going to do a cakewalk now. At the back." She held her Nehi in one hand and her tambourine in the other. "There's twelve cakes back there, so you can pick which one you want when you win. You all got requests?"

People in the crowd yelled the names of many songs at once, but Anneth cupped her hands around her mouth and hollered out "All Shook Up" so loudly that the little woman's head jerked around to find her in the crowd.

Anneth stepped up onto a nearby chair so the woman could find her. She finally honed in on Anneth and said, "Honey, we don't play no rock 'n' roll."

One of the guitarists stood. "Sure we do," he said. "I know that song."

Several people in the crowd clapped and squalled out, but some of them walked on back to the cakewalk as if ignoring all of this. Easter looked up at Anneth, who was still standing on the chair. She was smiling at the guitarist and gave him a wink. He winked back, smiling a crooked little grin, and the crowd clapped again. Of course Anneth knew him, Easter thought. The little woman stepped off her box as if trying to show her disapproval, and the rest of the band pulled back, leaving the guitarist alone on the stage. He looked back at them for a moment, then lit in on the song himself. Easter had never heard it before, but it definitely wasn't country. The man closed his eyes while he sang, as if he could feel it all through him. He moved around a little too much and arched back in a way that Easter found embarrassing.

Anneth stood on her chair and danced. Her eye never left the guitarist, and Easter could see that Anneth liked him simply for the way he held that guitar, his hand moving up and down the fingerboard, which was long and slender as a woman's calf.

Several people went out to dance—boys sliding their partner on the floor between their legs and throwing her over their shoulder—but most people were walking around the cakewalk table. Suddenly Lolie was beside Easter again. "He's supposed to quit playing," she said.

"What?" Easter said.

"So somebody can win a cake. He has to quit playing in the middle of the song so they can stop on the numbers on the floor," Lolie said. "Don't you know how to do a cakewalk, Easter?"

Easter just nodded, but really she didn't know how to do a cakewalk. She had only been to a couple of dances. Even when she was in school, she never went to any gatherings except church. It was most likely a sin for her to even be here. She didn't know why she had gone to church all her life; she just had. Serena hadn't exactly been devoted—she had gone to church sporadically, and on the holidays—and nobody else in her family went on a regular basis except Sophie and Paul. Easter had always simply wanted to serve God, in His house. It was a desire she couldn't explain, the same way she couldn't explain how she knew things before they happened.

The guitarist stopped singing abruptly, giving the guitar one final quick strum, and his eyes fell directly on Anneth, as if he knew that she would still be in the same spot. She stood on the chair a moment longer, then stepped down onto the floor again.

The band moved out and started playing "I'm So Lonesome I Could Cry." The cakewalkers started in again, but a sort of reverent silence fell over the place. Everyone loved this song. Easter could not stand it, as it was too sad. Loneliness was caught right in the notes of that song, and the players were picking it out of the guitar strings.

"That feller's coming over here," Easter whispered to Anneth without moving her eyes from him. "He seen you pointing and now he'll be asking you to dance, I guarantee."

Anneth busied herself with buying a bag of popcorn so that she could act surprised when he approached. By the time he had reached them, she had a small grease-splotched bag, and she took two kernels from it to place on her tongue. But he didn't even look at Anneth. He stood in front of Easter and looked her in the eye. She smiled nervously, not knowing what he was doing.

"Won't you dance with me?" he said. He was even better looking close-up. But it wasn't just that. Easter liked the way he stood, the way he held his shoulders square and solid.

"I'm Pentecostal," she said. "We don't believe in dancing."

He smiled. "Listen to that song, though," he said. "How can you not believe in music like that?"

Easter wanted to take his hand and go on out to the dance floor, but she hesitated. "I better not," she said. "I can't dance."

"If you can walk, you can dance," he said, and held out his hand.

"Go on, Easter," Anneth said loudly, hitting her arm. Then she leaned down close to Easter's ear and whispered, "Live, Sister."

"You just follow me. There's nothing to it," he said. "Come on before the song's over."

Easter took his hand. He led them out into the middle of the floor and put one hand on the small of her back. With the other he held her hand high in the air. She put her free hand on his shoulder the way she had seen other women do. Whenever Anneth danced with a man, she always held on to his belt at his hip. Easter wouldn't have dreamed of doing such a thing.

She tried to follow his lead and stumbled a couple of times, then fell into the rhythm of the music. "See there, you dance fine," he said. "You're Easter Sizemore, ain't you?"

"How did you know?"

"I've got inside information. I'm El McIntosh."

"El? Where'd you get a name like that?"

"My real name's Oliver, but everybody started calling me El. They say I look like Elvis, but I think they're crazy. I like 'El' better than 'Oliver,' though." He smiled and spun her around. "Why don't you do much dancing?"

"I go to church."

"Well, you done told me that," he said. "What could be wrong with dancing to such a fine song? David danced for the Lord, didn't he?"

"That's different," Easter said. She looked out at the crowd of onlookers and felt as if they were all watching her. She caught a glimpse of Anneth, who smiled widely and nodded her head in an exaggerated manner.

"You're too pretty a girl to be standing and watching everybody else dance," he said.

"To tell you the truth, I don't ever get asked to dance. Usually all the boys ask Anneth instead of me."

"Who's that?" he said. His breath smelled like peach pop.

"My sister, the one that was standing by me. You mean you didn't see her over there dancing on that chair?"

"No," he said, and she searched his face to see if he was lying.

"Every boy I know is crazy over her. Look at her," Easter said, and nodded her head in Anneth's direction. "Look how beautiful she is."

"You don't think you're beautiful?" El said, and pushed his thumb into the small of her back. "You are. You look like a good woman to me. That's what I'm looking for."

Easter felt the momentary impulse to agree with him. She started to say, *I do try to be good*, but swallowed her words, realizing how strange that would sound. She felt her face turning red.

"I want to come see you," he said.

Easter laughed and looked away. "I don't even know you, buddy."

"That's how you get to know somebody," he said. The song ended but he kept moving for a moment. Then he stopped but held on to her. "Will you let me come up?"

Easter caught sight of Anneth again over his shoulder. She was still nodding, fretting her eyebrows together. Easter could almost hear her whispering into her ear again: *Live, Sister.*

She felt the words assembling themselves in her mouth but had no intention of letting them fly on the air. And then she heard herself saying, "Come talk to me awhile and we'll see what happens."

WHEN SHE WASN'T watching Easter, Anneth had her eye on Matthew Morgan. She'd noticed him as soon as she'd gotten there. She'd liked him the first time she met him up there at the pine patch, but when he'd sung that song for her, she'd seen him in a new way. There was something gentle about the way he let the music lift him up off the stage. She had liked the way he moved as he sang "All Shook Up," but she liked seeing him singing "I'm So Lonesome I Could Cry," too—the way he seemed to be swept away by the song, like he could feel every mournful note.

And there were his bangs, which hung down in his eyes when he leaned over the guitar, and the way he didn't pause to brush the hair away. He moved his body in a way she had never seen, as if it were part of the music. When the song was over and he opened his eyes, she remembered why she had been so drawn to his face. Those eyes were like looking at deep water, the kind of water that draws you in on a hot summer day.

He looked out over the crowd while the lead singer tried to figure out the next song to play for the cakewalk. The people in the back were hollering out for something fast. Matthew looked out at Anneth and winked again and this sent a start through her legs. She knew that later tonight she would be kissing him, putting her fingers over his closed eyes.

And then it was as if she was being pushed back into the corner of the room without moving at all. The music slowed and blurred until it sounded like a record being played at slow speed. Everything about this place seemed pathetic to her—especially herself. She looked down at her cheap dress and worn shoes, noticed only the brightness of one of the sprigs of holly she had pushed into Easter's hair, its berry so red that everything else looked drab.

She felt the blues moving in on her—all at once, out of nowhere, like a wind that moved in and out of her body whenever it took the notion. It crept down the backs of her arms and up her neck. Her face felt flat and square; her mouth, drawn. She wanted to go somewhere and lie down and cry, and she didn't know why, but it was a real, solid thing that felt like a slow wave washing down into the pit of her stomach. It took the shine off everything.

She saw Easter coming back from the dance floor with that good-looking man but she slipped through the crowd and took her coat from the table near the door. She swung the door open, and the cold air hit her like a slap in the face. Anneth shoved her hands into the deep pockets of her coat and went down the steps two at a time. The men all tipped their hats to her and smiled, but she didn't acknowledge them. She passed them by and went to the purple shadows of the woods, where she struck a match and lit a cigarette with a shaking hand. She sucked in the smoke, hoping this deep breath would calm her, but it only made her more nervous.

She liked the winter air that slid up her legs. Her ears were in that state of cold between numbness and pain, and she liked that dull hurt, too. The sky was so big above her that it seemed like something that could come down and settle over every person on earth and smother them to death.

She heard footsteps approaching and reluctantly looked away from the sky. The lights of the schoolhouse lit the person from behind and Anneth couldn't tell who it was. As he came closer, she recognized the language of his body, the confident way he carried himself. Before he even spoke, she knew it was Matthew. "Hey," he said.

She took a long draw from the cigarette and listened to its crackle on the night's stillness before replying. "You're always saying that to me," she said.

"We finally took a break from playing," he said. "I been wanting to talk to you all night."

"I appreciated you playing that song for me," she said, staring him in the eye. "First time I ever heard rock 'n' roll in person. Just on the radio before."

"You like Elvis Presley, huh?" he said. His face was lost to the shadows, and she longed to see his eyes.

"I like all of it," she said, and looked skyward again.

"What're you doing out here by yourself?"

"I just wanted to be alone. Wanted to look at the sky."

"You want me to go back in, then? If you want to be alone."

"No," she said, and put her hand on his chest. She liked the way he smelled. He was wearing Old Spice. When she went to Conley's Drugstore, she always smelled all of the men's colognes. Easter said Anneth couldn't possibly remember her father's scent, but she did. She still missed his smell. He had worn nothing except an aftershave he sometimes splashed on. The drugstore didn't carry that brand anymore. More than that, he had smelled of coal—a rich, black smell that he couldn't wash out of his skin.

"I like the way you dance," he said. "I've been thinking about you ever since I saw you up at the pine patch."

"I've thought about you, too," she said, and moved her hand on up into the warmth of his neck. She felt along his square jawline, and he didn't move. Her thumb fit perfectly into the dimple in the center of his chin. Something in her didn't want her to have this good moment. But then again she wanted so much to touch him. She didn't care what anyone thought. She took a step closer to Matthew and told him her name.

"I already know your name," he said. He didn't move, as if he was afraid of her. She breathed in the whiskey on his breath.

"When you was up there playing that rock 'n' roll song, I was wishing that you were kissing me," she said.

He put one big hand on the small of her back and cradled her shoulder with the other. He pressed himself against her and put his mouth on hers. It seemed he was eating at her lips. She had never been kissed like this before, but she let him. She opened her mouth and let his tongue in. She put her hand against his back and pushed him closer against her, arching her leg into him. When he was done, she rested her head against his chest. The blues were still there, strewn out across her shoulders.

He put his face into her hair and took a deep breath. "God almighty, girl. That was about the best kissing I ever had in my life. And you are flat-out beautiful."

"So are you," she said, thinking of his eyes, blue as glass. She felt drunk and distant, like she was watching herself from very far away.

He kissed Anneth again and then walked her back so that she was leaning against a beech tree. She put her hands up into his hair and then held them flat against the sides of his face. He had shaved recently and the stubble felt good to her, like rough lumber. Then she pulled away. This felt too good, and she couldn't stand out here kissing him all night. She wanted to go home. She wanted to lie down, to be safe in her bedroom with the quilt pulled up to her neck.

"I need to go," she said.

He grabbed her hands and ran his thumbs over her wrists and looked into her eyes, even though she could not really see his face. "You want to get out of here?" he whispered.

"No, my sister is waiting on me. I have to get on home."

"No, I don't mean from the dance. I mean from here, period. I'm going to Nashville to play music."

She looked at him a long moment. She knew that she should say he was crazy, that she barely knew him. But she understood him; she could hear in his voice that he had a dream and he meant to pursue it, and she liked that. "I wish I could," she said. "I can't leave Easter, though. She needs me."

AFTER MIDNIGHT, WHEN they had all stood in a circle and sung "Auld Lang Syne," Easter let El drive them home. All three of them sat in the front seat, with Easter in the middle, looking at him while he talked. She held Anneth's hand, though. She knew that something was wrong. She had known the minute she saw Anneth come back into the school. When Anneth had the blues, it was spelled out plainly on her face. Easter could simply feel it. It was as if there was a warm air that moved off of Anneth, letting Easter know what she was going through. Sometimes Anneth missed school and lay in her bed until past noon, crying into her pillow. Easter could remember their mother doing this, inconsolable in her grief for their dead father. Yet Anneth had never known a grief so large. Sometimes Easter wondered if her sister had sucked up some of their mother's sorrow and carried it around with her. Nothing helped Anneth except, sometimes, Easter's singing.

Anneth barely spoke on the drive home. Occasionally El leaned forward and asked her a question, but she only answered yes or no and kept her forehead leaned against the cold glass of the window. She held tightly to Easter's hand, occasionally gripping it harder, as if pains were shooting through her.

El was a talker, and Easter liked the way he talked. He talked to her like she was another man. Like they were equals. There was none of this mush that a man usually fed a woman when he was trying to get her. He talked about his family and the hard way he was brought up and the new job he had just taken as a truck driver for Appalachian Freight, hauling coal over the mountains. And he asked about her, too, which was different from most men she talked to. He wanted to know all about her people and the way she was brought up and all that, but she couldn't bear to talk about it. There was too much to tell.

When they pulled up into Free Creek and El put the car into park, Anneth got out and slammed the door. Easter rolled the window down with the glass rattling against the frame and leaned out. "Anneth, ain't you even going to tell El thanks for the ride?"

Anneth waved a hand without turning around. "Thanks for the ride, El."

Easter rolled the window up. "I'm sorry," she said. "She gets like this sometimes. Next time you see her she'll be friendly as can be."

El leaned toward her a little. "It don't matter."

Easter held her purse in her lap. For the first time, she felt as if she had run out of things to say to him. His car heater was pumping out a warm flow on her legs and she hated to leave the closeness of the car and step out into the cold. And she didn't know how to say good-bye.

"I've sure enjoyed meeting you, Easter," he said.

"I've enjoyed it, too."

"You going to let me come back and see you?" he said. Even in the darkness she could see his smile. "I know where you live now, so you can't really keep me from it."

"I want you to," she said, and then felt foolish. "Come up one evening this week. I get home from work about three-thirty."

Then he leaned forward and kissed her without taking his hands from the steering wheel. She had not been kissed in a long time— not since high school—and it caused a knot to unlace in her chest. She kept her mouth tightly shut and her hands on her purse. She was very aware of the sound of the heater. He went to put his arms around her, but she backed away. She patted around on the door until she found its handle. "I'll see you," she said, and stepped out into the cold.

She listened to his tires splashing through the mudholes until he reached the paved road, where they hummed into the night. Then she could hear the sound of movement on the mountain behind their house. Limbs snapped underfoot, and last fall's leaves rustled as someone stomped on them. She knew it was Anneth, climbing up to the bald. Easter walked across the backyard and stood at the foot of the mountain. The black trees glowed in the moonlight.

"Anneth!" she hollered. "Come down from there."

Something was wrong. Otherwise Anneth would answer her. She eyed the mountain again, and thought there was probably enough light for her to find her way on the path. She put her purse on one of the porch chairs and walked toward the mountain.

Despite the light of the full moon, it was still dark. She heard small animals moving around in the brush on both sides of her. She was moving quicker than Anneth and could hear her clearly. It seemed that Anneth wasn't on the trail, though; there was the sound of too much brush being trod upon. It sounded as if Anneth was just climbing the mountain wildly, crashing through laurel bushes and letting branches snap off as she walked through them. Once, Easter heard the dull thud of rocks clattering down the side of the mountain, and she knew that Anneth was scrambling up the cliff face. Easter began to walk faster, nearly running. "Anneth!" she said again. This time she did not yell; she knew that her voice would be carried all the way to the top of the mountain on the New Year's night.

Slowly Easter made out her sister's shape in the darkness, at the bald. The field held thousands of wildflowers in the spring but now it was just a brown meadow full of sawbrush and dried weeds. Vine and Serena had always taken them there as children; Vine said it was a magic field, that flowers bloomed there out of season so they could show their colors all at the same time.

Anneth was sitting on the ground with one leg pulled beneath her. Her auburn hair shone in the moonlight and her face was hidden behind her hands. As Easter walked closer—cautious now, like someone approaching a deer—she could hear Anneth crying.

"Anneth?" Easter said, squatting down on the ground. She put her hand on Anneth's back and started at the cold her coat held. "What's wrong?"

"I don't know." Her voice was hoarse. "I'm so sad I don't think I can stand it."

Easter looked out at the field full of moonlight. There was no use in looking at Anneth; her face was lost to the shadows. "Did something happen at the dance?"

"No," Anneth said. "I was having a good time, but all at once, something just came over me. I don't know what's wrong with me, Easter."

Easter rubbed Anneth's back. As they sat, their breath plumed out into the air before they sucked it back in. The night seemed desolate and frozen. Far across the next ridge there was the cry of a screech owl, like a woman screaming for her life.

Anneth brought her leg down and ran her hands over her face. "I don't understand what happens to me. I can be having the best time, and then something hits me right in the belly. A great big sadness moves in on me and just overtakes everything."

Easter took Anneth's chin in her hand and held her face up so that the moonlight fell upon it. Anneth's face glowed within her hand. "You've got no reason in this world to be unhappy. Look at you— how beautiful."

Anneth ran the back of her hand over her eye and let out a

shuddered breath. "Sometimes when I see the night sky, I get that feeling you have when you think about eternity. You know what I mean?" She looked from the moon to Easter. "And I can't understand it, because it's so pretty to me."

"You just notice things more than other people," Easter said, and put her forehead against Anneth's. "You always have."

"I know I've got no reason to be unhappy," Anneth said, and got up. She stood with her hands behind her back, looking at the sky again. "But somehow I just feel like nobody will ever love me. Nobody but you."

"Good Lord, Anneth. Everybody who knows you can't help but love you."

"It don't feel that way," Anneth said, and started walking down the path. Before Easter even had time to get up and follow, Anneth was lost to the shadows of the woods.

Five

....

Things Change

ON NEW YEAR'S MORNING, the sky turned gray as the back of a tarnished spoon, gathered itself low and moaning over the mountains, and stayed that way for three months. The creeks froze solid enough to walk on. Snow fell big as torn pieces of paper, drifting down like it might never stop, as if the world might eventually be made completely of ice. If a woman had stood on the highest mountain in those parts, she would have seen a thousand columns of coal smoke making their way skyward. The wind tore through the valley, pushing drifts up next to porches, creating occasional twisters of white in the road. A trip outside took ten minutes of getting ready: wound scarves and high boots and two pairs of socks. A walk into the yard for a bucketful of coal or an armload of firewood caused chapped lips that caught like cockleburs against a scarf. The cold seeped through gloves like water.

But on Free Creek, heat bloomed in the breast of Easter Sizemore. She was so aware of the fever glow that she feared it might show up—a white pulsation that people could see from a long ways off. She felt as if light could shoot right out of the ends of her fingers. She couldn't stop herself from falling in love with El.

She awoke one morning and knew this. The realization was just as sudden as her sitting up in the bed. She sat there and watched morning light move around the room and thought of El. She had dreamed of him all night. It seemed she had spent the whole night walking alongside him, holding his hand as they made their way up a long dirt road with cedars on either side of them. The scent of the cedars had been overpowering and the light had been strange and beautiful, lavender colored. In this purple tint she had been able to see El's face in a new way. She could see below his skin, behind his eyes. And what she had seen pleased her: kindness. She had looked into his chest and seen a good heart.

She wanted to tell Anneth of her discovery, wanted to let her sister know that she finally felt something *more,* but once she let her feet touch the cold floorboards and walked down the hall, she saw that Anneth had gotten out of bed first and was already gone. The remnants of a hastily eaten breakfast—toast and a half cup of coffee—sat on the kitchen table, like a note to let Easter know that she had already left for the day. Anneth had taken a job working weekday evenings and weekends at the Depot Café in town, and she was devoted to going in for overtime when school was canceled because of snow. Every morning she arose early and caught a ride with Lolie. Lolie worked at Shoes Galore and spent her days frustrated not only by her omnipresent boss, Sissy Goins, but also by the fact that no one bought pretty shoes in the winter—only galoshes and heavy boots. Lolie was not afraid of driving in the snow. She had Israel put chains on her tires and she hit the road as if it were completely dry.

Easter's legs were sore. It felt as if she had really spent the whole night walking, just like in her dream. Once, she had dreamed of swimming in a great black lake—this was just before Serena died—and had awakened with her hair soaking wet. Another time she had a dream of flying through a snow-covered valley, and when she awoke, her room had been so cold that she had seen her own breath, even though the stove roared with fire in the living room. She had told no one about her dreams—not even Anneth—fearing that she would end up telling everything she saw and knew.

She lit the gas ring and put the coffee back on to heat. Outside, the mountain stood humpbacked in the new coating of snow. Red-birds flitted around in the yard.

Easter made herself a bowl of oats and sat at the kitchen table. She felt giddy. She couldn't wait to see El. She wanted to tell him that she loved him. She didn't know how people went about doing such things. It was something she had wanted yet feared all of her life.

Easter's mother had loved too much, and it had killed her. Every-one knew how big the love had been between her parents; it terrified Easter to think that she might be following her mother. She knew what had happened to her mother, although her grandmothers had never told her. She had seen it play out many times in her dreams, seen from high above, as if she was motionlessly perched in a tree and watching all of it in silence. She knew that it had happened just this way.

Easter was ten and Anneth just five. Serena was working in the house after she had fixed the girls breakfast and seen them off to school. Vine had gone off to Black Banks to check their post office boxes. Serena was so caught up in her chores that it took her a while to realize how silent the house was that morning. Birdie was always so noisy. If she wasn't crying she was usually sitting on her bed, combing out her hair and singing. That had always been a comfort to Serena—Birdie in there singing, "I sing because I'm happy, I sing because I'm free." But that morning there was nothing.

Serena went down the hall and found Birdie's room empty. The bed was made and Birdie's silver hairbrush and comb and mirror were all lined up neatly beside one another on the dresser. The little vial of lavender she kept in her pocket was sitting there, too. Serena hurried through the house, opened the back door, and looked out. There was Birdie, hanging from the locust tree in the backyard, long dead. A hen pecked at the grass beneath Birdie's feet.

When Easter had this dream-remembrance, she felt what Serena had felt. Serena was not really shocked, as she had been expecting this for a long while. Still, there was the sharp tear in her gut, as if someone had shot her in the stomach, and there was the sickness that swam up her back and across her shoulders, down her arms. Vomit rose in the back of her throat. Serena had midwifed Birdie into this world, and now she saw her swinging there in the tree. For a moment Serena felt she might die, too, from a sudden black grief.

Serena ran back into the house and pulled a drawer so hard that it came all the way out of the cabinet and crashed to the floor, silverware clattering out. She felt such an urgency to hurry that she thought of nothing else. She didn't want anyone to see Birdie hanging there that way, her face blue, her hair uncombed. She grabbed a butcher knife and ran back out of the house and to the tree. There was a chair that Birdie had used to climb up, and Serena sat it upright and stepped up to saw on the thick rope. Serena took Birdie in her arms as she cut the rope in two. She eased down from the chair and sat on the grass, Birdie spread across her legs. She didn't know how long she sat there, rocking her, but eventually she was aware of Vine standing there, back from town.

Vine didn't say anything. She lifted Birdie out of Serena's arms and carried her into the house. Birdie had never been much bigger than a breath and she looked even smaller in Vine's arms. It seemed that Birdie had become a deflated thing, her thin white wrists dangling down, black hair sliding over Vine's arm like water made of coal. Serena stood in the middle of the yard and watched as Vine went into the house, knowing that this would kill Vine, too. In that moment Vine's face and body both seemed to crumble in on themselves, and she was never the same. As Serena stood there, she heard Vine let out one awful cry, a sound like all the pain that Vine had ever known, made audible.

"Your mama went in her sleep," Serena told Easter for years and years. "I found her after you went to school."

Vine and Serena had Birdie buried in her high-necked blouse and hired the funeral director to come make her face look right, though no one they knew had ever used the funeral director before, as he was reserved for town deaths.

Easter willed herself to stop thinking about it. She couldn't handle reliving the funeral, too. When she became conscious again, she smelled the coffee burning on the stove. She jumped up from the table and found the coffeepot trembling on the burner, the aluminum bottom scorched black. The boiling coffee pecked against the sides of the pot. She wrapped a rag around her hand and lifted the pot over into the sink. When she ran water over it, a cloud of steam hissed up. Easter looked through it and out into the backyard. There stood the locust where her mother had died, right in her face all the time. She wondered why Vine hadn't had it cut down.

She didn't know why she was comparing herself to her mother. Her mother had loved too much, but she had lost her mind. El made Easter feel as if she had finally gained an understanding of the world. She knew that he wasn't perfect, but she had to keep telling herself this. She loved everything about him: the way he put on his hat, the way he ate with his hand wrapped around his fork, leaning over his plate to shovel in food as if it might be snatched away. She liked watching him drink a whole glass of milk without pausing for a breath, the *bump-bump* of his Adam's apple with each swallow. She loved his stories of growing up poor with nine brothers and sisters, his mother a widow woman who walked four miles to work at the telegraph office in Victory. He told her about his time in Korea and rolled up his shirtsleeve to show her the tattoo he had gotten while there: an eagle with a scroll in its claws. Whatever had been written within the scroll had been blacked out, and when she asked what it had said, he always changed the subject. She knew that it had been some woman's name. But she didn't care. He was hers now, and that was all that mattered.

They never went anywhere, although El occasionally wanted to go to a square dance or a honky-tonk; he loved a big crowd. But he always gave in when she said she didn't want to. Sometimes they went into town and watched *I Love Lucy* on the television sets in the windows of Mullins's Hardware. He went to church with her but she knew that he didn't enjoy it. He sighed loudly without meaning to, though he seemed to perk up when she sang and played the piano. Eventually, she told herself, he would be so moved by her singing that he would go to the altar and repent. She knew people were whispering about her at church — they thought it wrong for her to date a sinner — but she didn't care. She knew he had a good heart.

They spent most of their time at the house. He cooked for her. She had never known a man who liked to cook, but he had worked in the kitchen during boot camp. He fried hamburger steaks and made chili that was so spicy she had to have a glass of water nearby to eat it. They listened to the Grand Ole Opry on the radio and sat on the couch holding hands. Sometimes she caught Anneth watching them, but there was never envy in her eyes. She believed Anneth was happy for her, though she saw something else in her sister's eyes that she couldn't interpret. Then again, there was a lot going on with Anneth these days that Easter wasn't clear about.

Anneth had a secret life that was not secret. Easter knew about it without knowing how, but she made no move to interfere. Anneth was spending more time with Matthew Morgan than she let on. Still, Easter wanted Anneth to be happy, and as long as she kept going to work and school, that was all Easter cared about. What she didn't know was that Anneth thought she might be falling in love.

EVERY DAY AFTER he got off work at the mines, Matthew Morgan came to see Anneth at the café. He had black coffee and lemon pie, holding his tongue out so she could watch the meringue dissolve there before she slapped him on the back and walked away. Every evening he brought her home, and on the way she sat in the middle of the seat with her hand on his thigh. Sometimes they pulled into the road at the abandoned lumber camp and kissed. He cupped Anneth's breasts in his hands and she felt the heat of his fingers shoot through her skin. Although he always bathed up at the mine, she could still taste coal on his lips. He left the car running for the heat and the radio. They kept the volume down low, but when Sam Cooke or Patsy Cline came on, Anneth would push him aside and turn it up. While she sung he kissed her neck, but she was lost to the music. She closed her eyes, sang along, and felt as if she was completely alone in the world. Often the song would end and the deejay would come on to rattle off the closings due to the weather, though Anneth still would not respond to Matthew.

"Who's your favorite singer?" she asked one day.

"Buddy Holly, no doubt about it," he said. "If I could be as good as Buddy, I'd die happy."

"My favorite song of all time is 'This Land Is Your Land,'" she said.

He laughed and put his hand into her hair. "I thought you loved rock 'n' roll."

"I do, but that's the best song. I cry every time I hear it," she said. "Especially that part where he wonders if this land really was made for everybody."

"I would have never guessed that for your favorite song," he said. "It's kind of pinko."

"It's beautiful is all," she said, and then she put her hand on his crotch and began to kiss him again. She loved the way his chin scratched against hers, the way his hands felt moving under her blouse. She paused for a moment and looked at his eyes. If she stared into his eyes long enough, she could believe that she really loved him.

"You never cease to surprise me, girl," he said. He wrapped his arms around her and they sat there, not saying a word.

It was the last day of March when Matthew moved his mouth up from her exposed shoulder and along her neck and spoke with his lips against hers. "Marry me," he said.

"Not until I graduate," Anneth said, not missing a beat. She was aware of his disappointment—it seemed like a solid thing right there in the seat next to her—but ignored it so she could focus on the way an entire inch of snow balanced itself on a dogwood branch. She lit a cigarette and leaned her head back against the seat as she pushed out smoke rings, perfect circles that didn't break apart until they hit the windshield.

It must have been the unknown promise of spring that overtook the men that day, because El asked Easter the same thing that afternoon. The only difference was that Easter said yes.

THAT MAY, EASTER married El, and Anneth moved in with Sophie and Paul for a month so the newlyweds could have a proper honeymoon alone. They all agreed it would be for the best. For one thing, it would give Anneth time to adjust to the fact that a man would be living in their house. She knew the way a man's presence seemed to overtake everything.

When she wasn't at work, Anneth spent the afternoons sitting in the yard with her aunt and uncle. They cut up cabbage for kraut and peeled cucumbers for pickling. Anneth wasn't much good at this kind of labor, but she enjoyed watching the careful way Sophie and Paul worked together, like they were two parts of the same machine. She put slices of cucumber on her tongue and let them rest there for a long while before biting into the fleshy whiteness. She loved how a cucumber remained cool inside, no matter how hot it was outside. It tasted like a mouthful of solid, clean water. Sometimes Paul set up his quilting rack on the yard and they would all help choose the colors. Anneth wanted to put in all bright colors, but Sophie slapped her hand away from the pile of scraps.

"If it was up to you, the whole quilt would be purple and red. You have to throw in some darks to even it all out," Paul said.

Sophie let Anneth go out even on school nights, but only after Paul was asleep, which was easy, since Paul lay down just after it got dark every night. Sophie pushed fifty cents into Anneth's hand. "As long as you don't come in drunk and don't stay out too late," she said, and Anneth felt like kissing her slender hands. "Don't let Paul know it, either. Be careful."

Sophie liked Matthew. Anneth knew that Sophie was taken by his eyes, just as she was. He acted different around Sophie, like a gentleman. He called her "ma'am" and stood up whenever Sophie left the kitchen table on those evenings he came to have supper with them. It made Anneth want to laugh because he wasn't a gentleman at all. He was all the time trying to get at her titties and kept a fifth of Jim Beam under the seat of his car.

They always waited until Paul had gone into the bedroom; then Sophie would walk them to the door and lean against the wall while they put on their shoes. "Remember, don't be drinking and going wild," she said as they made their way down the porch steps.

One night, Anneth did get drunk. She couldn't help herself. Matthew had taken her in the back door of the Hilltop, where the band was playing. It was a Friday night and the place was packed. Anneth sat at a little table just off the stage, where she could look out and see everyone. Since she was with the band, the waitress kept her supplied with Pepsi and shots of bourbon. Anneth tilted her head back and let the whiskey slide down her throat, then wiped her mouth on the back of her arm like a man. When Matthew plugged in his electric guitar, and his buddy, Blake, sat down at the piano and they started in on "Whole Lotta Shakin' Going On,'" she couldn't control herself. She took the final shot of Jim Beam that would make her completely drunk and jumped up. She shook her hips to the beat, lifting her legs and holding up her skirt so her knees had plenty of room to move around. She shimmied her shoulders and put her arms up over her head and let her head sway about. They were almost as good as Jerry Lee Lewis himself and she had never had so much fun dancing.

The room spun around, shifted, like a boat crashing into giant waves. She spun with it, feeling more alive than she ever had before in her life. *I'm alive,* she thought. *I'm here, right now.* She leaned back and yelled out, then stumbled into a couple and leaned against the man's back, laughing with her face against his shirt until his date pushed her away. Even after the song ended and the band took a break, she kept dancing. Then the jukebox kicked on and played a slow country song. Back at the table, Matthew stood waiting for her.

"I think you've had enough, baby," he said.

"No, I haven't. You're wrong," she said. She put her face against the open space at his collar and kissed his neck. "Get me another shot of that whiskey."

"Sophie will hate me for letting you get this drunk, and it's about time to close this place down," he said, and kissed the top of her head.

"I don't give a damn," she said, "about nothing."

"Come on, Anneth. Straighten up, now." He caught the elbow of a passing waitress. "Bring her some coffee."

The waitress snorted in amusement, revealing teeth smudged with lipstick. Anneth stuck her finger up to point at the woman's mouth and laughed.

"We don't have no coffee," the waitress said. "Maybe some 7UP."

"Whatever will help her."

Anneth lay against his chest and ran her hands down his back to settle on his rear end. She tried to push her fingers beneath the waistband of his pants. "I want you," she said, as if out of breath. "Right now. Take me away from this place."

Matthew pulled Anneth onto his lap and held her, but he was unaware when she shed quiet tears on his shoulder. He didn't know that she was thinking of her own dead family: her grandmothers, her parents, all gone and never coming back. She saw each one of them in their caskets. Even if Easter said Anneth wasn't old enough to remember her daddy's dying, she remembered. Maybe memory lived on in your blood or crawled up under your skin. She didn't know. And now Easter was gone, too, in her own way. Down there in their house with that man. All Anneth had was Matthew.

IN THE CAR, she laid her head in Matthew's lap and didn't say a word. She watched the way light traveled around the cab of the car as they leaned into the curves between town and Free Creek. Matthew played the radio and rolled down his window so that the wind would move over her face. He must have thought she was asleep, because he never said a word. He drove slowly, as if prolonging the trip, and only occasionally forgot himself enough to sing along with whatever came on the radio. When the car slowed and bumped over the rickety bridge, she knew that they were home. She found the door handle and shoved out before Matthew could put on the parking brake. He had pulled into Paul and Sophie's, but Anneth wanted to see Easter. She started down the sandy road, aware of him behind her trying to catch up.

"Anneth, wait," he said, as if from very far away. "I said wait, now, damn it."

She could hear everything separately: the cry of the crickets, the scratch of the katydids, the squeals of the night peepers. The roar of the creek as it raged toward the river. She let all these sounds overtake her so that she didn't have to hear Matthew begging her to turn around. She glanced up at the sky to find a fingernail of moon on the blue blackness, pecks of stars like granules of salt spilled out across a dark tablecloth. Here was their house, where she had lived all her life with her sister. She could picture them within, Easter snuggled up to El's back. It was too much.

Matthew pulled at her arm, but she shook him away.

"Get up, damn it!" she hollered. "Everybody get up and look at this moon!"

"Come on, now, Anneth," Matthew said. "You've got to hush—"

"I said get up and see this beautiful night. Live, Sister! Easter, get up! Come out here right now, every sumbitching one of you, and look!"

Only when she saw Easter and El's shapes standing on the porch did she stop yelling. El was shirtless—his chest broad—and he leaned on the banister as if staring at a wild animal. Easter was rushing down the steps in her nightgown. With the yellow porch light behind Easter, Anneth could see right through the thin fabric. She looked at Easter's white feet, curved and long. Anneth had always made fun of Easter's feet, told her they looked like a boy's. Anneth took a step backward and then she was falling, falling right into Matthew's arms. His knees buckled and he sat down in the road with her head in his lap. When she looked up at his eyes, at Easter squatting down to plead and cry, Anneth knew that if she didn't make herself do something, she'd cry in front of every one of them. If she couldn't choke it down, she might come right out and say, *I'm hurting,* where everyone could hear. So she started laughing. She thought she might never, ever be able to stop.

PART TWO

....

The Land Waits

I am wealthy with earth and sky . . .
I am possessor and possessed.

—James Still, "Mine Is a Wide Estate"

Six

....

When Love Was Young

ANNETH DIDN'T LOOK back as they pulled out of Free Creek. They took it slow across the rough bridge and then Matthew turned onto the main road and gunned the gas, leaving black marks on the highway. The tires issued a piercing squeal. He reached across the seat and took hold of her hand.

"We're on our way now," he said. He looked very young in the early-morning light of high summer.

She was leaving home for the first time in her life. In two hours she would be in a different state, and before long they would be married. This was not the way she had pictured her wedding coming about, but she liked it. She liked that they didn't even have their rings yet. She liked the fact that she wasn't even going to have a real wedding dress. It was all spur of the moment. An adventure. And that was the best way to go about things. That was the way to make memories.

She held on to his hand tightly as they passed through Black Banks. At the stoplight, she felt like hollering out to the people on the streets that she was off to get married, that she was going to Tennessee. She wished she would see someone she knew so she could lean out her window and tell them. No one in this world knew what they were going to do, and she felt a thrill in having this secret. It would be dark before Easter returned from church and found her note. Anneth had taken a long time in writing it, although the note was not very long at all. She had chosen her words carefully and tried to use her best handwriting. She had used a piece of the stationery she saved for writing real letters. It was the smoothest paper, so cool and flat that she paused every so often to run her hand over it. The border was ivy and in the top right-hand corner there was a redbird perched among the greenery.

18 July 1960

Dear Sister,

I have run off with Matthew Morgan to get married. We are in love. We are not getting married because we <u>have</u> to. What I'm trying to say is that I am <u>not</u> pregnant, so don't think that. We're off to Jellico, where we can get married quick. I guess we will stay down there a couple days. Please do not fret. I know that you will, but just trust in me and believe me when I say this is for the best. This is what I want. Be happy for me. I will miss you terrible bad but soon we will be back together. I will call you from Tennessee later tonight. Until then, pray for me and know how much I love you.

As always, I remain yours,
Anneth Gail Sizemore <u>Morgan</u> (<u>!!!</u>)

Soon Matthew was driving them through the mountains toward Tennessee. She had never been this far away from home before and she kept pointing out things to him. He laughed at her amazement. He tuned the radio to a station out of Knoxville and sang every word along with Buddy Holly on "It's So Easy." Anneth knew this song, too, and their voices bled into one like they were meant to sing together.

"You harmonize good," he said when the song was over. "You ought to start singing with me."

She pulled her legs up beneath her and didn't bother to smooth her skirt out across her knees. The windows were down and the breeze went up her skirt, cooling her thighs. "I'd love to do that," she said.

"You'll try anything, won't you?"

"I sure will," she said. "I want to do everything in this life that I can. People just set around and talk about doing stuff all the time, but I intend to do everything. I want to sing and dance. And see everything that I can. This life's too short to set around dreaming and not doing it."

He ran his hand down the side of her face. "That's why I want to marry you," he said. "That's why I love you."

She scooted across the seat and sat next to him. She laid her head against his shoulder and breathed in his scent as he sped on down the winding road. She felt so comfortable there that she drifted off to sleep without meaning to. She had wanted to experience every moment of this, but the thrill had worn her out. She slept better than she ever had in her life — a deep, black sleep without any dreams.

Matthew awoke her when Tennessee came into sight. He moved his shoulder up and down to jostle her awake and she sat bolt upright in the seat, unsure of where she was for a moment. It was so strange not to awake at home. She missed the smells of the house, Easter's coffee, and her warm bedsheets.

"Look," Matthew said. "We're about to cross the state line."

They were going up a mountain, and as soon as it leveled off there was a small sign: WELCOME TO TENNESSEE, Y'ALL. The state flag flew from a thin metal pole. As they passed it, Anneth looked back to see the sign welcoming people to Kentucky. Tight painted letters spelled out WELCOME TO KENTUCKY, THE BLUEGRASS STATE, which Anneth thought was funny, since she had never in her whole life seen any bluegrass.

It was strange to think they were in a whole different state, because it looked just like home. The mountains were big shouldered and black, crowding close to the road in the gathering darkness. Jellico lay in a long, finger-shaped valley that she could look down into. There were several lit church steeples, and houses stood in rows on the mountainside. She could see their windows, rectangles of yellow from the lights inside. There was a drive-in theater down there and she could see the image on the screen. *Cat on a Hot Tin Roof* was playing and Liz Taylor was standing in the bedroom in her black bra and black silk slip hollering to Paul Newman, who was in the bathroom, trying to avoid her. This was the scene where he hobbled around on his crutches and fell. Paul Newman was so good looking that Anneth could barely stand it. And Liz Taylor was the most beautiful woman she had ever seen, besides her own mother, who could've put anybody to shame. Anneth thought she might get her hair cut like Liz's when she got back home. Matthew had taken her to the theater in Black Banks just last week to see that movie. She had cried and cried after seeing it, without really knowing why. Matthew didn't think it was a bit sad. But she did because she saw that it was a movie about people who had dreams that would never come true. That was the worst thing she could think of. The only thing worse, Anneth thought, would be to not have any dreams at all. At least she had her dreams, and now she and Matthew were on the open road and anything could happen.

The cars sitting before the screen were lost to darkness, but she imagined all the people down there, some of them eating popcorn without taking their eyes away from the movie, others necking in the backseat. Having Paul Newman and Liz Taylor on-screen together would lead anybody to make out. Gradually the winding road led them down into the town. The stores were already closed and dim lights burned behind the plate glass windows.

"Looks like everything's closed up. We'll have to wait till the morning."

"What will we do until then?" she asked, genuinely concerned. She thought they would pull up in front of a church and sleep in the car, or something to that effect.

Matthew laughed. "Get a motel room," he said. He had just played a show in Hazard and had plenty of money. He kept it rolled up and wound about with a red rubber band in his pocket.

She sat in the car while he went in to get their room. The light from the neon sign was beautiful to her. She squinted her eyes to get a better look at it. The neon border was the brightest pink—the way she imagined a flamingo to look in real life—and the word inside, VACANCY, was greener than a spring leaf. She had never stayed in a motel before; Easter would die if she found out that Anneth had done so before getting married. But they were going to be married in the morning, after all. Anneth decided that she would sleep with him tonight. It was just one day and it wouldn't make any difference. Besides, she hadn't been a virgin for a while now, though she had held off from going to bed with Matthew because somehow he had seemed different from those other boys.

She wanted to feel Matthew's hands running up and down her back. She wanted to kiss his eyes and breathe in his scent among the tangled covers of the bed. She wanted to get as close to him as she could. She had gone out with lots of other boys but she always came back to Matthew, and now she wanted to know him better than she knew anyone else in the world.

THE MOTEL ROOM smelled like stale cigarettes. Anneth tried to open a window but found that they were painted shut. Matthew came up to her from behind and put his arms around her. He slipped his hand inside her blouse and cupped her breast.

"Don't," she said. "Not yet."

He kept on, though. He kissed the back of her head and she turned around quickly and put her hands up into his wavy hair. He had used too much Vitalis but she liked the feel of oil in her fingers. She kissed him on the mouth. He walked them backward and fell heavily onto the bed. He leaned down and began to unbutton her dress and she watched his hands as they worked. His fingertips were big and square. He peeled her dress back and then he stopped and looked at her. He ran his hands over the cool silk of her slip.

"My God," he said.

Anneth had thought she would be nervous about her first time with Matthew, but she wasn't. She could hear the blood drumming in her ears and it seemed as if her heart was going to beat out of her chest, but she wanted to do everything. He undressed in no time, and when he was naked she was embarrassed at first. He lay back and was still for a long time, letting her run her hands down his stomach and up the inside of his thighs, discovering everything.

She sat up in the bed and pulled her slip over her head. She felt free. It was the freest she had ever felt, to be sitting there with nothing on, the neon light of the motel sign causing their room to glow. She had never been completely naked with anyone before. She would never go farther than her bra and slip, and most everything had taken place in the backseat of a car. Now it seemed she was seeing everything in flashes. She took hold of his hand and stroked his fingers. His mouth was cold on her breast, as if he had been sucking on ice.

"You have to be easy and take things slow," she said.

She was the one who sped things up, though. Her body took over and she let it. She rose up and pushed him back against the headboard. She crawled up onto his lap and wrapped her legs around his waist. He moved his hands up her back and his touch felt like rain on her skin. Chills ran up the backs of her arms. His mouth tasted like cigarettes and Pepsi. She pressed her lips against his until their teeth clicked together. She kissed his neck and then his chest, until she had made her way down his entire body.

She fell back onto the scratchy bedspread, and as he came down on top of her she said, "I love you," but it was lost to his moaning. And even when she made these words come out of her mouth, she didn't know if she believed them. She wanted to, though. She wanted desperately to love him.

MORNING CAME IN slanted white lines through the window. She awoke to sunlight in her eyes and the sensation of someone standing over her. She put a hand before her face to block the whiteness and saw Matthew standing beside the bed with his hand held out.

"You're going to sleep your life away," he said, and then she saw the rings he held on his outstretched palm. "I snuck out early and was waiting when they opened the jewelry store."

She sat up in the bed and he put the rings in her hand. They were just plain rings, like a hundred others she had seen, but they looked beautiful lying there on her palm. She felt the urge to slip hers on but knew this was bad luck.

"They're perfect," she said, and then realized that the sheet had slid off her breasts.

Matthew reached down and touched her nipple with his knuckle. "You better get ready," he said.

She put on her best dress—lavender, with big pearl buttons that ran from neck to hem—and a pillbox hat. She had taken a pair of scissors and cut off the black netting that came down over the bill of the hat, because it looked too old and matronly. Matthew had stopped in London and let her run into a department store to buy a crinoline. She never wore crinolines and she wanted this to be her only excess on her wedding day. She had told the old lady that it was for her wedding and the woman had gone on and on about how she ought to wait and get married proper, with her whole family there.

"Seems like Jellico is cursed for weddings," the woman said. "Everybody I know that gets married down there has bad trouble." Anneth lit a cigarette and just smiled at everything the lady said until she finally gave up. "Well, I'll give you a discount on account of it's your wedding day," she said.

The crinoline scratched against her legs but she liked the way it looked. It made her feel like a town girl and she danced around in front of the mirror to see how it moved on her.

As she studied herself, she realized that she finally wasn't a virgin anymore. She had thought that she had lost her virginity long ago, but truly she hadn't. She stared at her face and thought she looked different. She felt different. Like a grown woman. She had felt like a woman for years now, but she had only been fooling herself. She loved the sort of cleansed-out feeling she had, the way her breasts ached from Matthew's working on them, the little patch of heat atop her right shoulder where he had sucked forth a hickey. She put on lipstick and pinched her cheeks for some color.

They walked down the main street to the little drugstore that sold the marriage licenses. The day was unnaturally perfect, like a day out of a movie. The air was fragrant with summer smells and the ridges were misted with stripes of heat that had not yet moved down into the valley. People on the street were dressed up like they had somewhere important to go. Just as Matthew started to open the drugstore door, Anneth remembered that they had to have blood work done before they could be married.

"We'll have to go to the hospital first, won't we?"

Matthew pulled a certificate out of his back pocket and smiled. "I'm way ahead of you, baby." She reached for the paper but Matthew held it high, next to his head, as if making a presentation. "There's a doctor in Black Banks who'll sign a blood work if you give him a ten-dollar bill. This way they don't have to put a needle in that pretty arm."

The drugstore was packed with people eating in the green vinyl booths. Waitresses strutted about in smart pink uniforms and little white aprons, holding the coffeepots and loaded trays high above their shoulders as they navigated the crowd. Anneth could hear bacon sizzling on the grill. She sniffed at the burned-toast smell in the air and realized that she was famished.

There was an old man standing at the big cash register, shaking out the newspaper the whole time he read from it. The light from the bare bulbs overhead made a blinding circle on top of his bald head. Matthew tapped his blunt fingers on the counter and the old man looked up from the paper over his thick glasses. "Hidy," he said.

"Morning, buddy," Matthew said. He called every man he met "buddy," even if the man was older than him. "I was told this was the best place to get a marriage license."

"We'll sure sell you one," the man said. "Got your blood-work certificate?"

Matthew produced the yellow piece of paper from his pocket and handed it to the man without unfolding it. The man eyed it and then looked from it to Anneth a couple of times. He felt below the counter and pulled up a clipboard that had an ink pen attached to it by a long, beaded cord. "Fill this out and we'll be in business. Just get you a booth and have a bite if you want to."

It was nine o'clock in the morning, but Anneth ordered a cheese-burger plate with slaw and fries. The breakfast here was the same that Easter cooked at home — bacon, eggs, home fries, gravy, honey — but she only got to have cheeseburgers on the rare occasion that she had enough money to splurge in Black Banks. Matthew kept telling her to get whatever she wanted — the crinoline, the best room at the motel — so she did. She savored every bite, closing her eyes while she tasted the meat, pickles, lettuce, and tomato. The onion was sweet and full of juice. Matthew had long finished his breakfast before she was even halfway done. He filled out the forms and she put down her burger long enough to sign her name. He smoked one Chesterfield after another and made small talk with the waitress when she approached their table to check on them. He was so friendly he charmed people everywhere he went.

"You all from Kentucky, huh?" the waitress said. Her name tag identified her as Swella, a name that made Anneth want to burst out laughing. She wanted to ask her where her mother had come up with a name like that.

"How could you tell?" Matthew said with a smile, knowing their accents gave them away.

Swella looked him right in the eye while she talked to him, although she hadn't even glanced at Anneth. "I like the way Kentucky boys talk," Swella said, and put one hand on her hip. Her fingernails were bitten down to the quick and had been sloppily painted so that some of the polish ringed her cuticles.

Anneth leaned over the table and poked her finger into Swella's ribs. "Hey, honey?" Anneth said. Swella turned to her, startled. "Can't you see I'm setting right here?"

Swella blinked twice without saying a word.

"I'd hate to have to stomp your ass where you work," Anneth said. She eased back down in her seat as if completely relaxed.

Swella turned to twist off, but Anneth grabbed hold of her arm. "And I'm interested in some of that pie, too," she said, nodding her chin toward the coconut cream sitting beneath a glass dome. "Bring me a piece of that and a cup of black coffee. And do it pretty damn quick."

"I swear, girl," Matthew said, smiling. "You're a hellcat, ain't you?"

"She wasn't the only one flirting," Anneth said, and kicked his shin under the table.

Anneth finished up her pie and coffee while the old man looked over their papers. He sat right down in the booth with them and signed the certificate and pressed a notary mark into the page. He took Matthew's money and wished them luck.

"Where's a good place around here to get married?" Matthew asked.

"Usually people think of that before getting the license," the man said. He laughed and chewed on the toothpick lodged between his false teeth. He looked at Anneth while he laughed, but she didn't smile back. She never laughed out of politeness.

"That's why everybody comes to Jellico, buddy," Matthew said. "Because you don't have to think first."

The man seemed to find this awfully funny. He had to make himself stop laughing before speaking again. "What kind of preacher do you want?"

Matthew started to say, "It don't matter a bit," but Anneth cut him off. She placed both hands flat on the table. "We need a Pentecostal preacher. I want to get married Pentecostal."

"I didn't know you was so religious," Matthew said.

"Even sinners have their choice," Anneth said.

IN HER GRIEF, Easter dropped the letter and let it drift like a feather onto the creek. She watched it float away over the rocks and then into the quick current. On and on until it disappeared forever. Perhaps it would slide on down the many rivers until it found its way into the ocean. She wanted rid of the words Anneth had left for her. Without the letter, perhaps she could convince herself that Anneth had not run off. She had read it first in the kitchen, where she had found it, then on the back porch, and now, this last time as she stood beside the creek.

It all made sense, though. She should have known on the day of her own wedding, the way Anneth sulked around the corners of the room, trying her best to look happy but failing miserably. She should have known by the way Matthew brushed Anneth's hair back out of her eyes, the way he couldn't keep his eyes off her. And more than anything else, she should have known that it would all lead to this in those first strange days after El moved into their little house. Even when Anneth came back to live with them, she had stayed gone as much as possible, or stayed holed up in her room. Easter had thought it was simply because a man had not lived in the house since their father.

But Easter had been blind and foolish not to see that Anneth felt as if she had lost her sister. She had quietly finished up her days of high school and walked the graduation line, and then after another year of dating Matthew, she had run away to be married. There was nothing to be done about it now. Anneth was almost twenty years old and had been grown a long, long time. At least she hadn't gotten married at sixteen, as Easter had feared she would. Easter really didn't know why she was so upset; Matthew was a good man. Maybe that was the problem—he was too good. She doubted that Anneth's marriage to him could ever survive.

Easter went around to the back of the house and grabbed her hoe from its place leaning against the coal shed. She needed something to get her mind off everything. It wasn't just that Anneth had sneaked off to get married; Easter and El had been having trouble, too. Gabe had problems with Jimmie and had been coming down a lot lately. Sometimes Easter came home to find Gabe and El playing poker or sitting on the porch, drinking, singing along with the radio. Gabe liked to start trouble when he was drunk. It was an unexplainable thing about him, and she was just waiting for the day when Gabe would cause a great fight between her and El. Once, El had cupped her behind in one hand, right in front of Gabe. She had knocked his feet off the chair where they were propped up. "I won't have this going on here," she said.

Gabe had snickered. El looked up at her and she saw that he wasn't as drunk as she had thought. His face was so clear and flat with anger that she realized he wasn't drunk at all, but had only been playing along with Gabe, who looked near to passing out. "I'm a good man, Easter," El said. "I work hard, try to do my best by you. But if I want a beer every once in a while, I'm going to by God drink one." She knew that he had thrown in the "by God" especially to spite her.

She chopped the weeds hard, sweat rolling down into her eyes. The sun beat down on the top of her head and she lifted her hair off her neck. Even though it was pulled up into a bun, it had gradually fallen down and was hot on her neck. If she was smart, she'd go into town and get it cut. She wondered sometimes if she wore her hair long because she wanted to or because the church wanted her to. She wiped her brow and went back to work. She had hoed around the tomatoes and the corn and the beans before she realized that blisters were forming on her hands. Then she let the hoe drop and fell down on her knees in the rich loam, praying. When she finished, she realized that she hadn't prayed like this in a while. Serena had always prayed in the garden. Easter helped her with the hoeing and dreaded it when Serena felt the urge to pray, as her grandmother sometimes knelt for a half hour. It was disrespectful to keep working while Serena prayed, so Easter had to stand there waiting after she'd finished her own hoeing. Gnats swarmed around her face in the heat. Once, she had said, "Not now, Granny. Please." But Serena had gotten down anyway and looked around with a stern face. "No, I'm bound to pray now, honey."

Her knees were in that same soil where her grandmother had knelt so many times. But she was not as good a woman as Serena had been. Lately she had been full of doubt and lust and everything except goodness. She clasped her hands and prayed again, this time for her own forgiveness. With her eyes closed and her head bent, it was easy for her to realize that this was a strange thing, to be asking for forgiveness. Because really, what had she done to repent for? She knew that it wasn't what had already been done, but what she was about to do. Because for the first time she admitted to herself that she needed more, too. Maybe not an adventure like Anneth's — running off to Tennessee — but a change. She held her hands together tightly and tried to find the proper words. She had never prayed for herself before in her life.

THE IN JESUS' NAME Pentecostal Church was one block away from the drugstore. The building wasn't really like a church at all. It looked like an old storefront. There were curtains covering the big plate glass windows, and gold lettering on the glass: THREE SUNDAY SERVICES, PRAYER MEETING EVERY TUESDAY AND WEDNESDAY, ALL-NIGHT SINGING FRIDAYS, WEDDINGS ANYTIME. PASTOR R. C. SHEPHERD. The church must have recently moved in; customer bells still hung from the door. They rang out loudly when Matthew went in.

Anneth stood back in the open doorway and looked at the announcing bells. As the air from inside pushed out past her, Anneth sniffed and realized this had been a bakery at some point. The smell of cinnamon and chocolate still lingered. She suddenly felt so sad that she could hardly stand it. She wanted Easter here with her.

She walked on in and didn't hear a word as Matthew talked to the preacher. The faces of the people around her registered briefly. There was a tugging at the back of her lungs that made her worry that the old sadness she carried around might be blooming again. *Not now,* she thought. *Not on my wedding day.* Before long she found herself in a Sunday school room where she was to get ready, and now her homesickness for Easter hit her like a fist to the stomach.

She wanted to marry Matthew; she wanted to be married right now. But she wanted Easter and El as her witnesses. Not the preacher's gray-skinned wife, Zinnia, who smelled of mothballs and liniment, and his spinster daughter who wore glasses so thick that her eyes were magnified to twice their size behind the lenses. Zinnia had bouquets in the refrigerator standing in the fellowship hall. There were bunches of roses, daisies, and mums. Anneth chose the daisies. "I usually charge a half-dollar for them," Zinnia said, "but you're so pretty I want to give them to you."

Zinnia stood in the Sunday school room with Anneth and asked her if she needed anything. The daughter slumped in the corner with her arms crossed and her head cast down. She was pitiful and Anneth knew she ought to be friendly to the poor girl but couldn't bring herself to do so. Her mind was too occupied. Zinnia claimed to be a good hand to fix hair—she had always wanted to be a hairdresser, she said, but her husband thought it was a sin to fix up too much. "You're so naturally pretty there's nothing to add to," Zinnia said.

There was a small window in the room that looked out onto the backyard. A huge tomato plant grew there, where a block of sunlight came down between the house and the mountain, and its leaves pressed close to the window. She could see the red of a tomato just below the distorting glass. She stared hard at the plant, willing herself to do this alone. She felt a shudder go through her.

Zinnia put her hand in the small of Anneth's back. "Honey, are you sure you want to do this?" She lowered her voice and took a step forward so that her hot breath played in Anneth's ear. She looked behind her to make sure they were alone. "If you're not sure, don't do it. Or you'll have a life of misery."

"Yes, ma'am," Anneth said, and heard her voice as if from very far away. She did not meet Zinnia's eyes but kept her gaze on the tomato plant. The garden would be full of life back home. It was strange to think that the world was operating the same back there, since she felt so far away from Free Creek. She knew that as the crow flies there was very little distance between them, but it was too big a gulf. She wanted to fall against Zinnia and cry until she felt better. "It's just I wish my sister was here. I wanted her to see me marry."

Zinnia patted her back. "Oh, honey. I'm sorry. I know what you mean. I still miss my sisters from when I left home. That's part of marrying, though. Leaving your people behind. You have to cleave to your man."

"I'll never do that," Anneth said, her voice harder than she intended. "Leave my people behind, I mean. There's no way."

Zinnia just nodded, but it was obvious that she was only resigning herself to agree.

"I'm ready," Anneth said, but she wasn't. Still, if she didn't do this quickly she'd never do it at all. Zinnia opened a door and waved to begin the ceremony. The organ music started and Anneth felt as if she was about to die. She walked out into the foyer of the church and sucked up her homesickness and grief. She could feel tears standing on the bottom of her eyelids. But then Matthew stepped out in front of the altar and their eyes met. She shook Easter from her mind and walked on down the aisle.

MATTHEW GRABBED HER up from the car and carried her to the motel room. He had a hard time fumbling around to get the key into the doorknob but did it without dropping her. He laid her on the bed and kissed her so hard on the mouth that she couldn't even protest. Neither of them undressed. He let his trousers slide down around his legs and jerked Anneth's panties off. He kissed the insides of her thighs and she undid the buttons on his shirt, peeling it back so she could put her face against the flat muscles of his stomach. But then he was sitting up in bed and she was straddling him with her dress and crinoline and everything between them. She arched back, her hands against his chest, then held on to the sides of his neck, and his mouth searched for her lips, his hands moving on her hips. Cool beads of sweat broke out on the small of her back and a great warmth swam all through her.

Afterward they lay on the bed with the sounds of coal trucks rolling by the motel.

"Why don't we head on over to Nashville from here?" Matthew said. "We're only about six hours from there."

"That's an awful long way," Anneth said around a mouthful of crackers. She was hungry again and had pulled a pack of Nabs off the nightstand. "I thought the band had another show lined up this weekend."

"Yeah, but I'm thinking of trying to go solo," he said. He positioned himself on his side, put his elbow on the bed, and supported his head that way. "I'm tired of mining coal all week long and playing little clubs on the weekends."

"But I'll miss home so bad—"

"I've got a dream, Anneth."

She liked the way he said that. Just hearing him talk about dreams pleased her. When she talked like this to Easter or Gabe or Aunt Sophie, they barely paused in whatever they were doing, the silent equivalent of saying, *Oh, that's nice.*

"I want to be a real singer. I'd like to sing rock 'n' roll one of these days. But I've got it all figured out," he said. He got up quickly, grabbed Anneth a Dr Pepper out of the silver cooler he had packed in from the car, and got back into bed without ever taking a pause in his talking. "The easiest way is to get into country first—because I can play any country song there is. I can hear one verse of a country song and pick up the rhythm on my guitar. I know I can do it."

"I wish you could, Matthew," she said, and took a drink. The Dr Pepper was so cold that it hurt her teeth. "But I got a job to get back to. I told them down at the diner that I'd be back Monday. I'm lucky they let me off long enough to get married."

"If I make it in the music business, you won't never have to work again. We won't have to worry about nothing." He moved down and laid his head on her stomach and she put her hand in his hair. "I want more out of life than that. I want us to have the biggest life we can have, and I can make that happen. I want to give you everything you deserve."

She took another drink and looked out the window at the hills. There were no mountains in Nashville. Of this much she was certain.

Matthew rolled over so that he was facing the ceiling and took her hand and kissed it. As he talked, his words were warm against her fingers. "Do you know what it's like to have a dream? To want something so bad you can taste it?"

She turned and looked him in the eye. She could see sincerity there. He did not blink. She put her hand on the side of his face and held his gaze. "Tell me something, Matthew. The first time I met you, you told me you believed in magic. Just like that, without even having to think about it. Were you just telling me that?"

"I believe in magic," he said. "I do."

Anneth didn't have to think about it a minute more. If nothing else, it was an adventure. The thought of being that far away from Free Creek and everyone she loved didn't cross her mind at that moment. She didn't think about where they would live or how they'd get by until he got a good gig, or anything else. All she thought was that they were young and free and she loved the way that word—*adventure*—felt in her mouth. She whispered it to herself, and when Matthew asked what she had said, she only replied, "Let's go, then."

Seven

O Nashville

EASTER HADN'T BEEN fishing since she was a child, but the memory resided in her hands so clearly that when she felt the pluck of a bluegill on the end of her line, she immediately drew back her rod to set the hook and started reeling the fish into the boat. She couldn't help growing excited as the bluegill raced toward the river's bottom, pulling her line taut. Then it came up so close to the water's surface that she could see a zoom of its glistening back as it caught sunlight. She stood, causing the rowboat to rock and tremble, but did not lose her balance as she reeled the line all the way in and swung the end of the pole around so she could take the fish off the hook. The bluegill hit the wooden floor and flopped with such strength that it nearly made its way back into the water, its iridescent scales sending glints of sunlight against the sides of the boat.

"Here, I'll get it," El said, rising up from his seat at the end of the boat. He had been watching her quietly except for the loud clap he gave when she managed to get the fish into the boat.

Easter snatched the fish up off the floor with one quick motion and reached in to grasp the neck of the hook, working it back and forth. "I can get my own fish off, thank you very much," she said. "You seem to forget I'm a country girl."

El leaned over to unlatch the lid of the wire basket he had tied to the side of their boat and held it open while Easter dropped the blue-gill in. She dug into the cold loam of the coffee can to pull out another night crawler.

"What do you think about that, now, buddy?" she said to El. "I'm already beating you."

"We've only been out here twenty minutes," El said, smiling. He pulled his T-shirt over his head and sat there bare chested. She knew he had done this not because he was hot but because he relished the feel of the breeze against his skin. "You won't be ahead long."

"We'll see who comes away with the most when we get ready to go home," she said. She sat down and baited her hook, cast her line, and looked out over the winding expanse of the Black Banks River. She could smell the sandbar willows that leaned over the water, the dripping cliffs farther upstream. Here the shade was thick and blue and a breeze was always present, just enough to move the boat around in a slow little circle from the anchor. She heard the glee in her own voice and saw the peace of this place and instantly chastised herself for the tenth time that morning.

She had let El talk her into going fishing instead of going to church. In the last year her churchgoing had been their biggest problem. It wasn't that El griped about her going to church, really. But often the only day he was home from work was Sunday, and she couldn't blame him for not wanting to spend his only time at home within the confines of the church house. He wanted to be out fishing or driving up to Natural Bridge or simply sitting around the house with her. It was a dilemma—miss church to be with your husband, or go to church and not see him for another week. At first she had been relentless, not letting anything stand in her way of attending both services that were held on Sundays. She told him that he ought to enjoy going to church, that he ought to see it as a release, the way she did, but as soon as those words escaped her mouth she knew they wouldn't work on El. Because of course everyone didn't think of church the same way she did. It was a place where people wore their best clothes and talked in hushed tones — how could that be relaxing for most people? Slowly she began to see his point and started to attend only one service on Sunday — usually the Sunday morning meeting so that El could sleep late — but today was the first time she had not gone to church at all. They had left early in the morning and packed a picnic that they took up to Pine Mountain. They had eaten on the big rocks up there and laughed at the little cars on the roads below and climbed the mountain's rough trails to see the laurels that grew out of the cliffs. When they came to a place of slick, moss-covered rocks, El had taken her hand and guided her through. He had run his thumb across her palm and it had stirred up a feeling in her that felt very much like a kind of salvation.

Then they had driven back home, and El had talked all the way and made her laugh so much that she didn't even think twice when he suggested that she skip the evening service so she could go fishing with him. They had shoved El's little rowboat into the back of his pickup and driven down to the Black Banks River to fish awhile. When Loretta Lynn came on the radio, singing "I'm a Honky Tonk Girl," Easter was surprised to realize she knew every word of this song, as if it had been sung to her when she was a child and she had tucked the lyrics away in the back of her mind. She hadn't even been conscious of hearing this song before, but obviously she had heard it. When she sang, El tapped his thumb on the steering wheel and nodded his head to the beat.

The evening church service would be starting in ten more minutes, and here she sat, intent on catching another fish. What made her feel most guilty was that she didn't feel too bad about missing church. El was right — God could be found on Pine Mountain in those laurel bushes, could be found in the little ripples on the river's surface—but still, she should have felt worse than she did. She knew that this was the way people fell into temptation and forgot the ways of the church—she had heard preachers talk about that her whole life. She tested the weights of both pleasures: the ease of laughter between herself and El, and the sensation of the Holy Ghost racing up and down the backs of her arms. Both things filled her with joy. And it seemed that God could be more easily present in time she had with her husband than El could be in her own dialogues with the Lord.

She didn't want to think too much about it or it might all start to make sense. She would never believe the way Anneth and El did that church really wasn't necessary as long as you believed in something—but she found herself seeing their side of things. That was a mistake, not because she intended to be small minded, but because thoughts like that were not really thoughts at all. Instead, they were temptation.

She cleared her mind and focused on her line, waiting for another nibble.

"Do you think Anneth's all right?" she said.

"Why wouldn't she be? She's a grown woman."

"She's never been away from home, though. Running off to Nashville like some wild fool. Always looking for some kind of adventure."

"There's nothing wrong with that," El said. His worm made a plop in the water as he cast his line out again.

"I worry about her, though."

El gave her a quick glance, then went back to staring at the water. After a long silence he said, "You worry about everything. About Anneth. About the church."

She hated it when he said this, and he said it all the time. She didn't want to be seen that way, didn't want to be known as the worrywart old woman. She had been seen that way all her life, not only as a worrywart but also as old. Even when she was twelve, people had treated her like an adult, had laid burdens on her that were too much for a child to bear. She was sick of feeling this way. And perhaps that was why skipping church and giving herself over to fate, just throwing her soul out on the air the way a fishing line could be sailed across the sky with the flick of one's wrist, was suddenly so very appealing.

"When you married me, you knew that I went to church, El. You can't expect me to change now."

El reeled his line in and found a cleaned hook. He sat quietly while he baited his line. "I didn't know you went every time the door was cracked, though," he said. "I believe in God, Easter. Prayer's the only thing that got me through my time in Korea. But I can't abide going all the time. I can't live my life inside a church house."

"Nobody's asking you to," she said. A breeze rose up and caused their boat to turn. She could hear the creak of the anchor rope.

"I'll make you a deal," he said. "You go out with me like this every once in a while and I'll go to church with you now and then. I know that Bible pretty good, Easter, and it seems to me that Jesus spent as much time fishing as he did preaching."

"I don't recall him ever being in a honky-tonk, though. I imagine you'd like for me to go there with you on occasion, too."

"There's two things that give me a whole lot of pleasure, Easter: a cold beer and a day fishing. I can't deny that."

Before she could answer she felt a tug on her line. The fish pulled the end of her pole down toward the water, nearly jerking the reel out of her hands. "I got another one!" she hollered, and standing up, she began to crank the line in.

They drove into Nashville at daybreak.

Anneth was driving, and Matthew was slumped against the door, sleeping. She glanced at him but decided that she would not wake him for a while. She wanted to experience seeing Nashville for the first time alone. He had been to cities before; he had played in Cincinnati and Knoxville. But she had never been anywhere. She came over the hill and saw the skyline glistening there in the light of morning, and it made her feel like crying. She had never seen anything so strange and wonderful in her life. It was all laid out before her like a painting and she thought it strange that she was looking down on a place where thousands of people lived, all within one view. She imagined what the people inside the houses were doing right now. Most were probably still asleep. It was a Sunday morning and they had probably been up late. Some were in their kitchens frying up breakfast, getting ready for church. Others were throwing back their bedcovers and touching their feet to the floor for the first time this morning. These people were doing the same thing that people back home were doing. It struck her that she had never really thought of cities as places where people lived. She had always pictured cities as office buildings and lawyers on the street and nothing else. But now she could see the houses standing close as gravestones on the ridge. In the downtown there were the tallest buildings Anneth had ever seen. As she crossed the bridge, she saw that the city was tucked into the crook of the river, which was wide and green. She drove slowly and looked at the river. Sunlight caught in the whitecaps and sent glints of brightness up to her. Even without the sign, somehow she knew it was the Cumberland River, the same river that snaked around in her part of the world. If she got on a boat and rowed against the current, she would eventually get back to Crow County. She would come to the confluence of the Black Banks and Cumberland rivers and she would be home again.

Now here they were, but she didn't know where to go next. She saw a sign that said RYMAN AUDITORIUM, so she went that way. She figured if she got them to the Grand Ole Opry, that was a good place to start. Since it was early on a Sunday, the streets were empty. She'd figured cities would be places of great commotion at all hours of the day. But she passed only a couple of cars as she went down Broadway. She passed bars and record stores and churches with spires that pierced the sky. At the stoplight there was another sign. She glanced down the street the sign pointed toward and there it was—the Grand Ole Opry, just as she had seen it so many times in magazines. She couldn't believe it was real. And it was so huge. She ignored the stoplight and turned anyway. Another car came speeding through the intersection, and the driver laid on the horn as he passed behind her, barely missing her bumper.

Anneth slid the car alongside the curb and turned off the ignition. She rolled down her window and listened. There was nothing. Complete silence, right in the middle of the big city. It was cold in the shadow of the Ryman, but she liked the way it felt. She got out of the car quietly and lit a cigarette and stood peering up at the building as she smoked. She thought it was the most beautiful thing she had ever seen in her life. All those bricks, hundreds and hundreds of them. It seemed like a holy place to her, although she knew it was a sacrilege to think so. She thought of all the singers who had been through those doors and all the times she had sat listening to them on the radio back home.

She felt a sudden pang at not having Easter here with her to experience this. Easter claimed not to like country music, but Anneth knew that she secretly did. Anneth had seen Easter tapping her foot along to Patsy Cline, even singing the words to some of Hank Williams's songs. And she felt bad that she was out seeing the world while Easter had never even left Crow County. Anneth missed home already, but she wanted to see as much as she could. She wanted to see cities and oceans and deserts. She wanted to go up in the Empire State Building and stand on the lawn of the White House. She wanted to swim in the Pacific and wade in the Atlantic. And she intended to stand backstage at the Opry. She would be standing in the wings as Matthew made his debut. Maybe he'd let her sing backup for him. The possibilities were limitless. They were in Nashville now, and anything could happen. That's what Matthew had kept saying on the drive down from Jellico to Knoxville. He had stretched his arm out and laid his wrist on the steering wheel, leaning back with his leg propped up so that his knee was as high as the dashboard, smoking one cigarette after another. "When we get to Nashville, it's untelling what will happen," he kept saying. "This is the sort of place where your dreams can come true."

She walked down the side of the auditorium and saw the windows with their different colors of glass. The air smelled of the river— green and sweet, like the inside of a hickory-nut shell. She walked back around and hopped up onto the hood of the car and sat there looking at the Ryman. She sat so long that she slowly became aware of the streets' growing more and more crowded. She glanced at her watch and realized that it was eight o'clock—she had been sitting there for more than an hour. People would be going to church before long and then the streets would be full. She would never have another moment in Nashville like this, when the city belonged to her. When everything was quiet and she could take it all in without being disturbed.

Anneth got back in the car and sat on her knees in the seat, studying Matthew. He had reclined his seat as far back as it would go and had wadded up his coat to make a pillow. In his sleep he had hunched up his shoulders as if he were cold. His chest rose very slowly, so slowly that she could barely see any movement there, and she had a momentary panic that he might have died as she drove across Tennessee. Matthew looked completely different when he was asleep. Watching him, it was easy to question why she was with him.

She wondered if she loved him. Sometimes she was sure of it — love swelled in her chest when she saw his beautiful eyes. His face was so square and roughly hewn, but in his eyes she saw the child he had been. Within his eyes she saw the kindness that lurked inside Matthew, and that was what she believed in. That was what she loved. And she loved his hands, which could play a guitar better than anybody she had ever seen. She loved the way his fingers danced across the strings as if barely touching them, like a Jesus bug walking across the river. Now, even his hands were different, because on one of his fingers was the wedding band she had put there. It didn't look right; it was so new and shiny that it looked fake.

"Matthew," she said, and shook him gently. "Wake up."

Matthew rose up with a start, his eyes still half-closed. His knuckles popped against the windshield. "What is it?" he said. He opened his eyes all the way and looked around the cab of the car as if he didn't know where he was.

Anneth fell back against the driver's seat and folded her arms across her chest. "Well, I got us to Nashville."

Eight

Why They Call It Falling

SHE LOVED THE WAY it felt, to be standing up here with everyone listening to her. Of course, people always listened to her when she sang in church, too, but this was different. In church her voice stirred the Holy Ghost up and caused it to spread out over the people, and they fell back, slain in the spirit, pushed back by her singing, but still, they only cried out to the Lord. It had nothing at all to do with her, as was only right.

But here! Here the people were dancing and raising their beer bottles high and wolf-whistling to *her*. They leaned into one another and said she sounded like Patsy Cline, even better than Patsy. "Listen to that girl sing, hot damn, has she got a voice! Sing it, honey!"

She was singing a song she had heard only a few times—"Walkin' After Midnight"—when Anneth had played it on her record player in her bedroom as loudly as it would go. She couldn't help herself from growling out the words and leaning into the microphone and closing her eyes to feel every word of the song. The music took control of her and there wasn't a thing she could do about it.

So this was what backsliding was like.

Easter had heard people whisper about it all her life. She remembered when she was a child: a woman who was thought to be the most devoted churchgoer had given in to temptation and gotten pregnant out of wedlock. A backslider. And only recently, a man who gave his tithes every first of the month had suddenly broken down and gone back to drinking and dancing. Another backslider. And here she was, singing in a honky-tonk. Singing a country song, a song she hadn't even realized she knew all the words to until she had been prodded up onto the stage and opened her mouth. She couldn't even fathom how she had gone from simply missing church to singing in a bar with a bunch of drunks dancing down below her. But here she was.

The first couple of minutes of the song she had been enraptured by this, had let their admiration take over her better senses. But now, in this last verse, she realized that she was backsliding. She would not be able to go back to church without rededicating herself. She would have to start over from scratch, get baptized again and wash away her sins. An ache came over Easter, a fist that curled its fingers up in her very gut. She kept singing, but the initial thrill had gone. The people should have realized it, too—they should have known that she had lost the spirit of the song, but they were all drunk. When the final word of the song was sung, it was not even hers anymore. Her guilt had taken the joy away from her, and as they applauded wildly, cheering and stomping their feet on the wooden floor, some of them even standing on their chairs, their cigarettes clamped between their teeth as they clapped, she sped across the stage, looking away from them.

Even though she tried to push past El, he caught her in his arms and kissed her on the ear. His breath on her face smelled of whiskey. "They loved you, baby," he said.

Easter stepped back. She wanted to leave right then, but the crowd was still clapping and cheering. It seemed they wouldn't stop. The band was strumming along and looking to her. The lead guitarist hooked his thumb through the air, motioning her back.

"They're wanting you to sing another one," El said, smiling. For the first time she noticed that his teeth were large and filled up his whole mouth. She had thought she knew his whole face as well as her own.

"No," she said, and although she meant for it to be forceful, her voice came out as only a whisper.

She saw an exit door off to the side of the stage. As she opened it she heard the guitarist say to the audience, "Looks like she's a little bashful," and then the door slammed behind her and there was the sudden, complete silence of late fall. She folded her arms across her chest and looked out at the rows of cars. She wanted to cry but couldn't.

The door opened briefly and she heard the chorus of a George Jones song—she couldn't remember the name of it—and then El was right behind her. He put his hands on her hips and she could feel his breath on the back of her head as he spoke. "What in the hell's wrong with you?"

She turned around quickly. She felt like slapping his face. "That was wrong, El. It was wrong of me to even come to this place. I told you that I was a churchgoing woman," she said. Her mouth was full of so many words that she didn't know if she'd be able to piece them all together correctly. "And you ought to have respected that. You shouldn't have asked me to come here with you."

"We're young," he said, cooing to her, the way he talked when he wanted to get in the bed. "Got plenty of time to go to church."

"You should have married Anneth," she said. "Not me. You're just like her."

El put his hands on his hips. "Maybe you are, too," he said. "But you're too damn proud to admit it."

"I want to go to the house," she said, and started walking. She looked about the parking lot, trying to find their car. There were so many cars that it looked as if a church revival was going on inside. "Right now."

But then he was kissing her, and she felt herself relax in his arms. And all at once his mouth tasted good, and she had a sudden memory of when she was sick and her grandmother had made her drink whiskey and honey mixed together. It was the only time she had ever had liquor. She remembered the soothing feeling of it on her throat, and the way it made her drift off into a perfect, dreamless sleep. Her eyes were shut very tightly and she could see Serena leaning over her with the bottle. A flannel nightgown, her hairpins glinting in the firelight, Anneth peeking around her hip. "It'll make you feel so much better," Serena had said. "It'll cure you."

He guided her to the car and then they were in the backseat and he was moving on top of her. She opened her eyes and saw that a light misting of rain had fallen on the windows. She could smell the rain and El, and they seemed to mix into one clean scent that she wanted to drink up. His head was at her neck and then at her breast and she found herself moaning. She thought, *I am young*. And to her surprise, she saw that she had never felt this way before.

AFTER THAT NIGHT, her life was a stack of papers scattered by a strong wind. There was no recapturing every piece of it, no possible way of knowing when each page was sucked up into the sky. She had no idea how it all happened so fast. She kept going with El to the clubs and honky-tonks on Saturday nights and started sleeping in on Sunday mornings. Sometimes she would get up in time to make it to church but was too ashamed to go. Once or twice, she had gotten ready and even gone as far as putting her hand on the church's doorknob but had pulled away with a start, as if she had touched something hot. She couldn't possibly go back in there. The preacher's wife, Helen, came to the house, but Easter stood behind her heavy curtains and watched as her old friend knocked and peeked into the three rectangular windows on the front door. Helen stayed out on the porch so long that Easter thought she might never leave, but finally she turned, eased back down the steps, and walked across the yard to her car, looking back as if she knew Easter was watching her. Easter stopped answering the phone because she feared it was somebody from church, asking why she wasn't there. She always made El answer, and when the caller was someone from church, she made El say she wasn't home. The sins just kept piling up.

People started coming to the club especially to hear her sing. When she didn't want to go onstage, the crowd chanted her name, the men hitting their beer bottles against the tables. When she sang, people danced. Women stood at the edge of the dance floor with their eyes closed and sang along with her. It was a little bit like being in church, this feeling of unison, of being part of something bigger, and she liked that. It made her feel buoyant.

Standing up there singing, she wondered what Anneth would do if she saw her like this. She'd probably pass out, Easter thought. Anneth couldn't even have imagined Easter up on the stage, moving her hips, belting out songs. Easter didn't know if she would be able to do this with Anneth in the audience. Maybe Anneth's leaving had freed Easter in some strange way.

Still, every time she found one of Anneth's postcards in the mail, she couldn't help but cry. She had never thought that Anneth would leave, certainly not leave the state altogether. But she had a shoe box full of postcards to prove that Anneth was gone. Each card was different: the Grand Ole Opry, the Tennessee Capitol, the Parthenon, the Cumberland River, one with gold records on it, another with a view of the bars all along Broadway. Anneth wrote on the back of each one as if in a great hurry—as if her life in the city was far too busy to linger over her written thoughts or her penmanship. "We are living the high life!" Or "Here is where Matthew is playing right now!" Or "Oh, Easter, I miss you so, but it is so exciting here. You would never get over it in your life!" Easter knew better, though. Surely Anneth was homesick. Surely she missed Easter. She had to.

To lose herself, Easter listened to the radio all the time and learned every song that came on. El came home from work with a new record album every time he got paid: Marty Robbins, Patsy Cline, and Brenda Lee. Those were her favorites. One day he brought home an album by Wanda Jackson that Easter ended up secretly loving. Sometimes when no one was there with her, she would put on "Fujiyama Mama" and hold her hairbrush like a microphone, singing and moving along to the music. She had seen Wanda Jackson one time on television and was downright shocked, not only at how beautiful she was, but also at how subtly she used her body to emphasize every word of the song. She didn't do anything more than tap her foot, but there was all that fringe on her dress that made it seem as if she was moving all over the place. She was a presence to behold. Easter stood in her bathroom with the record player turned up as loud as it would go and growled into the mirror, though she would never have done this in public—the song was too dirty. But she loved the way it made her feel.

El talked her into driving over to Hazard for a talent show, and she won by audience applause—there was a big meter onstage that moved up and down with the intensity of the clapping. Then they went to Pikeville and she opened up the show for Conway Twitty, and one thing led to another and before long she found herself in Knoxville, Tennessee, on that Cas Walker show that everybody watched in the mornings. Hanging behind the stage was a backdrop painted with four raccoons up a tree and a man standing under them with a gun, which she thought a strange thing to sing in front of. They had to be there at four-thirty in the morning to begin taping, but she was wide awake when the big television camera moved near and a man leaned over to whisper, "Five, four, three," and then mouthed the rest of the numbers silently, counting them down on his fingers with great exaggeration.

As soon as she opened her mouth to sing "Sweet Nothings"— which everyone said she could sing just as good as Brenda Lee—she realized that thousands and thousands of people were watching her. She had heard someone say that the show broadcast to four states. Surely everyone back in Black Banks was seeing her. *The Cas Walker Farm and Home Hour* was the most popular show on television and people tuned in as much to see Cas Walker, a rich grocer, talk bad to people who owed him money as they did for the music, so that everybody not only watched this show but also talked about it. Why hadn't she thought of this before stepping before the camera? But what difference did it make, anyway? She wasn't going to church anymore, so they knew she was up to something. Her secret had been out long before she realized it. Instead of freezing at this realization, however, she sang louder. She broke loose and began to move around in a way she never had before. There was only a scattering of crew members and a couple of other people sitting in the folding chairs in front of her, but they were dancing around in their seats, too. She leaned back into the song, closed her eyes, and let the words rip from deep within. She smiled for the camera and winked to a woman sitting out there—she didn't know her, of course, but she had seen singers do this before and thought it looked professional.

When she was finished, the few people who were there jumped up, clapping and whistling. A man hit a switch and recorded applause filled up the studio. Cas Walker himself came out and put his huge hand in the small of her back. She stood there smiling into the camera without knowing what else to do. "Now that gal can *sing*," Cas said in his raspy voice. He tapped her back with the tips of his fingers and somehow she knew this was her sign to exit, so she moved out of the camera's range and Cas held up a piece of notebook paper and began to rattle off a list of people who had recently written bad checks at his groceries in Knoxville.

As soon as Easter was offstage, a man in a leather jacket grabbed her by the arm and led her down the hallway, back toward the waiting room. She didn't see El anywhere. "Honey, you can sing better than anybody I ever heard. Better than Kitty Wells."

"I sure hope so," Easter said. She couldn't stand to hear Kitty Wells sing.

"I want to sign you up for a record deal."

Easter laughed and pulled her arm away from him. "Shoot, buddy, you must be out of your mind. I just do this for fun."

"Fun?" he said, holding his cowboy hat with both hands. Easter thought cowboy hats were a stupid thing for country singers to wear. No one she knew wore them—and all she knew were country people. "We could make a fortune."

"There's no way I'd go on the road and do all that. I've got a husband and a home and people that I could never leave."

The man's face seemed to be growing redder. He shook his head and laughed, then clicked a business card out between two fingers, as if he had pulled it from his shirt cuff. "If you ever decide to, you let me know. I can make you into a star."

He was wearing cowboy boots and they made a hollow sound as they faded away down the hall. She thought he looked pathetic walking away with the fringe on his white leather coat swinging in rhythm with his footfalls.

She stood there listening to the show as it went on behind her. The studio was enclosed by a thick wall, but she could hear the muffled sounds of banjos and guitars, two young girls singing in harmony. She tried to picture Anneth and smiled at what she imagined.

She could see her sister walking down the streets of Nashville, swinging her purse and looking up at the buildings, holding on to the arm of Matthew, who had his guitar slung over one shoulder.

"I miss you bad," she said to the air, to no one. And then finally there was El with his proud grin. She felt something stir in her and suddenly she knew she was doing all of this for him as much as for her own enjoyment.

In the car, Easter didn't speak as she watched the big buildings going by. She sat up straight in her seat and peered down the road. "We're not too far from Nashville, are we?" she asked. "We could go see Anneth."

"God almighty, no," he said. "Nashville's way on the other side of the state."

He pulled into a Krystal and got them a sack of cheeseburgers to eat later, when it was lunchtime. The smell of grease and onions made her want to throw up. She rolled her window all the way down and positioned her head so that the warm breeze would hit her in the face. She closed her eyes, feigning sleep.

THE FIRST TIME Easter had hollered out in church, she was eleven years old, at a camp meeting she had gone to with her grandmothers.

Serena drove them in her battered car all the way over to Harlan, where the camp meeting had been set up, near the shoals of the Cumberland River, a perfect location for baptizing those who got saved during the services. It looked the way Easter imagined a Civil War army camp might have looked—rows and rows of white cloth tents on a flat piece of land in the crook of the river. They had left Free Creek in the blue dark of early morning and arrived here just as the smells of breakfast spread through the camp. At each tent, people sat huddled around small fires, drinking coffee and watching as their bacon fried. Everyone nodded or waved as Serena drove by, until she came to an empty spot where they could pitch the tent they had borrowed from the church.

The preaching started at noon and went until suppertime, then resumed again and lasted until midnight, sometimes later. They stayed at the camp meeting three days and nights, and Easter spent most of that time in the huge, open-sided tent that had been stretched for the preaching. It was the music that had drawn her here first. All those voices rising together, the clapping, the fast rhythm of the guitars and the tambourines. Such energy flowed out of that music that it overtook Easter: she could not sit still when she heard it. It made her aware of God churning all around her. And then the preaching was just as wonderful. Each day there were four different preachers, but the one who preached at night was her favorite. He wore a full suit and had wavy black hair and he had an amazing talent for balancing the open Bible on one outstretched palm as he paced back and forth in front of the crowd.

Easter went to the services even when her grandmothers did not. In fact, she realized that they had come to the camp meeting more for a getaway than to celebrate the Lord. They didn't even go to the services much, instead spending a lot of their time at the tent, where they braided each other's hair and laughed like girls. They spent hours down at the river, picking flowers or sitting and talking. She got angry with them when they tarried after supper, lying back on their bedrolls to sup their coffee or nibble on dinner biscuits smothered in molasses.

Vine didn't go to church anyway. She couldn't stand being inside for that long and told Easter that she liked camp meetings, tent revivals, and brush arbors because they were at least out of doors, where God could see you without obstruction. Serena went enough that the preacher knew of her wonderful voice; he always asked her to sing when she attended. No one could sing "The Great Speckled Bird" with as much conviction as she could, but she was not a devoted churchgoer. This embarrassed Easter; she felt as if both her grandmothers were heathens. She didn't know why she was so devoted. She simply was. She had always loved church. But it was at the camp meeting that she first felt that electricity run up her back. It was there that she was convinced that God was completely real and big, and that he could cause her to take off screaming and running the aisles.

On the last full day of the camp meeting, Serena awoke Easter very early, before the sun—or the rest of the camp—was up. When Easter opened her eyes, she smelled the sweet tang of apples frying. She breathed in the dampness of the tent; a thick dew had settled on it in the middle of the night.

"Get up now, Little Bit," Serena said. "We're going into town this morning."

Easter stepped out of the tent into a purple morning. It was late September, and cool, so she held her gray sweater together at the neck. Vine bent over the orange fire, stirring the apples. "Come here, baby," she whispered.

Easter stepped forward and Vine kissed her on the forehead. Her lips were cool. Vine nodded to the box of supplies they had brought. "Get that flour out, baby, and make us up a big biscuit dough."

Easter obeyed, sleepy eyed. She paused from her chore only long enough to drink the chicory coffee Serena had made. It was an adult taste that Easter wasn't used to. She had drunk only creamed coffee before, and felt that this was a sign that she had been accepted as a woman among them. She mixed up a dough and began to push it out across the small wooden table they had brought from home.

"No, bigger than that. Make a *big* old dough. Don't cut out biscuits, though," Vine said when Easter had rolled out the dough. She added a dollop of butter to the apples, stirred them again, then stepped over to Easter. "Look here, we're going to cut them out for turnovers."

Vine sliced the dough into squares, dropping a spoonful of apples onto each. She hummed to herself as she carefully folded each one into a neat triangle, pinching her fingers along the edge to seal the apples within. Vine put lard in a skillet and showed Easter how to fry the turnovers. As others began to get up and build their fires, red light showed at the horizon, but daylight was still some time away. The morning smelled wonderful. The riverbank was covered in kudzu, and the vines still held the purple scent of grapes. Easter noticed everything, as if the morning air amplified her surroundings.

"Eat one right quick if you want to," Vine said, handing Easter a turnover. Easter bit into the pastry and thought it the best thing she had ever tasted, the dough fried golden and lightly dusted with flour, the hot apples oozing into her mouth with each bite. She watched as Vine wrapped the rest of the turnovers—there must have been two dozen when she was finished frying them all—in waxed paper and stacked them in an egg basket.

They drove into town just as daylight completely overtook the sky. Light touched the buildings one by one as they drove down Main Street and then to the other side of town. They had to sit and wait as a train lumbered by; then they drove on around winding curves.

"Where we going?" Easter asked, but Serena only glanced back in the rearview mirror and said, "You'll see."

Easter scooted up and put her chin on the back of the seat. Far up the road she could see a line of campfires glowing in the light of early morning, and then she could see people sitting on the side of the road. They all stood when the car approached.

Some of them were holding shotguns. They were mostly men, but there were a few women, too. Their eyes looked dead. There was a grayness to their faces that Easter had never seen before. They stepped toward the car, but Serena got out quickly and said something to them that Easter could not hear. Vine looked over her shoulder and smiled at Easter. "It's all right, baby," she said. Easter could see that the people relaxed as Serena spoke to them. It was as if the tension went out of their shoulders, and their brows smoothed out. Easter thought it strange that there were no children about whatsoever, although there were at least twenty-five people.

Vine took Easter around to the trunk of the car and took out the box of apple turnovers and told Easter to hand them out. The people moved forward eagerly but stuck their hands out with trepidation, as though they didn't know if they ought to take the turnovers or not. Serena was unloading a stack of quilts from the car. In the weeks before the camp meeting, Serena and Vine and several other women had worked feverishly, producing twelve quilts in a matter of a month. They were not beautiful—just simple crazy quilts—but they were thick and sturdily made.

Vine was moving amongst the people, patting their arms and speaking to them in quiet tones. Easter longed to know what she was saying. It must have been words of wisdom or comfort, for the people all looked at her with thanks in their eyes. A couple of the women cried. Easter watched both her grandmothers and she could see the kindness in their faces. They were doing something good here; she knew that much. She felt this knowledge swimming around her, as surely as she had felt the Holy Spirit all about the camp meeting the night before.

When they got back into the car and headed toward the camp meeting again, Easter waited before speaking. A reverent sort of silence had filled the car since they had left the people, and Easter hated to break it. They were going back over the railroad tracks, and far down them she could see a deer, nuzzling at a tuft of grass that had pushed up through the tracks. She couldn't stand any more curiosity. "What were they doing, setting outside like that?" Easter said.

"They're on strike from the coal company," Serena said. "They've been treated like dogs."

Only then did she notice that Vine was crying quietly into her handkerchief.

That night, Serena and Vine both went to the late service with Easter. There was a woman with white eyes—Serena said she was an albino—who stood and sang without any music. Easter thought it the most amazing thing she had ever heard in her life. This woman's voice didn't seem to come from her mouth, but from her very soul:

> When the labor here is over at last
> And I lay these burdens down
> I'll sail away home to Heaven above
> For my savior I have found.
> I'll lay these burdens down at his feet
> And exchange them for a crown.
> I'll leave this world of trouble and sorrow
> When the sun of my life goes down.

The song started off very slowly, very peacefully, and then there was a shaking of a tambourine, and then a stomping of feet and the riff of a guitar, and the woman leaned back and let the words come more quickly, more joyously, until that was what filled the air: joy. It was unmistakable.

It all happened as if by explosion. It seemed everyone was singing along, clapping—their arms rising up from the sides of their bodies—and moving, churning like waves in a white-capped river. It seemed that energy took on a form, and although Easter could not see it, she was aware of it. She could see it coming from a long ways off, at the front of the tent. It began up there, where the wavy-haired preacher stood shouting over the music. His voice was lost to her, lost in the song, but Easter could see his mouth and she could imagine what he was saying, a beautiful prayer. The energy was the Holy Spirit and it began to move toward Easter, swimming up and over the crowd, knocking them back as it came. Some of the women shook their heads so furiously that Easter could see the bobby pins falling from their hair. Their carefully wound-up buns came loose and their long hair shook free.

Easter took hold of her grandmothers' hands. They stood on either side of her, singing along. She stayed focused on the energy that was moving toward her, closer and closer. And then it came to her and she hollered out—whether it was in fear or in ecstasy, she never knew. It was a guttural cry, the best feeling she had ever had, although it also felt as if she had been punched in the stomach. She let go her grandmothers' hands and began to dance in place at her seat, swinging her arms. Then the crowd rushed forward and their hands were upon her and it felt as if she was being lifted above them all. She felt as if the light of God shone upon her, and it was the warmest, most comforting feeling. It was peace, and even a child could recognize that.

When the feeling left her, she was so tired that she collapsed into tears, slumping against Vine. She vaguely remembered their leading her back to the tent. She fell into a dreamless sleep and awoke before daylight as Serena poked the fire, the sparks popping and growing brighter. Her grandmothers were up early, waiting to see the sun rise. She could see their shadows on the wall of the tent, huge, made bigger by the distortion of light. They leaned into each other, whispering while they sipped their coffee. They were so much like sisters that it caused her to have a pang of homesickness: she missed Anneth, who was back home with Aunt Sophie and Uncle Paul. Easter watched Vine and Serena, hoping that she would grow up to be like them.

Now, as she leaned against the door, with rain beating on the windshield and El thinking she was sound asleep, Easter remembered the kindness in her grandmothers' eyes when they were handing out the quilts and the turnovers. She tried to decide which had been the best feeling—what they felt when they helped those people, or what she felt that first time that God swooped down and caught her under the ribs. She thought it might be the same feeling, the way goodness feels.

Nine

....

Leaving on Your Mind

"WE ARE STILL HAVING the biggest time ever!" Anneth wrote on a postcard, then drew a line through her words. That wasn't enough. She scratched the nib of the pen back over the sentence so many times that the ink turned into a black mess on the heavy paper. She turned the postcard over and looked at it: a view of the Nashville skyline against a bright summer sky. She tore the card in two, then again, and let the pieces fall out over the table.

She had a whole stack of postcards she had bought at the Ernest Tubb Record Shop. She picked up another one — on the front was a picture of a banjo being strummed — and wrote:

Dear Sister,

I am so homesick I think I will die. I don't love Matthew. I have tried to, but I just don't. There's nothing I can do to change this. I miss you so bad I don't believe I can stand it.

Yours, as always,
Anneth

She tore that one up, too. She laid the pen down and watched as it rolled off the table and onto the floor. A cool breeze rose up from the river and washed through the open window and across her face. The closeness of the river was her favorite thing about their apartment. She liked to sit at this window, watching the barges go by, looking at moonlight that sometimes caught in the waves. If it wasn't for the Cumberland, she didn't think she would have made it this long in Nashville. Every other apartment they had considered either overlooked downtown or had no view at all except for the brick side of a building. All those places were nicer—some of them even had a separate bedroom—but she had chosen this one because of the river. The river was the only thing good about this place. The apartment was no bigger than that motel room they had stayed in at Jellico on their wedding night. There was nothing but this card table pushed up against the window, and their bed and two chairs. Their kitchen was more like an open closet with a half sink, a two-burner stove, and a refrigerator so small it looked like something that belonged in a child's playhouse.

They lived above Frosty's Pub, downtown where Broadway nearly ran into the river, and now Matthew played in the pub four nights a week. There was no one named Frosty that Anneth knew of, but the pub and their apartment were owned by a man called Sloan. He was shaped like a Jim Beam bottle and had one good eye; the other was covered by a white glaze, the result, Sloan often explained, of his holding a lit firecracker that exploded too close to his face.

Sloan was good to her. On the nights that Matthew played, Sloan let her drink on the house. He had been unaware of the amount she was able to drink, and she thought that he probably regretted his offer now. She had drunk Sloan himself under the table once or twice. Everyone at Frosty's was good to her, actually—the fry cook, Chester, who made the best cheeseburgers she had ever eaten, and the bartender, who flirted with her all night long, and even the waitresses. They were good old girls, all wild as bucks. She liked the way they strutted around in their short skirts and checked blouses that looked like those red and white tablecloths people took on picnics. She had entertained the thought of hiring on as a waitress at Frosty's, but she enjoyed sitting there drinking and watching Matthew too much. Although she sometimes didn't know how to feel about him, she never doubted his power onstage. She liked for everyone in the bar to know that she was his wife, even if she didn't particularly enjoy being married. Matthew said she didn't need a job, anyway. Sometimes in bed at night, he would lie with his hand under her gown, and say, "You don't need to work. One of these days we'll have so much money you'll be able to hire one of those girls to keep house for you."

He sure wasn't making much money right now, but that didn't bother Anneth. But sometimes she found herself flinching at his touch. Their lovemaking had held them together; no matter how much they fought or how badly she missed home, his body had always been a comfort to her. Somehow it reminded her of home. His skin possessed the scent of the mountains, a clean, sharp smell like leaves baking on summertime hickories. His mouth tasted like the water of Free Creek, so cold and metallic. Yet now she had begun to turn away from him.

She didn't know why she didn't love him. He was a good man, full of dreams and big notions. Sometimes he'd get up real early—even after playing late at Frosty's—and go down to the street vendor to buy her some flowers. She'd awake with him standing over her, the flowers held out. "Wildflowers, just like back home," he'd say. He wore the same two pairs of Levi's all week, interchanging them every other night, but he insisted that Anneth buy herself a new dress or skirt each time Sloan paid him. The only things he bought for himself were record albums, and most often he let her pick those out, too. A couple of times he had interrupted his set to dedicate a song to her, and everyone in the pub had turned to look at her as she winked at him. He wrote her little notes when he arose and left before she had awakened: "I watched you sleep while I had my coffee. You are so beautiful it hurts."

One night he asked her to come up onstage to sing with him. She jumped up and climbed the wobbly wooden steps to the stage, not realizing that her night of drinking bourbon had affected her until she looked out over the crowd. Matthew leaned toward her and whispered, "Let's do 'Let It Be Me,' okay?" They were always listening to that Everly Brothers record. Sometimes they even sang it when they walked down the street looking in shop windows. Once, he had insisted that they both sing it into the telephone when she called Easter to check in. Easter had said they sounded good, but went right back to talking as if it was nothing special. Anneth moved in close to him, her shoulders arched toward the silver microphone that they had to share.

They harmonized beautifully, their two voices merging into one palpable force as they drifted out over the crowd. She gave the song everything she had, hitting her pitch, going high and then low, remembering what he had told her: "When you talk, you do it from your throat. Singing comes from your belly." But she was amazed to find that she didn't really enjoy being up there onstage with him. She didn't know why, but it wasn't as exciting as she had thought it would be. To sing well, she had to close her eyes and not look at the audience. Most of them were watching in silence or dancing, but there were others who went right on arguing or laughing or slamming their glasses down on the table. She couldn't stand the thought of their not paying attention to the words of the song, so she sang higher and prettier. She opened her eyes on the final verse and saw that Matthew was staring at her, completely love-struck, singing every single romantic word to her and only her. The audience didn't even exist to him. And that's when she knew that he loved her too much.

They had been in Nashville only two months but she had spent two weeks of that in bed, pinned to the mattress by sadness, as if someone had gathered all the furniture in the room and stacked it on her chest. In one thirteen-day stretch, she got up only once. She walked down to the pay phone on the street, clad in nothing but her nightgown—barefooted, even—and called Easter. But the phone had rung and rung before Anneth realized that it was only noon and Easter was still at work.

She lay in the apartment all day with the curtains pulled together so tightly that when Matthew came in and jerked them back, the room was filled with a blinding light that caused her to pull the covers over her head, screaming at him until he made the room dark once again. Matthew sat on the bed for hours at a time, running his hand down the back of her head. "What's wrong, baby?" he'd say, his voice a coo, the voice he used on soft love songs. The only reason she'd remain still at all was that it took her a while to build up the strength to push him away. Once, she caught him off guard, and he fell right onto the floor when she pressed both her hands against his back. Even that did not anger him. She knew that he was good and that he loved her. But still, it was his devotion, his very goodness, that caused the gulf to rise up between them. Or maybe it was not possible for her to ever be satisfied by anything or anybody. It was the way she was made.

Everyone loved Matthew at Frosty's, though. All up and down Broadway there were plenty of singers and bands, but most of them were standard country groups that wore sequins and cowboy hats and did covers of Johnny Horton or Don Gibson. Sloan had put a big

sign out in front of Frosty's that read ROCKABILLY MUSIC WITH
MATTHEW MORGAN and the bar was packed every night he played.
Matthew had three good honky-tonk shirts set off by pearl buttons,
and he always wore cuffed jeans and loafers. He didn't wear a cowboy hat, either. Sometimes he played in his white T-shirt, his pack of
Chesterfields rolled up in the left sleeve. No one else was playing
songs by the Everly Brothers or Buddy Holly, either. And if it had a
beat he admired, he'd cover a song even if it had originally been sung
by a woman. "Stupid Cupid" was one of his most popular numbers.
It was just him and his guitar. The women loved him because of his
eyes and the way he moved around on the stage, and the men loved
him because he got the women all hot and bothered.

During the day, Matthew haunted Music Row, trying to get into
the offices of big producers. He was sure that if he could just get on
as a demo singer, someone would snatch him up for a contract. He
had managed to get into the offices of the Louvin Brothers and
claimed that he had met Loretta Lynn there, but the next time he
went, the secretary wouldn't let him in. No amount of rejection got
to Matthew, though. "It'll happen," he'd say, climbing into bed. "If
you work hard enough you can have whatever you want." Lately his
optimism made Anneth roll her eyes.

Now that the blues had left her—simply lifted and flown away
without her knowing why they had given up and moved on—
Anneth made a habit of going down to the river while Matthew was
traipsing the sidewalks with his guitar slung over his shoulder. She
needed water in her life. Back home she had had the creek, which
was so reliable and present, right there across from their house. It
was strange, how she could go just a few steps from the bustle of
Nashville to the riverbank, where it was quiet and still, as if the willows on the bank soaked up the noise from the streets above. She
loved it down there, but it made her homesick. It was the only thing

that resembled countryside in this concrete-and-brick place. Trees and grass and sand. There were lots of birds, too, although she never heard a whip-poor-will, even when she went down there after dark. And here was a winding path home. If the water flowed the other way, she could put one of her postcards on the river and it might find its way to Free Creek. She pictured Easter leaning over to pluck it off the rocky bank. The ink would be washed away, but the picture on the front—of the Nashville skyline or the Opry or banjos—would be intact and Easter would know that Anneth had sent it to her by way of moving water.

Nashville was loud and exciting and full of dancing and singing. She liked strolling down the sidewalks late on Saturday nights, when the drunks stumbled out of Tootsie's, and she loved waiting out behind the Opry to see which stars would hurry out the back door into waiting cars. But she couldn't stand it here. It wasn't home and that was all there was to it.

Down at the river she could spend an hour studying the sky, the way some people might look at a painting they love but secretly do not understand. Sometimes she perched on one of the big rocks down there and read. One of the waitresses had lent her a battered paperback copy of *Peyton Place*. But most often she skipped rocks, the way she had as a child. She got so caught up in it that the act made her feel as if she was floating back in time. She expected to turn around and see Vine standing up in the yard, her face dark in the light of the gloaming, hollering for her to come in to supper. She spent a long time choosing the perfect stone. It had to be flat, preferably oval or rectangular, and about the size of a coaster. She gathered a stack of suitable rocks and held them in one hand while she skipped with the other. She curled her hand, then let the rock fly with a flick of the wrist. She could make one skip six or seven times. Back home the creek was so narrow that she could make the rock bounce up the opposite bank, but here the river was too wide for that and the last splash left its mark on the water, a ring that moved out and out and into nothingness.

One afternoon, as she was about to let loose the last rock, Matthew caught her elbow in his hand, causing the stone to fly out and sink immediately. He stood behind her and kissed her cheek, but she turned her face away.

"Good news," he whispered into her ear.

She took a deep breath, not out of anticipation, but only because she wanted one last smell of the river before her thoughts were completely broken apart.

"A producer from Decca let me audition for him."

"Really?" She turned around and was caught up in his arms. She was so glad for him, yet she didn't feel that it was happening to both of them, the way she knew she should have.

He held her close and talked into her ear, as if it was a secret he didn't want the river to overhear. "He wants me to come back in and sing for a couple of his people tomorrow."

"It was bound to happen," she said. "I'm proud of you."

Then he kissed her, his fine lips on hers, his cold tongue moving into the warmth of her mouth, but she barely felt it at all. She kissed him back, but she wasn't even there, as if she was a part of the river running by the city, a river with no comprehension of what its waves touched or changed along its course.

EASTER COULDN'T SLEEP. The whip-poor-will was calling incessantly, and each time he made his mournful song, Easter pictured Anneth. She looked into the blackness settled over her bed and saw her sister lying on a riverbank, stretched out on a slender gray rock.

Heat radiated off El's long body lying beside her. She listened to his breathing—steady and peaceful—to see if he was asleep or not, but couldn't decide. It was a comfort knowing he was there, because the room was so dark that she couldn't even see him. All the windows were open and the night sounds came in and pressed into every corner of the room.

"El? Are you awake?" He didn't answer. She put her palm on his stomach, nearly starting at the warmth there. She shook him a little. "El. Wake up."

"What is it, baby?" His voice was clogged by sleep.

"I can't sleep. Let's get up and go outside." She sat up on the edge of the bed and found his hand, interlaced her fingers with his own. She tugged at him. "Come on."

She could hear him climbing out of the bed behind her, and as she led him down the hallway he tightened his grip on her hand. "Have you lost your mind?" His words were nearly lost in a yawn.

She opened the back door and stepped out into the darkness. The cool air made her feel as if she were stepping into a sort of cleanliness. There was more light out here but it was still strangely dark. The moon was lost to the clouds of an impending thunderstorm. She looked around and laughed when she saw the brightness of El's underwear. That was all he had on.

He sat down on one of the porch chairs and she positioned herself on his lap, her back to him as she looked out on the yard, trying to distinguish the shape of the black mountain from the black sky.

"What time is it?" El asked.

"I don't know," she said, and leaned back against him. "Three or four."

"What're we doing?"

"I just couldn't sleep," she said, speaking so low that her words were nearly lost to the cries of crickets and cicadas. "I wanted you with me."

The whip-poor-will called, over and over, and each time it did, the katydids and frogs grew silent for a moment. It was the most lonesome sound, but also soothing somehow. It sounded less like a bird perched up there on the old locust than it did like a small woman who was trying to tell them something.

"El, do you know what I want more than anything else in this world?" she said.

"I know what I'd like," he said. "To go to bed."

She turned to face him, although she could barely make out the shape of his face. "No, I mean it," she said with a little laugh in her voice. "Listen to me. I want a baby. So bad."

"Well, you know what a person has to do to get babies, don't you?" Now he was laughing at her.

She lay back against him and he latched his hands around her waist. She could feel his breath on her neck. With one hand he held her hair in a long hank. "We have to stop going to these bars and places, El. It's just not me. What I want is our own little family. Me and you and a child. That's what I want more than anything in this world."

He rubbed his chin against her shoulder, a motion so slow and intimate that it made her love him more than she ever had before. She took this as her answer. A promise made by skin against skin.

ANNETH SAT CROSS-LEGGED on the bed and smoked three cigarettes in a row with the ashtray perched on her knee. It was four o'clock in the morning and she watched Matthew in the gray shadows of the room. He lay on his stomach, naked to the waist, with the covers kicked down around his feet, and he was so brown that the sheets seemed to glow around him. She ran her hand down the cleft of his back, reached over, and snapped on the lamp, and then shook him awake.

"I have to leave, Matthew."

He sat up quickly, his eyes squinting against the light. "What?"

"I want to go home. I miss home too bad."

Matthew grabbed her hand but she pulled it away and knocked the ashtray off onto the floor. She climbed out of bed, stepped over the mess of ashes and butts, and pulled her suitcase out of the closet. She jerked the top drawer out of the dresser and dumped its contents into the suitcase. Matthew grabbed her from behind. He pressed himself against her back.

"Lay back down for a little while. You're not thinking right."

She pulled away and opened the next drawer, scooped up an armful of panties. "I know what I'm doing. I'll catch a bus to home. There's one leaving the station at six."

"You're just getting into one of your spells again. It's just them old blues talking."

She spun around and stood very close to his face, trying not to look into his eyes. "No. You know as well as I do. How can you possibly love me? I don't understand how you could continue to be good to me, the way I treat you."

"That's what being married is like. It's work," he said, and she realized that he was completely awake. She had the sudden urge to reach out and smooth her hand down his chest.

She sat down on the edge of the bed and looked up at him. He refused to sit, stood there with his hands on his hips. She thought he looked both ridiculous and beautiful standing there in his underwear.

"I don't love you," she said.

"Don't say that," he said, moving closer, his hands out.

"You're too good for me, Matthew. I can't stand to go on lying to you, because you're a good man. You deserve somebody who will love you back."

He sat down on the bed next to her and put his arm across her shoulders. She covered her face with her hands, knowing that he thought she was crying. But she wasn't. She felt exhausted by the charade she had made for herself and for him.

"I've got that audition. I'll get a contract—I know I will. And we'll be out of this apartment. I'll buy us a little house. Before you know it we'll have a mansion like that Belle Meade you love to look at. We were going to sing together."

"No, we can't sing together," she said, and stood again. She kept her back to him as she gathered her things. "I'm going home."

He didn't say anything while she packed her clothes. She folded her dresses neatly and found a string to tie four shoe boxes together. There wasn't much to pack. She hadn't brought anything with her and had long ago stopped talking about sending for her things. It was so quiet in the apartment that she fancied she could hear the waves of the river washing up on the bank below them. The windows were open but there wasn't even the sound of a car passing by or the distant laughter of drunks or anything. The night was completely still.

When she turned around, he was still sitting there, his palms upturned on his knees. "If it's home you want, I'll leave the record deal and everything. I'll go back and mine coal if it means having you."

Here was the kind of love she had been looking for all her life. But still, she couldn't make herself love him back, no matter how hard she tried. She leaned down and put her hand on his face. "There's no way I'd let you do that," she said. She pulled her gown up over her head and lay back on the glowing sheets. "Just lay here with me until daylight. Lay here with me and then tomorrow we'll go our separate ways."

He stretched out beside her, his long legs stiff and warm beside her own. She moved his underwear down without a word from him, let her hand linger as it cupped the heat between his legs, and then spread herself atop him. She held him as tightly as she could and spoke with her lips against the skin of his neck. "Love me one more time," she said.

ANNETH'S BUS CROSSED the Kentucky state line at noon. She sat up on her knees in the seat and propped her arms on the open window. The September air was warm against her face. Here there were hills that rose up with stripes of mist lying across the ridges. She could smell the earth and the leaves, water in unseen creeks that bubbled in distant valleys. "I'm home, by God," she said aloud, but no one noticed because it was so hot that all the windows were down. There was only a scattering of people on the bus, anyway, and most of them sat looking straight ahead, as if caught in a state between sleep and awareness. There was an old woman who sat across the aisle from her, sleeping with her mouth thrown wide open. Two little boys held on to the backs of their seats and made faces at Anneth. She stuck her tongue out at them and looked away. Behind her there was a young girl with eyeglasses and a pink scarf stretched tight over her head — she couldn't have been more than seventeen — who had held her baby ever since the bus picked her up outside Oak Ridge. Anneth had bought the girl a Dr Pepper, a slice of pickled baloney, and a pack of saltines at their last stop because she could tell the girl didn't have a dime.

"Sit down back there!" the bus driver hollered when he finally noticed that Anneth had her whole head out the window, drinking in the rushing air, but she ignored him until she was good and ready to get back in her seat. She watched the little towns race by: Williamsburg and Rockholds and Woodbine and Corbin, all interrupted by long stretches of countryside. People pumping gas and cutting down their cornstalks. Women sweeping their yards and hanging clothes on the line. Men who didn't look up from their bucking tractors, shirtless boys who waved and wolf-whistled as they stood amongst the tobacco plants they were supposed to be tending. The farther the bus went, the higher the mountains became—purple in its own shadows—and more and more creeks snaked alongside the highway.

It was three o'clock by the time the bus pulled into Black Banks. She had been gone for three months but it felt like ages, so she was surprised to see that absolutely nothing had changed. She felt the urge to run into the Depot Café and see everyone she had once worked with, but she didn't want to face them right now; her boss, Gloria, was probably still upset that she had run off. She used the pay phone at the bus depot, relishing the sound of her nickel dropping in.

"Come get me," Anneth said when Easter answered.

"What's happened?"

"I just want to come home," Anneth said, trying not to laugh.

"Well, I guess we can be there by late tonight."

"I can't wait that long, Easter. I'm dying to see home, to see you."

"Well, honey, it'll take me a big long while to get all the way to Nashville."

Anneth cackled, catching the attention of the other people who had gotten off the bus to stretch their legs before going on to their stops. The girl with the baby smiled, and the old woman, finally awake, shook her head.

"I'm home, in Black Banks," Anneth said. "I just got off the bus."

Ten

Trouble

BLACK BANKS WAS A boomtown now. Just when coal was petering out everywhere else, a new seam was discovered on the outskirts of town, and people drove from neighboring counties to stand in line for work at the Altamont Mining Company. On Mondays the foreman came out and walked down the line of men, spitting a stream of tobacco juice at their feet and sizing them up. Then he'd climb up on the porch of the office, lean on the rail while he conferred with his assistant, and run his finger through the air, stopping it to point at the strongest men. "You, you, you, and you," he would say around his cud of tobacco. "And you two boys there, you brothers? You all, then, too."

The timber business was booming, too. The lumber company felled trees and brought steam shovels in on the backs of eighteen-wheelers, their brakes smoking by the time they had made their way down the mountain. Coal trucks lumbered down Main Street, grinding holes into the pavement and belching out black fists of smoke that stained the yellow bricks of the courthouse, which sat in the square like a slumped cake.

But most of all it had become a crossroads. Trains and buses came in every hour, letting off people who squinted in the sunlight and seemed taken aback by the bustling streets of such a small town. Only about twelve hundred people lived in Black Banks, but sometimes it seemed as if there were twice that many milling about the train and bus station. When there weren't passenger trains, there were slow-moving freights burdened with their solid loads of coal and lumber. Sometimes cattle cars passed through, leaving the town with the rich green smell of manure and the cries of the live cargo, bawling and mooing at their rickety means of transportation. But mostly it was the passenger trains that kept the town alive. Women on their way to visit their families in Virginia had two-hour layovers that they spent in the dress shops along Main Street. They extended their slender feet to Lolie and asked for the latest pump while she tried to steer them toward the higher heels. Soldiers who were going to Ashland for assignment leaned against the magazine racks at the drugstore and propped their feet up on the backs of the seats at the movie theater. Shaking out newspapers and carrying briefcases, men from Baltimore and Cincinnati who had bought out the mineral rights from people twenty years earlier came to see how their mines were doing.

Anyone who had any money found his way into the Depot Café, so that Anneth was right at the center of all the commotion that Black Banks was becoming known for. She had managed to talk Gloria into giving her back her old job, and she liked being a waitress. She got the best tips of all the girls. The city men liked to watch her and she didn't pander to them and treated everybody the same, whether it was a broke college girl on her way back home or a Detroit lawyer who shook his head at the lack of fine cuisine. She refused any of the businessmen who asked her to accompany them on time-killing trips to the movies or for a drive to the lumber camp. She slapped the face of a man who couldn't resist the urge to pinch her on the ass. She sneaked grilled cheese sandwiches to young boys who asked for nothing more than a glass of water, even though she knew they didn't have any money.

After spending six months riding back and forth to town with Lolie every day, she had saved up enough money to buy a candy-apple red Falcon that Lonzo Morgan had for sale. This was her favorite part of being back home — being able to just get in a car and drive around curvy roads, putting her arm out the window so that her hand fluttered up and down in the rushing wind, her radio turned up as loud as it would go. Now that she had her car she could do anything she wanted to, could go anywhere without asking anybody for a ride. Her Falcon gave her a freedom that she could never have found in Nashville.

She had been home a year and was living with El and Easter, happy to be back on Free Creek. She knew that she was an intrusion — although they never made her feel that way — but she wanted to be in her old room with the sound of the creek, able to go out the back door and climb the mountain up to their field.

Apparently Easter had accepted that Anneth was a grown woman now, because she didn't chastise her too much on the nights she came in at three in the morning, drunk and hollering out in the yard. Then again, there wasn't much Easter could say, since she had quit church herself, a fact Anneth couldn't get over. Anneth didn't tell Easter, but this saddened her. She had always felt safe in the knowledge that Easter was praying for her, that Easter was living the good life and was happy doing that. It had never occurred to her that Easter might not enjoy going to church anymore. It hadn't even seemed possible.

Although Anneth went partying and came home singing and hollering, she had never drunk anything at the house before the evening of the heat wave, when El invited her to sit down with him on the back porch and have a beer. He held up the can of Pabst Blue Ribbon as she came around the back of the house, just getting home from work. "Want one?" he asked.

"I believe I do, buddy," she said. She sat down in the chair beside him, kicked off her shoes, and tilted the beer back. She wished that she didn't love the way it tasted, but she did.

EL PULLED ANOTHER beer from the ice chest and poked a pair of holes into the can with two quick stabs from the church key. "Match me?" he said, and Anneth nodded. They both turned up their beers and drained them in one long drink. Anneth wiped her mouth on the back of her arm and El sat back in his seat, letting out a long, jagged breath.

"I never seen a girl drink like you before," he said.

"I never seen a man who couldn't drink no more than you," she said, and tapped the corner of his chair with the bottom of her bare foot.

Easter stood behind the screen door and watched them. They had been out there drinking all afternoon. El had the day off from work before going out on a five-day haul to Pittsburgh and said it was too hot to do anything else but sit in the shade and drink. It was hot, a freak day of heat in mid-October. The mountains were at the height of their color and the red and yellow leaves baked in this sudden burst of warmth. Usually by now the first frost had fallen and Easter was already cutting down the cornstalks for fodder. She liked the idea of a heat wave settling down over the valley when everyone was already preparing for winter. This was God's way of letting people know that He was still in charge. Still, the heat was only an excuse to drink for those two.

Used to, Anneth wouldn't have dreamed of leaning back in a chair on their grandmother's back porch and getting drunk. Easter supposed Anneth thought it was all right now, since Easter didn't go to church anymore.

Easter had hoped that Anneth would chide her about not going to church, would cave in and tell her that she had respected her sister's reverence all these years, even though she had always said the opposite. But Anneth seemed glad that Easter had quit. Easter figured Anneth would have liked it even better if Easter was still going out to sing at the honky-tonks, but now she was caught in some of kind of purgatory between going back to the church and actually sinning. Easter cringed at the idea that it was sin that joined them so much closer than before.

"Come out here and sit with us!" Anneth called, spying Easter as she studied them. "You ever drunk a beer before, Sister?"

"Hell, no," El said. "She used to go right in them bars and sing her heart out, but never touched a drop of anything. I don't see how she did it."

Easter stepped out onto the porch as the screen door slammed behind her. She still held the damp towel she had dried the supper dishes with. She took two clothespins and latched it to the little line stretched between the porch posts. "I don't need to drink to have a good time," she said.

Anneth slapped her sister on the hind end. "Sit down here and talk to me," she said. "You never do sit still for a minute. Always working." Easter could see she was drunk. There was that permanent smile that made it so plain for everyone to see, that special laugh that Anneth reserved for when she was drinking. "Tell me what happened between Gabe and that Jimmie woman of his. I stay at the café so much that I never know what's going on."

"They quit is all I know," Easter said. "He's out running wild, and them not even divorced yet, hitting every honky-tonk between here and Hazard."

"Kind of like me!" Anneth laughed. She propped one foot up on the corner of El's chair and her dress rode up to her knee. It was a thin dress, anyway, a cream fabric with a sprinkling of violets, and was almost transparent at the neck, where Anneth had sweated. Easter felt like slapping Anneth's leg down. It didn't look right, the way her foot occasionally touched the side of El's knee. "You're the only one of us three that's worth a dime. Even if you did backslide, you're still the good one."

"I've been miserable since I left the church," Easter said. "And I intend to go back as soon as I get my head on straight. I'm done with singing in them honky-tonks. It's not how I'm made."

Anneth and El knew not to say anything when it came to matters of the church, but Anneth couldn't resist. She leaned over and rubbed Easter's back with her free hand. With the other she took a long drink of her beer, then propped the can on her lap. "Let's not get all serious, now. Tell me something funny."

"I thought it was pretty damn funny why Gabe and that woman quit, myself, considering the way Gabe brags about pleasing his woman and all that," El said. He was drunk, too. He never talked this much and certainly didn't cuss. Easter hated seeing him this way, that stupid smile etched across his face. Even his posture disturbed her. He looked as if he was about to slide out of his chair. "He walked right in on her with another man."

"You're lying!" Anneth squalled, leaning out so far that her foot dropped off the corner of the chair. "Surely not!" She turned in her chair to face Easter. "You never told me that part. Did he, Easter?"

"That's what he said," Easter told her, and tried not to sound as stiff as she felt, although she wanted to grab their beers and pour them out. She couldn't say much about their sitting here drinking. She hadn't exactly been a saint lately, and she was paying for it now. Her backsliding had given El the chance to do what he'd wanted to ever since they got married, anyway. Be himself. How was it that she had thought he wouldn't want to drink and carry on? She had been a fool. Just because he hadn't done it when they were courting, she had thought he was different from every other man she had ever known.

"It's a wonder Gabe didn't blow that man's brains out," Anneth said. "And Jimmie's, too."

"It hurt him too bad for that, I guess," Easter said. "He said he just walked out and got in his car and left. Went straight and filed for a divorce."

"Poor old Gabe," Anneth said. "I guess we'll be divorcés together. What's the odds of two black sheep in one family?" Then all at once Anneth jumped out of her chair and stood twisting around on the porch, snapping her fingers and bringing one arm up over her head. "Hey, Easter, I want to hear you sing a rock 'n' roll song."

"I don't sing no rock 'n' roll."

"You ought to hear her sing 'Seven Lonely Days,' though," El said, and fished down in the ice for another beer. "She can do it better than Patsy Cline ever thought about. That's what everybody says."

"I don't feel like singing this evening," she said, and stood, looking out on the yard. "I'm going to go take a bath. It's so hot I feel sticky."

Easter took her time. She never filled the tub all the way up, but tonight she did. She wanted to lie back and just not think about anything for a little while. The water felt like warm milk on her burned skin. She had gotten up early to hoe out her garden this morning but the sun had been fierce and had reddened the back of her neck and her arms. Her scalp even felt sunburned.

She wished that she could drift away, be aware of nothing but the water, but she couldn't. She kept thinking about El, the way he had turned out. El wasn't mean—he was always happy, in fact—but he liked to drink more than she had ever thought he would. And he loved going into those honky-tonks, liked dancing and hollering. His favorite thing was to talk her into the backseat of the car, almost as if he was excited by the notion that someone might see them tangled up like that. She had thought that he would eventually break down and go to church with her, but she had given up on that. She would be like all those women she had seen when she was growing up, the ones who came in looking tired and defeated, who seemed to get no satisfaction out of life except for going to church. The ones who, at prayer request, always stood with their shoulders hunched and said, "I want everybody here to pray that my husband will see the light and decide to start coming to church."

And Anneth. She didn't even want to think about that mess. Running off and leaving her husband in Nashville without even looking back, starting the divorce procedure. She was glad Anneth was back, and in her happiness Easter had tried to ignore that her sister was about to be divorced after living with her husband less than three months, but Easter knew what lay ahead. More nights of Anneth coming in wild drunk, running the roads with every man who had beautiful eyes or a certain body language or a good voice.

She splashed water onto her face and sank into the water, letting it overtake her mind as well as her body. She let everything lift from her, rise up with the dampness that drifted off the water.

She didn't know how long she rested like that. In a way it felt like a very long time, but it was probably only a few minutes before she started at the sound of the kitchen radio being turned up as loud as it would go. Ray Charles was on, singing that song "What'd I Say." Preachers all over the place were taking hammers to that particular record because they said it was about sex. She didn't know how they went about listening to records so closely— she simply heard a fast beat. Still, this was enough to break her peace, and even though she started to run more warm water and try to relax again, she couldn't. The spell had been broken now. She sighed and ran the cake of Ivory soap down her arms, trying to rid herself of the anger she could feel beneath her skin.

Easter glided down the hall, pulling the belt on her housecoat tight and patting the towel that was wound about her wet hair. The music was so loud when she came into the kitchen that the sound was tinny and distorted. The little yellow radio sitting on the counter fairly vibrated with Ray Charles's rough voice. Now she could hear what the preachers heard; it wasn't so much that the words to the sound were dirty as it was the way he was singing. There was a suggestion in every syllable. She went to the screen door and looked out, but no one had turned on the porch light. All she saw were the empty chairs and past them there was the blackness of night. She pushed open the door and stepped out, and then she saw them there. She stood on the porch and watched them, unable to move for a moment.

Anneth and El had gone out into the yard and they were dancing near the porch. They weren't dancing together, really, but were caught up in their own separate magics. El's eyes were closed and he held both arms over his head as he swayed in place with a strange little smile on his face. Anneth had her eyes closed, too, but she was twisting against the grain of the music, faster than the beat, her hips swaying and jutting. One hand was on her hip and the other was raking her hair back from her face. She threw her head back so that her curls tumbled down in her face again and she laughed, even though the sound of her glee was lost to the music. She moved close to El and turned her back to him, rubbing her whole body against him, her backside brushing his thighs. The dress hugged her hips tightly, the fabric revealing the gentle curves there. Easter wanted to step forward, to grab Anneth and shake some sense into her head, but she still couldn't move. The sight of them drew out all of her strength.

Anneth turned to face El and put her hands on the sides of his face, her fingers spread far apart so that her thumbs were nearly in his mouth. El didn't flinch. He either didn't realize or didn't mind that she was touching him this way. Anneth continued to laugh that low, quiet purr that seemed to catch in the back of her throat as she ran her hands down El's arms and then held on to his hips. She moved too close, the top of her head touching El's chin, and buried her mouth against his chest as she forced his hips to move back and forth. Then she arched her head back, her neck a long, elegant whiteness. El turned around, still snapping his fingers, his face placid and flat, and Anneth sidled up behind him and slid her hands into his front pockets.

Easter took two striding steps off the porch, as if stepping over a narrow creek from one mossy bank to another, and grabbed Anneth by the arm. Easter twisted her around. Anneth's eyes opened; her smile widened, then faded when she saw Easter's hand slicing through the air to strike her. She didn't even try to dodge the slap that Easter delivered. The sound of the smack was deafening—so loud Easter could hear it over the music—and then Anneth was recoiling, her eyes wide with disbelief, her hands to her face, one atop the other to cover the redness that spread there.

"I didn't—"

"I was looking right at you!" Easter screamed with so much fervor that the damp towel unraveled from her head and fell onto the sandy yard. The words tore from the back of her throat. "You leave here and never come around my house again. *Never!*"

Anneth's face seemed to flatten, her eyes hard. For just a moment Easter thought Anneth was going to say something else, but then Anneth turned and simply ran away; a few steps, and the purple flowers on her dress disappeared into darkness, into thin air. Into nothing.

Eleven

Life under Her Hands

EASTER WAS AWAKENED by the smell of river water. She recognized the scent even before she opened her eyes. It was the aroma of sandy banks and long willow leaves and small stones. She felt an overwhelming bloom of joy rise up in her chest. It was so sudden and real that she sat straight up in bed and clutched her stomach. Then she realized that she was carrying a child. It was there, just behind her hands, stirring, a gathering of veins and blood and water and all things that would eventually make it real and solid.

Her first thought was of El. He had been gone six days because she had ended up telling him to leave, too. He had defended Anneth, raved and thrown the chair off the porch, followed Easter as she walked to the creek.

"She's just young and drunk. She didn't mean a thing by the way she was dancing," he said, his hands out to her like someone asking for penance, although his voice was hard and sharp, a blade that was prepared to cut deeply.

"I seen the way you were dancing together," Easter said. "You've turned me against the church, started drinking, and now you want to dance vulgar with my own sister and want me to overlook that?" She crossed her arms. "I won't do it."

He turned his back on her and walked away. This made her so furious that she ran to catch up with him, her naked legs escaping the folds of her housecoat. "If you're going to take up for her, you pack your bags and get out of my house, too."

He stopped in his tracks, turned his head very slowly. He was completely sober now, she saw. Apparently he could snap his fingers and forget that he had ever drunk a drop.

"*Your* house," he said, and something in his face changed. "If that's the way you want it, by God, all right then."

Now she was sitting in her bed alone, realizing that she was carrying a baby, even though she hadn't seen her husband in nearly a week, since that evening when he grabbed a few of his clothes and left. He had been on the road since then, but usually he called her and checked in, told her of the things he saw along the highways of West Virginia and Pennsylvania, North Carolina and Tennessee. She had never felt so alone in her life, not even when her grandmothers or her parents died.

She was desperate to call Anneth, to tell her to come to her, but she couldn't do that. She hadn't seen Anneth, either, since that night. And she still wasn't ready to see her, although nothing had changed in her heart. She knew that what El had said was true, that Anneth was just wild and young and stupid in her own way, but still, she had disrespected Easter. Nobody got so drunk that they didn't know what they were doing. She had often heard Serena say that there was truth in wine. "A person only does what they truly desire when they're drunk," Serena told her once. "Instead of being out of your mind when you're drunk, you're even more *in* your mind."

Easter picked up the phone and called the Depot Café, anyway. Sophie had told her that Anneth had moved into the apartment that was tacked onto the back of the restaurant, perched on stilts over the river. Sophie had told Anneth to stay with her and Paul, but Anneth was determined to have a place of her own. Easter thought about how she had said "my house" to Anneth. It was Anneth's house, too, and always would be. She had told her that the day she and El were married, and she had meant it.

"Can I help you or not?" she heard a voice say. It took her a minute to remember she had called the café.

"Oh, I'm sorry," Easter said into the phone. "Never mind."

She hung the phone on the hook, giving up, since she didn't know what to say to Anneth. There was still too much distance between them. Every time she closed her eyes she saw Anneth dancing out there in the yard, the way the purple-flowered dress had clung to her hips, her head leaned back as she slid her hands into El's pockets. It was too much to think about right now. She was going to have a baby and hadn't even taken the time to be happy about it.

She had wanted this for such a long time. On her wedding night, when El first moved on top of her, she had closed her eyes, and while she had concentrated on the newness of a man and the feelings it stirred up inside her, she had also prayed for a baby. She had hoped to get pregnant that very night but hadn't. Now she counted back the weeks and tried to pinpoint when this child had been conceived. Impossible, since she and El had been doing *it* all the time lately. It pained her to realize that it had probably been one of those nights after they had been at the honky-tonk. El was always especially affectionate on those nights. He'd whisper into her ear: "Seeing you up onstage like that turns me on." She couldn't help but laugh. She never told him that it made her feel the same way.

She knew why she had wanted to get pregnant so badly: she wanted to see what it was like, being there for the beginning of life. She had spent so much time with death, known too many who had died. People talked about life; they talked about it without even realizing. Yet no one ever discussed death beyond the basics. At church, death was as simplified as it could possibly be. Your soul left, your body was buried, and your soul went either to heaven or to hell. In both places there was eternal life; one was miserable and one was joyous. But no one ever really talked about death at all. She supposed people were afraid of exploring their mortality, fearing what they might discover if they thought about it too much.

But with a baby it was different. For nine months she would have life right there in her belly, right under her hands. She would feel the baby moving and kicking, growing. She didn't know how her body would contain all of this. The idea of that joy alone was so big that she felt she might burst wide open, an explosion of white light.

She called El's supervisor at Appalachian Freight. He said he could radio El and get a message to him with no problem. "What is it you wanted me to tell him?" the boss asked.

"Just say 'Call home,'" she said, and thanked him before hanging up the phone. She sat there for the next thirty minutes with her hand on top of the receiver, and although she was lost in reverie she didn't even startle when the phone rang, its piercing bell so loud it could be heard all the way out to the garden.

"El, when will you be home?" she asked.

"You mean to *your* house?" he said. He was on a pay phone at a truck stop somewhere—she could hear cars and trucks speeding by. She could picture him leaning against the phone booth, his black hair slicked back, his big fingers tapping impatiently.

"I'm sorry about all that," she said. "I was wrong. It doesn't matter now—none of it."

There was nothing but the sound of a car horn on the other end of the line. He must have been standing beside the busiest highway in the country. It sounded like a train was going by.

"El, I'm carrying our child," she said, and heard the sounds of traffic. Then, in a jagged little breath, he told her that he loved her more than anything in this world.

THAT DAY, ANNETH worked at the café without really hearing anybody say a word. It had happened a lot lately. She saw people's mouths move, somehow knew what they were saying. She nodded, but she was somewhere else, not there in the café waiting tables. At the end of her shift she stepped out into the light of October and breathed in the smell of autumn, and this scent seemed to awaken her, but not much. She was all at once aware of the sounds of the town: a few cars speeding by, going far too fast for Main Street, the scratch of a broom sweeping the sidewalk in front of the record store across the way, a car door slamming and then a woman hollering to her little boy to wait for her. At five o'clock the excitement died, as the trains came in less frequently, and Black Banks seemed an altogether different place than it had that noonday.

Anneth felt as if there were weights attached to her jaw, pulling her face down. Why had the customers joked and talked to her at all today, anyway? Couldn't they see that her eyes were dead?

It wasn't just because of her fight with Easter—the biggest fight they had ever had. The blues came in and she had no control over them; they just swooped in whenever they took a notion. All she wanted to do was lie in her bed with the shades pulled down and her quilt pulled up. She felt a stirring in her gut, something like disgust, for no reason at all. Maybe she was disgusted with herself. It was all too much to take, and the only thing that would help would be sleep. Sleep was the closest thing to death, the only way to escape. Lately she had been having short, unexpected pangs of missing Matthew, too. She missed listening to him sing as he piddled around their apartment by the Cumberland. She missed looking into his eyes, studying the round veins in his big hands.

She had a few good friends, and Paul and Sophie, but deep down Easter was really all that mattered. She knew that Easter could have gone off to teachers college if it hadn't been for raising her. Easter had given it all up to take care of Anneth. It made her think of that

Ray Charles song "Ain't That Love," and she found herself singing it under her breath as she leaned against the wide window of the café: "When you cry, I want to cry some, too."

That *was* love, that desire to do for another person what wasn't any real help to oneself. She couldn't really think of anyone else besides Easter who had gone that far for her. Then she remembered that it was Ray Charles who had been singing when Easter got mad at her. She hated that she would never, ever be able to listen to him again without remembering that evening; she loved Ray Charles so much that it felt like losing a good friend.

She stood on the sidewalk with everyone walking by and cried. She was glad they could all see her. Lots of people were out, because town was closing down and people were going home for the day. Lolie threw the door of Shoes Galore open and came down the sidewalk, swinging her yellow purse, then started to holler out something before she realized that Anneth was in tears.

"Oh, baby," Lolie said, and took Anneth in her arms. Anneth leaned her chin on Lolie's shoulder but didn't embrace her, just stood there with her arms limp at her sides. "It's over Easter, ain't it?"

"It's everything."

"Work?"

Anneth shook her head. "No."

"Matthew?"

"Hell, no." She didn't know if she was lying or not.

Lolie hooked her arm in Anneth's and walked her up the street. "I tell you what. You come home with me. I'm going to cook you a big supper. Beans and salmon patties and fried potatoes. You can make the corn bread—you're the best hand at making it, anyway. And then we'll get all fixed up. And then me and you and Israel will go honky-tonking."

Lolie let go Anneth's arm and did a little rump shake. A carload of boys went by in a red Chevy. They leaned out the window and wolf-whistled. "Oh, baby!" one of them called. "*Hell,* yeah," yelled another.

"In your dreams!" Lolie hollered after them, but she was smiling and waving to the boys. "Come on, Anneth Gail," she said, and took hold of Anneth's hand. "We'll have a big time. God knows I could use a night out. I hate working for Sissy Goins. That bitch was on my case all day."

Anneth wanted to at least give Lolie a smile out of kindness, but she couldn't. "Not tonight," she said, and started walking away. "I just want to go home and be by myself."

Lolie caught hold of her arm. "You want me to stay with you?"

Anneth had never noticed how much older Lolie looked than her, even though they were the same age. Lolie's eyes were so kind, like an old woman's. "I'll be all right," she said, and gave Lolie a hug. She patted her on the arm and let go her hand. "Go on, now."

Anneth walked back up the sidewalk but paused at the door to the café, looking back down the street. Lolie stuck her arm out her car window, waving as she pulled away with her radio turned up so loud that Anneth could hear it.

THE MUSIC WAS a train that moved through the church, circled their feet and about their heads, pressed against their faces. It was a real thing that they could feel all through them. It caused their heads to jerk back, forced their legs to take off running up and down the aisles. This song seemed impossibly fast, the piano keys hit so quickly that one note overlapped the other above the moaning of the guitars and the steady beat of the drums. The drummer's arms moved in a great blur, his foot tapping the drum pedal with such force that the *boomp* of the bass drum could be heard over everything else. They couldn't help but dance, listening to music like that. Easter wondered sometimes if it was the spirit or the music that caused them to holler out. It didn't matter; whatever it was caused an exhilaration like she had never felt before. She threw her arms up into the air, closed her eyes, and swayed back and forth a moment before dancing down the aisle, all the way up to the front of the church, where the preacher jumped off the altar and put his hand on her forehead. And then she fell onto the floor, pushed down not by the preacher's hand but by the very breath of God. She was sure of this. She lay on the floor and convulsed as one of the women snatched a towel off the pile in the first pew and spread it over Easter's thighs.

Now everyone was on their feet and they were all dancing, crying, waving their hands. Ecstasy was a real thing, so palpable that Easter couldn't understand how it wasn't seeable. The music grew louder, so forceful that she thought the walls of the church might give out and simply fall over. But the music would keep the roof from caving in on them. The music would cause the roof to rise up and be carried off. She imagined it landing somewhere far away. In the ocean, perhaps. People would stand on the beach and put a straight hand to their brow as they watched the roof float by, the steeple like a grand sail.

Easter had gone back to church the Sunday after the argument, feeling lost and disoriented, but everyone there had come out of their seats to hug her. She had not been inside the church in two years, but they all acted as if it was only yesterday that she had been such a large part of the congregation. That was the thing she had always known about church people—you didn't even have to ask them to forgive you.

But she realized that she would have to ask El to forgive her for running him off. And somehow that didn't seem right. Because she hadn't really forgiven him in her heart. After she went back to her pew, and the preacher started preaching and people kept getting more and more anointed, she sat there and cried. People thought she was crying because of the preaching, because of the emotion in the room, but it didn't have anything to do with the service. She was crying because she was no fool. She knew that if El didn't change, she would have to quit him, baby or not. She wouldn't stay with a man who drank and didn't respect her religion just because it was the right thing to do for the church or for the baby—in fact, that would be even harder on a child. Nor would she stay because of her own pride. And she missed her sister.

After the service was over, the pastor took Easter's hand and leaned into her ear. "You'll be baptized again and rededicate your life?" he said. His breath smelled like a damp basement.

"Not yet," Easter said. "But soon." She couldn't be baptized until she had forgiven Anneth. No matter how much she missed her, she still hadn't forgiven her.

ANNETH UNBUTTONED HER waitress uniform and let it fall around her feet and then sat down in the horsehair chair by the open window in her slip. Here she could feel the breeze off the river. She let her photo album lie on her lap for a long time before opening it. It was November and the air held that burning-leaves smell of late autumn, but it was a nice evening and the wind was not so much cold as merely cool. For her supper she shook a bag of peanuts into a Coke and smoked two cigarettes, all the while looking down at the little plaid cover. This plastic photo album was small enough to fit in her purse but large enough to hold her family's history. Finally she opened it.

There was a picture of Vine, although Vine had never consented to having her photograph taken. It was an old superstition of hers. Serena had sneaked and taken this picture one day when they had both ventured to Vine's old homeplace on Redbud, which wasn't even a place anymore. Nobody called it that, at least. Now it was a coal-mining camp, Altamont, a dirty sprawl of houses that were shipped in on railcars. In the picture, Vine was standing near an old fence line, her fingers held out to a bush of touch-me-not flowers. Serena had taken the picture just as Vine began to look up, so that her face was lost in a blur, but Anneth thought she could see a glimmer of Vine's beauty, anyway. It was almost like her own face, lost there in that shadowy place. She liked the fact that Vine hadn't let her face be caught. No one would ever be able to look into her eyes and wonder what she was thinking when that picture was taken or try to ponder the secrets she kept hidden. And Anneth loved seeing the straight way that Vine stood, her long black skirts and her rough old brogans. But most of all, Anneth loved the way Vine held her hand out to the flowers, tempting them to open up and see the world. Vine had such beautiful hands; Anneth could remember them in Vine's old age, but here she could imagine them young and smooth, so graceful and long fingered, like a piano player's.

There was a picture of her grandfather Saul in his casket. She never could understand why people took funeral photographs. After Serena's death, Easter had taken down all the funeral pictures in the living room. Serena had decorated the whole front room with them and had hung them very high, some up over the windows. Anneth had read in a magazine that a picture was supposed to hang at eye level, and after she told this to Easter, her sister had redone the whole house that way. But she had not put the funeral pictures back up. Now they were stacked up in the top of the hallway closet, a dark place where they belonged. Anneth knew that it was mostly because Easter had to live with the dead, anyway. Anneth knew how Easter was visited by ghosts. It was an unspoken truth between them.

Anneth had studied this picture of her grandfather many times. There was nothing to see, really. Just a peaceful, strong-boned face and a pin-striped shirt with suspenders, which she thought was an awfully stupid thing to put on a dead man—especially Saul, as she knew that below the waist he had been crushed by the coal that had fallen in the mine and killed him. Easter had told her all about the way he died. He had bored a makeshift mine into the mountain behind their house so they'd have easy access to coal for their stove, and one day the earth simply swallowed him. Vine and Serena had dug him out, working for two whole days until they reached his death chamber. At that, Vine had thrown down her shovel and run up onto the mountain, leaving Serena to pack him out by herself. When Vine came back down she simply sat in her chair for a week, talking about their family's being cursed by her own sins. Nobody ever knew what she was talking about, so they ignored it. "I loved him like air," she had said, standing by his grave as the first clod of dirt was thrown onto his casket.

Anneth wished she had known him. Everybody attested to what a good man he had been. There were still people in Crow County who would bend over backward for Easter and Anneth just because he had been their grandfather. His goodness haunted them somehow, hung over their heads and caused them to want to be better people. On the rare occasion when Anneth felt guilty about drinking or running wild, he was the first person she thought of, even though she had never known him.

Many times, Anneth had sat at Vine's feet and listened to her talk about Saul, how she couldn't have asked for a better man. Vine had told how he drove her to North Carolina to see her people on the Cherokee reservation. Whenever she started telling that story, Vine always collapsed in tears, as if that memory was too intimate to put into words. Even as a child, Anneth had begged Vine to tell her more about that trip because it seemed like such an adventure to take off across the mountains. But Vine would never say more.

There was Serena, laughing with her mouth open, one hand on

her thigh, the other up to the side of her face. Anneth had never noticed before that between the fingers of that hand stuck a cigarette. She realized that she was probably more like Serena than anyone, although she had always identified with Vine. But Serena had been wild at one time—Anneth had heard tales—and had even gotten a divorce from her first husband, Whistle-Dick, back in the early twenties. She had eventually married Dalton, Whistle-Dick's brother, when she got pregnant with Paul. Anneth had only one real memory of her two grandmothers' being together, although they always were, of course. They were all the time at each other's house, breaking beans or quilting or going to town together. But there was only one time that she could recall vividly, when she was ten.

Anneth had been miserable. For three days the mountain had been on fire and they had worked all night to make sure it didn't cross the ridgeline. Nobody knew how the forest fire had started—lightning or a carelessly thrown match—but everybody in God's Creek and Free Creek had come together to save the mountain that divided the two places. They hauled buckets of water up on the ridge and dashed it onto the ground, over and over, a monotonous circle of everyone Anneth had ever known in her life. All her cousins and Sophie and Paul and Gabe and Lolie and the preacher and just everybody. She wondered where so many buckets had come from. She had been given the worst one of all, a wooden bucket that leaked and had a rope handle, which cut into her hands. She knew that they had to keep the fire away, though, and she didn't complain until Vine noticed that her hand was bleeding. Vine ripped a strip from her apron and wound it about Anneth's hand, and just when Anneth thought she'd send her on back to the house, Vine simply traded buckets with her. Vine's wasn't much better—lighter, since it was aluminum, but the handle was thin metal that seemed to bite into Anneth's cut.

"I'm sorry, Anneth Gail, but we need ever hand we can get," she said, and tilted back her head, pointing her chin down the mountain to the finger-shaped garden. "I've worked too hard on them crops to give them over to fire."

So Anneth kept on packing the water, watching the shape of Easter in front of her, her hair hanging down in her face, her face black with soot. Anneth dashed her water out and paused for a minute, watching as Serena and Vine worked side by side, digging at the ditch line the men had formed around the ridge. Their big hands, their hoes, worked in unison, as if they had memorized each other's movements. She had felt like she would pass out from fatigue when the sky finally turned peach with daylight.

Then Serena and Vine and all the men stood with their elbows propped on their hoes and seemed satisfied that the fire had been kept away. Serena unwrapped the apron strip from Anneth's hand and kissed her on the palm. Her kiss felt like something that might heal her. "Bless your heart," she said. "But look what you done. Saved this big mountain. Kept our garden safe."

When they got back down to the house, it had turned into the most beautiful summer day that Anneth had ever seen. It was as if all the smoke had been absorbed by the sunrise, and there was even the song of birds amongst the trees—a sound she hadn't heard since the fire had begun three days earlier. She was so tired she felt as if she was watching the world in snapshots. She was vaguely aware of Easter's arm around her shoulders.

"I don't believe I'll be able to sleep on such a pretty morning," Vine said, her hands on her hips as she leaned back and looked at the sky.

"We've been up all night," Serena said, pushing the girls along toward the back porch. "These children are killed."

"Let's go to the swimming hole, though," Vine said, and a smile broke out on her face. "To get rid of this smoke from ourselves."

They walked up the crooked dirt road to the place where the creek widened and deepened, a round place with high banks covered in ivy and trumpet vines. Vine stripped off her blackened dress and left it in a clump on the ground, then climbed up on the bank. She stood for a moment, lit from behind, so that they could all see right through her slip. Anneth didn't look away from her grandmother's shape, the dark buttons at her breasts, and the black triangle below her belly. Vine put her hands together in front of her and dove into the water, her skin so brown and smooth it looked like something that had been baked for the exact right amount of time. When she came up out of the water, her long hair floated on the water behind her. She ran her hands over her face and called for Serena to hurry up. "It feels so good!" she hollered, and her voice echoed against the damp banks.

"Come on, girls," Serena said. "Shed them old dirty dresses."

"We can't strip down right here in front of God and everybody," Easter said, shoving her hands into her armpits as if she was already naked.

"There's nobody to see," Serena said, and stripped down to her slip. She didn't climb up on the bank but ran right into the water from the shallow sandy beach where they stood. She went under, then burst forth from the water with her shift sticking to her.

"You all coming?" Vine called, and before they could answer, she started splashing Serena. They had a water fight, just like two girls, and for the first time Anneth realized that they had once been young and carefree. Anneth jerked her dress over her head, ran right on up to the bank, jumped off, and caused a huge splash with a cannonball. When she came up, Easter was still standing on the bank fully dressed, but she was laughing. Finally Easter waded into the water, dress and all. They splashed each other, and Anneth did a dead man's float to much applause, and Easter won the contest of staying under the longest. Anneth remembered her grandmothers then sitting on the ivy-covered bank together, clad in their wet shifts, leaning back as they watched their granddaughters caught up in the happiness of simply being alive.

She missed her grandmothers too much to look at either of their pictures for very long. She turned the page to her parents' wedding picture. They both looked so solemn. It was impossible to tell by this picture how much in love they had been, but from all accounts they had worshipped each other. They had grown up together, after all, and must have known each other better than anyone else in the world. Her mother was so beautiful—half-Cherokee and half-Irish, with black hair that fell in corkscrew curls down to her waist and blue eyes that nearly pierced the gray confines of the picture. And her father was equally beautiful. Big shoulders and a square jaw, dimples and one big hand propped up on her mother's shoulder. How she wished for a love like the one that had existed between them. It was no wonder her mother went mad when he died. It must have been like walking around with only half of herself.

And of course the next picture was of her and Easter and Gabe, their mother's elegant handwriting on the back:

Gabe—10
Easter—5 $^1/_2$
Anneth—5 months
At Free Creek, Kentucky, July 1940

They were all three barefooted. They always went barefooted in the summer, even though they had shoes. Easter had told her that they had been poor back then, but not so poor as to not have shoes, like some others. The mountain was full of leaves behind them, so lush that she could almost remember the warmth of the summer day when the picture was taken. Gabe already thought he was a man, standing behind his two sisters with his dark eyes and fretted brow. He leered at the camera as if he had better things to do. And Easter looked pitiful in her heavy, out-of-season dress, holding Anneth in her arms.

She slammed the album shut.

If Vine and Serena were here, they would tell her to go to Easter, to beg for forgiveness. But she knew Easter better than that. Easter rarely got mad, but when she did, her heart became stone. She had to come around on her own, and if Anneth went to her, words would be said that might cause unhealable wounds. So she would just have to wait. And she knew what her grandmothers would want her to do in the meantime: live. She wasn't going to let herself be trapped inside her own mind.

She jumped out of her chair and went to her record collection, knowing that music healed her the same way water could. She put on a Coltrane album and turned it up as loud as it would go.

She gave herself what Serena had always called a whore's bath—standing at the sink with a soapy washrag to clean all the important places—and pulled on her red honky-tonking dress as she shimmied to the music. She put on lipstick and ran a brush through her hair, took just a moment to study herself in the mirror over the tiny bathroom sink. She pictured herself walking into the Hilltop, waving with the same hand that clutched her purse.

PART THREE

....

Coal Tattoo

When coal flashed bright as diamond,
men might rise in the mineshaft's
after-silence, lift themselves
from their cairns, these men who seemed
marked for death now marked for life
by those black bruises or streaks
called coal tattoos, and claimed them
certain signs of God's favor,
the best good luck charms if curved
up like a horseshoe—though most
came slower, rubbed in the way
quickwater wears stone, and all
part of the dark they entered
to bury their waking lives in.

—Ron Rash, "The Marked"

Twelve

·············

Live Forever

ANNETH LAY ON THE beach at Blackhawk Lake in her gingham two-piece bathing suit and cat's-eye sunglasses and felt her back cooking in the sun. The heat was almost painful on her skin but she was too comfortable to move. There was nothing better than this, nothing more relaxing. She loved lying here upon this sand, everyone splashing in the water just below her, people singing along to songs that came onto the transistor radio that Lolie had hung high on the branch of a hickory so that the sound would carry farther. Right now "Hey Baby" was playing and it seemed everyone here knew it. Anneth loved watching all these coal miners and old mountain boys joining in to sing together as they stood in the water. They slapped one another on the shoulder or wrapped their arms about one another's necks and closed their eyes to sing as loudly as they could. She took a deep breath of the lake air—a clean, green scent—and when she moved her teeth, there was the grit of sand in her mouth. It tasted good, like raw potatoes.

Like everything else lately, it made her think of Easter. Whenever Easter peeled potatoes, she always slipped a raw piece into her mouth midway through her work and crunched it between her teeth, turning it over on her tongue. There was nothing in the world that Easter liked better than raw potatoes. A palpable grief curled up in Anneth's gut. Sophie had told Anneth that Easter was pregnant. "But don't go up there and upset her, now," Sophie had said.

Many afternoons when she got off work she would drive up to Free Creek and sit in front of the house, hoping for Easter to come running out the door to greet her and tell her to come in. But if Easter knew that Anneth was out there, she must have stood to the side of the window, peeking out without giving up her grudge. Now it had been nearly eight months. Every time Anneth had the thought of never talking to Easter again, she felt the blues threaten to spread out over her body at any moment. She tried not to think about Easter or the baby, but lying here on the lake with the good sun warm on her back, she could think of nothing else.

She rolled over, sat up, and lit a Lucky Strike. Israel and Lolie were standing waist-deep in the water, splashing each other. There was a scattering of children playing near the water's edge: collecting rocks, using a stick to write their names in the sand. Several boats had pulled up on the bank. Men sat in them, smoking and drinking beers. Anneth's mouth watered at the prospect of a cold Blue Ribbon; Lolie hadn't brought a thing but several bottles of RC and Anneth had already had three of them. She was cotton mouthed, and the cigarette was only making it worse.

The music went off and a man came on to announce the news in a monotone: something about the Cubans and JFK and Asia, the same thing that had been in the news for months now. After that it seemed the station just faded out of existence; first there was dull static and then nothing, and she could hear all their voices clearly down at the water. Above them all there was Lolie's high, clear laughter. Israel laughed, too, and Lolie punched his arm playfully and swam away.

Anneth closed her eyes as a cooling breeze drifted in off the lake. She could hear it passing through the leaves of the sycamores. Far away there was the sound of a boat motor, and closer, more laughter, and even before she opened her eyes she could hear Lolie's wet feet slapping on the sand. Lolie sank down onto the towel next to Anneth's and lay back as if exhausted.

"What're you laughing about?" Anneth said.

"Israel. I swear, he ain't got a brain."

"I wish he'd bum us a beer off some of them fellers down there."

Lolie sat up and put a hand to her brow to block the sun. "Them's coal-company men. Israel wouldn't ask them for nothing."

Anneth eyed the men more closely. They had pulled their boats in very close together and they leaned over the sides to talk to one another. One of the men was incredibly brown—Anneth wished she was that dark—and good looking, from what she could see. He had hair the color of a penny and he was wearing sunglasses. She had never seen a man wear sunglasses before. He leaned down and brought up another beer, then made two holes in the top with a church key. He caught her looking and nodded his head.

She held his gaze while she talked. "See that one staring me right in the eye? I bet he'd give me a beer."

"He ought to take a picture—it'd last longer," Lolie said. She tapped Anneth's box of Lucky Strikes and caught a cigarette between her teeth. "Don't you dare ask him for no beer. He's the mine foreman."

"He's tall. Look at them long legs."

Lolie elbowed her. "But he's a company man."

"Who cares? He's still sharp to look at."

"His daddy is one of the owners of the Altamont mine. They sent him down here from West Virginia to straighten him out, I heard. He was so wild that his daddy put this big job on him. He lives in that old house overlooking the camp, two stories and gingerbread on the porch. A real prick, Israel says."

Anneth got her bottle of baby oil and squirted out a handful, then coated her arms and the tops of her breasts and her belly. Her skin shone in the stark light.

"You'll burn up, all the iodine you put in that oil," Lolie said, and lay back down.

Anneth stood up and popped the back of her bottoms so they weren't riding up on her cheeks. "I'm going to get me a beer. You want one?"

Lolie put her hand around Anneth's ankle. "Them company men won't fool with no waitress. They're all highfalutin."

Anneth jerked her ankle away. "I'm not wanting *fooled* with," she said, and tapped her toe against Lolie's waist. "I'm wanting a beer."

He watched her closely as she walked down the beach toward him. But they were all watching her. She liked that, liked having so many eyes upon her. Some of the men who stood with women in the water even paused to look at her. The radio got staticky again and she could hear choppy voices—an announcer giving the end of the tobacco report, and then one talking about the Stanley Brothers playing a show in Bristol. Out on the lake a boat went by with a skier behind it, a white-capped wake trailing out behind.

She stopped at his boat and put one hand on her hip. "Hey, buddy," she said, "you got an extra beer?"

He fished down into his cooler and held one by the top, extending the bottom toward her. "Come and get it."

THE PAIN HIT Easter as if someone had shot her in the stomach and ripped her wide open. She was standing in the kitchen, fixing El's lunch pail. The tearing ran through her like a zipper and she dropped the ladleful of pinto beans she had been dipping into the pail. The beans and hot juice covered the top of her feet and she focused on this as she bent over, thinking it might ease the pain.

She fell back onto the floor and ran her hands over her big belly in long, quick motions. The blood spread across the linoleum like a blooming stain on cloth. Before she had even realized there was bleeding at all, the blood was in her hair and its metallic smell was rising up, making its way into her mouth.

"El," she hollered, but it only came out as a gurgle. But he was there all at once, still buttoning up his shirt.

THE DRIVE TO THE hospital seemed to pass her in a blur of houses and cars and mountainsides. By the time he carried her into the emergency room lobby, she had passed out. The pain was too much to bear.

When she came to, she saw the nurses' faces and she didn't even have to ask. She had known even before awakening. It was as if she had seen every bit of it: the doctor cutting open her belly and lifting out the baby, which was so blue it was nearly gray, then a scrambling about in the operating room as they tried to save the child. It was like a dream to which she couldn't recall all of the details.

A nurse came and took hold of her hand. She leaned over and said something, but Easter didn't really hear. The woman was saying, "Honey, I'm sorry," or "We did all we could," or something to that effect. Easter didn't have to hear her, for the nurse's face held all these sentences in the gathered wrinkles of her brow.

"I wanted him so bad," Easter said.

The nurse nodded and ran her thumb over Easter's knuckles.

"I want to see him."

"Are you sure about that, Mrs. McIntosh?"

"Bring him to me," Easter said in a whisper. The nurse stood there looking down at Easter as if she were some strange sight to see, and Easter mustered all the voice she could and screamed: "Now!"

El crept into the room as if she was something he feared. His face was stretched tightly across his skull and she could tell that he was trying not to show how hurt he was. But his pain couldn't equal hers; there was no way. They had torn the baby right from her, cut it away from her own live body, and how could he possibly know what that was like, to have a part of you lifted out of yourself, dead and blue? There was no way. She wanted him there, but at the same time she didn't want to share her grief with anybody. Not with him, not right now. He came to her bed and just fell over, his face against her breasts. She could feel his tears hot on her thin gown but she made no move to comfort him. She looked at the ceiling and squinted hard, as if she might be able to see God hovering over her. "Why?" she said. She thought of saying, *I beseech you!* the way the preacher often did; it sounded like the epitome of pleading, to beseech for something, but she couldn't muster any more words. She rose up a bit, wanting to understand, trying so hard to do so, but she couldn't and she felt her faith drifting up out of her, right through her heart and her chest and El's face and on up, up, until she realized that what she was reaching for was that very thing. She was trying to catch hold of her faith and not let it escape, but it was gone. It burned through the ceiling. She could hear it sizzle through the wood.

The baby was wrapped tightly in a striped blanket, so that she couldn't see any of him as the nurse stood there in the doorway, pausing before coming forward.

"Mrs. McIntosh," the nurse said, her voice caught somewhere amongst her teeth.

"Bring him to me," Easter said. "I have to see my baby."

It was as if the nurse became nonexistent and El dissolved into thin air, too, and there was nothing but the baby drifting toward her.

She put her hand up and he came to rest in the crook of her arm and she pulled the blanket away from his face. Perfect. Perfect in every way, fully formed, the fingers of his left hand slipping out to reveal a tightly clenched fist. Little nostrils and downy eyebrows and the prettiest lips. And right there on his forehead, a curved blue line burned into his skin, a mark that she had seen before.

The nurse was beside her again, and she was aware of El down at the foot of her bed, his hands on her legs, as if he wanted to be near for comfort but couldn't bear to look at their son's face.

"He has a coal tattoo," Easter said.

She was aware of the nurse's nodding. "We see them every once in a while."

"But it's a sign of survival," Easter said, speaking aloud for herself, not for El or the nurse or anyone else. She felt as if she was speaking just to convince herself that she was still there, that she was alive. "My brother has one, from being in a mine cave-in, when the chunks of coal fell on his arm. He never could get rid of that blue mark it left." She flashed back to when she was a child and had seen a man with such a blemish for the first time, Serena leaning down to tell her not to stare, that it was something for the man to wear proudly. Serena had whispered, "When the coal breaks your skin, it becomes a part of you."

"Babies have them sometimes," the nurse said. "Nobody really knows why."

"It's a sign that you're meant to live, though," Easter said, her voice trailing out of her mouth as if she could see the words forming themselves on the air, letters that came together and snaked out across the room to plaster themselves on the wall. She could see the words back there on the whiteness between the two long windows. The only word she focused on was *live*.

She heard Serena whispering in her ear again: *But it's a sign of sacrifice, too.* Easter pushed Serena's voice away from her, actually put a hand into the air as if to shove her grandmother aside.

"Easter, please. Let him go," El said, but his words meant nothing to her. She thought he was a coward, standing down there where he wouldn't have this baby's face burned into his mind forever. She had already memorized that face, the big eyes and fat cheeks and most of all the coal tattoo, a faint blue line like the jagged edge of a leaf, stamped onto his temple. She leaned over and kissed him on the coal tattoo. And there her lips felt a coldness that she had never known before, a cold like darkness stretched out eternal.

She dropped her head and held the baby up just enough so that it could be a sign for the nurse to take him. She knew if she didn't let him go now, she would sit here and hold him all night. She would hold him until they put him in the ground. She wasn't even aware of the nurse over her until her arms were empty—a great, barren lightness there on her chest where he had lain.

"What am I to do?" El was asking at her ear then, his voice a whisper, a call from very far away.

When she opened her mouth it felt as if her tongue was coated with chalk. She spat the word out, as if she were coughing up two pieces of coal: "Anneth."

Thirteen

···············

Bone Moon

ANNETH SEEMED ABNORMALLY aware of noise this morning. It was suffocating and loud, coming at her from all sides. She had been out too late the night before with that mine foreman, Liam, but it was more than just being tired; every sound ran all through her. Someone was playing "Where Have All the Flowers Gone?" on the jukebox, and even though she loved that song, she still thought it was too early for the Kingston Trio. A baby was crying; Anneth's boss, Gloria, was shouting out an order; and four men who had gotten off the seven o'clock train were being particularly obnoxious with riotous laughter. When she took their order they had made fun of her accent—raising their eyebrows and shooting knowing looks to one another when she spoke—and that was enough to make her hate them, besides their laughter, which was so loud and jovial that it seemed fake. She could hear the sizzle of the grill and the chairs scraping on the floor, forks clattering against plates, a girl who chomped on a cud of gum and popped her bubbles with the flat of her hand, then went about the task of pulling the bubblegum off her nose and cheeks. The sharp ring of the bell when an order came up. Too much noise. She needed a break and she had only been there an hour.

When she glanced up and saw that El had stepped in, it seemed the place grew even louder. He stood there looking about helplessly for a moment, as if he had never been in a restaurant before. There was something wrong. She could tell by his face. Of course there was. Why else would he come into the café? He had never been in here before as far as Anneth knew. It felt strange to see him, to be watching him across the room. It was as if she and El really had done something wrong, something like Easter had thought that evening, because she felt guilt wash over her. For a moment she considered running into the kitchen to hide from him, but then he saw her and as soon as their eyes locked she knew for sure that something was wrong.

"What is it?" she said, holding her tray against her chest. "What's wrong?"

"I was going to call you but I just didn't think it would be right," he said. He couldn't look her in the eye.

She put her hand on the ball of his shoulder, shaking him a little. "El, tell me," she said, hearing the pleading in her own voice. "Is it Easter?"

"The baby," he said, and looked away. "She's lost the baby."

Anneth rushed back across the room past the table of laughing men. She could sense them making a great show of turning to watch her walk past. The old man raised his coffee cup in the air and said, "Miss?" but Anneth went on past him without a word. The cook tapped his palm against the bell, which sent out its singular, high ring. She squatted down behind the counter to get her purse but took a moment to close her eyes and suck in a deep breath. When she got up again, El was still standing just inside the door as if he was waiting for someone to seat him.

"Let's go," she said. She breezed past him and threw the door open.

Outside, the air was damp with heat, so humid that it was hard to take a breath.

El was right at her heels. "Now wait a minute, Anneth," he said, trying to catch her elbow in his hand. "I'm not so sure you ought to just bust right in on her. It's been months since you seen her."

"I should've gone up there to see her. I was so damn afraid she'd run me off." She stopped and looked up and down the street, her voice swelling in her chest. "Where the hell's your car at?"

"Let's talk about this, now, Anneth. Wait one damn minute here." He shoved his hands into his pockets and didn't say anything else until she was still, looking him in the eye. "She's asked for you."

"But you don't want me going to her?"

"I'm just not certain it's the right thing," he said. "You all ain't even made up since that big fight."

Anneth spotted El's Chevy sitting in front of the shoe store and hustled toward it. "Sisters don't make up, El. They just go back to the way things were."

SHE HAD NOT felt as if she could completely break down until Anneth came. Now a great release moved up out of Easter's heart. She could feel it rising, bursting forth, when Anneth leaned down and wrapped her arms around Easter's shoulders. Anneth held Easter as tightly as she could. They cried with a grief that Easter reckoned could be felt all throughout the hospital.

She knew that their mourning was growing and growing until it became an actual, physical thing. It rose from them and moved out the window, a great wind that whistled through the trees down the mountain until it reached the town. There this wind of grief kicked newspapers along the sidewalks and blew the hats from the heads of a group of men leaving the Depot Café. It blew up the skirts of women on their way into the dress shop, caused trees to bend, set waves to peaking on the river. People felt it come out of nowhere, turned to watch it pass. The trees showed the white sides of their leaves to its approach, and as it moved across the hills the wind tore damp clothes from lines where they had been hung to dry. Tomato plants broke in two and tufts of leaf lettuce were lost. Their collected grief moved up the dirt road and took shingles from their own little house on Free Creek.

Anneth stretched out on the bed there with Easter, one arm behind Easter's neck and the other thrown across her waist. Before long, darkness overtook the world outside the long windows, and gray shadows moved about the room. By that time they had both fallen asleep, exhausted by their heartbreak.

ANNETH DID NOT really ever dream. It was more like remembering while she slept. She always saw the past in her dreams. Tonight, once again, she was observing something that had already happened. She was aware that this was a part of her life she was looking at, although it was something that she had only heard spoken of a couple of times. Asleep but not asleep, she stood in the middle of the road at Free Creek just as she had when she was five years old.

It was January and winter had set in like a chill that gets under the skin. The trees stood black and stark, the mountain shrunken with the loss of leaves. Vine told Easter and Gabe to get sweaters on while she dressed Anneth. They were going outside to see the bone moon and to check on Samuel.

Samuel lived far up in Free Creek and was rarely seen, but in the winter he often got drunk and started walking down the holler as if he had somewhere to go. Most people made fun of Samuel or downright hated him—they leaned out their car windows and threw pop bottles at him and called him an old drunk—but Vine and Serena tried to watch out for him. During warm weather he busied himself with the biggest garden in those parts, but once the winter sky took over, he turned to the bottle more and more. That night, Vine had wrapped up a chunk of corn bread in a piece of waxed paper for Samuel and was carrying it in her apron pocket.

"It's the bone moon," Vine said, and squatted down to put her hands on the back of each girl. "Look how full and white. But that's not why it's called a bone moon."

"Why, then?" Easter asked. She stared at the sky, and Anneth thought that she could see the moon reflected in her sister's eyes.

"It got its name because it always rose in the month when people were about to starve to death. They'd gnaw on bones to get by, or make bone soup," Vine said, and stood on popping knees to take hold of the girls' hands. "I wanted you to see it, to remind you how lucky we are, to always have plenty to eat."

They all stood there looking up in silence for a long moment before Vine squeezed the girls' hands. "Let's go make sure old Samuel's not passed out by the creek again," she said. "I worry about him when it starts getting cold."

"Samuel's crazy as a lunatic," Gabe said, walking behind them. He thought he was too big to have his hand held.

"Samuel's in a bad way," Vine said. "We have to be good to people who are in that kind of shape."

Anneth studied the sky and wondered if a bone moon put out more light than others, because it was the brightest night she had ever seen. The skeletal tree limbs were touched with silver and the dirt road was white. She put her hand in front of her face, and her skin seemed to glow in the moonlight. As they walked, Vine hummed beneath her breath a song that Anneth didn't recognize.

"Samuel!" Gabe hollered, cupping his hands around his mouth. His voice echoed up the mountain, over and over.

When his voice had died out up on the ridge, there was complete silence for just a moment. Then the gunshot broke apart the night, and Vine jerked Anneth and Easter up and held each of them by the waist, pressed against her hips as she ran back to the house amidst more gunfire. She screamed for Gabe to run, to run as fast as he could, and then there was the sound of men hollering and cussing and all at once the night seemed very dark as the girls were pushed into a closet. One block of light fell on Vine's face as she leaned down to them. "Don't move from here," she said before she closed the door. Anneth scrambled over shoes and boxes, trying to reach Easter again, but she couldn't find her. She called out her name in a great panic before Easter's arms slid around her. "Be quiet," Easter said. They listened to the hollering on the other side of the closet door—Serena telling Gabe to get in the closet, to get down—and to Vine's heavy shoes clomping across the floor to get the shotgun. A pounding on the door, a man hollering outside.

"Shh," Easter said, patting Anneth on the back. Anneth marveled at her sister's bravery. Only ten years old, but already so old, it seemed. Easter prayed silently, but Anneth knew what she was doing because she could feel Easter's lips moving against the back of her head. She could feel the prayers filling up the closet around them.

"Send him out here," yelled a man.

"I told you, Samuel's not here," Serena shouted. "It's just me and Vine and these children. You're drunk and out of your mind, ever one of you."

"He can't just run off from a poker game without paying his debt, Serena."

"John Henry, I want ever one of you to leave this place, now," Vine said, and in her mind's eye, Anneth could see Vine holding the shotgun up, keeping the men at bay.

"We know you hiding him," the man called. "I seen him run on your porch."

Vine's voice, big and bold: "Get off our land or I'll blow your brains out. You know I will, too."

And then more gunfire, three reports of a pistol. Anneth heard a bullet zip through the air of the closet. She thought she could feel the wind off the shot.

Someone was knocking on the back door, but not pounding. Just a peck that grew weaker and weaker until it was nothing at all, until it seeped into complete silence. Then the back door creaked open. A thud. Anneth shuddered with tears, afraid that every one of them had been killed. Perhaps she and Easter were the only people left in the world. She felt movement and then a line of light and then she realized that Easter was opening the closet door and peeking out. Through the thin opening they could see Serena and Vine sitting down on the floor at the back door with Samuel stretched out across their laps. Gabe was hiding beneath the kitchen table, his eyes large as he watched the blood from Samuel's chest seep out onto the floorboards.

"They've killed him," Vine said, her voice a sob that barely escaped her mouth. "Over poker money."

Easter pulled the closet door closed again and put her arm back around Anneth's shoulders. "Just sit here, baby," Easter said. "Set right here with me."

Anneth relaxed against Easter's chest and as her eyes adjusted to the darkness she realized that a stripe of the light from the bone moon was stretched across the tops of their feet, coming in through the space at the bottom of the door.

ANNETH CAME AWAKE with a start, but she didn't jump from the bed or even move. It was the middle of the night and she was asleep in Easter's hospital bed with Easter lying there beside her. She could tell by the gray pallor of the night sky through the open window that it was nearing dawn. She eased from the bed and walked backward to the door, feeling her way through the room with her hands as she watched for any sign of Easter's waking up.

The lights in the hallway seemed very stark. Out here was the noise of the hospital: nurses' plastic soles squeaking on the tiles and an IV cart being wheeled down the hall. An old man moaned.

Anneth wiped the sleep from her eyes and straightened her wrinkled blouse on her shoulders as she walked. She needed a cigarette and a Dr Pepper. In the waiting room off to her right was El, asleep and gray faced as he sat in an orange plastic chair, leaning against the wall. Anneth realized that she hadn't even asked him how he was. He had lost a child, too. She felt so sorry for him, asleep like that. He wouldn't leave Easter's side, which was more than she could say for herself. Why hadn't she tried to make up with Easter, knowing that she was pregnant? Anneth would never forgive herself for being so proud and stupid. Yet Easter had forgiven her.

Anneth only had to put her hand on El's arm to rouse him. He jumped and swiped one hand through the air as if knocking someone aside.

"What is it?" he said.

Anneth put her hand on his shoulder so he wouldn't get up. "It's all right," she said. "It's just me."

She sat down in the chair beside him. "I'm so sorry, El. It's just not right, this happening."

"I hate it, Anneth," he said, and put his face into his palms. "I hate it so bad."

Anneth ran her hand around his back. "I know it," she said, suddenly aware that she had to be strong right now. Funny how Easter had always been the strong one, always taking care of everybody else.

People thought that Anneth was a strong woman—the way she could drink so much and fight when that was called for and stay up all night partying. But she wasn't strong at all. And maybe people didn't think this, anyway, she reasoned. Perhaps she had been the only one to think that, while everyone else knew that Easter really was the backbone for both of them.

"Somehow this was all meant to be," Anneth said, and tapped her cigarette pack against the meat of her palm so a Lucky Strike would slide out. "Who knows why."

"Did she tell you about the coal tattoo?" he said, looking at her as she lit her cigarette. There were unshed tears in his eyes.

She shook her head no. "We never spoke a word," Anneth said.

"She kept saying how it was a sign of survival, that the tattoo alone should have made him live," El said, "but she didn't understand what else that mark can mean."

"What?" she asked. She had seen lots of people with coal tattoos, but never a baby.

"My uncle had a coal tattoo," El said, and pushed up his sleeve. He tapped a finger on the whiteness of his forearm. "Right there, just a faint little hint of blue, like a permanent bruise. One time, me and him got drunk together. Just set and drunk all night long, talking and playing cards. I knowed he had been in a mine collapse, that he had survived what had killed a dozen other men. He never did like to talk about it, but I was drunk, so I said how he must have been proud of his coal tattoo, that it was a sign of survival. But he said he didn't think of it that way at all. To him it was a sign of sacrifice. He said, 'It reminds me of all them other men who died down there, died trying to make a living to put food on the table for their family.'"

Anneth looked away. Out the window she could see daylight spreading across the sky like a bloodstain. "But what could that baby be sacrificing itself for?" she asked.

"That's not what it means," El said. "That mark was a sign to her—to us—that a sacrifice was on its way to help us."

Anneth thought that El might be talking out of his head, so racked by grief that he wasn't thinking clearly, but she nodded anyway. She patted the top of his hand as she got up. "Well, I believe you need some breakfast," she said, and put her cigarette out in the ashtray that stood in front of the seats. "Let's run down to the café while she's resting good and get you a bite."

"I don't want to leave her," he said.

"She knows that, but you need to eat." She put out her hand to help him up.

Fourteen

....

When No One's Around

EASTER TOLD EVERYONE that she was all right. She clasped her
hands together in front of her and was aware of putting on her most
saintly face when she said, "I lost the baby for a reason," and "God
works in mysterious ways." She didn't believe either of these things.
Especially about God's working in mysterious ways. This just was
not true to her mind anymore. God worked in blunt, obvious ways.
There was no mystery to it at all. He had not allowed her baby to live
because He hadn't wanted to. He didn't want her to have a child. Because He didn't *feel* like it. Because He could.

She would never have said any of these things aloud because that
would have made it too real. If she put it into words, she might start
to completely believe what she said. She hadn't told El the way she
felt. Not even Anneth—especially not Anneth. Despite their recon-
ciliation, there were still days when Easter couldn't bear to speak
Anneth's name aloud.

She peeled potatoes without watching her hands. Her eyes focused on the invisible air, like someone in a wide-eyed coma. She
sat like that, her hands moving knowingly, but in her mind there
was only one thought that kept repeating itself over and over, like a

record when the needle's stuck in a groove: *It's not fair. It's not fair. It's not fair.* She cleaned the house and hung clothes on the line and tended to her garden with this mantra in her head: *My baby is dead. I did everything right but my baby is dead.* But most of the time she blamed herself. It was because she had backslid. But surely God couldn't be that cruel, cruel enough to punish someone in such a way.

Everyone tried to make sure that she was never alone, as if they knew how her mind worked when the house was all silence. When Anneth and El were at work, Sophie came down to sit with her. Anneth moved back in with them, and for a month she slept in the same bed with Easter. At first, El took off from work, but then he realized that Easter had no use for him, so he spent most of his time on the road. When he was home, Anneth cooked for him and sometimes they sat in the kitchen talking long after the meal was over. Easter could hear them, even though they were whispering.

"I've never seen her like this," Anneth said. "I know it's a hard thing on a woman, but I'm starting to worry."

El's chair scraped against the linoleum as he got up, and Easter reckoned he did this so that Anneth wouldn't be able to look him in the eye. Easter thought he most likely went to stand at the sink, leaning on the counter as he looked out the window on the backyard. What did he see there? Their dying garden. The locust where her mother had hung herself. "It's been almost three months. Maybe she ought to go back to the doctor."

"Doctors don't know their ass from a hole in the ground," Anneth said. The clink of her coffee cup being put on the saucer. The scratch of her lighter flint. A loud exhalation of smoke. "Her grief is too thick to bear."

The next morning, Easter awoke to find Anneth sitting on the edge of her bed, studying her face. Tears fell down Anneth's cheeks, but she didn't wipe them away.

"What is it?" Easter said.

"I need you to get up, now, Easter," Anneth said. "You need to get up and go to church and start living again. If you don't, I don't believe I can stand it."

Anneth wiped her face with the back of her hand and leaned down to kiss Easter on the forehead, and then she was gone. When the room became still with her exit, Easter wondered if she had truly been there.

Easter got out of bed and sat down at her dressing table, the same dresser Serena had used since she was very young. Easter ran her fingers over the hard maple, trying to feel the history that lived within the wood. She wondered what heartaches Serena had pondered sitting here. Easter saw that her face was completely changed, marked by this curse that had befallen her family for so long now: death. Her grief was stamped into her eyes. She had always been serious, even as a child, but her eyes had once been wide with wonder for the world. They weren't anymore. All her life she had believed in magic just as strongly as Anneth had, but now that was gone. There was no magic in this life, only grief and an occasional glimmer of joy. She hadn't pinned her hair up in weeks and it hung limp on her shoulders, down to the small of her back. It had once been the color of honey but now it seemed darker, as if it had darkened in soaking up all her grief. She lifted it up and watched as it dropped lifelessly to settle against her gown again.

The Bible said that a woman's hair was her glory. The church had taught them to never cut their hair, to display it for God's pleasure. Suddenly this struck Easter as incredibly stupid and contradictory. The church spoke against vanity, yet the women tried so hard to make their hair grow long and beautiful. It was hypocrisy that fell around her shoulders, and she felt as if it would smother her to death.

Her sewing kit sat there on the dresser, and she unlatched the lid and withdrew a pair of scissors. It didn't take long to cut her hair to shoulder length. With each slice of the scissors she felt lighter. If she cut it short enough, she might lose her anchor to the earth and simply float away. People would be out in their yards and sense her drifting over them like a balloon that has escaped a child's grip. She'd simply put her arms out and let the air carry her. She'd close her eyes and be lost forever, content to swim away through the sky.

When she finally stopped cutting her hair, she plucked it from her lap and shoulders and cupped it in her hands. She held the hair to her face. She didn't cry, though. She didn't have any tears left. She let the hair fall onto the dresser and collected herself, patting the jagged edges of her new hairstyle. She remembered the little net full of her great-grandmother Lucinda's hair, in the cedar box. She thought she might put her own locks there, too, but she wanted rid of it. She would throw it onto the yard, and the birds could use it to build nests. She looked in the mirror and let out one choked laugh. Women always cut their hair when they wanted a fresh start, didn't they?

The house was impossibly quiet with both El and Anneth gone off to work. She knew that Sophie would be down here any minute to sit with her. El had given strict instructions for her not to be left alone. Was she on suicide watch? She wondered if El and Sophie and Anneth sat in the living room together and whispered about the way her mother had gone mad and how Easter might do the same.

She moved through the rooms as if walking in a dream, her feet unaware of which way they would step next. Outside, it was already autumn. She had no memory of the summer's fading away after the baby's funeral. The cold ground felt good against her bare feet, though. She stepped quickly through the yard, grinding the heels of her feet into the sand as she crossed the road. She climbed down the crooked rocks and waded out into the creek. The water sent a chill all the way up to her thighs. Maybe her mother had chosen to exist somewhere outside herself. Maybe that's why she had stood in the creek stripped of clothes. Easter wished she could make her mind go to this place, but she couldn't. She was completely aware of standing in the creek, clad in her nightgown, with her head dizzy from its new and unexpected lightness. She closed her eyes and turned her face to the weak sun. No cars passed on the road; Sophie still hadn't made her way up here. No one to see her and think that she had finally lost her senses. After a long time she scrambled back up the rocky bank.

She'd start trying to live again. Even though she knew it was a false start. She was sure that she wasn't ready yet. She couldn't put her heart into it, but she could make a show of getting up. So she would go about acting as if she felt better, when in fact she felt worse than ever. She didn't want Anneth and El to be hemmed in by her grief. There was no use in four lives' being lost.

She heated up the coffee Anneth had left on the stove and was sitting at the kitchen table when Sophie appeared at the back door, breathing hard in her attempt to hurry. She stepped in the door apologizing for taking so long, but Easter just took a drink of her coffee and waited for Sophie to notice that she had cut off her hair.

"I'm up," Easter said. "I'm awake now."

EASTER KNEW ANNETH didn't want to go back to her apartment in Black Banks, but it was obvious that she did want to get back to seeing Liam, that mine foreman she had taken up with down at the lake. Easter didn't know much about him but she knew that Anneth was sleeping with him. She could tell by Anneth's eyes. So it wasn't too hard to force Anneth out of the house. Easter missed her: her loud music and cigarette smoke and high laughter. The way she whistled the whole time she washed dishes or fried an egg. But

Easter needed to be alone, and most of the time, after they were all duped into believing she had recovered, she was left to do what she wanted. And all she wanted to do was nothing. She sat and remembered the baby's funeral. It had been the hottest day of the year and the leaves had wilted in the sunlight. The heat had lain in white stripes across the graveyard ridge. The littlest casket, impossibly little. The scent of the soil so rich and present on the hot air. Nothing but the songs of birds. That was all she heard. She didn't hear a word the preacher said or the singing or anything. Just the birds. A redbird that sat on a high branch and called, "Birdie, birdie, birdie." Its song was her mother's name.

Even when she went to church, her mind drifted above her and cowered in the high corners of the room, looking down at her as she sat motionless in her pew. It wasn't right for her to be there, anyway. She still hadn't made the move to be baptized again and she never felt really whole. It wasn't right for someone to leave the church, do their sinning, and come back without having had their sins washed away. No matter if she had been baptized way back when she was a child. She needed that cleansing again. But how could she do that now when she secretly doubted God's very existence? For weeks she refused to go up and sing. People stood during services and requested that she sing particular songs, but she only looked at the preacher and shook her head no.

No.

She sat in church with the people singing and shouting around her, the preacher's voice reverberating through the building like the dynamite blasts from the Altamont mine, but she wasn't there. Not really. She was floating above them all, a ghost that hovered with her back to the ceiling. And while this happened she thought of Anneth.

Anneth was wild and didn't care which way the wind blew. She was selfish and looked out for her own happiness, no one else's. True, she had stayed with Easter and tried to nurse her, but some days Easter could see that Anneth's heart wasn't in it. Still, Anneth had had plenty of men—Easter seriously doubted if Matthew Morgan and Liam Trosper were the only men Anneth had ever slept with—but she had never gotten pregnant, only to suffer a stillbirth. If Anneth had a desire to get pregnant, no doubt she would. Anneth always got what she wanted. Things just fell into her lap as if she had a special deal with the world: *Let me have a big time and I'll grace you with my presence.* In the event that Anneth were to get pregnant, if she wished she wasn't, the baby would be magically taken away. God would do that for Anneth. He would snap His fingers and Anneth would miscarry and that would be that. But it would only be because Anneth wanted to miscarry. That's how it seemed to work. Because things always worked out that way for Anneth. But not for Easter. No matter how hard she tried. No matter how hard she worked to serve God, to sing, to play the piano for His glory. No matter how much she followed Christ's example and treated everyone with compassion. No matter her sacrifices or anything else, nothing ever went the way she wanted, and her only really selfish wish—to be a mother—had been taken from her.

She knew that she would never carry another child. She could feel her womb withering within, like an orange that is tossed out on the yard. It was just like that, like an orange that shrinks in on itself and becomes a grayish white hollow thing. *Withered.* That was the perfect word; that word said exactly the way she felt inside.

But not Anneth. God smiled on Anneth. Easter didn't know why, but it seemed that way. The preacher was constantly saying that good things come to those who serve the Lord, but it wasn't true. It seemed to Easter that sinners had it better than anyone. They didn't make any sacrifices, and things just seemed to go the way they wanted. It was high time she admitted it to herself. Why couldn't everyone else see that this was the way it was? They had all been fooled. God didn't watch out for Christians. On the contrary, He let them suffer while the sinners got everything they wanted.

Of course, Anneth thought she wasn't a sinner at all. As long as she prayed to God and was aware of His presence and tried to be a good person, Anneth figured she would get into heaven. Easter had been exhausted long ago by such foolishness. If that was the case, then everyone would get into heaven, wouldn't they? Because if it was that easy, everyone would sign up.

Her mind raced with these thoughts all the time, so much that she feared she might be going mad. She thought of these things when she drove into work at the school cafeteria, as she took the students' lunch money, as she told her co-workers good-bye. She watched autumn play out, and then winter, and then spring, and her thoughts never varied. She thought about her loss when she cooked, when she ate with her family, when she stopped for groceries and perused the aisles as if she was really interested in what she bought. Sometimes she got home from the store and put up the groceries and realized that she didn't even remember taking these things from the shelf. She ended up buying things that neither she nor El ate: limes, sardines, canned corn.

One day in late March, she came home with groceries for a baby. She took each item out of the bag very slowly: boxes of baby cereal, zwieback toast, and animal crackers; a bunch of bananas; and thirty-two jars of Gerber baby food in every known flavor. She gathered all of it around her on the floor and sat in the middle of it, rocking back and forth without crying.

Later, she bagged the baby groceries up and put them on the porch of the church, hoping somebody who needed them would find the bags and think they had been sent there by God. She hurried back up the road—moving quickly, as if she didn't want to be seen leaving food for a baby on a church porch—and realized that the ghosts she had known all her life were scurrying alongside her. Her mother was there. Easter couldn't see Birdie, but she could feel her. As Easter walked up the road, Birdie walked in perfect stride with her. She put a hand out and placed it in the small of Easter's back. It was like being touched by the Holy Ghost itself, a jolt that passed all through Easter's body. The touch felt like peace, like the promise of contentment spreading through her bones.

In that moment Easter saw that it was time to stop this. The realization came to her as quickly as that, and it felt as if she had let out a breath that she had been holding for nearly a year.

She looked at the mountains, red with buds that promised to open and usher in spring, and felt a wave of gratitude wash over her—because she had survived this, hadn't she? She would never be completely over it, of course, but she had made it through to the other side. She hadn't gone mad, the way her mother had. She was alive. Still, she felt two holes in herself. There was the place where her womb had been. Now it wasn't even so much as an empty place, because it wasn't a place at all. It was a place that used to be. But the other hole was deep and round and black: the place where her faith had resided. She remembered now, watching her belief and trust in God floating up through the hospital ceiling. She didn't know how one went about rescuing something that had floated so far away.

Fifteen

....

Big Time

ANNETH AND LIAM were a dangerous couple. Dangerous because there was so much excitement balled up in their relationship that it threatened to explode at any minute. Liam was exactly like her in one major way: he liked to have a big time all the time. He liked nothing better than to be traveling the open road, pushing the gas against the floorboard as hard as it would go, sailing by other cars even on the curviest roads, the radio turned all the way up. He would drink a beer in one long pull, only to slam the bottle onto the bar with such force that the glass threatened to crack. He spent money as if he couldn't stand to have it in his pockets. When Anneth said she had always wanted to go to Cincinnati just to shop in the nice dress stores up there along the river, he insisted that they get into his car and drive there. When she read in a magazine that Natalie Wood had once stayed in the Seelbach Hotel in Louisville, Liam took the day off from work and escorted her into the hotel's ornate lobby and rented the biggest room they had. They drove down to Knoxville and danced in every bar, went to Mammoth Cave and crept through the damp caverns while drinking from the flask he had sneaked in. Their life together was a wild, drunken ride.

Lolie disliked Liam because he was the foreman, but she couldn't deny that he knew how to have a good time. At the Hilltop Club he danced to every song and bought every round of whiskey and beer that was brought to their table. By the end of the night, Israel and Liam were all hugged up, singing as they staggered toward the car. Their friends would not even come over to their table because of Liam's being there, though. They disliked him because he was the boss over the biggest job-supplier in Crow County and that was all. He had a job to do and he did it well. If they couldn't see past that, Anneth thought, if they couldn't look and see that he was a normal guy just like the rest of them, then that was their problem and she didn't care.

In the spring, Liam finally took Anneth to meet his parents in Huntington, West Virginia. As soon as they turned onto the driveway that took them atop Huntington's highest mountain, Liam changed completely. He sat up stiffly, turned the radio down low, and took the curves with careful calculation. Once they stepped into the mansion, Anneth couldn't understand Liam's trepidation. His parents seemed as welcoming as they could possibly be. A lifetime of witnessing the snobby antics of rich people in movies had not prepared her for their friendliness; she had imagined them turning their noses up at her red dress and the camellia in her hair. Liam's mother, Edith, wore a ring on every finger and kept a sloe gin fizz in her hand, but she had embraced Anneth upon meeting her, even kissing her on the cheek. His father, Stanton, was just as outgoing and gave a wink to Liam. "You've finally found a real looker," he said. He was tall and dignified with his salt-and-pepper hair and well-fitted suit. It was strange to see people dressed up for dinner, but this made her feel sophisticated.

She did not like the house, though. The rooms were meant to be beautiful but didn't strike Anneth that way at all. It felt like a museum.

There were antiques in every room, and Anneth wouldn't have been surprised to find velvet ropes and little signs instructing her not to sit on anything. There were fresh-cut flowers in every room, though, and their perfume filled the air. Back home there was a rumor that the owner of the Altamont Mining Company had a bathroom completely made of coal—walls, tub, vanity, even a commode—but she looked through the entire house and could find no evidence of such extravagance.

Still, she quickly noticed that Liam's big spirit shrank in that house. Talking to his father, Liam hunched his shoulders, his thoughtfully nodding head the opposite of his usual hyperactivity. At dinner he sat across the table from her and instead of rolling his eyes at some pretentious comment his father made, as he would usually have done, Liam kept on nodding in agreement. He spread the cloth napkin on his lap with such formality that Anneth laughed out loud. She couldn't help it.

He gave her a look and she tried hard to remain quiet as long as she could. But when Liam's father started talking about the mines—asking how production was coming along, instructing Liam that he had to prepare for the change from deep mining to strip mining—she felt the need to say something. As soon as her words escaped her mouth she realized it was the wrong thing for her to have said here, but she didn't give a damn.

"If you switch over to strip mining, people are going to turn against the company," she said.

Their forks all became still, even Edith's, which was halfway up to her mouth. Edith returned her fork to her plate and took a drink of her gin.

Liam's father finally spoke. "Why is that?"

"Because strip mining tears up the land too bad," Anneth said. She took a bite of her salad and chewed gingerly around her words. "People there are used to deep mining because it's hidden — back in the mountain. But strip mining, it's too hard on the land."

Liam's father held his fork and knife over his plate as if posing for a picture. "Well, strip mining is much less expensive."

"Yeah, well, you don't have to live there and look at it, do you?" She got angrier with each word she spoke.

"There's just a lot you don't know about coal mining, Anneth," the man said.

"I'd hate to think I don't. My daddy was killed in the Altamont mines," she said loudly, and before she knew it she had jumped up, causing her chair to fall backward. She stood leaning on the table, waiting for him to say something else. He looked completely taken aback. "So I know plenty about mining, buddy."

"Nobody's died in those mines since I bought them," Liam's father said, choosing each word carefully. "I take care of my men."

Anneth felt stupid, standing there while the rest of them sat looking up at her. She bent and righted her chair, then sat back down and picked up her silverware again. She took another bite and chewed with her eye on Liam. She didn't know what she expected him to say. To her dissatisfaction, he didn't say a word. She turned back to Liam's father. "All I'm saying is that you have to do right by the people who live near your company."

"I have always tried my best to do that," Liam's father said, and smiled at her. She saw what a practiced smile it was, the face of a businessman, a door-to-door salesman. "And besides, with strip mining, the accident rate is cut in half, at least. When you don't have men going back in the mountain, you don't have to worry about roof collapses and disasters like the one that killed your father."

Edith reached a hand across the table and patted Anneth on the wrist. "I'm so sorry about your father," she said. "You have every right to be angry." Her rings were cold against Anneth's skin.

Liam's father seemed to think it best to forget Anneth's outburst and go forward with the conversation. "We need to start going through all the broad form deeds that came under our ownership when we bought into Altamont," he said, looking Liam in the eye.

"Those broad form deeds are dirty," Anneth said before Liam could reply. She knew all about these deeds, which had been in the news so much lately. Bought by the companies ages ago, the deeds were to the mineral rights to people's property. A person could own his land and see his whole yard mined right around his house and not be able to do a thing about it. She knew that this was not a proper thing to say to Liam's father but she didn't care. Somebody needed to tell him. Those sloe gin fizzes that Edith had pushed on her had given her just enough prodding to say what she wanted.

"What do you mean, dear?" Edith said, and kept her eyes on Anneth as she tilted her head back for another drink.

"Everybody is against them," Anneth said. "Most of those deeds were bought for a quarter an acre or something. And then fifty years goes by before the company comes back and says they're ready to mine the land. It's not right."

All three of the Trospers were exchanging looks now, as if Anneth were part of the museum exhibit currently occupying their dining room, an exhibit that had unexpectedly opened its mouth and spoken out, not only once, but twice now. Suddenly she didn't like any of them.

Liam's father was looking at her with such a strange grimace on his face that she thought he might have taken a bite of something obscenely bitter. "Well, the thing is, they did sell the mineral rights," he said after a long silence broken only by the loud click of the grandfather clock's pendulum. He had a way of speaking that made him sound as if he were on the news, explaining something very important to the simpletons who watched him. "So the law is the law, Anneth."

Anneth didn't like the familiar tone he took with her. Liam's parents had both told her to call them Edith and Stanton, but she had not told them to call her Anneth. It had never crossed her mind to do such a thing because no one back home called you by anything but your first name, anyway. But now she was insulted by his boldness, the way his mouth curled around her name like she was a child he had to call down. "That doesn't make it right, *Stanton*. That's just a shitty way to act."

Liam put the tip of his shoe against her leg. She wadded up her napkin and threw it on her plate, then got up and walked out of the room as if she were off to simply take a stroll on the veranda. She decided that her exit had been too graceful, so when she got to the door she slammed it behind her. She stood on the porch and lit a cigarette and wished that their visit hadn't turned out like this, but there was nothing she could do about it now. She wasn't going to sit there like a dog and just take whatever was dished out to her, and they could go to hell if they didn't like it. She sure wasn't about to go back in there and spend the rest of supper with nothing more than the silver sound of forks clattering between them.

Liam came walking backward out the door, kissing his mother on the cheek. Liam's mother stood within the crack of the door and looked at Anneth with longing, as if she knew her very well and was sad to see her go. She bent her fingers twice in a wave and slowly shut the door.

"Let's get the hell out of here," Liam said, and held her lightly by the elbow as he led her back to his car. As he drove back down the driveway he put his hand on her thigh and looked over at her with a smile. "You were amazing in there," he said.

"I was pissed off in there," she said. She took a hard draw on her cigarette.

"Well, I loved it," Liam said, "seeing him struck down like that." He slapped the steering wheel and let out a high laugh.

"Well, you sure didn't act it," she said, and turned to watch the mountains go by out her window. She wondered who Liam was exactly, a man who could walk around like two different people. There were a lot of things she didn't know about him, and it wouldn't occur to her until much later that she should have realized this before it was too late.

AN UNNATURALLY THICK dew had fallen in the blue part of night, just before the world started to awake. In that time when daybreak is still hours away, the world knows it is approaching and prepares itself. Even before grayness shows at the horizon, things begin to stir. Animals move about. Trees take in deep breaths of the cool air, anticipating the heat that will descend upon them by midday. The ground opens its pores and yawns against the dark.

It was during that time that the dew had fallen, a dampness that moved down through the air and touched the leaves and the moss and the ferns along the creek. The dew was thin and beaded, so that it seemed to arise from the earth instead of coming down on it, but it was there nonetheless. The dew stood like sweat on the old rocks and made undecipherable, beautiful patterns on the glass of car windows, on the petals of flowers.

Anneth sat down in the woods and felt the dew soak into the seat of her dress. It was cool on the backs of her legs. She wasn't sure how long she kept her eyes closed but when she opened them, all was awake, as if she had wished it into being. Birdcall filled the mountain behind her, echoing far back into the deepest, most shady parts of the forest. Suddenly it was morning, clear and peach and lavender. The scent of summer came out of the ground and surrounded her. She could smell everything: the field of wildflowers atop the mountain, the creek water, the dew.

She had awakened in the middle of the night and sat up in her bed, trying to orient herself to the darkness of the big house over-looking Altamont. Liam snored beside her, his back hot and sticky against her elbow. The house creaked and moaned around her, set-tling into its patch of earth. She threw back the sheet covering them and carefully slipped out of the bed. She dressed silently, eyeing his naked body in moonlight. She grabbed her keys off the kitchen table and went outside, standing in the driveway with the coal camp spread out below her. There were so many lights down there that it almost looked like a big town. The coal company had built a church down there and its steeple was white against the black mountainside, watching her. Judging her. This was the first time she had stayed all night at Liam's house and already she didn't like the place. It wasn't that she felt guilty for being with Liam. The last few months they had been together many, many times. But there was something about his house at Altamont. She knew there were ghosts there. Altamont had once been known as Redbud, and Vine's family had lived there before the mining company took it away from them. Now the valley belonged to Liam's family, who had bought it several years back. She wished she had reminded Liam's father of this fact, too, since in ac-tuality he was now mining her family land, stolen from them.

Anneth had awakened with the thought of Easter and was not able to go back to sleep. It was three o'clock in the morning when she put her car into neutral and let it roll to the bottom of the driveway before cranking its motor halfway down the mountain. The car glided above the silent curves of the mountains as she drove toward Free Creek, knowing that she had to see Easter. Once she bounced across the old bridge and pulled up into Free Creek, she saw that there was no one stirring. She had expected the lights in the house to come on at the sound of her car engine. She had thought she would see the flutter of curtains being pushed aside as Easter looked out to see who was in her driveway. But there was no movement at all and the world was a perfectly still place, as if she was the only person left on earth. So she had walked around to the back of the house and sat down on the big rock near the foot of the mountain, the trees close around her. The trees were bigger in the heart of summer, their leaves huge and crowded, and they surrounded her like a womb while the dew fell, as the forest brought itself up out of sleep.

She didn't know why she felt the desire to sit and study the little house where she had grown up, where Easter and El still lived. But she didn't want to disturb anything until daylight. The blue part of night was perfect and ought not be bothered.

Now daytime was instant, and down in the holler she could hear cars being started as people left for work. Roosters crowed and dogs barked. She kept sitting there while lights came on in the house—probably El getting ready to go to work. She sat there awhile longer—an hour, she supposed—while Easter cooked breakfast for El and they sat drinking coffee together. Anneth didn't move until she heard the door open and watched as El went to his truck and pulled out onto the road. Didn't he even notice her car, parked on the side of the road?

Anneth arose and went to the back door. She was aware of how silently she moved across the yard. The damp grass didn't make a sound beneath her feet. She stood at the screen door, breathing in the only scent that would ever conjure up the aroma of home for her. That big house in Altamont would never be hers. Her body didn't fit correctly into its space. Here she could smell the breakfast Easter had cooked—tenderloin and biscuits—and that familiar scent of home. The house smelled of all the good things that had ever happened there. The overlapping scents of so many meals, Ivory soap, and talcum powder.

Easter came into the kitchen without even realizing that Anneth stood behind the screen, watching her. She moved like an old woman now, slightly bent. Her hair was a wild mess, even though Anneth could never remember its being out of place when Easter used to get up in the mornings. It had finally started to grow out a little after Easter had hacked it all off. She was still wearing her gown, and this was the thing that convinced Anneth she was needed here. Easter never got out of bed without immediately dressing. She rarely left her bedroom without first putting on a freshly pressed dress and placing tortoise combs into her hair.

"Sister," Anneth said, and Easter dropped the cast-iron skillet she had just taken from the stove. It made a dull metal thump against the enamel countertop. The screen door let out a high, familiar screech as Anneth opened it and stepped into the kitchen. Easter's hand had rushed up to her heart in surprise, and she took it down slowly, letting her fingers settle on the edge of the counter. Anneth felt the great distance between them as they stood three feet apart in the kitchen of the house where they had grown up together. The gulf there seemed to churn and sway.

Anneth took a step forward. "I woke up in the middle of the night, worried to death about you," she said.

Easter brought her arms up and let them cross her breasts, her hands on the tops of her shoulders. "I want to die, Anneth," she said.

ANNETH TOOK HER up on the mountain. It took some coaxing; Easter said she had to force herself to get out of bed in the mornings, much less climb that steep path. But Anneth would not hush until Easter went with her. Anneth needed to go there as badly as Easter did. It was the only place where she could get her thoughts in order. They walked up the path with their arms intertwined, the songs of the mountain twirling around them. Anneth talked non-stop, thinking she would not give Easter time to think about anything else. She told Easter how good Liam was to her, told her what asses his parents were and about their beautiful but lifeless house on a mountain overlooking Huntington. She told Easter of their adventures traveling around the state, how Lolie and Israel were finally coming around to liking him. She could tell that Easter wasn't even listening to her. When they got to the summit, Anneth paused for a minute in the shade of the woods before stepping out into the field of wildflowers, her favorite place in the world. She felt as if she had spent her childhood here, running, lying back, pulling out the stamens of honeysuckle to drink their juice. This was her church, the one place she prayed.

"Granny told me that she and Vine used to come here all the time," Anneth said. "They was like sisters, wasn't they?"

Easter just nodded.

"I wish you'd tell me tales about them sometime. I don't know nothing about our family."

Easter let go of Anneth's hand and put her fingers out to touch the pink blooms of a trillium. "Granny brought me here one time when I was real little. When you was a baby," she said, her voice low. Almost a whisper. "She set down in the flowers and cried, but she wouldn't tell me why."

"They had so many secrets," Anneth said. "Reckon we'll be thataway one of these days?"

Easter stepped out into the field, and her hair shone in the stark sunlight. Anneth walked closely behind her, so close that she had to take small steps to keep from stepping on Easter's heels. The smell of the flowers rose up to swim around them.

They sat in the middle of the field, in a patch where no flowers grew. Anneth couldn't stand to crush them. The wind rose up out of the valley and smoothed back their hair, and the sun was hot on the tops of their heads.

"I know that you've been living a lie," Anneth said. "I knowed you weren't healed yet. There's no shame in grieving over that baby, Easter. Give yourself time."

"I'm scared, Anneth," Easter said, her voice firm and steady now. "I'm ashamed to say it out loud, but I've been doubting God. I can't understand why He'd take the baby from me. I'm a good person—I know I am. I try to be."

Anneth took Easter's hands again. She couldn't help but tear up, hearing Easter admit this. Only now did she realize the weight of Easter's grief. For Easter to say such a thing, she must have been in the lowest place of her life. She must have been past sadness, into a black, hollow place.

"I don't believe in God anymore," Easter said, leaning forward, her eyes large. "How can anybody live in such a world?"

"That's all right, Easter. I believe strong enough for the both of us," Anneth said. She ran her finger across the air. "How can you doubt there's some kind of God when there's a morning like this? When you hear music or open your mouth to sing? There's no doubt about it, Easter, and you know it."

Easter started crying again, but this time there were no tears. Her body simply convulsed and she had to put her hands to her face out of shame. "Why did my baby die, then?"

Anneth took Easter's shoulders. "You can be mad about it, Easter," she said. "Just because you believe in God don't mean you can't get mad at Him. That's what your problem is. You believe, but you can't accept that you're angry. Be mad, Easter. Let yourself be mad."

"I am mad!" she yelled.

"Good," Anneth said. She put her hand on Easter's chin and pulled her face up. Easter's eyes were closed and tears trembled down her cheeks. "I don't believe I could live if you didn't believe, though, Easter. I couldn't make it without knowing you were always praying for me, always watching over me. You can't give up," she said, running her hands over Easter's sheared hair.

Sixteen

················

Little Lives

THAT SUMMER, EVERYTHING grew wild. Easter's garden burst out of the confines of its tilled ground and snaked into the yard surrounding it. When El mowed he had to carefully lift the cucumber and squash vines, then replace them once the grass had been chopped away. The tomato plants were abnormally large, bearing fruit that was so perfectly round it looked unnatural.

Easter arose every morning — saying a quick prayer of thanks that school was out and that she wasn't having to go in to work at the cafeteria — and went straight to her garden, where the bite of her hoe in the earth was the only sound until everyone else arose to fire up their cars and leave for work or children ran out of their houses to play. She hoed the garden even when there were no weeds because she liked to. But often this did not take long at all, and she secretly wished that weeds would grow rampant and that she would have to stay out in the garden until midday, when the sun beat down so furiously that she could hear it.

Once the beans came in, she got her wish and was bent in the garden half the day, shedding the vines of their load. Her back ached after picking the bucketfuls of beans, but she relished the tight knot of pain at the base of her spine. It was the irrefutable proof of a day well spent.

Every evening for a week she sat on the porch in the cool of the day, stringing and breaking the beans to put up for canning. On the last night of that week, El came home from a long haul to Pittsburgh and sat on the porch with her.

She studied him closely as he sat in one of the folding chairs they had recently bought for the porch. He stretched his tired legs in front of him, obviously grateful that they were no longer cramped up in the cab of his truck after the long miles between Pennsylvania and home, and leaned his head back against the chair. He had brought home a case of Pabst Blue Ribbon and was drinking one now, silently eyeing the mountain in front of them. When he sat like this, drinking his beer and leaning back in his chair, Easter always thought of that evening when she had caught him dancing with Anneth. She did not think back on this event much and still felt somewhat foolish over her reaction to seeing them dancing like that. Even as she had slapped Anneth and told El to leave, she had not believed that he had really done anything wrong. She knew him well enough to know that he would never betray her. He was not that kind of man. Still, letting Anneth rub up against him was a kind of a betrayal, Easter thought. Even if he hadn't seen it that way—even if he had been too drunk to see it that way—the thought of it still caused doubt to rise up in the back of her throat.

She broke the beans—five loud cracks at each knuckle of the bean—and let them fall into the bowl she had set on the floor beside her chair. A breeze moved through and lifted one corner of the newspaper she had spread across her lap to catch the strings and the brown places. There was a rhythm to bean breaking that she enjoyed. It was persistent enough to make her consider tapping her foot, but at the same time it was the music of monotony, and this sound always made her reflect on her life and the excitement involved.

She knew that it was outer forces that made her think this way. People were always going on about how you had to have some fun in your life. How you had to have adventures. But she had never wanted to be anywhere else but Free Creek. She didn't feel an empty place inside herself because she had barely ventured out of these hills. She did, however, feel funny because she did not share these desires that the rest of the world seemed to have. She had never studied movie magazines and wished to be an actress, had never envied the people on television. The rest of the world was what was messed up, coveting everything they laid their eyes upon.

She thought about people who drove through Crow County or flew by on the new highway without even realizing there was a whole town beyond the mountains on either side of them. If they saw this place, if they drove by Free Creek and saw her house with her and El sitting on the porch while she broke beans and he drank his beer, she knew what they would think. They would consider these people on the porch and wonder how they stood living such little lives, stuck in a small town where nothing ever happened. A place where the stores closed up at dusk and nobody famous ever came to speak or sing in a concert hall. A place where nobody important in their eyes had ever been born or lived. They would feel sorry for the people on the porch and the smallness of their existences and be thankful that they themselves lived in places where there were fancy restaurants and tall buildings and jobs that you had to get dressed up for.

But her life did not feel little at all to her. All she had ever wanted was the peace of a life well lived, a good man, and the knowledge that her family was safe. Those were big things. In her mind, those people were the ones who led boring lives, always watching the parade go by, wishing that they could be something they were not. So full of dreams, all of them, Easter thought, dreams that would never, ever come true.

El drained a beer, then grabbed up another one and opened it with the church key. Three bobs of his Adam's apple as he drank and a barely audible "Ahh" when he brought it down to rest on his thigh. She couldn't understand how someone could put so much store by a cold beer. It was something that was beyond her, the sense of satisfaction that a man got from just sitting on his porch and tasting that amber, fizzy taste as it ran over his tongue. Easter wondered what his dreams were. She had never even thought of this before.

"When you were young," she said, breaking the spell of quiet that had befallen them, "what did you want to be?"

El thought for a moment and didn't look away from the trees, as if he was aware of animal eyes watching them from there. "I don't know," he said. "I never really thought about it."

"Everybody has dreams."

"I wanted to be a soldier," he said. "And then I got shipped off to Korea and seen what it was really all about, so I got out of the service as quick as I could."

"Did you ever want to leave here?"

"No," he said. "My brothers did. Every one of them left here, you know. But I never could bear the thought of it."

She watched her hands. She had been breaking beans since she was six years old, taught by her grandmothers, who had sat on either side of her, giving directions. She could have done this in her sleep.

"Why?" he said. "Did you?"

"No."

"But you had dreams," he said. She loved the way he said this, the expectation in his voice. She detected a little quaver there, as if he expected her to tell him something that would change them forever.

"I wanted to be a teacher. I had a scholarship to Berea College."

He didn't reply because he knew why she hadn't gone. She had told him all of this when they first met. The death of her parents, then her grandparents, Gabe too old to matter, so that it felt as if it were only the two of them in the world. Anneth and Easter.

She finished the last handful of beans and threw them carelessly into the bowl, then wadded up her newspaper full of strings and put it on the porch floor. "But if I had gone to college," she said, "I never would have met you."

"That wouldn't have been good," he said, and winked at her.

"El, do you love me less, because I can't have a baby?"

He leaned forward quickly and put both his feet on the floor. He shook his head. "How could you think that, Easter? Can't you see that I love you even more on account of that very thing?"

She ran her hands over her face, glad that no tears came, although his words caused a great release all through her body. She had been wanting the answer to this question for so long that his reply was a balm.

He looked at her for the first time in their conversation. "I went to that square dance hoping you'd be there," he said.

"What?" A strand of her hair blew down between her eyes and she tucked it behind her ear. "You never told me that before."

"I seen you in town," he said, his voice distant and dreamy, a sound she had never heard coming from his mouth before. "About a week before that. You and Sophie out Christmas shopping. I liked the way you walked down the street with your arm in hers, laughing at something you saw in the window. I liked the way you carried yourself, the way you seemed so at ease with the world."

Easter had never thought of herself as being confident before, but now she realized that she was. Confidence came from not caring what anyone in the world thought. Anneth bragged about not giving a damn what people thought about her, but Easter knew that her sister did. It was Anneth's darkest secret.

"I asked this buddy of mine if he knowed who you were, and he did, but he said 'She's a church girl,' like he knowed I wouldn't want to fool with anybody that was Christian. But somehow I liked that even more. It was like you were the first woman my own age who I could respect, somehow."

Easter felt as if she was only just beginning to know her husband after all these years together. After all they had been through together.

"And so from then on, you were the only girl I wanted. Something about you I just liked."

"I wish you had told me this a long time ago," she said, and only then did she notice that darkness had completely overtaken the backyard. The cornstalks scratched together out there in the blackness.

He plucked another beer from his cooler but didn't open it right away. "I'm telling you now," he said. "I'm trying to tell you that I've loved you for a long time."

She laughed. "Sometimes I don't know why you'd love me."

"Because you're the only thing I ever really wanted," he said. "I like my life. I like driving them loads of coal down the long highways, like eating in truck stops and listening to the radio while the land goes by. But I think what I love most about my job is that I know I'll get to come back home, to this place. I think about that a lot. Parking my truck up there behind the church and then walking down the road to our house. Finding you in the kitchen or in the garden. That's all I ever wanted."

Finally she got up and sat down in his lap. She laid her head on his shoulder and looped her arms around his neck. "Will you do something for me, El?"

"Anything." His word was a breath against the top of her head.

"Go to church with me in the morning. Just this once."

"I will," he said, and spread his big hand out on her back.

Seventeen

....

Dog Days

THEY CAME DOWN out of the shadows of the mountain and stepped into the white light of a Sunday morning. The crowd was large and they were all singing. Their voices drifted down the river and carried to people who lived near the water's edge. Dozens of people singing, all of their voices lifted in the same harmony, forty mouths making their lips work around the same words. There was harmony in their voices, but also in the way they moved down onto the river's bank, as if they had practiced so their legs would move in the same stride, so their arms would swing in rhythm.

This morning there were six people who were to be baptized. Amongst them were Easter and El. Easter had started crying as soon as the crowd started singing and walking down the worn path that led to the river's edge. She was filled with such a pure joy that she cried from the effort of containing it within her chest. She let the tears fall freely from her face as she joined in with the others:

I'm going to live right now.
I said I'm going to live right now.
I woke up this morning,

Thinking 'bout that glory.
I'm going to live right now.

She ran her thumb over El's hand as she held on to it. He walked along very stiffly, and watching him from the corner of her eye, Easter wondered if he was as moved as she was. When he became very still and straight-backed like this, Easter knew his heart was full up. She hoped that he felt this pressing of joy against his rib cage, the way she did. She wanted him to know how it felt to be at peace.

The people kept singing until the preacher waded out into the water and held his Bible high in the air. His shirtsleeves were rolled up, and sunlight glinted off the little waves, making golden pockmarks on his face. He began to talk, but Easter did not really hear him. She was looking for Anneth. There was a great crowd of onlookers on the riverbank. Most of them were from the church, but there were lots of people who had come to see the baptism. She saw several people crying, moved by the sight of the first woman who walked slowly into the water. Easter leaned to this side and that, trying to catch sight of Anneth standing on the shore, but she couldn't see her anywhere. Anneth had assured her that she would come.

One by one they made their way into the water, and finally it was El's turn. Just before he went out, Easter stood on her tiptoes and kissed him on the cheek. "I love you," she whispered in his ear, and in that moment she loved him more than she ever had before. She had a sudden, startling thought: *He is only doing this for me.* She didn't want that; she wanted him to serve the Lord because that was what he most wanted to do. But she would always keep this in the back of her mind, that he was only going to go to church because she'd asked him to. This was a good thing, to think he'd do something this large for her, but still it wouldn't be right. She shook the thought from her mind, for fear of spoiling the beauty of this day. He had made the decision on his own, just as he had decided on his own last Sunday to get up and go to church with her. She had not prodded him to the altar, had not forced him to confess his sins and be saved. Now, all at once, she heaved with tears as El stood there in waist-deep water. He kept his head down and looked at the water while the preacher said a few words. Then the preacher put one hand over El's mouth and the other at his back. Then they were dipping back, like dancers, until El was under. It seemed he stayed under forever, but when the preacher brought him back up, El lifted his arms high in the air and kept his eyes closed, and his mouth moved. He was praying; he was full of the spirit. Slowly he began to speak in tongues and the preacher was lifting his own arms high into the air, shouting, "Praise Glory!" The spirit drifted from El and hit the people on the bank. Some of them jerked back as the Holy Ghost descended upon them. Several people began to speak in tongues and cry and call out to the sky, but Easter was so overtaken by gladness that she could do nothing except put her hands over her mouth and laugh. She had never been so happy in her life.

ANNETH STOOD AMIDST the trees, watching. No one was aware of her, and she loved this feeling of spying, of not being known. There was a crowd of people on the bank, and when El was baptized, they all got into the spirit of things. They were shouting and waving their arms and hollering. She knew this was because they all thought El had been a bad sinner. When church people saw a bad sinner be baptized, they got real happy, Anneth thought. She saw Easter standing down there, the next to be baptized, and it made Anneth want to cry. It filled her with a great sadness but she could not put her finger on its source. Easter just looked so pitiful there, her arms thin, the wisps of her hair flying out of the bobby pins, which caught sunlight. Anneth wanted nothing more than to run down the mountainside and wrap her sister up in her arms. She thought of all the kindness Easter had shown to her since she was born. She had been a sister and a mother both.

"I love you so much," Anneth whispered. Only the leaves heard.

Anneth squatted down on her haunches and eyed the ground, looking for snakes. Now it was the dog days of August, when snakes went blind and struck at anything, when dogs went crazy or slept in the shade all day. Anneth wondered what dog days did to people, for she had felt different lately. She had always carried a stone of grief around, but these past few days it had grown heavier.

She lit a cigarette. The strike of her match was so loud that she looked up quickly, afraid it had drawn the attention of the people down on the shore. But there was much noise down there and of course nobody had noticed. She was wearing last night's dress and it reeked of smoke and whiskey. She had been out all night with Lolie and Israel and Liam. She had nearly overslept but had awakened in Liam's bed just in time to get into her car without so much as brushing her hair and speed along the winding road until she got to the baptizing place. She sat down on the mossy ground while Easter waded out into the water. She didn't know if she could bear seeing Easter be put under. She didn't know why. But when the preacher swooped Easter back, Anneth started, as if she were afraid Easter might drown, and she sat up very straight-backed, peering through the trees. It seemed as if Easter stayed under forever, as if she might never be brought back up. Anneth had a sudden thought that the preacher was holding her under, that he was drowning her. As her panic spread all the way up her back, the preacher brought Easter out of the water, and the whole crowd started singing again and all their hands went into the air, praising the Lord. Easter shook all over as she walked out of the river. She paused halfway out, standing in the water with her arms raised and her eyes closed. There was so much joy on her face. There was complete peace. And Anneth knew why she felt this terrible sadness: she feared that she would never know what that felt like, to know for certain that what she was doing was what she most wanted to do in her life. To have that look of assuredness and happiness upon her face. She was positive that such knowledge would never come to her.

THE CROWD MOVED back up the riverbank and climbed the steep path up the mountain to the road. They were singing again, "Meeting in the Air," and their voices silenced those of the birds who sat watching in the trees lining the path. Something told Easter to look up, and when she did, she saw Anneth standing there amongst the trees. No one else had noticed her, for she stood within the shadows of the great hickories and sycamores leaning over the river. She started to let go of El's hand and run through the woods to her sister, but then Anneth simply put one hand up as if she were about to wave but couldn't force herself to do so. A big smile covered her face and she nodded. She kept her hand up, a palm frozen in the air, and Easter knew this meant to move on, to stay with the singing crowd as they made their way back up to the mile-long line of cars that sat on the side of the road.

Eighteen

Night Swimming

THERE WAS NO freedom like swimming, no feeling in the world. It was like flying.

Anneth came up from underwater, wiped out her eyes, and looked at the pitch darkness surrounding her. Liam was standing very close to her, and although she could barely see his face two feet in front of hers, she could tell that he was smiling. He took great gulps of air, and when he breathed out she could smell the beer on his lips. She could smell it on herself, too. The scent was so strong that it seemed to be seeping out of their very skin. Besides that, there was the smell of lake water and she noticed that the night had a smell all its own, too: the cool that drifted down over the valley drew up the aroma of the woods and the sand and the moon itself, it seemed. He put his big hands on her waist and then ran one of them down her thigh. She turned away from him and he held her from behind; she wanted to take in the world around her. As her eyes adjusted to the darkness, she could make out the mountains' crooked forms across the lake. There was a scratch of moon, and the only stars were gathered close to it as if bits of the moon had chipped off and floated just within its orbit. From far across the water she heard a screech owl cry out, and then there was nothing to hear at all except the lap of the little waves around their bodies and Liam's breathing against her neck.

She went under again, leaving him, and swam toward the shore. She loved the sound of being underwater. She thought this was probably how death sounded: a low, black rumbling in your ears. Nothing but roaring and darkness. The feel of rushing through the water was exhilarating. She kicked her feet and scooped the water away with her hands, building up speed, then let herself sail, like a bird drifting. She relaxed and imagined she was not surrounded by water, but by wind. *I am flying,* she thought. *This is what it feels like.*

She glided along like that until she felt her body rising to the top. Once there, she let her arms drift out to her sides and became completely still. She opened her eyes to the night sky and saw that a few more stars had come out. But they were tiny glints and probably no one else was seeing them. They were only visible because of the complete darkness here on the lake.

Then Liam was suddenly behind her. He had followed. "Ain't you afraid to be swimming out here in the dark?" he said in a whisper.

"Hell, no," she said aloud, and her voice seemed to break up some kind of wonderful silence that she had not really noticed before. "I'm not afraid of nothing."

"Not a thing in the world?" he said. She put one arm around his neck and one hand on his face. She could feel that he was smiling. He had crow's feet at the corners of his mouth, and she found them very appealing. Beads of water caught there.

She thought about it a minute. "Well, maybe the hydrogen bomb. That's all I can think of."

He picked her up in his arms. He carried her up on the bank and fell onto his knees with her spread across his lap, and she lay back, knowing what was going to happen. Here, out of the water, she was aware of her drunkenness again. When he kissed her, she became very dizzy and finally forced his lips away with a laugh. She didn't know where this had come from, but she was so tickled that she kept laughing. He smiled above her. "What is it?"

"I'm just so drunk," she said. In the whole year since Easter had lost the baby, she had only been out drinking a few times, always nervous that she might get a call from El, telling her she was needed. But now she could give herself up to the world and go back to the way she had been. She had been the strong one and she hadn't liked it. Now it was time to go back to being Anneth. She ran her finger across Liam's lips.

Liam put his hands under her bathing suit and peeled it away. The sand was gritty beneath her back, but it was a good feeling. She lay there and when he came down on her, she put her arms around his neck and arched her head back and watched the sky while he moved above her.

She kissed him and ran her hands over his back, moved beneath him in rhythm, but she didn't feel as if she were there at all. She felt like she was part of that sky, drifting on outstretched wings, sailing back home, back to Free Creek. She imagined what she might see and hear there tonight. Nothing. Dark little houses, the sounds of the creek and katydids. All the windows were opened in their house. In her mind's eye she hovered over the bed that Easter and El were now sharing again. She watched them sleep. Easter on her back, her hands folded on her chest like a woman lying in her coffin. Easter's brow fretted, disturbed by a dream. Or maybe she sensed Anneth there, staring down with intensity. In the shadows of the room she could see Easter's eyes open, and then Easter rose from the bed. She sat up, looking about, knowing someone was in there with her. But never thinking to look up to the ceiling.

Anneth realized that she had not had a good night's sleep since leaving that house, since the night she and Matthew Morgan had taken off to Tennessee to get married. She pictured that now, too, the surprise of being on the open road as Matthew pushed the gas to the floor and they sped over those winding roads toward Jellico, and then her taking over and driving them to Nashville. Sometimes it felt as if she had lived two or three lifetimes, for that seemed ages ago. It seemed as if it had all happened to another person.

Liam was lying on the sand next to her now, breathing hard, one arm beneath her neck and the other laid across his own stomach.

The world was spinning. She felt that she was in sync with the turning of the earth. Lying there, she could actually feel it moving round, getting nearer to daylight. She rose quickly—so quickly that it caused her to lose her balance for a moment, but then she righted herself and ran back down the beach and out into the water. When she had run far enough, she put her hands together in front of her and dove in, slicing through the water, free.

THEY DATED FOR two years, spending their entire summers on the lake, and one day, as the boat drifted out into the middle of the big water, Liam did exactly what Anneth had known he was going to do. He opened the glove compartment of his boat and withdrew a small box. He held it out to her on his palm, his other hand holding on to a beer.

"It's been two whole years now," he said. "I want to make an honest woman out of you."

She looked at him, his brown eyes, his dark skin, which was strange only in that the soles of his feet and the palms of his hands were so white. He was a beautiful man. Slim and broad shouldered and long legged. She knew she didn't love him. She would never love him, either. At least with Matthew she had thought she might. But with Liam, she knew the only attraction was that he liked to have a big time and that he had that nice car and this fine boat, which was the finest one to ever float upon Blackhawk Lake. Besides all that, she loved the way he looked at her. When his eyes were upon her, she knew that he was thinking she was beautiful. He told her that all the time. They might just be driving along silently and he would reach over, cup her chin in his hand, and say: "You're the most beautiful woman I've ever seen."

"I want to have a real wedding," she said. "With a veil and everything."

He laughed and leaned over to kiss her. With his lips still against her, he said, "You can have anything you want."

Nineteen

Tell the Truth

ALL WHITENESS, A WHITENESS like eternity, and Easter thought for a moment that she might be dead, before she realized that she had opened her eyes from a long night's sleep only to see the ceiling illuminated by the blinding light of an August morning. Usually she came awake with a start, always pushed out of rest by a dream that escalated until she could bear no more. But this morning she had felt as if she was drifting up from the bottom of a still lake, her arms extended, the last bubbles of air in her lungs forcing her to the surface, and once there, she had opened her eyes with no more thought than she might give to blinking. She lay flat on her back for a long moment, trying to orient herself. It was the morning after Anneth's wedding and they had stayed up late, everyone gathered at Easter's house after Anneth and Liam had pulled away with cans tied to their bumper, heading to Virginia Beach for their honeymoon. Easter had so much to do: she had to work in her flower bed, and the garden needed tending in the worst way. Busy helping Anneth with the wedding, she hadn't chopped the weeds out in a week.

She sat up and the white light of August filled her head. It crackled behind her eyes and flashed across her brow. She had never felt a headache like this before in her life. She lay back down and the pain eased somewhat but still pulsated around her eyes. If she kept her eyes open, the daylight was too much to bear, and if she closed them she could see the pulsing, as if she were seeing the traces of her every heartbeat in the corners of her eyes.

She immediately began to pray. A headache like this was more than it seemed. Used to, when the pain like this came she would deny it to herself. But now she knew that the headache was an admonition she had no way of warding off.

The headache lasted three days. In that time, Easter was barely able to leave the bed. She grieved over missing the last full days of summer, the blinds drawn tight against the sunshine. Sophie had to tend to her. The pain was blinding, so bad it made her vomit into the dishpan Sophie held for her.

"Bless your heart," Sophie said, and held a wet washrag against Easter's forehead. "I tell you what, honey, you sure have suffered a lot for something you don't seem to want."

Easter eased herself back on the pillow. She spoke over her cracked lips. "What do you mean?"

Sophie rewet the rag in a bowl of cold water sitting on the nightstand and wrung it out. She didn't look at Easter. "You know good and well what I mean."

"No," Easter said, "I don't."

"Every time these headaches come, they let you know something, don't they? Everybody knows," she said. "I don't know why you try to hide it."

"There's nothing to tell," Easter said, glad for the opportunity to talk about this curse she had, a curse that some people saw as a gift. They didn't understand, though. "That's the thing. Sometimes I see a little glimpse of something. Vine or Serena whispering to me. A flash of bad times coming. But when these headaches strike me, all

I know is that something bad is going to happen. What's the use of a gift that makes you throw up?"

Sophie laughed and ran her hand over Easter's forehead, then stood. She took the dishpan and the bowl of water.

Easter closed her eyes and listened as Sophie walked down the hall, humming. Easter knew that Sophie wanted more information—it was the first time she had ever asked Easter anything about her seeing—but she didn't know what else to tell her except the truth. All Easter was sure of was that her forewarning didn't involve Anneth, even though she was the one who was off traveling. In her sleep the night before she had seen Anneth walking the beach, bending to pick up shells. Anneth threw her head back in laughter, her curls blowing around in the salt wind of midnight. But that meant that only Anneth was protected. Something bad approached for someone Easter loved, and each throb across the top of her eyes had let her know that much.

Still, she worried about Anneth as she lay in the bed, trying to go to sleep. Why was it that her sister was always trying to fill up some hole inside herself with the help of a man? Anneth didn't love this man any more than she had Matthew Morgan. At least with Matthew they had looked good together. Liam Trosper was all wrong for Anneth, in every way. There was something about his face that was immediately unlikable—a smugness, a slight upturn at the corner of his lips that seemed to announce that he thought he was superior to everyone. He was good looking, but in a dark, forbidding way that made Easter want to avoid him. The thing was that he was *too* good looking. His whole face was like a mannequin's, unreal and placid in its features. A truly good face had to have some imperfections to even it all out. But Liam's face was not like that at all. It seemed that someone had cut pictures out of a magazine—two dark eyes, copper-colored hair, a strong chin, a steep, straight nose—and pasted them together to make the perfect face. And within perfection lay something akin to blandness. It wasn't just that their looks didn't match. Although blunt and loud, Anneth was never impolite and made everyone feel as if they were important. Liam, on the other hand, seemed to be entertaining people without caring what they thought or said. When someone talked to Liam, he looked just past their face, biding his time until he could break in and speak again. It seemed the only voice he wanted to hear was his own. Easter suspected that this stemmed from having been raised with plenty of money. Rich people were different from everyone else and that was all there was to it.

And people like Anneth Sizemore didn't marry the sons of coal operators. Coal mining had put bread on the table for her family for years—but poor, regular girls didn't mix with the company men. Rich people and poor people didn't do things together, period, much less get married. That stood between Easter and Liam, but it also stood between Anneth and Liam.

Easter had told Anneth as much the day she announced their engagement. Anneth had come to the house while Easter was cutting lavender to hang up on the porch rafter to dry, and she would always connect that scent to the day Anneth told her this news.

"When are you going to learn that you don't need a man to take care of you?" Easter said, drawing the blade of her knife against the lavender. The thick aroma washed over her face. "Just be still awhile and don't jump out and get married again, Anneth. It's a mistake."

"I don't think I need a man to take care of me," Anneth said, and lit a Lucky. Easter felt like snatching the cigarette from her sister's mouth and throwing it onto the ground. "We have a good time together. Wouldn't you rather I marry him than keep on doing what we've been doing out of wedlock?"

Easter saw the little grin on Anneth's face. Anneth wanted to shock her but she had underestimated Easter's sophistication. Easter couldn't care less what they did in the bedroom. "I just don't know when you'll learn." Easter wiped her hands on her skirt.

"That's so easy for you to say," Anneth said, her voice building with each word. "You've always had a good man. The best man anybody could hope for, but half the time you take him for granted."

"That's not true."

"You better look back in time and check on that, honey. Because it's true. Everybody knows it, especially El. I don't know why he's put up with you all these years."

"Hush, Anneth. That might have been the case once upon a time, but it's not anymore. I know what a good man I've got. I'm happier now than I've ever been."

"You still don't know how good you've got it, though." Anneth's words came out with puffs of smoke. "And you don't appreciate that, don't know how hard it is to find that in a man. You're so lucky—"

Easter had a sudden flash of her own baby, dead in her arms. "Don't tell me about being lucky," Easter said, and started to add, *Or I'll slap your face again,* but she stopped herself. She got up and walked toward the house with her handful of lavender, leaving Anneth behind. Anneth leaned back on one arm and smoked with the other, looking at the sky. Easter stepped up on the porch and looked back at her. "Mark my words," she said. "One of these days you'll regret marrying that man."

There was no use worrying about it, though. Anneth had married him and run off to Virginia Beach for her honeymoon, and when she came back she would leave her little apartment behind the Depot Café and go to live with him in the Altamont Coal Camp, a sprawling, dirty place that sat in the shadow of Redbud Mountain on Vine's old land. Easter finally went to sleep thinking of this place with its grit and its noise. She dreamed of being down in a coal mine and feeling as if she might never come up to sunlight again.

The next morning the headache had left. It was snuffed out all at once, like a candle flame. Easter threw back the covers and was buttoning up her dress by the time Sophie came back into her room.

"Get back in that bed," Sophie said, hooking her finger through the air.

"The pain's left me," Easter said, and slid her feet into her shoes. She had work to do.

ANNETH STOOD ON the beach and looked out at the ocean. It was very early, still dark, but she had not been able to sleep. She'd left Liam snoring in the hotel room and come down to the beach in nothing but her gown and a robe she had found in the hotel closet. There she would be able to see the sunrise. Daylight came very quickly here, unhindered by mountains. The sun showed itself over the ocean like a great light that was spreading its wings, and then suddenly it was morning, clear and white.

Her big sadness was upon her this morning, but she tried to shake it away. It was a burden to be ecstatic one minute and in the throes of sorrow the next. She felt like two different people, and when she awoke to find herself in this stage between joy and sadness it was even worse, a vast purgatory that seemed inescapable.

Now, sitting here on the beach she had always wanted to see, she watched the waves roll in and felt nothing but an overwhelming sorrow. Everything made her sad, this vast ocean with its power and glory, the water going on and on until you couldn't even tell where the ocean ended and the sky began. The flight of gulls above her, the relentless wind and the white sand and the seashells. She didn't think she could stand living in a world where everyone didn't pay attention to these things. Maybe that was the reason for her grief.

But she knew that she had made a bad decision. How could she have been so stupid as to marry a man she didn't really love? She had sworn that she would never do that again, after Matthew. It still broke her heart to think of the way his face had looked when she left him in Nashville. But she hadn't loved him. And she didn't love Liam, either. She just thought that being married to him would make her happier. He had plenty of money. He liked to go places all the time. He was always interested in having fun. But none of that mattered, really. She was just beginning to see that the only thing that really mattered was finding someone who would listen to you when you spoke. Really listen. Someone who missed you when you weren't around. All these realizations had come to Anneth the day she saw Easter and El be baptized together. Because there existed a respect between them now that hadn't been there in the past. Finally they were a true couple, joined not only by their marriage certificate but by something much deeper as well. Perhaps it was their shared grief that had finally been the key for them. Or maybe they had grown to know each other in a way that Anneth felt she would never know a man. Whatever it was, she had seen the love that existed between El and Easter the day of the baptism. And from that day forward she had known that she was searching for that same thing. She had spent her life looking for magic without realizing that it existed in things like that: the bond between two people, the power of family. There was no magic in her relationship with Liam. Only fun. And everybody knew that the good times didn't last forever. Why was it that she had to wait until her honeymoon to discover all this?

She had agreed to marry Liam because he had a boat, because he had taught her how to water-ski. He never let his Coleman cooler run out of ice or Pabst Blue Ribbon. He knew how to have a good time, and when they talked they discussed only that: the next thing they were going to do. At least he would keep her busy. That was the problem with people nowadays, though, she thought. They married someone just because they had things in common. If two people liked the Beatles, then they thought they had a match made in heaven.

People—including herself—forgot to look at the really important things. But now she realized that what was much more important than having similar favorites was the simple things: the ability to have comfortable silences, a sort of telepathy achieved just by glancing at the other's face, a surrender of pride.

And then there was the conversation she and Liam had had last night. If he had told her that before, would she still have married him? Because now everything was so clear to her.

They had gone to a bar on the pier. People drank and looked out at the black water, and the band played until two in the morning. They had taken shots of rum and been served drinks that came with orange slices and umbrellas. They had done the limbo and the twist until their legs were sore. Once back at the hotel, Liam drank more until he finally ended up on a crying drunk. She did not like to see men cry. Some women were moved by this, but it did nothing for her. And especially the way Liam cried, an all-out, blubbering mess of boo-hooing. He sat on their balcony with his face toward the ocean and let the tears flow. She finally pulled a chair up in front of him and asked what was the matter.

"I killed a girl," he said. "Back home. We were drinking, all night long. It was daylight when I realized I should take her back. And then . . . I just drove right off the mountain. Didn't do nothing but break my arm, but it killed her. She went right through the windshield."

Anneth didn't say a word. She knew what he would say next before he even opened his mouth.

"Daddy got me out of it, though."

"And that's why he sent you to Altamont," she said. "Gave you the hardest job he could find in the company to straighten you out."

He nodded, his hands covering his face now. She should have gone to him, held him until he felt better, but she couldn't find it in her heart to do such a thing. Instead she went on into the room and lay down on the bed, smoked three cigarettes, and dozed off for a few minutes. He had passed out on the balcony, sprawled in the metal chair out there. When she woke up, she went down to the beach.

She was never satisfied. Matthew had been completely selfless and devoted himself to her and she had lost respect for him because of it. Now there was Liam, who didn't love her but loved the way she danced, loved the way she strutted up the beach in her two-piece, loved the way she leaned back and drank an entire beer without taking the can from her lips. A man who had been given everything and didn't appreciate any of it. Two completely opposite men and neither of them pleased her. She was impossible.

She plucked a rock from the sand and threw it into the surf.

"Maybe I am crazy," she said to the ocean.

PART FOUR

....

This Land

They cannot see
A river is a vein in God's arm.

—Ron Rash, "The Preacher Who Takes Up Serpents"

Twenty

Paradise

IN EARLY SEPTEMBER, Easter put together a party both to welcome Anneth and Liam back from their honeymoon in Virginia Beach and to give Gabe and his new wife a good send-off. Gabe had recently announced that he and Evelyn would be moving to Dayton, Ohio, to find work. Easter grieved over the loss of her brother and the marriage of her sister, and she figured the best way to nurse all of this was by way of a good meal.

Easter and Sophie had cooked all day, hustling around the kitchen as if they could predict each other's movements. At the first redness of dawn, they had killed, cleaned, and cooked a hen, then rolled out a great dough that covered the kitchen table, and pinched off dumplings to go in the bubbling broth. Sophie had tended to the shucky beans, which took all morning to cook. Easter had taken ears of corn, snapped off tomatoes and cucumbers from the garden. By the time everyone arrived, Sophie was still fretting over the beans, and Easter was slicing up cucumbers and tomatoes while the smell of corn bread filled the kitchen, along with the heat, which was so thick that Easter thought it might be visible. She had opened all the windows in the house but it was still like a furnace.

Anneth held court as she sat on top of one of the tables in the yard and smoked in an exaggerated manner. Easter walked out to tell them all to come in and get a plate, but she stood watching her sister for a moment, resenting her for not coming in to help, but also admiring the way she held them all in her grasp. Anneth was talking about seeing the ocean for the first time and the navy ships and the long drive to Virginia Beach. Liam sat in a chair in front of her, holding her bare feet in his hands and watching her talk.

"It's the scariest thing, that ocean. I wasn't scared of it—I jumped right in—but to sit and look at it for too long, it's so *huge* and powerful. Looking out at it, you know good and well that the ocean can kill you if it wants to."

"Lord have mercy," Lolie said. "I don't believe I ever want to go to the beach."

"Oh, yes, you do," Anneth said, and took a quick drink from her Dr Pepper before continuing. "It's so beautiful, Lolie. The most beautiful thing. Just endless, that water. You would never get over it in your entire life."

"What was your hotel like?" This question came from Evelyn, Gabe's new wife, whom they had known their whole lives. She had been raised just up the road but Easter had never entertained the notion of Gabe's even dating the likes of her. Evelyn was as old as Gabe but was somehow childlike, with bangs that were so long they quivered in her eyelashes (which grew to be annoying because Easter noticed that Evelyn blinked *a lot*) and two perfectly rounded blots of rouge. Evelyn was clearly mesmerized by Anneth, who looked like Elizabeth Taylor that day with her off-the-shoulder blouse and full skirt. She wore dangling pearl earrings that seemed to point out her bare shoulders, and her fingernails were painted red as a pepper.

"Oh, it was so fancy," Anneth said, blowing out smoke. "We had a concierge that did everything for us."

"A what?" Evelyn said, moony-eyed, leaning in with the question.

"A concierge," Anneth said, enjoying the way the word worked its way out of her mouth. Easter knew that she was enjoying knowing such a strange new word, too. "This little man that is there for your every whim—"

Easter slapped her hands together. "Let's go in the house, boys," she said. "Dinner's going to get cold."

They had waited until late afternoon to eat so they could sit outside in the shadow of the mountain, once the sun had moved behind it. Easter sat at the end of the two long tables in the yard and looked at everyone. This was the first time since the baby's death that she had been completely happy. She watched them all talking and leaning forward to laugh with one another, eating the food she had raised in her own little garden and made with her own hands. Here was everyone she truly loved, sitting on the patch of ground she had known all of her life.

Anneth sat at Easter's left and Gabe at her right. Anneth talked nonstop. She had brought Easter a box of seashells and wouldn't hush until Easter held one of them up to her ear so she could hear the ocean. Anneth had stood there, slowly beginning to smile as she watched for a sign of recognition on Easter's face. And then, there it had been, the roar of waves on the beach. "It's magic," Anneth had said.

Gabe seemed to be crazy about Evelyn. She was the first woman Easter had ever seen him really talk to; all during dinner he whispered into her ear, delighted by the reply of her laughter, and he even kissed her on the cheek right in front of everyone. Easter had always thought a kiss on the cheek was more intimate than one on the lips. When a man kissed his wife on the cheek, you knew that he loved her because he wasn't really getting anything out of it, wasn't receiving the thrill of her lips, so it was a completely selfless act. Still,

Easter had to marvel at his attraction to Evelyn, who was a mouse of a woman. He had always liked women that he could boss around, though, a thing Easter could not understand. Most men she knew enjoyed a woman who couldn't be broken.

She caught El staring at her as he sat at the other end of the table. Israel was saying something to him, but El was simply nodding as he looked into Easter's eyes. He had been studying her while she watched Anneth and Gabe and Evelyn. She saw how much he loved her in that look, the way his eyes couldn't break away from her, staring at her so long that Israel eventually noticed that El wasn't even responding, so he turned his conversation back to Lolie.

They ate until they couldn't hold any more—the beans and dumplings and boiled potatoes, then the lemon pie and banana pudding. They scooted their chairs back from the table and patted their bellies. Gabe and Israel both unlatched the buttons on their pants. Anneth and Lolie smoked cigarettes and leaned on the table with their elbows. For such a small bird, Evelyn could eat more than any of them and was still picking at a large slice of coconut cake when the rest of them had already finished and simply sat there talking.

Finally Sophie stood up and spoke loudly. "Now, girls. Me and Easter worked like dogs all morning cooking," she said, and ran her finger through the air, pointing at each of the women. "It's time for you all to wash the dishes."

Easter appreciated Sophie's demands, but she couldn't stand the thought of women being in her kitchen without her supervision, so she was the first to fill the sink with soapy water.

"You go on and rest," Anneth said, a cigarette bobbing up and down between her lips. "We'll take care of all this."

Easter snatched the cigarette from Anneth's mouth. "You know I'm funny," she said, and ground the Lucky Strike out in the ashtray. "I'll help you."

Easter and Anneth washed the dishes together while Evelyn and Lolie ran in and out of the house, packing in dirty dishes. Sophie couldn't stand to sit still, either, so she joined in, too. While they worked, they sang the same song their grandmothers had always sung while washing dishes. Easter started the song off, and then they all joined in, Easter's and Anneth's voices harmonizing while the others' voices drifted in and out with the slap of the screen door. They sang:

> Who's gonna shoe your pretty little foot?
> Who's gonna plait your hair?
> Who's gonna kiss your red ruby lips?
> Who's gonna be your man?
> Is that you, Reuben, Reuben?
> Where have you been so long?

Sophie came in with an armload of plates and sang along as she slid one after the other into the hot water. She leaned against them in song, her voice high and more beautiful than Easter had ever noticed before.

> The longest train that I ever saw,
> It was near a coal town long.
> And the only man that I ever loved
> He was on that train and long gone
> Is that you, Reuben, Reuben?
> Where have you been so long?

Sophie went out to fetch the rest of the dirty dishes. Evelyn leaned against the refrigerator with a dreamy look on her face. "Oh, there's nothing in this world like hearing two sisters sing together," she said, and clapped her small hands together. "Sing another one."

Easter smiled at her. "You have a pretty voice, too," she said, and she meant it. "You're our sister now, too, since you've married Gabe. That's the way this family is."

Evelyn took a step closer and put her knuckles against her lips before speaking. "That means a lot to me, Easter. I never had no sisters of my own, you know."

"It's a damn shame that you all are leaving," Anneth said.

Evelyn stepped even closer so that she stood just behind the two of them, her face peering between their arms as if the dishes they were washing might be something to see. "I don't want to go," she whispered.

"I hate for you all to go, too," Easter said. "So bad."

"I could've killed my brother. He was down here last weekend, bragging to Gabe about how much money they were making up there in the refrigerator factory, said we could waltz right in there and get a job. But I don't want to leave home."

"Gabe says you all will just stay long enough to save up some money," Easter said, but she wished she could be as reassuring to herself. She couldn't stand the thought of Gabe going north. She knew what happened when people went up there. They moved off and got jobs in factories and lost their accents and became different people, and when they came back, they were changed forever.

"That's what everybody says," Evelyn said. "But then they only come back for Christmas and Easter."

"Well, the company doesn't need as many men since they've started that strip mining, which is ruining everything," Easter said. She washed out a bowl and handed it to Anneth for rinsing. As she looked over her shoulder, she watched as Evelyn seemed to deflate, sinking back until she found a chair at the kitchen table. "And I begged Gabe to not leave, but he can't stand being out of work. He's been so unhappy since the mine closed, and you can't hardly blame him for that."

Anneth rinsed the bowl and spoke in an even voice. "You know good and well that Liam would have give him a job at the Altamont mines," she said.

Evelyn and Easter exchanged knowing looks.

"He didn't want to go asking his new brother-in-law for a job, I guess," Easter said. "It's done now, anyway. It'll all work out, though, Evelyn."

Anneth jabbed Easter in the ribs. "Let's sing 'Downtown' for her," she said.

Easter was glad her sister had the good sense to know when to change the subject. "Lord, no," she said. "I don't sing that old rock 'n' roll no more." She put her hands into the hot water and savored the prickle of its heat.

"Please!" Evelyn cried, just like a little child. "Oh, please do, Easter."

Anneth started singing and moving her hips around while she ran plates under the rinse water. Even though she hadn't sung a rollicking song in what seemed like ages, Easter started tapping her foot, too, and then the three of them were singing so loud that everyone out on the yard stopped talking and listened.

EVERYONE STAYED UNTIL twilight began to overtake the sky with streaks of purple and yellow. They had played horseshoes and sung and eaten dessert once again, but mostly they had talked, and when darkness settled over them, they were still talking, some of them sitting in the stiff chairs around the table, but others lying back on the grass or on quilts spread on the yard.

While Anneth was going on and on to Evelyn about the golden dome she had seen on the state capitol in West Virginia, Gabe sat down on the quilt beside Easter. He put his hand atop hers, and his skin was rough and callused. Gabe hardly ever touched anyone.

"I'll come home every weekend," Gabe said. "And I don't want you worrying about us."

"I will, though," Easter said. "I don't understand why you don't talk to Liam about getting on at Altamont. He's a foreman, Gabe. He could do whatever he wanted to."

Gabe looked away, his eyes hard and trained on Liam, who was telling Paul a long, animated story about his childhood. "I don't want nobody to know it," he said, "but I did talk to him about it. I hated to, because I don't like to ask nobody to help me out, but I didn't want to leave here, Easter. So I went into his office and asked him about giving me a job."

"What did he say?"

"He told me he'd do all he could, that he'd pull a few strings and call me. Said the coal boom was over and that Altamont was having to make cutbacks like everybody else, but he'd find something." Gabe still wouldn't look at her. He plucked a piece of grass from the ground and rubbed it between thumb and forefinger. "But he was just keeping me hanging on. He didn't try to help me, never even mentioned it again."

Easter looked across the yard, and when her eyes met Liam's he smiled at her like a little boy seeking approval. She couldn't help but pull her mouth in tightly and look away.

Twenty-one

....

Altamont

ANNETH HATED ALTAMONT, the dirt and grime and noise, the barren landscape where the trees had been clear-cut. And the distance from both town and Free Creek. But most of all what she hated was living in the big foreman's house while friends of hers lived in the camp down there in the valley. It didn't feel right. She was meant to be in one of those shotgun houses that had arrived preassembled on a railroad car, not in this fine home with the upstairs bedrooms and the gingerbread on the porch, sitting perched on the side of Redbud Mountain like a giant tooth that had fallen out of the sky.

And the worst part was that this place was—in a roundabout way—her own land that was being mined and hauled away. She remembered so many stories about this place, could recall the way Vine's face changed when she spoke of Redbud. She had told them of their grandfather's proposal down there where the river met the creek, had described the neat little Cherokee houses sitting in the valley so vividly that as a child Anneth had often pictured the settlement. Vine had told Anneth that she had a special place up on Redbud Mountain where she went to sit and watch the world, an outcropping that overlooked the entire valley. Now those rocks were nowhere to be found. They must have been removed to make way for the very house she now lived in. The mayor had built this house himself back then, and his presence somehow lingered, a feeling in the air that seemed to dull the light and affect the temperature of the place. It made her sick to think that she was somehow part of tearing up what Vine had always called Redbud Camp, although everyone now called it by the name of the mining company—Altamont. It caused her to lie awake at night. Therein was planted the first tree that would grow up in the middle of her marriage to Liam. It was the first of a forest.

Being married to Liam turned out not to be at all the way Anneth had imagined. They had been married almost a year now and in those months the bad episodes had just piled up. She couldn't count the times she had heard women say, "As soon as I married him, his true self came out." That was certainly true of Liam, and she guessed that it was true of many men. She had thought it would always be like their summer on the lake. The freedom of swimming, the speed of his boat slicing through the waves, their kissing as they lay back on the sandy bank with the heat of the sun on their legs. Cold beer in the cooler and a good song always on the radio, the smell of coconut lotion and baby oil. But once they had returned from their honeymoon, Liam had become a different person. She remembered the way he had been when they visited his parents, and realized that he was that way all the time now. Most of it was because the company had put extra pressure on him. Since his father was part owner of the mine and living the easy life up in Huntington, everything fell onto Liam's shoulders. Everyone was saying that the coal boom was over, after all. It had lasted longer in Crow County than it had in most other places. He stayed at the office all the time and had to be up at the mine sometimes, too.

When he came home he took a long shower with the bathroom

door closed and then sat on the porch in nothing but his Levi's, looking out at the coal camp while he drank a beer. Anneth stood in the doorway and watched him from behind. "What is it?" she asked.

"Nothing. You wouldn't understand."

She walked across the porch quietly and leaned on the rail in front of him so that he had no choice but to look at her. "I won't understand if you don't talk to me."

"It's the mines. They're wanting to start strip mining and using the broad form deeds. People around here won't go for that."

"You can't let them do that," she said. "Talk to your daddy. He'll listen to you."

His face darkened and he finished his beer. "He's never cared what I had to say, Anneth. Couldn't you see that when you went up there?"

Often he drank until midnight, sitting there staring out at the lights of the coal camp. And then he would come into the bedroom and get on top of her without so much as a kiss, pulling up her gown and biting at her lips until she had to push him away. And sometimes he slept out there on the porch in that stiff wooden chair.

Other nights he didn't get home until after dark. Often she was already in the bed and he ate his supper cold, finding it in the oven, where she had left his plate wrapped in aluminum foil. She had had her suspicions about his whereabouts. If she ever found out that he was having an affair, she thought she might shoot him, to wound him at least as much as her sense of pride would suffer at the thought. But she had followed him into town once and seen that he had simply gone to see his lawyer. And several nights she had walked down to the foreman's office to see if he was still there and had peered in to see him leaning over his desk with a hand to his forehead as he listened closely to someone on the phone. His father, no doubt.

She wished she had never quit her job. Most of the time she had nothing to do. It would have been impossible to stay on at the café, though. Altamont was so far out in the mountains that it took an hour to get to Black Banks and almost as long to get to Free Creek. There was no one to visit because everyone she knew was at work during the week—Easter at the school, Lolie at Shoes Galore. Sophie didn't actually have a job, but she was so busy she didn't want to sit and visit with Anneth. She was always going about the business of quilting or sewing or canning or something. Anneth was made tired just by watching her dart around the house. And even though Anneth had been out honky-tonking with lots of the people who lived down in the mining camp, they were all busy during the day, too. The men were miles back in the mine, and the women were tending to their children and their chores.

So she occupied herself by spending money. Every day she walked down to the post office and found her box stuffed with catalogs from Louisville and Chicago. One thing she liked about being married to Liam was that she could buy anything she wanted. She had never had money before, and she loved being able to flip through the catalogs and circle dresses and shoes with one quick swipe of her ink pen. The catalogs bored her after a while, and she found herself making the long trip into town once or twice a week. There she could walk into the dress shop and just pick out whatever she wanted. She loved meeting up with Lolie at noon and taking her out to eat and being able to pay for their cheeseburgers. She bought clothes for Easter and left them hanging on the door while Easter was still at work—otherwise Easter would never have accepted them.

Sometimes she sat on the bench at the bus station, smoking cigarettes and watching all the strange, different people getting off the bus. Occasionally she spotted someone who obviously needed some money, and she'd approach them and insist that they take a ten-dollar bill. There were young men who were out of work and old women who wore ragged dresses, and lots and lots of girls with babies on their hips, most likely going to Ashland to see their men before they were shipped out. President Johnson was sending more and more boys to Vietnam. Anneth always remembered her own bus ride and how poor so many of the people had been, the way that one girl with the baby hadn't had enough money to buy breakfast.

Most of all, Anneth loved going into the record store and buying three or four albums at once. Nobody else in town did that. Used to, she had to save up her tips for weeks just so she could buy one single record after she had paid all her bills. But now when she left town she strutted down the street with so many bags and boxes that she could barely carry all of them. Most days she sat in the house with nothing to do but play solitaire or listen to her records. She liked to read but rarely found books that satisfied her. She had a stack of magazines that arrived in the mail with her catalogs, but they were mostly things like *Silver Screen* and *Look* and *Life*. The pictures didn't take very long to look at.

When she couldn't work up the energy to drive all the way into town and couldn't stand sitting in the house any longer, she went for long walks up onto the ridge that Vine had explored as a girl. She sat down in the woods and listened to the world. Mostly all she could hear was the drone of the coal tipple down there in the valley, but sometimes she could find a cove between two mountains where the noise of the coal camp was not able to enter. Here she could hear the growth of ferns and the clicking of the earth beneath her back and the music of falling water. She studied the sky through the bobbing leaves and ran her hands down the trunks of trees. She listened to the songs of birds as if they might be telling her something important and cupped her hands to drink from a creek—spewing the water back out, since it was now tinged with sulfur dredged up from the mining. She walked along whistling and was sometimes aware of being followed. She would turn very quickly, expecting to see Vine trailing along behind her, but there was nothing but the trees, although sometimes she thought they were watching her, too.

And sometimes she went down to the camp and visited with a few people she knew. She hesitated to do this because it made her feel like they thought of her as the rich lady who came down to study the poor, although she didn't feel this way at all. She would have traded places with them in a heartbeat. Those little coal-camp houses held much more warmth than her big house on the hill with the long hallway and the gingerbread on the porch.

The only place she felt truly at home in the camp was at Jewell Stubefield's. Jewell was married to one of the miners and had her camp house fixed up with doilies on the furniture, and nice cotton curtains she had sewn herself. Jewell was the kind of person who kept fresh flowers on the kitchen table. When Anneth was especially bored she went to Jewell's house for a long while. They played records and danced or worked in Jewell's flower garden and sometimes Jewell would read to Anneth from whatever book she happened to be obsessed with that particular week. Once a week, Anneth took her into Black Banks to check books out of the library.

Jewell was much more beautiful than she realized. Anneth thought she looked like a country version of Grace Kelly with her blond hair curling in and her big blue doe eyes. Jewell got up every morning at daylight to fix her husband a big breakfast; then she started cleaning her house so that she was finished by noon. After that, she read the books she got at the library. Jewell wanted to be a writer. Usually when Anneth got there, she could tell that Jewell was happy to see her but also a bit disappointed that she wouldn't be able to spend her afternoon reading. She always met Anneth at the door with a novel in her hand.

"What you reading this time?" Anneth said.

Jewell held the paperback up. *"A Long and Happy Life,"* she said.

Anneth liked the cover. It showed a good-looking boy with a motorcycle and a girl in a pretty red skirt. They both looked wild and free. "And this one is *mine*. I bought it this weekend when we went to Pikeville. It's the best book I've ever read in my life."

Jewell said this about every new book that she found, and Anneth told her so.

"No, I'm serious about this one. It's about people like us, Anneth. You'd like it."

Anneth tapped Jewell lightly on the arm. "You're serious about everything, Jewell Lynn." Anneth opened the refrigerator and helped herself to a bottle of Pepsi. "I'm bored out of my skull. Why don't you get ready and let's go to town? I'll take us out to lunch."

"I can't today," Jewell said, and marked her place in the book with a grocery receipt. She placed it carefully on the little shelf with her other paperbacks. "It's too late. We'd never get back in time for me to have supper ready."

"I can't stand just setting around the house," Anneth said. She took a long drink from the bottle. "It drives me crazy."

"Just wait till wintertime," Jewel said. "They're saying it's going to be bad this year. You got lucky this past winter. It barely snowed. Hey, you got a smoke?"

"You know I do, honey," Anneth said, and pushed her purse across the kitchen table.

Jewell lit the cigarette as if famished. "Anyway, you remember the winter before last? That's when me and Doug moved in up here. The longest winter I've ever seen in my life. Just snow and more snow. And so cold you couldn't stick your foot out. I thought I'd crack up. I like being in the house all day, being able to read and write, but knowing that I can't get out, that's what kills me. I didn't leave this house for two months solid, Anneth. The company sent in groceries for us because the road was too bad to get out."

Last winter, Anneth and Liam had still been newlyweds, so she hadn't paid much attention to the weather. But now she thought of the road: ten miles of dirt and mud from the main highway. If a bad winter was on the way, it would undoubtedly be impassable.

Jewell closed one eye against the smoke that washed over her face as she exhaled. "How's life with the big boss man?"

"He's good to me, gives me whatever I want. Leaves money just laying around like it's nothing at all," Anneth said. "I didn't even know he made so much money. But I hate that house. And I hate this place. I never thought I'd live in a coal camp way up in the head of nowhere."

Jewell held the thin curtain back from the kitchen window and peered out. Her face glowed in the light that fell there. "I kind of like it here. I never do get lonesome. I like hearing the coal cars running all day long and the way the whole place is lit up at night by all the lights on the tipple. And even how we're all stuck here together in the winter. It makes you appreciate your neighbors more. I love it when Doug comes home in the evenings and pulls off all his clothes behind the screen right there on the back porch."

Anneth leaned forward, smiling. "You love him, then, don't you?"

"Of course I do," Jewell said, and looked at her strangely, about to say more. But there was a big ruckus out on the porch, someone stomping their feet as if they were clogging. Jewell mashed out her cigarette and hurried to the door. "What're you doing? Don't worry about muddy shoes. Just come on in. It'll sweep up."

A broad-shouldered man stepped in and Anneth couldn't take her eyes off him. He had style. He wore a necktie and a pressed white shirt with the sleeves folded up a cuff or two. He also had on a hat, the kind men had worn when Anneth was a child, but he looked to be about her age. He wasn't a bit good looking, but he had a nice smile, which he immediately showed to Anneth. It seemed to over-take his whole face, running up to wrinkle out his forehead and cause laugh lines at the corners of his eyes. He tipped his hat to her without taking it off his head. "Hidy there."

"Hidy," Anneth said, and took another drink of Pepsi while Jewell introduced her.

"And this is my brother, Glenn," Jewell said. "He delivers bread for Sunbeam, so he comes to see me every time he brings a load out to the company store."

"I might come more often, now that you're here," he said, eyeing Anneth. She just smiled and tilted up her bottle again, taking a long chug of the pop.

"Anneth is married to Liam Trosper, Glenn," Jewell said, chiding him with her eyes.

Glenn changed the subject. "I mostly come so she'll fix me a bite to eat for dinner," he said. Anneth noticed his hands, folded over the back of the kitchen chair where Jewell had been standing. His fingertips were wide and square. The noon whistle sounded up at the coal tipple and they all turned that way for a moment as if they would be able to see something accompanying this noise.

Anneth snatched her purse up off the table and scooted out of her chair. "I guess I better go on, if I'm going to town, before it gets too late," she said to Jewell, and then added to Glenn: "You got a good little sister here, Glenn. She keeps me from going crazy, living way back in these big mountains."

"She's going to be a writer," Glenn said, and put one of his big hands on the back of Jewell's neck. Anneth kissed her on the cheek and gave Glenn a crooked smile as a way of saying good-bye.

Once she was in her little Falcon, speeding down the crooked road toward town while "Paint It, Black" played on the radio, she found herself smiling. Maybe it was the fact that Glenn had been flirting with her. Men hadn't flirted with her much since she hooked up with Liam, because he was the mine foreman. Or maybe she was just smiling at Jewell, who was such a good friend to her, in some ways even better than Lolie. Or maybe it was that she was flying down the road in her own little car with the Rolling Stones on the radio and it was warm enough to have all the windows down and her billfold was full of cash in her purse. Either way, she was happy and she said a quick, eyes-open prayer that it would last.

Twenty-two

....

Out of the Smoke

OCTOBER, AND THE MOUNTAINS were on fire. The fires had not come to Crow County but they were so vast and raging that the smoke covered half the state, and the world could only be seen through a gray haze. The smell was thick but oddly comforting, like the scent of a campfire. It was not especially cold, but someone peering out the window might think as much; the sun was a white orb sliding in and out of smoke.

Easter had been in the house for three days, waiting for the smoke to lift, when she decided she couldn't stand it any longer. She didn't care what the radio said—breathing this faraway smoke couldn't be any worse than what people did to their lungs on a daily basis, she thought. She put on her mackinaw and ventured out to work in her garden. The corn was long gone and its fodder needed to be cut and gathered. She went down the rows chopping with a tobacco knife, and the stalks fell like dominoes, collapsing onto one another, the scratch of their dry leaves making much noise. She stood up the piles of stalks, big enough for her to barely reach her arms around. She took a length of rope and tied the fodder, as if she were latching a belt onto a friend too large to do so herself. Before long, six fodder shocks stood in each row. She hoed out the old bean vines, which crackled like twisted paper, and the dead tomato plants, and she took the tobacco knife to the thick stalks of the sunflowers, too.

She worked like a woman who had to be done in time to go somewhere important, the chop of the hoe beating out a rhythm in the soil. She did not sing or even hum. She hated this death in her garden and wanted to rid the ground of these old vines and plants. She couldn't stand seeing their brown skeletons standing in the rows she had so carefully prepared last spring. They reminded her of the baby, of her own womb, just as dead and parched. Of course, everything reminded her of the baby. It had been almost three years and she still thought of it more often than seemed normal. She had only now begun to accept that she would never be able to carry a child. She said the word aloud—*barren*—and found that it was the dullest word she had ever uttered. There was nothing beautiful about it at all, which was only right, since it meant such an ugly thing.

She relished the feel of the hoe's strike and heard nothing but the bite of metal into dirt. She snapped out of her reverie when she felt someone behind her. She let the hoe dive into the loose soil and turned, her eyes trying to find the shape of a man amongst all the smoke, which was funneling into the valley like a morning mist now.

Liam came walking out of the smoke with one hand to his brow, as if leaning against a strong wind. "Easter?" he hollered.

Easter leaned on her hoe and breathed out with exasperation. She knew that the dread she had carried in her belly like a stone would see the light of day now. She didn't know what Liam would tell her— something bad, real bad, like Anneth being dead or the fires coming into Free Creek, or something that would change them forever— but she knew that she had been waiting for this moment for a year now, ever since that last bad headache.

"Easter?" he called again, as if he could not make her out plainly, although only the backyard lay between them. The smoke seemed to distance them in every way. Even his voice seemed to come from very far away, as if she stood at the mouth of a mine and he called out to her from the very heart of a mountain.

She grabbed hold of her hoe and carried it like a shotgun, propped up on her shoulder, as she walked across the yard to see what was the matter.

"What's wrong?" she asked.

"Do you have time to set down and have a cup of coffee?" Liam said. He looked as if he hadn't slept in days.

"Tell me if something's wrong, Liam. Is it Anneth?"

"No," he said, eyeing her with suspicion. "Everything's fine. I just need to talk to you."

In the house she struck a match to the gas ring and warmed up the coffee. She shed her coat—the scent of smoke rolling off it—and hung it on the back of a chair at the kitchen table while he sat down. He kept his coat on, a blue painter's coat with a patch on either side of the zipper. The one over his heart read WILLIAM—his real name—and ALTAMONT MINING COMPANY read the one opposite.

"El on the road?"

"He took a load of coal up to Cincinnati." She poured coffee into two cups, and steam curled up over her arms as she carried the cups to the table. "Where's Anneth?"

"Still asleep when I left this morning," he said, and sipped his coffee. "I reckon she's at the house."

"So what brings you up here, Liam?" There was no use beating around the bush, she thought. She realized she had never had a conversation with him in the year he had been married to her sister.

"I wanted to come up here and talk to you in person," he said. He didn't look her in the eye but watched his left hand. He traced and retraced the ivy print on the tablecloth. "Do you know what a broad form deed is, Easter?"

"That's what a mining company uses to mine coal on land that don't belong to them," she said, and then she realized why he had come. The knowledge washed over her like cold water.

"Well, not really. Mining companies buy the mineral rights to a piece of property, and this is all written up on a broad form deed. Your great-uncle—Aaron Sullivan—sold the mineral rights to the mountain that runs behind your house, that whole ridge that runs between Free Creek and God's Creek."

"My grandfather's brother? His brother disappeared ages ago. Left his wife and baby."

Liam nodded. "Before he left he sold the rights."

"This is nineteen *sixty-six,* Liam. That was almost fifty years ago. And he didn't even own this land." She looked at Liam and realized that this meant nothing to him. He couldn't care less. "So you all intend to put a mine in there and there's nothing we can do about it."

"Well, that broad form deed gives the company the right to mine it, and it'll stand up in court," he said. "But I'm here to tell you that we'll do it as proper as we can. It'll just be the ridge and we won't be mining on any of the land around your yard. Just up on the mountain."

"You make it sound like you're doing me a favor," Easter said. "Where will the mine entrance be?"

"Well, that's the thing, Easter," he said. He slipped his finger in the coffee cup handle and tapped his thumb against the cup's brim. "No, the coal business is in bad shape now, Easter. The boom is over. So they're all turning to strip mining. It's cheaper. They'll cut down all the trees and then they'll come in and doze the mountain down until they get to the coal. There won't be a mine entrance. The whole mountain will be dozed."

"Why do you keep saying 'they' when it's you that will be doing it?" She could feel heat spreading up her neck, taking over her face.

"I don't have a say in it, Easter. You know good and well that my father is only a part owner in Altamont. I'm trying to do right by you, to come up here and tell you in person."

"To tell me in person," she said, sitting back in her chair. "To tell me that the land my family has owned for as long as anybody can remember is going to be tore down. That I'll look out my back door and see a mountain cut down to nothing, hear bulldozers and steam shovels all day long. And you can just take it. You know them broad form deeds are dirty. They probably bought that land for a quarter an acre."

"They probably did," he said, his voice level and calm. He was a businessman, she saw. He was talking about all of this so easily. And he really thought that he was being a big man for telling her face-to-face. "But the fact is somebody in your family got the money and they spent it ages ago."

"But they just sold it thinking a mine would go back in the mountain. Not that it would be destroyed. Once you strip that land, it'll be changed forever. All those trees, the field of wildflowers up there." She was trying not to talk loudly, but she couldn't help it. Her voice kept rising up and up. Her own father had given his life for Altamont and now they were going to destroy her land. Almost everyone in her family was dead and now her land was going to die, too. "This is your own wife's land. She'll quit you over this."

"I'm sorry, Easter, but there's nothing I can do about it," he said, displaying both his hands palm-up now. "Nothing."

"You do something," she said, her voice deepening as she spoke.

"I knew it would be this way," he said. "That's why I wanted to—"

Easter rose from her chair. "Don't you come in here and act like you're being the good guy, Liam. We'll fight this with all that's in us.

My grandmothers loved that mountain more than anything. They would have killed anybody over it, they would've—" And then her words dissolved into tears and she chided herself for letting her emotions overcome her this way. She hadn't wanted to break down in front of him. He would think they were the tears of a simple woman and he'd not have the sense to see that she was crying because she was so angry. He wasn't smart enough to see that with each tear she shed, the heat of vengeance rose up in her breast. She felt like grabbing him by the shirt collar and throwing him out the back door.

"My hands are tied," he said.

"Get out of my house," she said. "Don't you ever foot my doorstep again."

He took the last drink of his coffee and looked up at her when he set the cup down. She thought he would say more, that he would try to convince her that he was a good man who couldn't fix this. But instead he got up and walked to the door without a word. By the time he stepped off the back stoop, he had disappeared into the smoke of midday.

ANNETH WAS BEGINNING to believe that all of her marriages would end with her running away. First Matthew, and now she was trying to get away from Liam, too, but this time she was driving in her own good car and Liam was not crying. That wasn't his style. Instead he had screamed and raged, raking his arm across the dining room table to send dishes crashing to the ground. He hadn't known whom he was messing with; Anneth sailed a plate past his head, releasing it with a click of her wrist the way she used to skip rocks on the Cumberland River. If it had hit him just right, it could have decapitated him in one clean cut, she thought. She felt strangely ecstatic. She knew one thing for certain: she'd never have to live in this place again. She could leave this noise and grime behind her. She stopped in the camp only long enough to tell Jewell good-bye and promise her that she'd be back to see her.

Now she was rolling out of the camp with two suitcases and three cardboard boxes in the backseat. She'd have to go after the rest of her stuff later. All she had taken the time to round up was a few clothes and shoes, all her record albums, the Bible box in which she had been keeping souvenirs since she was a child, and her family pictures. Upon moving to Altamont she had been so lonesome that she had taken all the pictures out of the photo album she kept in her purse, and put them into frames. They were all back there in a box now except for the one of Vine that she loved so much, the one that showed Vine in this very place, sticking her hand out to brush the petals of touch-me-not flowers. Since she had come to Altamont, her connection to her grandmother had grown stronger. She must have absorbed some of the strength that was left behind in the soil.

She stopped her car for just a moment on the bridge. Down there was the confluence of the river and the creek where her grandparents had become engaged. It was so strange to think of them being young there, so many years ago. They could never have imagined that they would have a granddaughter who would pause here and look at that place and wish herself back in time. How the air must have smelled then, and how light must have gathered in that triangle where the two waters came together. She saw them down there on a summer's day as heat bugs screamed in the trees, the water so white and wild. Now the creek had been weakened and made orange by the mines. The river's banks were the place where the people in the camp dumped their garbage.

She pressed hard on the gas and flew around the curves, the huge mountains slumped on either side of the road. A thin rain had fallen and seemed to make the smoke from the forest fires thicker and more acrid. The scent seeped in through her heater vents and filled the cab of her car. It was only four in the afternoon but she had to turn on her headlights because of the smoke. They didn't help.

She drove and was barely aware of driving, her mind churning. She couldn't believe she had married a man who was going to tear up the land she had loved all her life, a man too stupid to see that she loved that land more than him. He couldn't even fathom the idea of loving a place, and she couldn't comprehend the idea of someone's not understanding how that felt, to love a place so much that you could cry for it, that you could hurt for it.

"It's just a mountain, you fool," he had said, the veins in his neck pulsing up. "Trees grow back."

Liam could have stood up to his father, could have told him that this was his wife's land they were dealing with. It was his one chance to be his own man. If he loved her as much as he had said he did, he would have quit the company in protest and tried his best to keep her. But that still wouldn't have been good enough for Anneth. Not really. Because if it wasn't her family's land, then it would be someone else's, wouldn't it? And how could she be married to a man who would do that to anybody? Mining was one thing, but going in and stripping somebody else's land was another. She had seen the strip mines before, horrible scars on the face of the earth. It just wasn't right.

When she pulled down into Free Creek she let the car slosh through the mudholes of the narrow road and took her time pulling into the driveway. The smoke was thicker here, since the fires were closer. Maybe this rain would drown the forest fires and stop any more destruction. Some people were saying that the Altamont Mining Company had set the fires themselves because it was on land that they had been fighting to strip-mine. Anneth thought it possible.

She walked around the back of the house and listened to all the familiar sounds of Free Creek: A dog barking far up the road and then being answered by the echo of its own bark against the cliffs. The rush of the creek and the high sound of someone striking a wedge with a sledgehammer to split kindling. Other than that, there was silence and she had never been so glad to hear it in her life. Up at Altamont there had been the ever-present drone of the coal cars. People said you got used to it after a while but she had lived there a year and had never stopped being aware of the groan of machinery.

Instead of setting down the cases to take hold of the doorknob, she balanced herself on one leg and tapped the toe of her shoe against the back door three times. "Easter!" she hollered. "Open the door!"

Easter opened the door and Anneth pushed past her. "Oh, honey," Easter said. "He told you, didn't he?"

She stomped on down the hall to her old bedroom. "Yeah, and I left the sumbitch, too."

EL GOT HOME from his trip at dark and brought with him an autumn thunderstorm that shook the earth. As soon as he stepped in the back door, lightning lit up the backyard and thunder boomed up the valley, repeating itself in echoes as it shuddered along the mountainsides. The sky opened up and a hard rain began to pelt the earth. Anneth and Easter were sitting at the kitchen table waiting for him, already clad in their coats and galoshes.

"You might as well not take your shoes off," Easter said, and stood up. "We have to go up to Sophie and Paul's."

"What are you all up to?" he asked.

"I'll tell you when we get up there," Easter said, "so I don't have to tell it twice."

They ran up the road in the pouring rain, splashing through the mudholes. The plastic umbrella that Anneth carried turned inside out and was jerked clean of her hands to bob down the road. She ran on, ignoring its wild dervish behind her. Lightning cracked down the length of the creek as they stomped up onto Sophie and Paul's high porch.

They stood crowded up under the porch for a moment to catch their breath and saw one another only when the lightning lit the world up as though a photograph was being taken. Without the flash, all was lost and black.

El hollered over the tail end of thunder. "What's all this about, now?" He was about to get mad. He hated suspense so much that Easter had once caught him looking for his Christmas presents in the hall closet.

"Altamont's wanting to take the mountain," Easter said. She took off the plastic bonnet she had fastened around her head and shook it out.

Sophie appeared in the doorway with her glasses glinting in the lightning. She held the door open against the driving wind. "Get in here!" she said, and wouldn't step aside until each of them had filed in. She stood small beside El. "I kept you a plate back from supper," she said.

El nodded and sat with Paul at the kitchen table while Sophie warmed his plate in the oven. Anneth and Easter took off their wet coats and galoshes to drain beside the door and came in, lifting their hair and wiping the water from their eyes, as Sophie withdrew an apricot-nectarine cake from the oven. They didn't speak of the real reason they were all together as they went about cutting the cake and pouring out glasses of buttermilk and seeing that El had everything for his supper.

Eventually Easter wiped the milk from her lips and leaned her elbows on the table to explain everything to all of them. Then Anneth told them how she had left Liam, her voice so loud and dramatic it seemed to stand in the room for a long time, since no one made any reply. They were all thinking of what they could do to save their land, but nobody said anything, and it seemed they had all silently agreed to listen to the dying storm as it moved away across the mountains toward Virginia.

After a long time, Paul spoke. "Usually they take years to mine the land even after they notify you."

"What if they don't wait years, though?" Easter said. "What if tomorrow morning they're up there with their dozers?"

Paul gave her a defeated look. "I read in the paper about one family that wrote to the governor and he stopped a company from stripping their land."

"Governor won't help nobody else," Sophie said, shaking her head. "That was just to look good in the paper, and he won't do it twice."

"I could talk to Liam about this," El said, talking around a toothpick. "You know, man-to-man."

"Or we could fight," Easter said.

"We could lay down right in front of them dozers," Anneth offered.

El plucked the toothpick from his mouth and held it between forefinger and thumb. "They'd run right over you, too."

"They'll have to, then," Easter said. "Because there's no way I'll let them tear down that mountain. I've been going to that field of wildflowers since I was a little baby, and my mother went there, and so did her mother. So you might as well get ready for a fight. Because that's what they're going to get."

She didn't say more and she didn't have to. They all knew that she was serious and they all knew what she wasn't saying—that their land was the most important thing they had besides one another. That loving the land was a given, not something one could choose, the same way you love your sister or brother even when you don't want to.

Twenty-three

....

Another New Life

EASTER WAS LEANED over the side of the bathtub with her head under the faucet, washing her hair, when she heard Gabe call for her. She kept scrubbing at her head, trying to put this sound out of her mind. It was a sign, she knew. Gabe was off in Dayton and something had happened to him and now she was being made aware of it. His voice was so plain to her, even under the torrent of water running over her head. She rinsed all the shampoo from her hair and was wrapping a towel around her head when she heard him again. And then she knew that he was really there, in the house.

Holding the lopsided towel, she bounded out of the bathroom with water still running down into her face, and there stood Gabe and Evelyn in the kitchen. She hadn't seen them in more than a year. He hadn't come home once since moving to Ohio; he couldn't get off work long enough to make the long trip down and back up. She didn't say a word, simply went to him and wrapped her arms around his neck. Still holding on to him, she put one hand over his shoulder to take hold of Evelyn's chin.

"Are you all home for good?" Easter could tell by their stance that they were. This was no short visit back to Free Creek.

"We couldn't stand it anymore," Gabe said. "I come home from work yesterday and told Evelyn to pack everything we had because we was going home."

"I was tickled to death," Evelyn said.

They sat at the table and drank coffee and told her of their adventures in Ohio while Easter went about cooking. Both Evelyn and Gabe had told her not to, claiming they had stopped at the Burger Boy in London. Easter said they needed some home cooking. She cut up potatoes and fried them in a cast-iron skillet, opened a can of salmon and shaped it into patties that she slid into popping grease, stirred up a bowl of corn bread. Evelyn went on about the way all the houses were clumped together right on top of one another.

"We lived in these tract houses and they all looked alike," Evelyn said. "I never could tell them apart, and the first week we were there I went into the wrong house. I had three bags of groceries and pushed the front door open with my hind end and there set a whole family, looking at me like I was crazy."

Gabe laughed around a mouthful of coffee.

There was something different about both of them. Gabe looked defeated, somehow, as if he had been away too long and had been broken by too much work and not enough respect. Evelyn seemed to have gained some strength in Ohio, though. She held herself differently, sat up straighter, finished Gabe's sentences. Maybe she had gone up there and gained some independence, too. Easter was glad for this.

"We saved just enough money to buy us a little house trailer," Gabe said. "Didn't save much, rent was so high. But enough. I have to find work somewhere, though."

"You'll find something," Easter said, and didn't look up as she coated the potatoes with a layer of salt. "And you move that trailer in right here beside the house. No use paying lot rent."

"You read my mind," Gabe said. "I was going to ask you."

"You don't have to ask. This is your land, too."

Gabe got up to pour another cup of coffee. He tipped up the pot and a thick mahogany stream gurgled out. "What's old Anneth up to these days?" he said. "She still with that sorry Liam?"

Easter flipped the salmon patties. "Oh, Lord. You don't want to know."

GLORIA WAS WIPING down the counter and kept her eyes on the wet rag instead of Anneth. "Do you think you can just waltz in here and get your job back anytime you want it?" she said.

Anneth took a drink of coffee and a pull off her cigarette before answering. With an exhalation of smoke, she said, "You know I was the hardest-working waitress you ever had."

"What am I supposed to do, fire one of the girls to make room for you?" Gloria's tone was firm but Anneth could tell that there was a little smile on her face. She knew that Gloria would hire her back.

"No," Anneth said. "But if you hire me back you could stay at home like a proper old woman and not be down here every day. You let me run this restaurant for you, Gloria, and I'll do it for the same wage I had when I was a waitress. The only other thing you have to give me is to let me stay in the apartment out back for free."

"I don't *have* to let you do jack shit," Gloria said, and came around to sit on one of the red stools next to Anneth. She took a drink of Anneth's coffee and cringed at the sugar Anneth had poured in. "But I'm going to, out of the goodness of my heart."

Anneth leaned over and wrapped her arm around Gloria's neck. "I knowed I could count on you."

"But I'll tell you something, Anneth Gail," Gloria said, pulling away and making her face serious. "You've quit this job twice now. Once to run off to Nashville like some kind of fool, and again to marry that prick, even though we all told you he was bad news. So if you leave me again, I'll flat-out never speak to you again. Am I clear?"

"Crystal," Anneth said.

Gloria jumped down from the stool and walked up to the front door to turn the sign around from OPEN to CLOSED. "And I'll need you to work late tomorrow and help me put up these Christmas decorations." She lifted a line of shining garland from a box on the table by the door and then turned to pull down the shades on the plate-glass windows. "Now, why'd you quit Liam?" she said, with her back to Anneth.

Anneth stubbed out her cigarette. "Because the company's planning on mining the ridge behind Easter's house and he wouldn't put a stop to it."

Gloria peeked out the side of the shade to watch the passersby. The gold letters on the window glass made backward silhouettes against the glowing shade: ƎⱯ⅄Ɔ TOԀƎD.

Gloria spun around on one heel to face her. "Is that why?"

"Mostly." Anneth laughed. "Why, do you know of a better reason?"

Gloria looked at her without smiling.

"What?" Anneth said, and slid down from the stool.

"I didn't want to tell you, Anneth, until you figured it out on your own," Gloria said. She went back to the counter and started rolling up silverware in paper napkins. Fork, spoon, and knife, then roll. "But I'm going to tell you now because you'll have an easier time of divorcing him this way. The state won't give you a divorce on the grounds of him not helping you with that land."

"He had somebody else," Anneth said, and felt as if someone had poured cold water over her head. She couldn't believe she had been so stupid, and in front of her face she saw a dozen different hints that she should have recognized: the way he sometimes stayed out all night, how he couldn't face her when they were eating breakfast, the way he went weeks without touching her.

"I just didn't want to hurt you," Gloria said, and put her hand atop Anneth's. "That's why I didn't tell you. I thought you'd surely know it before long."

"Who is it?"

"There's no use in——"

"If I'm going to use it against him in the divorce, I have to know."

"You promise me you won't go down there and whup her? I don't want you landing in jail."

Anneth crossed her arms. "I can't promise you nothing. Just tell me who it is, now, Gloria."

"Sissy Goins." Lolie's boss down at Shoes Galore. Lolie had been hating old Sissy ever since she had started working there and would most likely cheer Anneth on if she went down there. Still, Anneth could hardly believe that Liam would want somebody like Sissy, who walked around like she had a corncob up her ass. What in the hell had been the attraction? She'd never, ever understand the way people's minds worked. Anneth grabbed her purse off the counter and started toward the door.

"Don't, Anneth," Gloria called after her, although she didn't stop rolling her silverware. "Please. She's not worth going to jail."

Anneth put her hand against the door and opened it halfway. "I won't be going to jail," she said.

Anneth relished the click of her heels against the sidewalk as she made her way toward the Shoes Galore storefront. Small loud-speakers attached to the corner of the building pumped out Christmas music. Anneth felt almost happy in her fury and sang a line or two along with Brenda Lee as she growled about rocking around the Christmas tree. Anneth stopped long enough to peer through the windows of Shoes Galore and saw Lolie putting up boxes of shoes.

As if sensing Anneth there, Lolie turned her head and, spotting Anneth, rose up to wave.

Bells hanging from the doorframe rang out as Anneth stepped inside the store. Lolie's smile faded as soon as she saw the look on Anneth's face. "What in the world's the matter?"

"Did you know about Liam and Sissy and not tell me?" Anneth said. She knew the answer as soon as she asked, though. She had known Lolie all her life and could read her face.

"What are you talking about?" Lolie said. "Surely he wouldn't have *her*."

"Is she here?" Anneth asked, and Lolie nodded and then pointed toward the back, where thick maroon curtains divided the store from the shoe storage. Anneth picked up a black patent leather pump and inspected it carefully. "Go get her for me."

Sissy parted the curtain with an elegant hand and stepped out. She was wearing a smart blue dress with a Peter Pan collar and two-tone heels that caused her feet to arch unnaturally. Her hair was perfectly done, since she went down to the beauty shop every other day to have it styled. She had a kind, heart-shaped face that betrayed her true nature. She was so prim and uptight that Anneth couldn't picture her in the throes of a heated affair, but something about her hands gave Sissy away. She held them together in front of her as if she was about to wring them out of nervousness. Anneth tapped the sharp heel of the black shoe against her palm and tried to see something in Sissy's face that announced her trepidation. Surely Sissy would be scared to find her lover's wife standing in her store. But she was a perfect actress, smiling with freshly painted lips and asking, "Can I help you?" as if Anneth was someone straight off the train, just browsing for a new pair of shoes.

"I was wondering if you enjoyed screwing my husband," Anneth said.

Sissy took a step back. "I don't know what you're talking about."

"Sure you do. You know, screwing. When Liam gets on top of you and moves around and you holler out and act like it's really good. Letting my husband screw you and knowing good and well that he was married to me. You had to know I'd find out eventually."

"Lolie, get her out of here," Sissy said, walking backward into the counter.

"Kiss my ass, Sissy," Lolie said.

Anneth brought the shoe up and swung it through the air, stopping it just before it slammed into the side of Sissy's face. Sissy drew back in anticipation of the blow and let out a little scream. When she realized the impact wasn't coming, she put her hand up to her cheek as if checking to make sure she really hadn't been hit.

Anneth and Lolie looked at each other and burst out laughing, shaking with glee for a moment before Anneth forced her face to grow serious again. She threw the shoe down at Sissy's feet. "Honey, you can have the sorry bastard," she said, and turned to walk away.

She paused at the door and put her forefinger to the side of her mouth. "I wonder what *your* husband will think of all this?" she said, and walked out with the bells ringing merrily, announcing her exit.

THE WINTER MOVED like a slow song into the mountains. It started quietly, the cold a guitar strumming that grew until it was joined by the banjo feeling of frost, the cutting wind a crescendo that rose like the sawing of a fiddle. And then the snow fell, bringing with it a large quiet. A new year rolled in and then all was still once again, the earth tucking itself away for a winter's sleep, the season as big and gray as a bass plucking out a funeral song.

Anneth felt as if she was waiting for something all winter. When spring came, she was still grieving the failure of another marriage but didn't dwell upon it. She didn't miss Liam one bit and laughed uncontrollably when Lolie came to tell her about Sissy Goins's husband beating Liam so badly that he had to have six stitches below his eye. She told everyone that she was glad to be rid of him, but she carried a lump of disappointment in the back of her throat. Twenty-seven years old and twice divorced now. She loved Free Creek but at the same time she couldn't have stood living there for long. Living there had meant that she had to stay with Easter and El and watch how well their marriage had worked out. She was glad for this, but still it had reminded her of her own failures. So she was happy to have her little apartment behind the café.

She spent some money fixing it up better than she had when she'd lived there before. She and Sophie sewed curtains—Sophie doing all of the work while Anneth picked out the loudest colors—and she hung pictures and bought a metal stand to put her record albums in instead of just piling them up on the floor. She lined up her seashells from Virginia Beach on the back of the toilet and framed photographs she had taken of the ocean. It didn't matter that these were photos from the honeymoon of her recently dead marriage. She thought a bathroom decorated in ocean things made it seem cleaner. She bought herself a wooden bookcase at a yard sale and got Jewell to go with her all the way over to Morehead, which had a bookstore. There she had Jewell pick out all the books she had announced as her favorites—*A Long and Happy Life, To Kill a Mockingbird, Spencer's Mountain,* and two or three more—and bought them all, plus a copy of *Jude the Obscure* for Jewell. She found a Lava lamp and was so fascinated by it that she decided to take it home as well. Liam's affair had given her the right to a quick divorce—the courts paid more attention to infidelity than they did wife beating or anything else, it seemed—and the judge had also been moved to award her a lump sum of cash, which Liam had handed over in an envelope stamped ALTAMONT MINING COMPANY. She spent all of the money, wanting to rid herself of his cash. She felt like it was blood money.

One night after a long day at work she was sitting in her apartment, soaking her feet in Epsom salts and leafing through a magazine as she listened to the Grand Ole Opry, when Matthew Morgan came on to sing. Ernest Tubb introduced him as "the best feller you ever met," and then Matthew was singing a song he had written, "Love Me One More Time." The song was about a girl who didn't know how to be loved, and Anneth couldn't help thinking it was about her. She *knew* it was about her. She pictured the joy on his face as he belted out his song, which was so beautiful she knew he was going to get famous for it. When he was finished there was thunderous applause and then Anneth felt like bursting into tears when Matthew thanked the crowd and said, "I want to say hello to everybody back home."

Anneth was so proud for him. He had made it, had worked and worked until his dream had come true. She was glad it had happened for him, if not for herself. "You did it, buddy," she said to the radio.

She spent that whole spring partying. There was nothing else to do. She went out honky-tonking with Lolie and Israel or Jewell and her husband, Doug. Sometimes Glenn came, but she brushed off his attempts to take her home. The second time he came, Anneth danced to nearly every song with him. He was a good dancer and one of the few men she had ever met who seemed to genuinely enjoy dancing as much as she did and not just as a way of courting, like most other men. By the end of the night, Anneth was half-drunk and felt like letting someone hold her, so she leaned her body against Glenn's while they slow-danced. It felt good, just to be held in such a way, to be taken care of for a little while. But when they got back to the table, Jewell had demanded that Anneth come with her to the bathroom.

Jewell stood in front of the bathroom mirror and put on lipstick. Anneth had never seen her wear any makeup of any kind before.

Somehow it made her look young and foolish. Jewell was too naturally pretty for makeup, and Anneth was just drunk enough to announce all this. When she did, Jewell acted as if she hadn't heard her and clicked the lid back on the lipstick. She looked at Anneth in the mirror. "I don't want you and Glenn going together."

"Why, don't you think I'm good enough for your big brother?" Anneth said, and laughed.

"No," Jewell said, and turned to face her without a smile. "I don't think he's good enough for you."

"That's a hell of a thing to say about your brother."

"Well, you've been a good friend to me, Anneth. And I love Glenn. But he's too jealous. He'd try to control your life. Why do you think he's never been married? Because every woman he's ever had got tired of him looking over their shoulder."

Anneth hooked her arm through Jewell's and walked them toward the door. "No matter," she said. She opened the door, and the sound of the bar was suddenly raucous all around them. "A man is the last thing on my mind right now, anyhow," she said into Jewell's ear. She meant it, too. Her divorce had just been wrapped up and she had no intention of even looking at another man for the foreseeable future. Often she thought that she might never have another man, period.

THAT'S WHAT SHE thought, anyway, until one night when she found her shoulders heavy with the blues and whiskey. She had had a rough day at work and had gone to her little apartment to numb herself. She had already smoked a whole pack of cigarettes and gone through half a fifth of Jim Beam when someone knocked on her door.

It was Glenn. He stood there in a freshly pressed shirt and a hat, which hardly anyone wore anymore. Didn't he realize it was 1967?

People were going around naked out in San Francisco, and even people in Black Banks had given up on hats. But still, it was strangely sexy. She liked it that he didn't go by what was in style. The hat showed off the strong bones in his face, gave a shadow to their angular lines and clefts. His eyes were unnaturally dark, though. Black. Lolie said that Glenn's eyes made him look creepy, but Anneth didn't think so. They added to the mystery of his face. He was a big man: broad shoulders and thick forearms, and Anneth liked that about him, too, now that she thought about it.

"Hell's bells," she said, and held the door open wide. "Come in and get drunk with me, Glenn."

He did. The drunker he got, the more appealing he became. She liked the way he hooked his glass back through the air and drank his whiskey with the ice cubes clicking against his teeth. She turned on the radio and they danced to "Brown Eyed Girl," and Glenn sat back on the couch grinning while Anneth pantomimed "Ode to Billie Joe" and "To Sir With Love." She flopped down beside him and put her legs up on the coffee table.

"How old are you, Glenn?"

"Thirty-three."

"Damn, buddy," she said, and slapped his leg. "You're old. That's how old Jesus was when he got crucified."

"I know that," Glenn said.

"And you've never been married?"

"No."

"Why not?" Even though she was drunk, she remembered what Jewell had said. "Can't you keep a woman, buddy?"

"Never found nobody that I could stand that long," Glenn said.

She laughed. "I never realized that until I was already married to my men." She tapped a finger against her chin. "Let's see. What else can I ask you? I know—Stones or Beatles?"

"Stones."

"I can't choose between them, but that's still a good choice," she said. "Oh, here's a good one. My old standard. Do you believe in magic?"

He laughed. She knew that he wasn't as drunk as she was. "Yeah, I guess I do."

"Tell me what's magic to you, then."

He put his arm around her shoulder. She closed her eyes and relaxed when he started to massage her neck. She knew he was making a move but she didn't care. It felt good. And the room was spinning, around and around. "Finding somebody that you love, I guess. That's as big a magic as can be found."

She started to kiss him. She looked at him, considering what he had just said, but then she saw on his face that he had only been humoring her. He had said this because he had read her mind and knew exactly what she wanted him to say. So instead she punched him on the arm. "You're so full of it," she said, and laughed like they were old friends. She didn't drink any more after that and just let the whiskey ease out over her whole body. That sadness was so thick, so all-encompassing, that she knew if she didn't keep on laughing she might start crying.

"You're welcome to the couch," she said, and pushed herself off her seat. She meandered over to her bedroom door and looked back at him, pitiful as he sat there with his hands atop each of his knees, looking at her in a way that was much too akin to how Matthew Morgan used to stare at her. She didn't want another man who worshipped her. And Glenn would expect her to worship him, too. She had never done that for any man. This was all far too much to think about right now, so she locked her door behind her before she stretched out diagonally across the bed without even turning down the sheets. Even before she had had the chance to pass out, she heard him leave.

Twenty-four

What Flowers Know

ANNETH KNEW AS soon as she saw him. It wasn't love at first sight—she didn't even believe in that—but there was a connection there, something ancient. He was beautiful, of course, but it was more than that. It was as if she liked him right away not because he was good looking but because his looks said something about him. His hair was the color of rich soil, perfectly parted on the right side to reveal a line of pale scalp. The bones in his face were so straight and solid that they looked as if they needed someone to smooth out the sharp angles. She moved around and looked at him from behind so she could see the way his green uniform stretched tightly across his broad back. Maybe it was just the uniform. Soldiers always caught her eye when they came into the café.

But no, it was more than that. She liked the careful way he was studying the laminated menu that he had taken from its place between the ketchup and the napkin holder. He was poring over it as if choosing his meal would prove to be the biggest decision of his life. Most of all what she loved about him was the way he was tapping his foot beneath the table to the beat of "Crimson and Clover," which was playing on the radio behind the counter. She didn't think he even realized that he was moving his shoulders a little bit to the music. She couldn't help moving, either, and the waitresses stood on each side of her snapping their fingers and finally bumping their hips up against her. They all laughed and the men at the counter smiled as if paralyzed by their sudden vision of the three women all dancing together. As the song went into that strange part where Tommy James's voice distorts, Anneth strutted across the café and went to the soldier's table.

He was still studying the menu. Now he had it lying on the table and he had his hands spread out on either side of it as if he was keeping the table from floating up off the floor. His hands struck her—long fingers that looked like they were meant for picking a guitar.

He looked up at her, and his smile revealed that one of his front teeth was chipped. He put his tongue to the back of this tooth as if the damage was recent, and this sight caused a little start to run all through Anneth.

She pulled out her ticket pad and put the tip of her pencil to the paper. "What can I get you, soldier boy?"

"I think I'll have that lunch special." He put his fingertip to a line of text on the menu. "And a cherry Pepsi."

Anneth turned her wrist and glanced at her watch, already knowing what time it was. "Well, really lunch service was over ten minutes ago but I guess I can pull some strings for you," she said, and gave him a wink.

"I'd sure appreciate it," he said. He didn't take his eyes from her face as he put the menu back in its place. "I've been craving a BLT all day for some reason."

"Anything else?" She ripped his ticket off and then slid the pad into her apron pocket. She shoved the pencil behind her ear.

"You all could turn that radio up a little."

She smiled. "You like this one?" she said, just as the song went off and a reporter came on to talk about the space program.

He nodded. "You got that album?"

"No," she said, "but it's next on my list. I buy a new one every pay-day."

"Yeah, it's a good one," he said.

"So you're headed overseas?"

"Vietnam, here I come, baby," he said, leaning back in his chair.

"You enlist?"

"*Hell*, no," he said. "My number came up."

"I hate that for you."

"It's all right," he said, but he wasn't very convincing. "It'll be an adventure."

She took a step backward. "I guess I better get your order turned in," she said, and turned away before he could say more. She latched his ticket onto the stretch of line between the grill and the counter with a clothespin. The rush had slowed down, so there was nothing for her to do except roll silverware. This was something she had learned from Gloria: when everything else was caught up, roll silverware. Silverware rolls were something you could never have too much of. Anneth spread out her napkins and put the utensils in and then rolled them up with a twist of her wrists. She still hadn't gotten used to the fact that she was the boss now. Gloria had stopped coming in every day and let Anneth run the café, but Anneth still waited on tables when it got busy. Even if it was hard work, it seemed more tiring to her to be figuring out schedules or doing the payroll, which were only two of her new responsibilities. While she worked she kept her eye on the soldier. She wished she knew his name, but the sun had caught itself in the gold name tag on his jacket, so that she hadn't been able to read it.

Finally the cook tapped his palm against the bell and the soldier's order was up. When she leaned over his shoulder to sit his plate down in front of him, she caught his scent. His skin smelled like the mountains on fire.

"There you go," she said, and he immediately picked up the sandwich in both hands. She saw now that the cook had forgotten to cut it in half, but this didn't seem to bother the soldier at all. "You need anything else, just let me know."

"What time do you get off work?" he asked, and took a bite of the BLT. For a brief moment his lips shined with the juice of the tomato. His tongue darted out around his lips.

"I'm working a double today," she said. She felt foolish, standing here while he ate, but he seemed starved to death.

He held on to the sandwich. "I was wondering if you'd want to go to the movies with me," he said. "My next train doesn't leave for three hours."

"You sure don't beat around the bush, do you?" she said, but already she was thinking whether it would be possible for her to leave. They wouldn't be busy this evening; already the crowd was thinning out, and since another train didn't run until much later, there would be no crowds. Besides, she was the boss now. She could leave when she wanted to, really. The waitresses could handle it. They certainly weren't busy right now. They were standing behind the counter, laughing at themselves as they sang the chorus of "Dizzy" along with the radio.

"I'm going to Vietnam," he said. "I don't have time to beat around the bush."

"I don't even know your name."

He started to extend his hand, then wiped it on his thigh with a sheepish grin. He put his hand out again and when she put hers within it, his fingers closed over her own and caused a ripple to run up her entire arm. "I'm Bradley Stamper," he said.

She held on to his hand for too long, and when finally she let it go he dipped a french fry into his ketchup and looked up at her with anticipation. Before she even realized she was going to say anything at all, she said, "All right, then."

TODAY WOULD HAVE been her baby's sixth birthday. Easter pictured what he might have looked like as she climbed the mountain up to the wildflower field. He would have looked like El: hair black as a thousand nights, broad shoulders, and big hands. She thought he might have had Anneth's eyes—green as river water—and her own voice. He would have been able to sing. And maybe they would have done this together, walking along this path. He would be used to her bursting out in song and would still be at that age where he wasn't ashamed to join in with his mother. He would have been solid and long limbed, his posture that of a grown man as he walked along with a straight back and a confident gaze, studying the world around him like a young prince who recognized how blessed he was. She could almost see him there, moving in front of her on the narrow path, pausing only long enough to quell his curiosity about a spiderweb stretched between two trees or the quartz that sometimes washed up out of the earth along the path. He seemed so real that she felt the momentary urge to run up behind him just as they reached the top of the mountain. She wanted to scoop him up in her arms and twirl him around until he laughed.

And maybe they'd sit there and talk. At six he would be old enough to carry on a real conversation with her. She would call him Little Man and tell everyone how they had long discussions and how it amazed her because talking to him was just like conversing with a grown-up. She wondered what he would talk about. A six-year-old's greatest interest would most likely be the woods—bugs and birds and the wonderful possibility of spotting a snake stretched out on a big rock, sunning itself.

But when she picked up her speed and bent low, running fast to that spot where she thought he was, there was nothing. Not even so much as a ghost. It seemed to her that when she put her hands out to take hold of him, there was a crackle in the air, a moment of something changing forever.

She stood in the middle of the field and then turned very slowly, taking in everything around her. On one side of this mountain Serena had lived and raised Easter's father. And on the other side had been Vine's home, where Easter's mother had grown up. She wondered if her parents had sneaked off and met here. Perhaps they had had many secret rendezvous here, so in love that they didn't even speak but ran toward each other through the flowers, anticipating the feel of the other's mouth on their own. Sinking down into the flowers, electrified by the touch of naked skin. And her grandmothers had come here so many times to sort out their troubles. Vine had always said that this was a magic place, that a person could understand things better when she was on top of a mountain, surrounded by flowers. Even though it had been a year since Liam had announced his plans to strip-mine this mountain, Easter knew that it was only a matter of time. These things moved slowly. She had already been to the courthouse and written letters to the governor, but she was anticipating the day when she would hear the first bulldozer. And she already knew what would have to be done to save their land.

Easter sat down and dotted her finger onto the bumpy surface of a Queen Anne's lace. There were tiny bugs that worked furiously amongst the hundreds of small flowers that made up the lace. They had been blooming everywhere the day Vine had brought her up here and told her about stillness. She had said that being still was a thing easily gained, a thing that could heal. Easter didn't remember why her grandmother had told her such a thing, but she could see Vine's mouth forming these words plainly, as if she were remembering it from only yesterday. "Stillness saved me once," Vine had told

Easter, and the Queen Anne's lace had swayed like curtains around them. Easter had been ten and had not been ready for the things that she would be shown, but as soon as these words escaped Vine's mouth and Easter began to wonder what her grandmother had been saved from, she knew. It all came to her like images stretched out across the summer sky. She saw all of it: the door of her grandmother's house being thrown open, a man coming in to grab her by the arms and push himself down between her legs. And then the glint of the knife as Vine pulled it across his neck. Easter saw the blood and his last breath and everything.

Easter did not want to know family history such as this, but there was nothing she could do about it. The vision came to her like a sudden flurry of birds that flew down to overtake everything. But now, all these years later, she began to understand it all better. *Be still and know that I am God,* she thought. Her favorite Bible verse. And stillness had saved her grandmother once. So that's what she had to do as well, to be still and let everything fall back into place on its own. For six years she had been walking around telling everyone that she was all right because it wasn't acceptable for a woman to mourn too long over a child that had never even uttered one cry, a child who had never even moved. *Still-born,* she thought. *He was still.* So what kind of knowledge must he have possessed, if stillness brought one closer to the recognition not only of God but also of one's true self? Perhaps the baby knew too much, so he never made an effort to open his eyes. "Stillness is a habit easily gained," Vine had whispered.

So that's what Easter tried to do. She lay down on her side in the middle of the field and pulled her knees up toward her chest. She put both hands together as if in prayer. The wind moved over her like a cool hand and all around her the sounds of the world intensified. Birdcall and the scratching together of leaves. It seemed she could hear the red ants that moved along the ground in front of her face, carrying white granules that looked like rice. And she even thought that she could hear the slow, gradual growth of the flower stems. She was eye level with the stems of the Queen Anne's lace, delicate and thin and green. The flowers weren't delicate at all, though. They survived just by being still. People thought that they had to always be in motion, had to always be working. People thought that if you were too still, you would die. But Easter knew now that this was a way to gain life back. She had been keeping busy and only acting as if she were alive for the past six years, and it had been exhausting. She lay there surrounded by the flowers, waiting for her womb to be healed.

Twenty-five

. . . .

A Comfortable Silence

"LET'S NOT GO to the movies," Anneth said as she came out the door of the café. Bradley had gone on out and waited for her on the sidewalk bench. "It's a good day for a drive."

He followed along behind her as she walked quickly down the street. "You've changed clothes," he said. He made a show of taking in her peasant blouse and bell-bottoms. "How'd you do that so quick?"

Her car keys clinked together like wind chimes in her hand. "I have a little apartment there on the back of the café," she said.

When she opened the door to her Falcon he paused for a moment and laid his hand flat on the shiny roof as though he was savoring the warmth of metal. "This is sharp," he said.

"It'll fly, too," she said. She fired up the engine and floored it, peeling out to prove to him that the Falcon had plenty of power. Just a short distance, and they were out of town and on the winding roads through the mountains. She held on to the steering wheel tightly and sped around the curves. She wanted to show him how her car could make you feel as if you had taken flight.

"My favorite thing in this world is just going for a drive," she said, glancing at him and then back to the road. He looked completely comfortable over there, as if he were accustomed to having someone else drive him everywhere he went.

"You're an easy girl to please, then," he said, smiling at her with that chipped tooth, which she wanted to run her own tongue over.

"I love the movies and dancing and the lake, but what I really love is just driving along and looking at these mountains," she said. "Sometimes I drive all the way to the state line just so I can see all the churches and little houses and lives that I pass by. People out in their yards going about their business. Kids on their bicycles. Rows of corn just stretching on and on down in the bottomlands. There's so much to see."

"That's the way I'm trying to look at the war. Something new to see," he said quietly.

"Are you scared?"

He nodded and rubbed his palms together like he was cold, then relaxed against the car door, propping one arm up on the window frame. "Sure I am. Anybody'd be crazy to not be scared of going off to war. Especially with all that's happened lately. All that mess at My Lai. Even people who supported the war are against it now."

"Lots of people are against it, but even some of them support the troops."

"You can't have it both ways," he said, looking out at the horizon. "You can't be against the war and support the troops, too. It can't be separated."

"I don't know about that," she said. She had never thought of it this way, but none of it made any sense to her. To her way of thinking, protesting the war *was* supporting the troops. War was something she didn't understand at all and she always thought it was a bit odd anytime people acted as if they did understand. But she liked the confidence he had, the way he believed in what he was about to do.

Somehow Bradley made more sense to her than President Johnson or Walter Cronkite ever had. She didn't know how she felt about Vietnam, but she didn't want to talk about it anymore.

"So where do you come from?" she asked, and as the road straightened to follow the length of a long valley, she balanced her wrist atop the steering wheel.

He told her that he was from the next county over and on his way to Ashland to be deployed, just as she had suspected. His mother and sister had cried for a solid week when he got back from boot camp, after realizing that his being drafted was a real thing and that he was actually headed for war. It hadn't seemed real to them before. He couldn't bear to watch them grieve anymore, so he told them he had to leave two days earlier than planned.

"I have a cousin in Ashland I'm going to stay with until I'm shipped out on Sunday," he said.

And then he went on as if he needed to tell someone his entire history. He told her about growing up in Laurel County and about his father, who was a strict Pentecostal preacher. "But a good man," Bradley said, looking at her. "Not a hypocrite like some of them." And then more about his mother, whom he seemed to worship, and his sister, who was sixteen and desperately trying to be a hippie. He told her about getting drunk in Hazard and having to spend the night in jail when he was only eighteen; told her about the time he spoke in tongues when he was twelve. She didn't interrupt with her own stories but simply listened to his voice full of carefully chosen words and emphases. She realized the power that storytelling gave him; she knew that if he told his stories he would become immortal in a kind of way, and wasn't that what anyone ought to do when faced with going off to war—share their lives with someone and make their stories a solid thing that could be carried on and given to others?

As they drove, the light began to change and the sun sank lower in the sky. Before long there was a line of red at the horizon, and even though darkness was still a couple of hours away, the world was bathed in an eerie kind of twilight. Glancing over, she saw how the strange light emphasized his cheekbones and the straight line of his nose so that she realized how much younger he was than her. She was twenty-eight now and he was at least seven years younger, but that didn't matter. He talked to her in a way that most men her age had no idea about. He went on and on but it didn't seem as if he was only talking about himself to brag or to inform her. It seemed as if he was sharing a piece of himself.

They rode along in a comfortable silence for a long while as he looked out at the mountains and she kept her eyes on the road. It didn't seem that they had run out of things to talk about at all. On the contrary, it was like they were relishing the close space they both occupied. He stretched his arm out across the seat and then his thumb rested on the back of her shoulder. This seemed the most intimate thing to her, the ease he felt between them so that he didn't even notice touching her in this way. When they went over potholes or little bumps in the road, her shoulder rocked back so that his hand became more obvious there against the thin fabric of her blouse. All the way the radio had been playing quietly, turned down so low that she could barely make out the music, but then she was aware of the soft voice of Paul McCartney singing "Blackbird."

She turned the radio up and tapped her thumb against the steering wheel and sang along. Bradley joined in and sang the last verse in his deep, smooth voice. "Blackbird, fly," he sang, stretching the words out, and it seemed he was saying these words right to her. There was something so sad about that song that she wanted to cry, yet it also made her feel like she could do anything she set her mind to. What she really wanted to do was pull to the side of the road and kiss Bradley. She wanted to run her hands down the angles of his face, and more than anything else, she wanted to just lay her head on his chest and be still with him as dusk settled on the land.

"I guess I need to take you back," she said. After all, there was a war waiting. "Next time I'll take you to the state line and show you the place where I always stand and look back at the mountains."

He turned and looked at her as she drove. When she looked at him he said: "Just keep driving."

"But you'll miss your train."

"I can catch the later one. Right now what I want more than anything is to be with you."

By the time they crossed the state line and got out of the car, the air had cooled and the sun had spread itself out across the far horizon. They stood beneath the purpling sky and looked at the ridges, stretching for miles and miles, as if the whole world was made up of mountains. As the gloaming moved in, Bradley looked at the sky as if everything was new and different to him. "There really is something about the light in August, just like they say," he said. She thought this the most beautiful phrase she had ever heard in her life.

The wind rose up and slithered around them, pushing Anneth's hair back in a wild flurry. He put his hand on the small of her back. Then she saw the strip mine over there, a great, barren spot amongst the dark green hills. The whole top of the mountain had been chewed away by dozers, and all the trees had been cut to reveal acres and acres of yellowish red dirt. There was a layer of coal that had been left exposed by the workers, who had left for the day. Anneth couldn't bear to look at it. She caught the glint of dying sunlight shining on the river far down in the valley and focused on this, but Bradley had seen the strip mine, too.

"I can't understand anybody doing that," he said, and when she looked at his face she saw that sadness lived there. "Tearing up the land like that. It just kills me."

And it was that easy, that instant. In that moment she knew that she loved him more than she had ever loved anyone else. She knew what this would look like to others. Easter would say that Anneth fell in love with every boy she had ever met. But this was the first time she had ever felt anything, right in her soul.

Twenty-six

....

The End of the World

HE DIDN'T CATCH the train that ran later that night. And then didn't catch the one the next day, either.

After they drove back into town that first night together, she invited him into her apartment and he changed out of his uniform and into a pair of jeans and a madras shirt, which made him look even better, she decided. It wasn't the uniform after all, she thought. They sat out on her porch, watching the river while they talked. They drank all the beer from her refrigerator but never felt drunk. Anneth fixed a stack of 45s on her record player so that the only real silence was in that moment just before the single dropped and the needle found its way to the groove.

There was so much to talk about. Anneth told him things that she had never told anyone, not even Easter. As they talked she could feel herself healing inside. She saw suddenly that she had been afflicted—not only by her blues, which came and went as they pleased (and which she enjoyed in a strange way), but also by a need to feel that she was part of somebody else. She had never, ever thought she needed that. In fact she had relished being different, being a rebel. She had liked it that women talked about her behind cupped hands, that men turned to watch her walk down the sidewalk. But now, sitting here with Bradley, she realized that what she loved most about him was that he accepted her for just who she was. He didn't raise an eyebrow when she told them that she had been married and divorced twice.

"All that matters is right now," he said, and she would have loved him for that if nothing else.

She crawled up onto his lap as he leaned back in the rocking chair there on her porch. And then they were kissing and his lips felt just as good as—even better than—she had imagined. She unbuttoned his shirt slowly, admiring the thinness of each white button, and then pushed the separate sides of the shirt back to reveal his chest and the silver chain that encircled his neck. An oval medallion hung from the chain, and she held it on the tips of her fingers and leaned in close to look at it: a man carrying a child on his back. Around the oval were the words SAINT CHRISTOPHER PROTECT US.

"It's beautiful," she said.

"My sister gave it to me," he said. He put his chin on his chest so he could see the medallion and then held it between his fingers. "It's supposed to protect travelers."

"It's Catholic, though."

"He's a saint," Bradley said. "But I guess he'd protect a Pentecostal boy just as easy as a Catholic."

He put his hands on the sides of her face and pulled her up to kiss him. When her lips were upon his, she felt drunk. Kissing him was like dancing, like moving to the music. She felt his hands behind her back, unlatching her bra and then moving around to cover her breasts. She took hold of his fingers and brought his hands up so she could kiss his palms. She relished the roughness of his calluses, every line and crease holding another story that he could share with her. His fingers smelled like the woods. When she held them to her face she could smell the musk of pines, the sweetness of hickories. She felt like crying out at nothing more than his touch, at the warmth that bloomed between them when she put her chest against his and laid her head on the nape of his neck.

They lay there like that with the darkness watching. She could see the sky above them, a blackness like death with a smudged glow where the moon was supposed to be. The wind was cool against her back and as it ran over her it swam through the trees, too, causing the leaves to awake and stir. Here she lay, naked to the waist, completely fallen for a boy she had met only ten hours ago. She knew that he would stay the night here with her and then he would leave her and be gone for good, but even so, she wanted to be right here. There was something that had happened between them that she couldn't explain. All she knew was that this was the first time she had ever felt completely safe. She didn't care if it looked like another stupid notion of her open heart. She was filled simultaneously with such joy and such sadness that she didn't know if the tears that went unshed in the corners of her eyes were from happiness or grief. She had finally found the man she wanted and she wouldn't be able to have him. War didn't stop for love or anything else. It bulldozed right through all of that without a second thought.

So she simply held him and was so comfortable there within his arms that she fell asleep. She was only vaguely aware of his carrying her into the house and awoke just enough to open her eyes briefly and run her hand over his lips as he put her on the bed. He stood for a moment beside her, looking down as if he didn't know what to do next.

"Lay with me," she heard herself say, extending her hand. He crawled into bed with her and pulled her as close to him as he could get, laying his head on her naked chest. She put her hands into his hair and was asleep again in no time, dreaming of absolutely nothing.

EASTER HAD DREAMED of the end of the world, and the feeling of dread stuck with her all day. It had not been a dream of fire and brimstone. Instead she had spent the night wandering through an abandoned world, the last person on earth. Everyone else had been sucked up to heaven or sent down to hell. She alone had been left in the purgatory of a stilled earth. She had seen herself walking up the road, passing empty houses, cars stopped in the road, after people had floated up out of them into nothingness. In her dream she had walked into town and seen silent storefronts. A broom lying on the sidewalk after the sweeper had been whisked away into the end. The only sound that of a record player that had been left playing in one of the apartments over Shoes Galore. She had never heard the song before.

She tried not to think of the dream as she drove into town and parked in front of the attorney's office. The world had obviously not ended: cars sped by with their radios cranked up loud, women sashayed down the street with their purses hanging from the crooks of their arms as they went from the drugstore to the grocery to the post office. Easter was here to find out if she could save her land. The attorney had said on the phone that there was not much hope of doing so, but she had brought all the proper papers and intended to see if they could discover some loophole.

She started to stop in at Anneth's apartment to check on her. There was no phone at Anneth's and when Easter called the café that morning they said she had called in to tell them that she wouldn't be coming to work. Easter glanced at her wristwatch and figured it could wait. Anneth was probably just hungover.

She went into the lawyer's office and found an old woman sitting at a large desk. She was typing in such a practiced, fast rhythm that Easter felt the urge to tap her foot to the beat.

"I'm here to see Mr. Patton," Easter said.

The receptionist barely glanced up. She never stopped typing as she nodded her chin toward the row of chairs against the wall. "Be a few minutes," the woman said.

Easter sat in the leather chairs of the attorney's waiting room and studied the mahogany paneling. She ran her hands through the stack of magazines on the end table near her. *Life, Look,* and *Coal* magazine. She paused at this and picked up the magazine, flipping through the pages to find that it was an industry magazine. Articles about augering and draglines and coal-washing techniques. Looking around, she saw a polished wall behind her that bore a large print showing a coal tipple at night. Snow glowed on the mountainside beneath a full moon. A Mack truck seemed to idle beneath the coal tipple as a load was dropped into it, a sign that the tipple never closed, not even for the night or winter or anything else. She stood and looked at it more closely before she realized that the words AL-TAMONT MINING COMPANY were printed on the truck's door in small, neat lettering. She threw the magazine down on the seat and walked out of the attorney's office and back out into the daylight of the white street.

WHEN ANNETH AWOKE the next morning, he was still asleep. She studied his face, tracing his eyes and eyebrows and his nose and his mouth with her finger. They had both slept in their pants, their legs tangled up like grapevines. She ran her hand down his smooth chest, starting with her thumb on the silver medallion and working down until her fingers dug into the waistband of his pants. She stopped there and went into the kitchen.

Anneth made coffee, then fried bacon and boiled water for oats, whistling a song she couldn't remember the name of. She thought she might have made up the tune out of thin air. She scrambled eggs and slid pieces of bread into the toaster, briefly wishing that she had listened when Easter tried to teach her how to make biscuits. She put plates on the small table beside the window and realized that she had never set the table before. She never had people over to her apartment and usually ate on the porch or in front of the television. She rolled silverware in a napkin, just as she did at work, and crowded the center of the table with jars of jelly and honey and a bowl of butter. She wished that she had a flower to put into a glass of water, but she didn't want to go outside. There was a clump of wildflowers that grew down on the bank of the river behind the row of stores on Main Street, but she didn't want to leave this cocoon they had made for themselves.

He padded onto the linoleum of the kitchen in his Levi's and stood stretching in front of her, rubbing the sleep out of his eyes.

"That's the best night of sleep I've had since getting my draft notice," he said.

"Set down and eat," she said, and raked eggs from the skillet onto his plate.

She sat down at the table and held both hands around her cup of coffee. She had no appetite. "You must think I'm crazy," she said, "to just take off riding with a boy I don't even know and then let him stay all night at my house."

He blew onto a spoonful of oatmeal, leaning over his plate. "I'd say you were in love," he said, and she thought he might laugh or at least show her his toothy smile, but he simply put the spoon into his mouth. She wasn't used to men saying what they felt, being so honest and bare. Bradley meant every single thing he said. Maybe being sent off to war freed a person to be completely real.

"I'd say I've gone crazy over you in only one day and night," she said. "It seems foolish."

"Why should it?" he said. "Just because that's not the normal way people do things? It doesn't matter."

"You have to be in Ashland tomorrow, don't you? If you're not, they'll court-martial you or something?"

He nodded, swallowing his coffee. "If I don't report, I'll be a deserter," he said. "I have to go."

"I could drive you," she said. "The only train tomorrow is the evening one, at six."

"That'd make it that much harder to leave you." He wiped his mouth with his napkin and put his elbows on the table. "Let's just have these two whole days together. And I'll leave on the train. I'll write you every day, and when I get back I'll come for you."

She looked down at her coffee. "I want you to."

The rest of the day they sat together and talked and kissed, and when darkness came they didn't turn on a lamp. Anneth put a stack of 45s on the record player, but one of them—"Love Me Two Times" by the Doors—got stuck on there and kept playing for more than an hour before they got off the couch and walked toward the bedroom. Anneth turned the phonograph off. They undressed in the gray shadows of night and did not speak.

Twenty-seven

....

Proof of Life

SHE FEIGNED SLEEP as he moved around the room in the shadows of early evening. When it had been nearly time for him to leave, they had lain down to sleep together one more time. There was nothing more comforting or intimate than sleeping with him. Sex hadn't brought them so close as sleeping together had.

He packed his clothes and took a quick bath and put his uniform back on. She could see him buttoning his shirt and straightening his tie in the floor-length mirror that was fastened to her wall, even though she lay with her back to him. She didn't want to get up and tell him good-bye. If she did, it would be finalized. She knew she would have to at some point, but for now she just lay there and tried to keep him with her as long as she could.

He carried his bags out to the front door and took his time coming back into her bedroom, as if he was memorizing the apartment. When he came into her bedroom he stretched out beside her in his meticulously ironed uniform. He kissed her on the forehead.

"I love you," he said. For a moment she thought these might be the simple words of a soldier who needed to utter such a phrase so that he could hold on to this moment for later, when he smelled death, but she knew that he meant it. She could see the truth in his eyes. And a man had never said it to her this way, either, emphasizing each word—because each one was equally important, really. People always made a big deal about the word *love,* but it was really the other two words in that sentence that mattered.

She had never cried over a man in her life, but after she kissed him and he walked out, she buried her face in the pillow and wept, trying to block out the sound of the train when it approached. And then she heard it leaving, each turn of the great metal wheels on the metal track a sign that he was getting farther and farther away. Each scratching grind of the train taking him closer to the war. When she couldn't hear the train anymore she sat up in the bed with a start.

"Oh, my Lord," she said, feeling the warmth there, the spirit that stirred within. "I'm pregnant."

Twenty-eight

Mysterious Ways

ANNETH DECIDED THAT this baby would be her secret. She told only Easter, Lolie, and Jewell the story of her two and a half days with Bradley. No one else needed to know. She wasn't ashamed, but she wanted to keep the story to herself. It was no one's business, and telling it seemed to lessen the meaning of what she and Bradley had found in each other. In the months since he had gone, she had come to accept that she would never see him again. She hadn't received one letter from him and carried disappointment in her womb along with the child each time she went to the post office. For the past few weeks she had been going to check her post office box two or three times, as if the postmaster passed out letters on an hourly basis instead of filling the boxes a single time in the mornings. She slid her key into the small gold door, and each time her disappointment loomed bigger when she discovered nothing more than catalogs or bills.

She didn't have a second sight like Easter, had no dreams or visions. But she did have a feeling in her gut and she knew that Bradley was never coming back from Vietnam. This was as plain to her as the memory of his face, which she saw swim before her every morning when she awoke.

She bought a newspaper every morning, checked the state casualty lists, then threw the paper away without glancing at the other headlines. She was only looking for proof of what she already knew. If she saw his name there, spelled out in black letters, at least she might be able to go to sleep at night. She became obsessed with the war news on television. She rushed home from work and ate at her coffee table, never looking at her food. She memorized the cadences in Walter Cronkite's voice, could anticipate the calm quiet that came over him when he studied a piece of paper he had been handed. She sat on the floor, close to the television screen, hoping for a glimpse of Bradley when the news crews traveled with platoons. She sucked in her breath upon seeing a soldier that resembled him; then the camera would focus in on the boy, who always turned out not to look like Bradley at all, and she let her breath out. She didn't know why she looked for him amongst the living. She would be more apt to find him in one of the battle scenes when the reporter had to speak loudly over the gunfire in the background. She imagined that he had been shot in the heart as soon as he stepped off the helicopter and into the lush jungle. She saw his arms flying out in the rush to accept death, the way his body crumpled, his helmet staying on when his head hit the ground. Or he might be propped up against a tree as if resting, the only sign of death the slouch of his shoulders, the way his chin rested on his chest.

She had once quietly opposed the war—quiet in her opposition only because she wasn't sure what was right—but now she snapped the television off when it showed the protesters. She joined the others at the café when they condemned the hippies and the cowards. She refused to fashion two fingers into the peace sign, something that had once filled her with a sense of pride and great power. She bought a marker and a pack of construction paper at the drugstore and squatted down on her kitchen floor to let the marker squeak out

"We Support the Troops" in her careful handwriting. She taped this sign not only in the window of her own apartment, but also in Easter's living room window and on the front door of the café.

Beside her bed she kept a notebook in which she wrote a letter to Bradley every night. If she was completely wrong and he was still alive and she happened to find a letter from him in her post office box, she would post a large manila envelope with all her letters inside to his return address, and he would receive all of her love and desperation by way of the postal service. Some of the letters went on and on even though she knew her words were in vain. They were all letters to a dead man.

When she couldn't stand being the only one to harbor this knowledge anymore, she went to Easter. After work she asked Easter to go for a walk with her up on the mountain to see the wildflowers before the autumn frosts. Already the scent of fall was in the evening air.

They sat in the middle of the field and the sun was warm on the tops of their heads. This had always been their place of secrets, where they revealed the mechanics of their hearts to each other. Both of them knew that their grandmothers' ghosts loitered here. Now Easter sat quietly, waiting, and Anneth knew that Easter was no fool. Easter knew that Anneth had brought her for a reason. Anneth let it all out at once, like a gallon of paint that is tipped over on a new rug.

"Easter, I can't raise this baby by myself," she said. She put her hand atop her belly, where the baby had lived for three months now. She knew that it was impossible, but already she felt movement there. The gathering of blood and bone, an energy that glowed within. "I'm not ready."

"You will be," Easter said. "When you have a baby, something in you changes. Like a light switch. When my baby was born, a change washed out over me and I felt like I could do anything. It was only a second before I realized that he was stillborn, that I wouldn't get to put this change to use, but I felt it all the same, Anneth. When you have a child, you become more powerful than you ever were before."

"No," Anneth said, and then stopped. She couldn't say more, although her mouth was full of words. She looked at the sky as if the clouds might give her a way to say what she needed to put into a sentence. She hoped that Easter would be able to interpret the shape of her face and know what she was asking of her. She steeled herself, as if about to face a cold wind, and then looked her sister in the eye. "I want you to raise this child."

"I'll help you all I can," Easter said. "You know I will."

"No, I want this baby to know you as his mother," she said, and wondered why she knew it was a boy. "I'm not ready and I won't do right by him."

"Yes, you will, honey," Easter said. There was a lightheartedness in Easter's tone, as if she was amused by Anneth's worries. She put her hand on Anneth's back and held it still there. "You'll be a good mother."

Anneth stood. "I won't!" she said, louder than she intended. She coveted the confidence in Easter's face, wished that she could believe in herself as much as her sister did. In many ways Easter was stupid and naive. Could she possibly believe that everything worked out for the best, that all things happened for a reason, considering what had happened to her own baby? Anneth couldn't understand why Easter wanted to keep up this charade. Easter had had her own crisis of faith; she knew what it was like to have doubt. Easter knew as well as anyone that some things just didn't work out and that was the way it was. That was the way life was. Anneth wished her sister could admit this now.

"What if Bradley comes back, though, Anneth?" Easter said, looking up at her. "What will you do then?"

Anneth held her elbows in her hands. "He's not coming back," she said. "He's been gone three months and I haven't heard a word from him. I can't even write to him to tell him about this baby because I don't have his address. It was stupid of me, to think this could all work out, to think that I could love somebody I only knowed two days."

"We can find out where he is. We can fix all that."

Anneth squatted back down and rested on her knees. The ground was warm. "Some things can't be fixed, Easter." She spoke slowly, feeling as if she was assembling the words in her mouth just before they came out.

"You don't want to find him, because you're afraid of the reasons he hasn't written to you. Either he's dead or he's just put you out of his mind. All we'd have to do is call the army recruitment office to find out where he is."

Anneth looked up at her, a look that told Easter to stop talking. "Now I'm asking you, Easter. I'm asking you to stick by me through this, and when I have this baby, I want you to take him. I want you to raise him just like your own and I'll go about my life and be a good aunt. It's the best for both of us. You were the one who was meant to be a mother."

"If I was meant to be a mother, God would have given me a child."

Anneth took Easter's hands. "Maybe this is His way of giving you one."

THEY WALKED DOWN the path holding hands, something they hadn't done in years and years. Easter could remember the last time vividly: the day of Serena's funeral. They had gone up to the field to comfort their grief and had come back down completely changed. It was as if they had left their childhoods behind on the mountain. They had both been thinking of themselves as women for a long while by that time, but Easter knew that day—which seemed so very long ago, ages almost—that they really were grown now.

Back at the house, Easter stood in the yard and raised her hand when Anneth backed out of the driveway and drove away without looking back.

She felt drunk with the possibility of having a child. She went into the house and started supper. El would be home soon and she wanted to tell him this news over food. That was the best way to give tender information, at the kitchen table. She breaded pork chops and set them to frying, then stirred up a corn bread batter and fried that, too. The sizzling was a comforting sound, the smells of good food filling the kitchen. She sliced the ripe tomatoes she had picked that morning and couldn't help herself: she doused a slice in salt and ate it greedily, the red tang filling her mouth in an explosion of taste so good that she could barely contain her satisfaction when she swirled the juice around in her mouth. Already she was thinking of how it would be to stand here at this counter and turn to see a little baby sitting in his high chair behind her, smiling up at her as he waited for her to finish supper and tend to him again. Or maybe he would be crying and reaching his arms toward her and she'd hold him on her hip the whole time she cooked, a little dance they'd do in the kitchen as she moved around taking skillets off the stove and setting the table. She'd sing to him as she did this, and her movement would be so soothing to him that just when the food was all ready, he'd be asleep, his head laid upon her shoulder, his lips slightly parted. She had dreamed of that so many times.

She knew that it was crazy, knew that it was impossible that all of this could work out as Anneth believed it could, but Easter shook all that away. She let herself visualize the possibility of joy. She didn't want to think about the many ways this could all become complicated. It made sense, in a roundabout way. Anneth wanted to give her the biggest gift she could, a sacrifice she could make for Easter. And at the same time, Easter could make a sacrifice for her, to raise the child she would carry for nine months.

Twenty-nine

Making Plans

As it turned out, Anneth liked being pregnant. Her first trimester had been uneventful, although everyone had told her that she would be miserably sick. Women were always giving her advice, always telling her about their own pregnancies and labors and childbirths. She didn't understand why her swelling belly seemed to give people permission to talk about all these very private things. But she did enjoy their chattering, the fussing that they did over her. Even at three months her belly was especially large, and because of this her customers at the café treated her differently than they ever had before. Now when businessmen came in they didn't eye her as she walked away, or flirt and wink. They pushed out the extra chairs at their tables and told her to sit down while she took their order, hesitated to ask for more coffee when their cups ran dry. All her life, people had watched her when she crossed a street because they enjoyed the way her dress hugged her hips, the way her long legs sliced beneath her skirt. Now they smiled at her with respect, as if you had to be a good person to get pregnant. She knew this was not true.

Some people were rude enough to come right out and ask her

who the father was, but she would not say. She enjoyed carrying this secret with her, knowing that people were wondering.

Everyone tried to help her out. Sometimes she came home to find that Easter had sneaked in and cleaned her apartment for her, the floors swept, the furniture smelling of lemon polish, the dishes all stacked neatly within the cupboard, the boxes of food all turned face-out in the pantry. She immediately set everything askew again. She jerked open her dresser drawers to find that Easter had folded up all her clothes. She ran a hand through her panty drawer and made the bath towels hang unevenly on the rack, let the dishes pile up in the sink again without even running water over them. Unlike Easter she had never had a desire for order in her life.

When she was alone she sat in her apartment without turning on a lamp and let the night seep into each room. Often the blue glow of the television was the only light. She spread a quilt out over herself and watched the war news and simply remained still. Each day she seemed to be growing more and more unlike herself and began to see that the reason she liked being pregnant was that it gave her a reason to be still. She could do nothing now, without feeling guilty about it, and this was a great comfort. Sometimes she dozed off and right away she had short, muted dreams. She saw Bradley standing on the overlook, pointing to the strip mine on the ridge opposite them. "I can't understand that," he had said. "Tearing up the land that way." She often awoke with a start, thinking that she would find him leaning over the bed, peering down at her.

Yet each night she felt herself sinking further and further into a melancholy that she had no control over. Nor did she desire control over it; perhaps if she just gave herself over to that heavy feeling that settled over her entire body, she might drift off into a long sleep that would take her away from everything.

That included Glenn, who started to show up more and more.

She didn't know why he wanted her, but he did. She lay on the couch and watched television and he sat there holding her feet in his lap, running his thumb over her ankles.

"You ought to marry me, Anneth," Glenn said one night. "It's not right for a woman to be pregnant and not married."

She sat up and folded her legs beneath herself. "You're living in the past, Glenn. It's almost nineteen sixty-nine."

"That don't matter," he said. He had a way of looking right at her when he spoke that she hated. It was like he was studying her all the time. And she still hadn't gotten over that flicker of rage that had passed over his eyes when he had found out she was pregnant. He hadn't said anything, but it was obvious that he felt betrayed. "It's still not a proper way to bring a child into the world."

"I don't give a damn what nobody thinks," she said. She started to add, *Besides, I love Bradley. Not you. Never you.* She bit her tongue, though. There was no use being outright cruel to Glenn. At least he was there. "Why would you want to marry a woman who's carrying another man's baby anyway?"

"Because," he said, "I care for you."

"Well, I've tried not to lead you on, Glenn. I like to go out dancing with you and all, but not—not anything like that. You've been a good friend to me, but that's all."

She thought he might never stop staring at her but finally he turned his head and got up stiffly. He grabbed his hat off the coffee table, righted it on his head, and took his jacket from the coat-tree by the door. "If you need anything, just call me," he said, and left without another word.

When Glenn was gone she felt incredibly alone. She didn't know why; his presence didn't mean that much to her. But she found that she couldn't stand being in this apartment anymore. It reminded her too much of Bradley, as bad as she hated to admit that to herself.

There were not many people who could look at a couple of rooms and see that their greatest love affair had played out in such a small space, but hers had. Less than three full days and one drive and this little apartment were the extent of the only romance that had ever really meant anything to her.

She threw a few things into her overnight case and drove toward Easter's.

With each curve in the road toward Free Creek the baby shifted and swayed, as if dancing in anticipation of being at Easter's house. Perhaps he already felt a connection to that old place, just as she did. She turned on the radio and twisted the knob until she found a station playing "Piece of My Heart." She loved the way Janis Joplin screamed out those words. She began to sing along and felt the blues lifting off her shoulders a bit as her headlights washed over the dark trees of autumn. The closer she got to Free Creek, the better she felt, and she wondered if it was this closeness to home or simply the music that was healing her.

The baby rolled over again, causing her to put her hand over her belly. She wondered why women had this instinct, to comfort the baby anytime it made some sort of motion. Maybe this was maternal instinct taking over: the baby moves and the mother rushes to comfort it, to make sure it's all right. She patted her belly to the beat of the song, knowing that she loved the baby already. Loved the way he curled into her bladder, kicked at her kidneys. Easter had said that giving birth to him would change her forever, but he had already changed her. For the first time in her life she felt as if she was worth something. But each time this overwhelming feeling of love came over her, she told herself that she wasn't good enough for this child.

THE MORNING AFTER Anneth had shown up at their house late in the night, Easter awoke to find that El had gotten out of bed before her. She smelled coal burning in the stove and knew that he had recently stoked the fire. The creaks in the floorboards sounded very loud on the quiet. She looked into the extra room and saw Anneth was asleep. Easter stepped in and studied her as she lay in the gray shadows of the room. Anneth had taken clothespins and fastened the curtains together so the room wouldn't be bathed in sunlight as soon as dawn hit. She had always done this when she lived here, and Easter realized that it was a little quirk she missed.

Anneth looked so beautiful lying there. She was one of those people who woke up looking exactly the way they had gone to bed, a hair barely out of place, no lines on her face. Easter put her hand on Anneth's arm, felt her cool skin. She pulled the quilt up to Anneth's neck and looked at the rise of Anneth's stomach beneath the covers. Life stirred within, such an amazing thing that Easter couldn't fathom it. That was the reason, Easter realized, that people continued to believe in God despite the horrors of the world: because miracles were still constantly on display. Things didn't get much more miraculous than a baby's being carried around in a woman's belly and then being delivered one day. She could have stood there and watched Anneth sleep forever—hers was such a peaceful, undisturbed rest, a kind of tranquillity that Easter had really never known, with her vivid dreams every night. She closed the door, feeling as if she had been spying on her sister. It was an intimate thing to watch someone sleep.

Easter looked outside and saw no sign of El. She could tell by the morning's blue haze that it was cold. The trees had been at their height of color yesterday, but today they stood bare and black limbed as if they had shed all their leaves in one night. She pulled on a coat and slipped her bare feet into El's work boots.

The autumn air was so cold that it felt like a cleansing water. She knew he was in the shed out back even before she saw the crack of yellow light around the door. She pulled open the door and found him putting together the crib they had bought when she was pregnant. That seemed to be ages ago, another lifetime.

He looked up from his work and turned with the screwdriver clenched in his hand like a weapon.

"El," she said. She tried to interpret the way she said his name. It sounded to her like an expression of wonder or amazement. She hoped that it didn't hold the tone of pity, although she was sure that that was why she had decided on saying his name. He did look pitiful there, bent at this task not only of assembling a crib but also of nudging along a dream they had both shared for so long.

She stepped up into the shed and pulled the door closed behind her to keep out the cold. She moved toward him quickly and put her arms around his waist, laid her face against his chest.

"It doesn't seem right," he said, "to be planning on taking a baby from Anneth. But in a way it makes perfect sense. Sometimes I think we're crazy to even consider this."

"The best things that happen in life rarely make good sense," she said. She spoke quietly because she didn't want to break the morning silence that existed outside. It seemed that even the creek had stopped its incessant gurgling. She felt as if she and El might have been the only people in the world. Maybe they and Anneth in there sleeping and no one else. That wouldn't be so bad.

"I just want to do the right thing," El said. "Just whatever's best for this child."

"I know it," she said. "Me, too."

"But I don't know what is best, and I don't want you getting hurt again."

"God knows all things," she whispered, and for the first time in many years, she actually believed this when she said it.

Thirty

Something Ancient

THEY STOOD ON the mountain with their arms interlocked, their jaws tightening against the cold, their eyes hard and unblinking. Paul was working at the sawmill, El had just left to go on the road, and the dozers had come too unexpectedly for anyone to join them. Israel and Lolie and lots of other people down in Free Creek had promised to stand against the company with them, but it had all happened too quickly. So there was only Anneth, Easter, and Sophie.

The men had already cut down the bigger trees to make way for a road up the mountain. But there was still the brush and the felled trees, and here was a dozer that shook with life as it sat there at the foot of the mountain, waiting for the order to go forward. It would push aside the limbs and pull out the stumps until it reached the summit, where the real work would begin. Behind the dozer sat a red Ford pickup with ALTAMONT MINING COMPANY painted on the door. Easter could see the silhouettes of two men sitting in the truck, smoking cigarettes and moving their heads as if they were caught up in a passionate debate. Behind them was a coal truck, a Mack truck with headlights like big round eyes that looked strangely evil. Easter thought it might have been present simply to suggest a bigger threat. The company had known they would face resistance.

Easter wondered what the driver of the dozer thought of them. Here was Anneth, seven months pregnant but looking as if she could sit down and have the baby at any moment. Sophie, who was not more than five feet tall even with her beehive hair. And Easter herself—could he see that the grief of the last few years had thinned and weakened her, had cleaned her completely out? Or could he make out that this same grief had made her stronger, had made her more adamant than ever to fight for what was hers, to keep alive all of her family that she could? Did he see in all three of the women's faces that they would not surrender their land? Easter looked at the driver sitting up there—his face dark and unrecognizable because of the morning's new sun behind him—and knew that there was no way he could realize that Sophie had the courage to kill anybody that crossed her family, despite her thin wrists and kind eyes. And there was no way he could fathom the rage that Anneth was able to unloose when the need arose.

It seemed more likely that he saw three women and found this laughable. He tapped the gas, and a metal lid lifted on the exhaust pipe to allow three blasts of black smoke to burst out onto the morning air. The lid closed again and it rattled there atop the pipe, with thin wisps of smoke seeping out around its edges.

The doors of the Ford came open and the two men stepped out, flicking their cigarettes off into the woods. The women held one another's arms more tightly, pulling themselves together into a whole. As the men came closer, Easter felt the mountain behind her, its presence so big and real that she thought she could feel it breathing, something ancient and alive.

She could see that one of the men was Liam. He must have known that they would put up some resistance or he wouldn't have come.

The mine foreman never went out on jobs like this. He had on his work coat, and his hands were shoved in the pockets as if he was freezing. His head was slightly bowed so that he didn't have to look them in the eye until he was standing very near. The other man hung back, hesitant to approach them.

"Why are you all doing this, now?" Liam said, shifting his feet. He looked into each of their faces. "You know this is just going to cause trouble."

"That's what we intend to do," Easter said. "We're going to cause you as much trouble as we can to stop this."

"It won't stop us," Liam said. His words sounded rehearsed. "The law is on our side."

"You prick," Anneth said, but it seemed that something stopped her from saying more, as if her throat had filled up with dirt.

"Sophie, you need to get these girls out of here," Liam said. "I don't want to have to call the law."

"What are you telling me for?" Sophie said. "I'm the ringleader."

Liam shook his head and looked hard at the men behind him. They turned back toward the truck, Liam throwing his hand into the air to make a signal for the driver of the bulldozer, who tapped the gas again.

"Let's go," Easter said. They moved forward together and climbed into the dozer scoop without difficulty, settling in as if it was a wide, deep porch swing. They sat back against the cold metal. Easter brought her hands up and saw red soil on her palms, like clots of blood. She closed her eyes and started praying: *Lord, keep us in the palm of your hand.* Sophie was between the two sisters now and they both leaned against her, holding hands, unable to speak. There was too much to say. Within the scoop they could feel the vibration of the motor. The driver hollered but they couldn't make out his words, so he tapped the gas again to startle them. Easter flinched at the sudden jolt but steeled herself against the dozer bucket. There was no way she was going to move now.

More hollering, and then the scoop lifted and swung out, dumping them onto the ground in front of the dozer. Easter fell on all fours and saw Sophie tumbling down to land beside her. But Anneth held on to the edges of the scoop, wedging herself in and refusing to let go.

"No!" Easter screamed as the scoop rose higher, the driver pulling the lever back and then forward so that Anneth would fall out. "She's pregnant!" But Easter's voice was lost to the roar, so she prayed into the loudness. Out of the corner of her eye she saw another truck pulling in down there by the road. On its trailer sat a second dozer. The men climbed out of the high truck and went about undoing the chains as if they had to fight off three women every time they starting mining a new piece of land. Easter looked back at the mountain, its winter trees black and skeletal. She thought the mountain might rise up and avenge them, but it didn't. She thought of the birds that were usually gathered here and figured they had moved back into the deepest parts of the forest.

The driver brought the scoop down, a great heaviness being released. When it hit the ground, Easter could feel the impact in her ankles and up the backs of her calves. Sophie was beside her, hanging on to her arm, hollering words that were lost on the air. Anneth still had her feet firmly planted against the edge of the scoop, and her back pressed against the metal. There was nothing to read on her face. She had her eyes closed and Easter thought she might be praying, too. The driver swung the scoop in the air and brought it down again, the sound of its striking the ground a dull, wide vibration through the earth.

And then Anneth was tumbling out of the scoop, rolling toward them with her arms out to soften the blow of the ground. Easter pulled her up onto her lap, wiping dirt away from Anneth's face.

"I'm all right," Anneth said, pushing her away. "Get away. Don't let them think they've hurt me."

"But the baby," Easter said. "I want you to go back to the house."

"If you think I'd leave you all now, you're crazy."

Easter took in everything in flashes, as if her eyes closed between images: The dozer rolling toward them now, chunks of dirt caught in the metal tracking that wound about the wheels. The trees, their limbs bending down in a slight breeze as if leaning over to watch the action below. The sky rolling gray and low. And then as the dozer rolled closer and closer, they all knew what they had to do.

They interlocked their arms and sat down. The driver didn't stop until he was so close that Easter could smell the soil caked across the bottom of the scoop.

The driver jumped down and came to lean over them, his hands on the tops of his legs. Now she could see that it was Lonzo Morgan. Easter had known him all his life and started to say as much but didn't speak.

"Stop this now, girls. Please. You're going to cause me to lose my job because I can't do this. I won't," he said. His brow was fretted and his eyes were full of frustration. "When I tell them that, they're going to fire me."

"I'm sorry, Lonzo," Easter said. "But this is your mountain, too. Everybody that lives here—it belongs to them as much as it does us. It always has."

"Please," he said, but Liam grabbed his shoulders and caused him to stand straight up. Liam talked so close to his face that Easter thought their lips might touch.

The three women lay down as the dozer continued to tremble at their feet. The men all came and stood around them, as if they were women who had fallen from the sky. Easter closed her eyes and knew that Anneth and Sophie were doing the same. The ground was cold and filled with the hum of the dozer. In an odd way the vibration was comforting. Easter remembered all the times she had walked this old mountain, all the songs they had sung as they climbed its paths. All the times she had run in the field of wildflowers that swayed there in spring and summer. Anneth laughing as she fell back in the purple asters. Her mother walking out of the field clutching a handful of jonquils. Her father holding Easter when she was just a baby as he looked out over the view below them.

There was a flash of whiteness above her, and when she opened her eyes she saw a photographer leaning down with his camera.

And then there were hands on her. She pivoted her head back to find the sheriff and his four deputies, their pistols hanging from their sides. Down by the road she saw their police cars, the lights flashing against the mountainside. The sheriff, Lee Storms, and one of his men had hold of Anneth, and the deputies gathered around Easter and Sophie. Easter had known Lee for as long as she could remember. Serena had campaigned relentlessly for his election; he had been sheriff for more than twenty years.

"Just go limp," she hollered to Anneth and Sophie. "Be still."

They were carrying Sophie away, one man holding on to her ankles and the other with his hands in her armpits, carrying her away like a gutshot deer. Sophie had followed Easter's advice and simply relaxed as they carried her away. They had tried to grab Anneth but she had gotten to her feet and was backing away as they closed in on her, telling her to just go with them peacefully. But she wouldn't.

Easter saw Lonzo Morgan climbing down from the dozer, hollering. One of the deputies was holding him back, too. "Let go of her, by God!" Lonzo hollered.

Easter let them lift her and felt each flash of the camera as they carried her away, but then she saw a policeman grab Anneth from behind, his forearm caught under her neck in a choke hold as she fought against them. Easter bucked out of their grip, falling to the ground and scrambling to her feet. She ran toward Anneth. As she did, she said a short prayer, asking that God be in her hands.

WHEN THE MEN caught hold of her, Anneth imagined that she was drowning. She was sinking down and down, to the very depths of Blackhawk Lake, to the bottom of the Cumberland River, giving herself to every body of water she had ever known on intimate terms. She saw herself putting her arms out and being carried away by the current of Free Creek, washed against the rocks. There was no going back to the surface; there was no strength left in her legs to burst back up to the top of the water, where sunlight would be white and blinding. The man she loved was dead, and the baby in her belly would never know his father. She had failed at everything in her life. The cop had his arm clamped tightly beneath her chin and held both her wrists within one big hand. She relaxed against him, drifting down and down and down into blackness. She had been trying to act strong for as long as she could remember and now she was tired.

It was not surrender. Not really. Because hadn't Easter told Anneth that the best way to defeat the company was to let them think that she had been beat? The only way to win against something so large was to fool them. She might lie still and be carried away in peaceful protest, but no one would ever *keep* her down.

She thought of water swirling around her, the pulls and eddies of a river nudging her southward. Out of the corner of her eye she saw Sophie being carried away. The sheriff was hollering to his men and walking backward with his arms hooked through Sophie's, the heels of her shoes making little rows in the leaf-covered ground. Anneth could see that Sophie was making herself appear even smaller and more fragile than she really was for the benefit of the reporter, who ran alongside, snapping pictures.

But then Anneth heard Easter cry out, "Let her go!" She turned her head, saw her sister breaking away from the other men.

She had never seen Easter move so fast before. She was heading for the men who held on to Anneth. Anneth felt like putting her hand up and saying, *No! Let them!* But she didn't. As soon as Easter reached them she drew her hand back, and her mouth formed words that Anneth couldn't make out, and then Easter delivered a blow to the side of the man's head. He dropped Anneth's ankles and crossed his wrists in front of his face for only a second before grabbing for Easter. She was screaming at them, her face knotted up in rage, and moving toward the other man who still held on to Anneth.

Anneth put one hand on her belly to protect the baby, and with her other hand she reached up behind her head to grab hold of the cop's groin. She found what she was looking for and twisted the mound of flesh with all the strength she could muster. He dropped her like a sack of flour, and she came down hard on the frozen ground.

They had Easter now—one of the cops was carrying her, his arms wrapped around her waist as she kicked at the tops of his thighs. Anneth caught the brightness of a camera flashbulb again. There was the sound of the dozer's motor being revved up and a cacophony of yelling and confusion.

"Now, ma'am," one of the deputies said, running up to calm Easter, but she spat in his face. She brought her legs up and kicked him in the stomach. He stumbled back and then rushed forward, snatching up her moving legs. The two men carried Easter toward the police car, and Anneth couldn't do anything but stand there on what was left of the place she had known all her life.

THE MEN PACKED them down the mountain like corpses, like dead bodies they had found lying in the woods. The women were completely still. Easter closed her eyes against the white morning sky and kept them closed until she was in the back of the police cruiser, holding on to her sister.

Thirty-one

A Convergence of Voices

The Louisville Courier-Journal

WOMEN PROTESTERS JAILED

BY SHIRLEY O'MALLEY

THREE EASTERN KENTUCKY WOMEN were arrested and removed from their ancestral land yesterday after lying in the path of a bulldozer that was about to start strip-mining the mountain under the protection of a broad form deed.

Easter McIntosh, 33, Sophie Sizemore, 54, and Anneth Trosper, 28, all of Crow County, resisted arrest when police were called in to remove them from the path of the dozers. The fight resulted in two of the deputies being hit in the face and stomach. McIntosh was the only woman jailed after being charged with assault and trespassing. Trosper and Sizemore were released on bond but refused to leave the jail without McIntosh. When Sheriff Lee Storms refused to allow the women to stay in the jail without being charged, Trosper slapped his face, thereby forcing him to arrest her as well.

Trosper was visibly pregnant (see photographs below, courtesy of the *Black Banks Tribune*) when deputies forced her down to the ground and carried her to an awaiting cruiser. A midwifery team from the Black Banks Hospital was called in to examine her at the jail but declared that she had not been harmed. Citing her pregnancy, Storms declined to jail Trosper despite her assault.

"We never had any intention of hurting Mrs. Trosper or the other women," said Storms. "The situation was handled with the utmost professionalism. You should note that my deputies are the ones who suffered scratches and bruises, while the women showed no marks."

In the past few years, eastern Kentucky residents have been rising up in opposition to broad form deeds and strip-mining practices, citing irreversible damage to the environment. The most sensational of these confrontations occurred in 1965 when a 61-year-old woman named Widow Combs was arrested while trying to protect her farm. Combs went on to be a major voice for landowners' rights. Fifteen arrests have been made in five counties in the last six months alone.

The three women will be given a court date on Monday.

Easter awoke to singing.

She couldn't imagine how she could ever have gone to sleep, anyway. She had never expected to find herself in jail, but here she was, awaking on a slab of a bed beneath a green blanket that looked as if it had been washed so many times it would crumble the next time it was taken from the washer. The jail smelled of concrete — a cold, damp scent like the inside of a cave. She took the cell in and then stood on her bed and looked out the square window over her bed. The window was simply glass crisscrossed by embedded wires. There was a latch on the window so that it could be opened for an inch of air. When she pushed the window out as far as it would go, the volume of the singing heightened, and through the crack she could see people crowding the street in front of the jail. There must have been a hundred people out there, all their voices rising up into one. They were singing "They'll Never Keep Us Down."

She could see people that she went to church with—everyone in the congregation must have been out there—as well as Anneth, hanging on to the arm of a man Easter did not know, and Sophie and Lolie. Everyone she had known her entire life, and faces she didn't recognize. There were deputies out there, too, pushing the people back, moving about in the crowd. Reporters and photographers. Then she saw El, pointing his finger at the deputies lined up along the sidewalk. He was shouting at them but his words were lost to the singing. She put her hand against the glass, her fingers spread apart, and whispered, "El." She tapped her knuckles against the glass, but none of them could see or hear her. They sang louder and louder as if with each verse they garnered more strength in their lungs, more power behind the words.

She closed her eyes to soak in their singing and then slid down the cold wall and sat in the middle of her hard bed. It amazed her that people had gathered like this. She had never seen anything like it. They were all fed up and had grown used to seeing people protest over the past few years. Now it was their turn. The best weapon they had was their singing. The crowd sang every song that Easter had ever known. The songs were all full of the same power, each word so strong that all those voices together could have broken down the walls of the jail if they took the notion. Sometimes in between singing she could hear Anneth yelling at the police or the people chanting, "Let her go! Let her go!" or the booming voice of the pastor who led everyone in prayer. It must have gone on for an hour.

The door at the end of the hall opened on creaking hinges and then she could hear footsteps coming toward her. Everything was amplified against the gray cement floor. She pulled her knees up to her chin, situated her skirt so that her legs were covered, and leaned against her legs with her eyes closed. She heard a harsh scraping across the floor and when she finally looked up she saw the sheriff sitting backward in a heavy desk chair in front of her cell. He shook his head and tapped one finger against the chair's back.

"You've caused me an awful lot of trouble, Easter," he said. "All this mess has had me on the phone to reporters in Louisville and Nashville and everywhere all morning."

"Good," Easter said. "You've good enough sense to know that that's the whole reason we did it, Lee. How do you think the photographers came to be there? I called them."

"You're a smart woman, Easter. But the law says that they have the right to mine that mountain."

"The law's not right, and you know it."

"I don't want to keep you in here," the sheriff said. He shook his head again, looking away. Easter was suddenly very sorry for him, his bald head catching the glare of the bare bulb hanging over him, dark circles beneath his eyes. He looked like a good man who was trying to do the right thing; this was spelled out clearly on his face. "I didn't want to put you in here at all, but you didn't give me much of a choice."

"There has to be something you can do to keep them from mining that mountain, Lee. You're the law in Crow County. That land has been in my family for a hundred years. If I lose that mountain, I lose a part of myself."

From outside she heard Anneth begin to sing "This Land Is Your Land." The crowd was silent around her. Both Easter and the sheriff looked toward the window the way someone would face a radio to hear it better. Anneth had always loved that song. In the seventh grade she had been given a paddling for singing it; the teacher said it was something only Communists sang. It was a dangerous song that some people were afraid to love. She had heard Anneth sing it many, many times before, but it had always been to the accompaniment of the record. Here her voice was distinct and powerful on its own. There was an uncertain quaver in her delivery, but somehow this caused the words of the song to make much more sense than they ever had before. *This is your land we're fighting for, too,* Anneth was saying to all of them. Easter would have given anything to have seen Anneth's face; she knew that it was full of conviction. She wondered if everyone out there was turned toward Anneth, watching her.

The sheriff didn't speak until Anneth had finished and silence lay over the street once again. Easter turned to face him and couldn't help smiling, but he tried to look past this when he shifted in his seat and shook his head.

"Easter, I watched you grow up," he said. "I thought the world of your grannies, both of them. And I have to say that you're one of the finest people I know. But you acted like somebody wild yesterday. I didn't have no choice but to put you in jail, the way you hit my officers and went on."

"They shouldn't have put their hands on Anneth. You know I'd kill anybody over her. She's all I have in this world, besides El."

"Well, there was no use in acting that way."

"She's pregnant, Lee."

"And that's exactly why she shouldn't have been out there laying in front of bulldozers and acting a fool like that."

Easter folded her hands in her lap. "You have to help us," she said.

"All I can do is let you out of here so you can go to the courthouse and ask that the broad form be looked over. If your uncle sold that land and it wasn't his to sell, you'll be all right."

Easter nodded. "That's what I should've done before all this."

"It wouldn't have mattered. If you hadn't done all this, the judge wouldn't even look at the deed." The sheriff got up and pushed the chair back against the wall. "I'll tell you something. That picture of them carrying Anneth away—big pregnant belly and all—got picked up by the wire service and is on the front page of every newspaper on the East Coast. I don't believe they'll ever bother that piece of land again."

"I'll still go to court and get the deed fixed proper," Easter said.

Lee put his hands into his pockets and jangled the coins that lay within. He let out a long sigh. "I think one night in jail was enough for that slap you gave to my deputy, but you sure hurt that man's pride," he said. "It'd be good of you to apologize to him."

"I think I'm a big-enough person to tell somebody I'm sorry," she said.

He unlatched the key chain attached to his belt loop and sorted through his keys. He unlocked her cell and held her by the crook of her arm as he walked her down the hallway and back to sunlight.

Thirty-two

....

Promises Kept

WHEN ANNETH RECEIVED the letter, she knew—just by holding the paper within her hands, just by smelling his distant scent on the stationery—that he was no more of this world. But there were other reasons to suspect his death, as well. The letter had been written only a month after his leaving her on the train, but it had taken nearly eight months to get to her. There was no obvious reason why. The envelope bore an army and air force postal mark over Bradley's quickly written "Free" where a stamp normally went. The postmark date was only two weeks ago. She suspected that he had written the letter, addressed the envelope, and shoved it in his bags, meaning to mail it later. Perhaps after his death someone had fished it from his belongings and slipped it into the mail. The words in the letter proved that if he truly was alive he would have written more to her.

28 September 1968

Dear Anneth,

How is this cruel cruel world treating you? Ha. Fine I hope. As for myself I'm okay I guess but I'm sure homesick. Everything is really different when you are all by yourself on the other side of the world. All I do is think of home. My folks and brother and sister and you. You more than anything. Looking back it seems kind of crazy, what we did. Falling in love after knowing each other two days only. But I do love you, Anneth, and being so far away only makes me more certain of that. I count the days until I am back to you. I am saving about two or three hundred dollars a month and that will really add up after a year. Plus the GI Bill will help me out and send me to school. We will be able to get married in high style. I guess that's springing one on you, huh? We never really talked about that but it seemed to be right on the tips of our tongues. When I said I'd be back for you that's what I meant and you knew it too I am sure.

Being over here makes you think about things like that all the time. That's all that can keep me going, just planning on the future. I have to believe in that to get me through. I've just been here two weeks and already I have seen hell in the flesh. It is too much to talk about and I'm not allowed to talk about it in letters anyway. I can't even tell you where I am. They say it is a "secure location" but I don't know how they come up with that because it sure doesn't feel too secure when the fighting hasn't stopped here in two days. I never understood the war really until I got over here and I can't explain it but now that I am here I'm going to fight for my country. And just fight to get back to you. I will write to you every day and now that you have my address you can write to me, too. Please send me a picture of you too since I left without getting one and have regretted that every day. I want to show you off to the boys.

I've bored you long enough. Just know that I think of you every minute and that I love you. We'll be together soon.

Love always,
Bradley

And that was all.

She turned the paper over, as if there might be more. She tore the airmail envelope open and looked inside, hoping to find some secret message, but there was nothing. The address was strange, nothing like her own post office box number, but instead was a mess of numbers and letters mixed together with "APO–San Francisco" as its final line. She knew that she could use this address to find out if he was really dead. She could call the army and have this address traced to find out about him, but she knew that she would never do that. Though she knew he was dead, if someone actually told her this from the other end of the line, then there would never be a glimmer of hope left. There would be nothing. She folded the letter back up.

She put the letter inside her souvenir box and then slid the box back under her bed. She decided that she might as well marry Glenn Couch and leave it at that. Glenn would be good to her. He had a well-paying job and would take her anywhere she wanted to go. After the baby was born he could whisk her away to the beach or somewhere so she could forget that she had given away her child. He would take her to bars and honky-tonks. There was something dangerous about Glenn, she knew. He loved her, that much was true, but he loved her in a different way than Matthew had. Matthew had loved her without asking for anything in return, but it would be different with Glenn. He would want her to worship him as much as he worshipped her. And that was never going to happen.

But still, she had spent her whole life looking for someone to love her and she knew that he did; she might as well snatch up any love she could get. She thought she could live a lie for the rest of her life. Suffering like that would help to numb her, too. She could walk around like a whisper and no one would ever know the difference. People walked around dead all the time, going through the motions of life without really being there at all.

Hadn't her own mother done this? But unlike Birdie, she would bear her grief, she would go through life with this suffering resting on her neck like an oxen yoke.

She lay back on her bed and ran her hand over her stomach, trying not to love the child inside. She could fool herself with all the reasons she thought up to marry Glenn: his money, his love for her, his patience with her. But she knew the real reason she would marry Glenn: to betray Bradley. If she waited on Bradley, he might never come back. He really would be dead over there. But if she married Glenn, perhaps Bradley would show up one day. She knew there were no happy endings and this was the only hope of his surviving. This could be her sacrifice for him: marry Glenn and never, ever be happy, just so Bradley could live. Because it would be too easy if she just waited. It only happened in the movies that women waited and then the returning soldier just appeared out of nowhere, a survivor, a changed man in every way, back for his sweetheart.

If she betrayed Bradley, then Bradley might live. And more important, this betrayal would harden her heart. A heart of stone didn't feel anything at all.

Easter lay atop El on the couch, comfortable in the steady rise and fall of his chest. It was already hot, although it was only May, but Easter had set the box fan up in front of the screen door and a cooling breeze washed over them as the blue shadows of evening began to fall across the living room. They were watching the evening news. Nixon declared that he was going to start pulling troops out of Asia, but then the scene switched straight to pictures from Vietnam. It didn't look as if there was hope for it to slow down anytime soon. She saw soldiers firing into the distance, the launch of a missile, helicopters cutting into the sky. It was all a chaos of running men and black smoke rising into the air. Children crying and bloody bodies lying on the ground. She found herself looking for

Bradley, then realized that she didn't even know what he looked like. Still, he was very real to her. She prayed for him every night as he fought over there. He was the father of her nephew, the nephew she would raise and call her own. It took only one second to think something that she would always feel guilty about. She would never forget this moment, this thought running through her mind: if Bradley came back, they wouldn't get the baby. As soon as the thought came, it went, and then she was so ashamed at herself for thinking this way that she started crying.

Easter watched the images of war through her tears, but it was all too much—her own selfishness, the war, everything—and she had to look away, turning her face toward the couch and closing her eyes against what was always present, just barely out of reach.

El spread his hand out across her back but didn't say anything. She knew he was watching, too.

Without missing a beat the news anchor left the war behind to talk about Apollo 11. Easter could hear the smile in his voice, the tap of his stacked papers against his desk. As he talked she imagined pictures of astronauts working and smiling, a shot of Apollo 10, which had just been sent up.

"This world's gone crazy," Easter said. "Boys dying left and right and people all excited about men trying to walk on the moon. It's not right."

"We need something good to happen right now," El said in his even way. "It'd be something if they did end up walking on the moon."

"It's a scary time, though. Everything that's been happening."

"You'll be safe here with me," El said.

She knew this was true, but it didn't make her feel any better. Often she felt as if she were going through life grieving over something that hadn't even happened yet.

ANNETH TURNED THE volume on the television all the way down and ran her finger along the spines of her record albums, trying to find the one to match her mood. She scanned past everything until she arrived at *Dusty in Memphis*. She set the needle onto the first groove, and the strings of "Just a Little Lovin'" came on. She danced around barefooted in her living room, closing her eyes and swaying as the music built and fell away again. She realized that she hadn't danced in months and months. At first her legs seemed too heavy to lift, weighed down by sadness or frustration or something else she couldn't put a name to. But before long she felt light as a paper doll.

As soon as she had found out she was pregnant, she had sworn to herself that she wouldn't drink, but right now she needed a beer in the worst sort of way. She was glad she didn't have any in her refrigerator or she would have drunk one. Maybe she could be drunk on this music instead. It was the closest she was going to come tonight, anyway.

She twirled around, listening to Dusty Springfield and dancing in place as she watched the silent images on the television screen: Those long green helicopters and the shiny leaves of the jungle blowing in the sharp wind. Soldiers sitting in the open doorways of the helicopters, their legs hanging right out the side as they moved higher and higher into the sky, up above the fires and the smoke and the bullets.

She couldn't take it anymore; she turned the television off. She sat down on the couch and pulled the phone up into her lap. She would never stop loving Bradley, but she had to go forward with her life. If she sat in this apartment and waited on him, she'd go mad. She picked up the receiver and dialed Glenn's number.

Thirty-three

You'll Never Leave Harlan Alive

SHE SAID SHE DIDN'T want to wait until the baby was born. She wanted to go right now. True, her belly showed all of her nearly nine months of pregnancy, but the justice of the peace in Harlan had probably married plenty of girls in her condition.

"I don't care what anybody thinks," Anneth told Glenn.

"I don't, either, as long as I can have you," Glenn said. "I'll be right there."

"No, in the morning. It's too late right now," she said, feeling as though they were planning a trip to the grocery store instead of to get married. "Just come early."

She went to bed and slept like a dead woman, never moving throughout the night. In the morning she arose and dressed as if in a daze, slow and sluggish as she pulled on her dress suit and fixed her hair. When she opened the door, Glenn picked her up in his arms and she let him hold her a minute as she looked over his shoulder out the open door at nothing.

All the way to Harlan, Anneth leaned against the car window and watched the world pass by. There was a mist of rain, just enough to keep them from rolling down their windows, and she looked through the tiny beads of water on the glass to see the houses sitting on stilts beside the road, the gardens that were just beginning to grow full and crowded with bean vines and the bluish green leaves of potato plants. They drove over Buffalo Mountain, past the dripping cliffs and the places where she could look down and see the whole valley spread out below them. They passed several churches and little stores that sat close to the road and a couple of girls who were twirling around in their front yard, their faces up to catch the light rain. Glenn had come up behind a loaded coal truck and had to slow down while the truck tried to make its way up the slope, and she got a good look at the girls. They had left their shoes on the porch and were holding hands, dancing round and round barefooted on the wet grass, their legs long and brown—sisters who loved each other and would spend their whole lives loving each other.

Anneth felt cleaned out. She felt as if a great big hand had reached inside her and simply scooped out everything: her heart, her lungs, her soul. She leaned against the window and tried not to cry. Glenn was talking to her, asking her if she was all right. She didn't answer. How could he marry her when she was acting this way, not even looking at him? He must have been crazy, too. The glass had been made cool by the rain now, and she pressed her face against it, closing her eyes against a world that was all shrouded in gray now, a place that held no magic at all.

EASTER HAD NOT been so hurt since losing her own child. When Anneth called her from Harlan to let her know that she had run off to marry Glenn Couch, Easter hadn't even been able to say anything, and Anneth hadn't given her much of a chance.

"Bradley's never coming back, I've told you," Anneth said that morning. Easter could hear cars passing in the background and knew that Anneth was standing on the street talking into a pay phone. She could also hear a hollowness in her sister's voice, the sound of defeat. "And Glenn understands everything. He knows I'm going to give you the baby, that everything will come together just fine."

Easter wanted to say, *You've lost your mind, Anneth. Please come home right now. Don't do this. Don't marry that man.* But she couldn't. She wasn't able to say a word, something that would haunt her forever; even on her deathbed she would recall this morning when her sister made the biggest mistake of her life.

"Now, I know you think I'm crazy, Easter," Anneth said, "but this is the right thing. It's what I have to do right now. I've laid and cried for the past nine months and I have to get through this. If I don't do something, I'll crack up."

Easter listened to the distance between them. *You'll leave yourself behind in Harlan,* she thought. Easter wasn't even sure why she was so dead-set against Glenn. Maybe he could change. But Easter knew he wouldn't. She knew this was a mistake and there was no explaining that. She *just knew.*

"Please, Easter." Anneth was crying now. She had never begged Easter for anything, but now she was. "Say something."

But she couldn't. Easter put the phone back on its cradle and sat there, hugging herself against the realization that her sister had finally turned herself over to that big sadness she had carried around with her all her life. She had lost her mind, running off with somebody like Glenn Couch. He was just like Matthew—crazy over her—but unlike Matthew he was a fool. Easter could see in his eyes that he was the sort of man who thought he could make Anneth love him. Didn't he know that nobody could *make* Anneth do anything?

And suddenly she knew that Anneth's offer to give her the baby was a decision based on the same thoughtless logic. There was nothing she could do now. Anneth and Glenn were probably already in the office of the justice of the peace, saying their vows, a man half-crazy with lust for a woman he could never have gotten if she were in her right mind, and a woman whose belly showed that she was ready to have a child at any moment. Easter feared her sister would never make it back home before going into labor.

Easter tried to pray. But once she found herself on her knees beside her bed, her mind drew a blank. She didn't know what it was she intended to pray for, because it seemed that everything was done now. There was no turning back.

Thirty-four

....

These Sacrifices

EASTER STOOD LIKE a scarecrow in the garden and watched the birds settle on the branches around her. There were dozens of them—perhaps a hundred. All redbirds, birds that never traveled in groups this big. They fluttered down like drops of blood to settle on the tree limbs and perched there to watch her. She stood very still, afraid that any sudden movement might scare them away. Somehow she wanted their presence here with her, but they unsettled her, too, the way they sat staring down at her.

She had been hoeing. She had chopped out the rows only yesterday and the weeds had not had time to come back yet. She had awakened with the feeling that she was waiting for something and had made herself go out into the garden to pass the time. Now she knew what was going to happen. Anneth had always had a special affinity for redbirds, had even told Easter how she and Vine had witnessed a flock of birds converging around their yard. She waited a moment, turning her head slowly to take in all the birds; then she dropped her hoe and stepped out of the garden. As she moved, the redbirds flew away in a noisy fluttering, a pleasing sound like water falling on rocks.

Easter snatched her keys from the nail beside the back door, and as the screen slammed behind her she heard the phone begin to ring. She knew it was Glenn, calling to say that Anneth had started having labor pains just as they got into Black Banks, freshly back from their wedding. She didn't need to talk to him. She got into her car, sped up the road, and stopped in front of Sophie and Paul's house, where she kept her thumb on the horn until Sophie stepped to the door, looking out with squinted eyes. Easter leaned over to clatter down the car window. "Come on! Anneth's having the baby!"

GLENN AND JEWELL were already at the hospital, sitting on the hard chairs in the waiting room. Lolie was there, too, talking loudly into the pay phone. Glenn jumped up when Easter and Sophie came in, coming toward them as if he wanted a hug. Easter folded her arms across her chest, her key ring hanging from one finger and sending out little ringing notes.

"I tried to call you," he said.

"How did you talk her into it, Glenn?" Easter said. She looked at him a long moment, holding her lips together tightly, as if she were sucking on a piece of hard candy. "You caught her at her lowest and talked her into running off and marrying you. Why would you want that?"

"I love her, Easter."

Easter let out a scoffing breath. "I don't understand you, Glenn. And I don't trust you, either." She stepped closer to him. "But if you ever hurt her, you mark my words, I'll kill you."

He tried to act as if he had not even heard her. "She wanted you to go into the birthing room with her, but the baby just came so quick."

Jewell stepped forward, smiling. Easter had never met her but could see why Anneth loved her so much. Just the way she stood with her hands clenched in front of her suggested her kindness, her actions the opposite of those of her brother, whose presence took up the whole room.. "He's the prettiest little thing," Jewell said, and put a hand on Easter's arm.

"He's already born?" Easter said, recoiling from the both of them. Glenn nodded without looking at her.

SHE EASED THE door open, and as soon as she saw Anneth lying there in the gray shadows of the hospital room, she couldn't help thinking back to when the roles had been reversed, when Easter's baby had been born. Anneth had walked in without a word and had climbed into the bed with Easter. She had simply lain there with her, helping to soak up some of her grief.

Easter was glad to see that the baby was not there. She had expected that he might be, and she wasn't prepared for this yet. When she drew near to Anneth's bed, Anneth opened her eyes and smiled.

"I'm sorry I wasn't here for you," Easter said.

"It's all right," Anneth said, and patted the bed so that Easter would sit there. "It all happened so fast."

Easter took Anneth's hand. "And he's all right?"

"He's perfect, Easter. See, I told you he'd be a boy."

"You know you've made a mistake, marrying Glenn, don't you?" Easter knew this wasn't the proper time, but the words had to be said. "That man will try to rule your life. Can't you see that?"

"I see it now," Anneth said quietly. "I see everything so much plainer now than before."

"We'll fix it," Easter said. "We'll get you away from him and—"

"Let's not talk about all that now, Easter. It'll be all right. Everything will work out just fine."

The door opened and a nurse stepped in with the baby fussing in her arms. A little shudder ran through Easter at the sound of life. As the nurse made her way across the room, Easter felt her arms open-ing up, moving to take hold of the child. The nurse bent to put the baby in Anneth's arms and he stopped crying. Only then did Easter realize how she had fooled herself. This was not her child and he never would be. She saw how Anneth's body curved in toward the baby's, the little fist broken free of the tightly wound blanket. She could see the love that Anneth possessed for this baby standing like a mist above the bed. It was that clear and she knew what was going to happen.

She felt as if she was unable to move or even speak as she looked down at the baby. Perfect and moving, even in sleep. Alive. Thin blue eyelids with long lashes, a thick layer of downy hair. The fist clench-ing itself tighter and tighter, causing the tiny chips of fingernails to grow red and then whiten. A jolt ran through her—pure joy or in-cubated grief, she didn't know which.

She leaned down and kissed Anneth on the forehead. Beads of cold sweat met Easter's lips.

"Look at him, Easter. He's the most beautiful thing I've ever seen in my life."

Easter ran her thumb across his forehead. Impossibly soft, brand new. She leaned down to his face and drew in his scent, the cleanest smell, complete newness. She breathed it in as deeply as she could. She searched his face and head for any sign of a coal tattoo, but there wasn't one. She was thankful for this. Her own baby had been the only one to bear that mark of survival, a sign that this moment of healing would come to all of them.

"You were right, Easter. What you said," Anneth whispered. "As soon as I had him, I felt like a different person. It was like a light switch being turned on."

Easter nodded.

"All my life I've been looking for magic in all the wrong places,"

Anneth said. "Some kind of proof that magic truly does exist in this world. I didn't even realize that magic was in everything, that it happened every day. But now I know."

Easter sat on the edge of the bed and Anneth leaned over, trying to open the blanket, but she was too weak. "Unfold that and look at his little toes," Anneth said. "I love his feet the best of all."

As her hands worked, Easter tried not to think of her own baby, who had been wrapped in an identical blanket—white with red and turquoise stripes. She refused to let those images ruin this moment for her. She would not go through life looking at this baby and comparing it to her own. That wouldn't be fair to herself or to the child.

"What name did you decide on?"

"Clay," Anneth said, still in a whisper, as if terrified of waking the baby. "I wanted to name him something to do with the land. Bradley loved the land as much as I do. So that was the best name I could think of. Do you like it?"

"Clay," Easter said, holding his hot feet in her hands. "It's the best name."

They sat there in silence for a long time, looking at him. When he pursed his lips or wrinkled his forehead in sleep or opened his fist in a sudden burst of unexplained alertness, Anneth laughed. Finally Easter took hold of her sister's free hand, smoothed her hair back out of her face, and chose her words carefully.

"I can't take this baby from you," she said. "You love him, even more than you admit. It was stupid of us to think we could do that, to think that I could act like I was his mother and you just go about acting like he's just a nephew to you. We were crazy, and I can't take him."

"I'm not good enough for him, though, Easter," Anneth whispered.

"You don't believe that anymore. I know you don't," Easter said.

"When you had this baby, you quit believing that about yourself. You can't tell me you didn't."

Anneth tightened her fingers around Easter's hand. "What will we do, then?"

"We'll raise him together, Anneth," she said. "That's the way we've always done things."

Anneth didn't say anything, but her eyes agreed. When Easter was satisfied with this response, she stretched out on the bed beside Anneth. There was such comfort here, a good silence that can only exist between people who love each other. She put her arm across her sister's waist so she could touch Clay's hands. They would lie here and maybe the three of them would drift off into sleep together. She listened to their breathing, quiet and remarkable, a proof of life that sounded like a prayer.

Acknowledgments

A DEBT OF THANKS to Alice Adams, Grant Alden, *Billboard* magazine, booksellers and librarians across the nation, the Brosi family, Dub Cornett, Cracker, Hilary Elkins, friends at Spalding University's MFA Program, Shelly Goodin, Joy Harris, Wanda Jackson, fellow members of the Mezzanine Family Troubadours, Ron Rash, Grippo Reynolds, Jack Riggs, Ingrid Robinson, and Brad Watson. Extra special thanks to the following: Mike Croley and Pam Duncan for always being there when I need them most; Jane Hicks for wisdom and words; David Baxter, who gave me a CD called *Coal Mining Women;* Donovan Cain, Patty Loveless, Deborah Thompson, Billy Edd Wheeler (who wrote the song "Coal Tattoo"), and Zoe Speaks for their music—all of them have mountain souls; Marianne Worthington for being such a good buddy; Kathy Pories, friend and editor. To my good and patient wife, Teresa; my daughters, Cheyenne and Olivia, who give me joy every day; and my entire family, whom I hope to make proud. And to my uncle Sam, who has a coal tattoo.

In memory of those workers killed on February 20, 2003, at the CTA explosion in Corbin, Kentucky; the laughter of Jeanne Braselton; the goodness of my uncle Albert Ray House; the dignity of the

Daniel Boone Parkway; and the spirit of all those people who have had to fight for their land, especially Widow Combs, a frail sixty-one-year-old woman who lay down in front of bulldozers to protect her family's land in Knott County, Kentucky, and was forced away by authorities two days before Thanksgiving Day, 1965.

The
Coal Tattoo

A Reader's Guide

Silas House

A Conversation with Silas House

Bev Marshall and Silas House met at a book signing in Jackson, Mississippi, in 2002, and instantly became friends and fans of each others' novels. Since that time they've corresponded and occasionally had the opportunity to read and sign together across the South. Just after *The Coal Tattoo* was published, Bev completed the manuscript for *Hot Fudge Sundae Blues*. Now with three published novels each, Silas and Bev met again in Jackson at a favorite local watering hole to talk about their latest books. Here is a part of the lively conversation that ensued.

BM: Silas, you know how much I admired *Clay's Quilt* and *A Parchment of Leaves,* so I could hardly wait to read *The Coal Tattoo,* and now that I have, I must tell you that I absolutely loved it. I actually cried at the end when Easter asked Anneth what she named the baby, and Anneth said, "Clay." We readers had come full circle, and I marveled at how you wove the stories of these strong women through the passage of time. Did you have this grand plan of what you were going to accomplish, when you first began writing the trilogy?

SH: No, not at all. I didn't know that my first three books were even connected until I started writing *Tattoo.* I knew that my third novel was going to be about two sisters, mostly because I grew up in awe of the relationship my mother and her sister had and also because I've always been fascinated by sibling relationships. So I started out writing about these two sisters and about thirty pages in I realized this was Easter and Anneth, whom I had written about earlier in *Clay's Quilt*. And then I understood that they were the grand-daughters of Vine and Serena, whom I had written about in *A Parchment of Leaves*. So you don't have to read all three books to understand what's going on, but I do think it makes for a richer experience if you're familiar with all three books.

BM: I loved all four of those female characters. For a guy, you seem to have a nearly uncanny wisdom about the hearts of women. I especially loved the idea that, although Easter and Anneth are as different as Kentucky is from New York, they possess an uncondi-tional love for and understanding of each other. Can you tell me more about how you perceived their relationship and what caused you to be interested in the bond between them? Were you influ-enced by the relationship between your mother and her sister, which you mentioned?

SH: Well, my mother was orphaned when she was nine years old and her sister, Sis, was ten years older. So in many ways Sis was a mother-figure to her. They were always incredibly close, even closer than sisters normally are. They had this unconditional love for each other. Yet they were really different: one devout and calm, the other wild and restless. I loved that these two hugely different women could always put their differences aside because of their love for each other. It's a great metaphor, I think, for the way we should all be. It'd be a much better world if people could love one another despite their differences instead of hating one another because of their differences. The kernel of truth about these two sisters comes from my own mother and aunt, but it's heavily fictionalized. These characters just did their own thing and I let them, and I think that's the main rea-son they come off as being real. They're in charge when I'm writing.

BM: Speaking of metaphors, before you wrote this novel, you told me about the literal "coal tattoo" that sometimes occurs on the skin of the miners in Appalachia, but it seemed to me that the coal tattoo was symbolic of much more than the hardscrabble lives of miners. Am I right?

SH: Oh yeah, definitely. I just love the title of this book because it stands for so much. Besides being about these two sisters and their struggles and joys, this book—to me—is very much about the love for a place. So I think the coal tattoo is just a perfect symbol for how the land gets beneath our skin and becomes a part of us. Throughout this book Easter never leaves Free Creek, and when Anneth does, she keeps getting pulled back there. The land is a part of them and eventually, when they're threatened with losing that place, they fight hard for it. I love that. I didn't know that was going to happen at all.

BM: Well, one of our own things is music. We both included the lyrics of songs in our novels, but in *The Coal Tattoo*, the range is incredible. There are fiddles and rock and roll, country and gospel. Easter sings in church and then later she's onstage in a honky-tonk. What role does music play in your life and in the lives of your characters?

SH: Well, I think that's a reflection of how I grew up. My mother was (and still is) a great gospel singer, so I was exposed to that all the time. Went to church with her all the time, even sang with her in churches and nursing homes and revivals. And I still love gospel music. But at the same time, my aunt Sis and various cousins were taking me to see rock concerts, and we used to spend hours playing 45s by people like Bob Seger and AC/DC and all the great rock bands of that time. Aunt Sis introduced me to the blues and jazz. My sister took me to the drive-in to see *Grease* seventeen times.

BM: No way!

SH: I'm serious, *seventeen* times. We were obsessed. Olivia Newton-John was my first love. Meanwhile, a neighbor next door was always playing classical music for us. My father always had his truck radio tuned to a country-music station, so I grew up hearing people like Loretta Lynn and Don Williams. People in the family were expert banjo and guitar players. So I was exposed to just every kind of music growing up and it was very much a part of my life. Still is. I never go a day without listening to music. And I will tell you this: When I know what kind of music my character really loves, then I know my character completely. If you think about it, it makes a lot of sense. Because can't you tell a whole lot about a person when you find out what their favorite song is?

BM: I agree with that. So what is your favorite song?

SH: Well, there are so many. But if I had to narrow it down to just one, it'd be "Keep on the Sunny Side" by the Carter Family. What I love most about it is that the title is a bit misleading. The song isn't saying if you do right and be positive everything will go your way. If you listen to the song closely you'll see that it's saying that life is hard and full of obstacles, but if you try your best to do right, that'll at least make things easier. That's such a great, unsentimental message. Now that I think about it, that's really what I'm trying to say with my books, too. And I love that almost everyone I know can sing at least the chorus to that song. It's a great communal song.

BM: Trying your best to do right. If only everyone followed the advice in that song! Now, let's go back to that honky-tonk. I could nearly smell the spilled beer, hear the music, see the smoke curling above the characters' heads. I suspect you've been in a few honky-tonks yourself. Doing research, Silas?

SH: Well, Bev, you've been right there with me a couple times, now (laughter). I guess I have done a lot of research. I mean, before we had kids, I used to love to go out to bars every Saturday night. We would go and dance for three or four hours straight. Still do every once in a while, but now it's usually at friends' houses. I've seen my fair share of spilled beer and smoky clothes, that's for sure. And I love trying to capture that on the page. I always put a lot of singing and dancing in my books. It's hard to write about people dancing, or describing someone singing on the page, and that's one reason I love to do it. I love a good challenge. But at the same time, I've spent some time observing in those bars. I went purely for my art (laughter).

BM: (Laughing) Right! All for art! We writers are just forced into those places for our craft. But, Silas, besides our mutual love of dancing and singing, we share commonalities in that we both grew up in rural areas. And while we share a love for our land and our people, your Appalachian heritage is very different from mine. Your description of Easter and Anneth's mountain is so vivid, I thought of it as a character with human qualities. Is a passion for one's land an essential element in your work?

SH: It's just something I can't help but use. It's a part of me, the same way the music is, I guess. I don't actually think very much about that when I'm writing. I do want the place to be a character in my work, and in this book in particular I thought it very important that you feel as if you had actually been to the places that are mentioned. I wanted you to smell it and see it and feel the quality of the air in these places. So I hope I pulled that off.

BM: You certainly did. I moved those mountains down to Louisiana and walked on them while I was reading *Tattoo*. How did you accomplish that?

SH: Basically, I guess if you have a real passion for the place you're writing about, that passion is bound to bubble up on the page. I think a lot about what a thin line exists between the reader and the writer. Most of the time when the reader is reading they can somehow feel what the writer was feeling when he or she wrote the words. That's one of my favorite things about writing.

BM: One of my favorite things was the scene in *Tattoo* where Anneth, Easter, and Sophie take their stand against the strip-mining company. I was simultaneously terrified and thrilled. I nearly cheered aloud for them. Did you know what would happen before you wrote that scene?

SH: No, once I realized they were going to stand up to the bulldozers I just wrote that first line of that chapter, where they're gathering there on the mountain, and then it all just came very quickly. That's one of those times when I went into a weird sort of trance-like state while writing because I just saw it all like a movie in my head and somehow enabled my fingers to type out the words. That's when writing is so much fun—and often, I think, when writing turns out the best—when the story and the characters just take over and do their own thing. That's one of my favorite scenes in the book. I've read that in public only once because it's a very emotional scene for me, that sense of unity and love for the land. I love that they actually fight for their land, literally, hitting and kicking and spitting. I was drained when I wrote that scene, which is a great feeling in this context.

BM: I experience that, too. I know exactly what you mean and how you felt, and I also sympathized with both Easter's and Anneth's struggles to reconcile their Pentecostal faith with their desires. How do you perceive the role spirituality plays in our lives?

SH: One of the main reasons I write is to try to understand that very thing. I think it's evident in my writing that I'm very interested in spiritual and religious ideas. It's a major theme that runs through my work. I have a pretty good handle on my own spirituality, but I'm still trying to figure out religion. It's a complicated thing, which makes it such great fodder for literature. And it also makes writing more interesting for me, since it helps me to work all that out for myself. I think the best writing comes out of something that is very personal, when you're absolutely putting yourself out on the page, completely revealing yourself. I think I reveal that search for understanding, and it's something that writing has really helped me to understand better.

BM: Your quest for truth in your work is another thing I admire about you. Writing really is an act of discovery, isn't it?

SH: Definitely. Writing is actually a very selfish thing, in many ways, because the writer gains so much from writing, don't you think? When I write, I'm writing to figure something out for myself. Every novel I write helps me to understand myself and the world better. And it's interesting that you say that—about truth—because I never thought of it that way. But I am desperate to find out the truth about things, and that's usually what compels me to write.

BM: You know what I love most about your novels? It's that when I've read the last word, closed the back cover, I just feel good. Hopeful, happy, satisfied. There's not a hint of cynicism in your books. Is this what you wish for your readers to feel and how do you accomplish this without succumbing to sentimentality?

SH: First of all, thank you for saying that. I think if you're investing your time in a book, you sure ought to leave it feeling satisfied. When I'm writing a novel, I'm always trying to arrive at a moment of hope, I think. When I read, I don't want to necessarily read about happy people, but I do want to see someone getting happy, or end on a note of hope that these characters I've lived with for three hundred pages will find their place in the world. And to be honest, I think there's too much cynicism in modern literature. Most literary novels are so much gloom and doom. To me, it's much more challenging to pull off an optimistic novel without becoming sappy. I try very hard to walk that tightrope. Throughout this book people say "I love you" to one another. And I think a lot of literary writers cringe away from that; they're afraid to put that into writing or into their characters' mouths. But we're supposed to be writing about real life, and in reality, people say that to one another (and mean it) all the time. So, I think I'm able to avoid sappiness because I'm just writing about real life and not avoiding those things.

BM: Real life! Yes, but our childhoods weren't always rooted in reality. I grew up in a family of storytellers, who embellished every tale they told; and I know that you did, too. What effect do you think families like ours have on writers?

SH: There's no doubt my family shaped me into a writer. I don't know how one can avoid being a writer when they live in a family of such vivid storytellers like mine. In my family, when someone comes home from work and is asked how their day was, they never just say "Fine." They tell you an *epic* about their workday. I think growing up like that I learned from an early age how to exaggerate and make a story better than it actually was. Writing is like that, too. Situations have to be somewhat exaggerated to drive home the essential truth, you know? But I think the main thing is that growing up around all those stories instilled a love of language in me. I just love the way words can be strung together and turned into something powerful and lasting. I love the power of words, and I learned that by listening to stories.

BM: Okay, now I understand the genesis of your stories, but how do you set those stories down? My readers always want to know something of my writing life: my habits, my schedule, do I do my own laundry? What's your writing day like?

SH: I have a time set aside to write every day, but I rarely write during that time. I always tell people that I write every minute of the day. Instead of having to go into a room and sit down in front of a computer and turn the "writing thing" on, I'm constantly having to turn it off so that I can live as a normal person. So I write during every waking minute. That's what I love about writing—everything is usable. Nothing is wasted. If I'm having a bad day, then writing is a catharsis for that. And if I'm having a good day, I'm able to sit down and use that in some way, too. I'm the most disorganized writer I know. I don't have any kind of outline or any idea of where my story is going. But that works for me. I also spend as much time as I can outside. Some of my best writing happens when I'm taking out the garbage or mowing the yard or plowing my garden or doing things where I'm in motion. I get much more done during those times than when I'm sitting at my computer.

BM: I know what you mean. I'm often working out a character's dilemma when I'm folding laundry, doing the dishes, or driving to the Piggy Wiggly. But, Silas, a plow and a garden? Do you really do that?

SH: Well, it's not like I have a mule pulling the plow, Bev! (Laughing.) Although really we *ought* to do that instead of wasting so much gas. I plow my garden every spring with the tractor my father and I share. I've always raised a little vegetable garden. When I was writing *A Parchment of Leaves*, I raised a huge garden because my main character, Vine, was a great gardener. I felt like I'd be able to know her better if I worked out in that garden every day, and I did. That's where Vine was created, while I was pulling corn and hoeing my beans, things like that. So ever since then I've raised a pretty big garden. Some people say it's therapeutic and all that, but mostly it's just hard work, which is good for you, plain and simple.

BM: Knowing you as I do, I'll bet you're most likely doing some more hard work right now. You've already begun working on another fabulous story set in Appalachia. True?

SH: Well, sort of. In my new book, the location is never named. The town is, but I never tell you what state or what part of the country it is. I make it very clear that it's a rural place—because a rural place is what I know best—but because of the nature of the book, I think it's important that it could be set in any little rural place in America. The new book is set during the Bicentennial Summer—1976—and is from the point of view of a ten-year-old boy. It's about a house divided, about a family at war. I think we live in a very divided country right now, one that's going to be divided for a very long time, so it's timely in that way, even though I've had the book in my head for ages. In many ways it's my most autobiographical work, since my father is a Vietnam vet. But it's a very complex thing and is emotionally devastating, but in a good way, if that makes sense.

BM: Perfect sense! And I can't wait to read it. Will you send me a copy when you're done?

SH: Since you asked so nicely, I will. You know I'd do anything for you, sister.

Reading Group Questions and Topics for Discussion

1. Did you know what a coal tattoo was before reading this novel? In what ways does the occurrence of a coal tattoo stand as metaphor or as symbol for the characters in this story? What different meanings does it have?

2. The character traits of Easter and Anneth are often juxtaposed in the novel. Easter realizes early in the story that there "was no name she could put to the difference between them." How do the sisters' differences keep them in conflict? Bring them together? How are Easter and Anneth alike?

3. Is Easter jealous or resentful of Anneth's wild and carefree approach to life? Is Anneth jealous or resentful of Easter's more grounded and careful approach to living?

4. How have the sisters' grandmothers, Vine and Serena, affected the sisters' development as women, as sisters, as mothers?

5. How does Easter's devout religious faith both enrich and hinder her life?

6. Consider the scene where Easter is returning home after singing secular music on a popular television show (after she has left the church). She recalls the childhood memory of her grandmothers bringing her to a camp meeting where she had two first experi-

ences: An anointing by the Holy Ghost *and* helping her grand-mothers minister to striking coal-mining families. Does Easter view both of these experiences as religious?

7. Easter seems to possess mystical abilities, while Anneth seems obsessed with looking "for magic anywhere she could find it." Easter wants to reject these mystical abilities, preferring instead "the peace of a life well lived, a good man, and the knowledge that her family was safe," while Anneth continues to look for magic every day. Do the women ever reconcile themselves to their different quests? How?

8. Why does Anneth keep marrying men she doesn't love?

9. What are the narrator's attitudes toward the coal-mining industry in the early part of the novel? What are Anneth's attitudes toward coal mining in the first half of the novel? What are the major factors that cause Anneth to view coal mining differently later on?

10. Discuss your own experiences with, and dispositions about, coal mining. Did you know what a broad form deed was before reading this novel? How does coal mining affect Black Banks? The environment at large? The economic and political infrastructure of Crow County?

11. How does the author explore class differences in this novel? Consider coal miners vs. Altamont Mining Company, churchgoers vs. nonbelievers, rural people vs. city people, Kentuckians vs. others? Does Silas House set up an "us vs. them" outlook in this story? Why or why not?

12. How does the author animate or enliven abstract concepts like faith, love, depression, and grief?

13. Water is a recurring motif in this story. Anneth is said to know water "on intimate terms." What do you think this means? What are the different connotations for water that are explored in this novel? In what ways do the characters consider water as a personal emblem?

14. Redbirds also have a recurring role in this story. How do redbirds (and other elements of the natural world) help direct Easter and Anneth?

15. Do you agree or disagree with Vine's suggestion to Easter that "stillness is a habit easily gained"? Why?

16. What accounts for the fierce loyalty Easter and Anneth hold for their small place on Free Creek? Do you think this allegiance to land is unique to eastern Kentuckians?

17. With which character(s) do you most closely identify? Why?

18. How do the chapter titles and the epigraphs from the book's four sections contribute to your knowledge of the characters, plot, settings, or themes of the story?

19. *The Coal Tattoo* can be considered a companion book to Silas House's first two novels. If you have read *Clay's Quilt* and *A Parchment of Leaves*, how are these stories threaded together?

© JUDITH VICTORIA HENSLEY

Silas House is the author of *Clay's Quilt* and *A Parchment of Leaves*. He is the recipient of the Kentucky Book of the Year Award, the James Still Award from the Fellowship of Southern Writers, and many other awards. He lives with his wife and two daughters in Lily, Kentucky, where he was born.

ABOUT THE TYPE

This book was set in Caslon, a typeface first designed in 1722 by William Caslon. Its widespread use by most English printers in the early eighteenth century soon supplanted the Dutch typefaces that had formerly prevailed. The roman is considered a "workhorse" typeface due to its pleasant, open appearance, while the italic is exceedingly decorative.

Don't miss these touching novels by
Silas House

Clay's Quilt

A heart-stirring story of one man's search for family—and the townspeople who join him as he fashions a quilt of a life from what treasured pieces surround him. A tender novel in the great Appalachian tradition that will charm readers' souls.

"A young writer of immense gifts . . . One of the best books I have ever read about contemporary life in the mountains of Southern Appalachia."
—Lee Smith

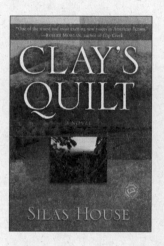

A Parchment of Leaves

It is the early 1900s in rural Kentucky, and Saul Sullivan wants to make Vine, a beautiful Cherokee woman, his wife. Though her mother disapproves, Vine is determined to marry Saul—but she's not yet prepared for a future that will test her spirit and her ability to forgive.

"With simple eloquence, [House] captures the rhythms of a woman's life, the passages from courtship to marriage to motherhood."
—*The Atlanta Journal-Constitution*